MW01026878

Shadow Knows

A Cameron McGregor Novel

To Pat

[signature]

Dennis Russell Dunklee

A combined edition of <u>Non-Stop Flight</u> and <u>Shadow Knows</u>

This combined edition of <u>Non-Stop Flight</u> and <u>Shadow Knows</u> is a work of fiction. Names, characters, places, other than cities, townships or villages and public spaces, are products of the author's imagination or are used fictitiously including any connection, or reference to Travelers Aid Society or Travelers Aid International. In addition, any resemblance to actual events, locales, business establishments or persons, living or dead, is entirely coincidental.

Never trust what only you can see,
even salt looks like sugar.

unknown

CHAPTER ONE

Loneliness. Dulles International Airport, just outside of Washington, D.C., at three o'clock a.m. Somewhere, the sound of a vacuum cleaner. A beat-up old umbrella, unclaimed, goes around and around all night on a robotic carousel. Any airport's late night or early morning atmosphere breeds a feeling of being lost and lonely, sort of like an unclaimed item, to stranded passengers who have patiently removed their shoes for the third time that day, gulped down overpriced fast food and slumped for hours in chairs of cold fake leather and peeling chrome. Often, trapped in flight delays, they may have many hours to see, hear and sense, without freedom of choice, their fellow passengers. And, as they grow more invisible, the moving world around them takes on a life of its own. A life like no other in the wee hours of the morning. There's almost always someone coming or going—foreign travelers, diplomats, sports stars, avid fishermen and resolute golfers, soldiers, politicians, musicians, but...not at that time in the morning. Vacationers and conventioneers, meeters and greeters, children hugging grandparents, sisters bidding tearful good-byes, couples sharing a quiet moment, and young and old sipping coffee in a coffee shop...hardly ever at three o'clock in the morning.

Clearly, some people love the excitement, the exotic mix of travelers, the allure of greeting people who have traveled to places one may only dream of visiting, but it's never this way for stranded or abandoned passengers at three o'clock in the morning. Their situations, whatever they might be, whatever caused them, tend to bend and obscure their ability to fully grasp reality. The world around them can seem to be cloaked in a mysterious fog.

That morning, Cameron McGregor, a tall, rangy man with intense eyes, a sly grin and a slightly grizzled appearance, arrived at Dulles at precisely seven-thirty a.m. He was covering for a fellow Travelers Aid volunteer who was not feeling well and had to miss his eight to eleven o'clock shift. McGregor, to whom promptness was a virtue, always figured that, if he wasn't thirty minutes early, he was late.

"*Buenos días*, Maria Rosita Guadalupe Florez," he said, smiling at the small industrious women pushing a massive dust mop.

"*Hola, Señor* McGregor! Are you changing shifts?" she asked.

Maria was just one of hundreds of housekeepers and custodians at the airport, but she was quite different from many of her counterparts, he knew from experience. She was always smiling—always had a pleasant greeting for everyone. She kept busy and was meticulous in her work, and she had a soft spot in her heart for those, like him, who volunteered to assist travelers at Dulles.

"No, just filling in. How are things going for you?" he asked.

1

"Oh, *Señor* McGregor, I'm just happy! Where are you working this morning?"

"I'm in the main terminal until eleven o'clock—are you going to help me with my Spanish if I need you?"

"*Lo siento mucho, Señor* McGregor, I leave at eight o'clock. But, listen, there's—how you say—a young women, if she's still there, sitting in the back row of the waiting area right behind the Travelers Aid desk. She's been there since I don't know when, but I visited with her at three o'clock this morning. She says she's from *Alemania.* I think she's—how do you say—*varados aquí?*"

"Maria, help me here. I think you're telling me that you think 'she's stranded here,' and does *Alemania* mean Germany? Is that what you're saying?"

"*Si, Señor* McGregor!"

"Three o'clock this morning?"

"*Si, Señor* McGregor!"

"I'll see what I can do, Maria," McGregor said. "Thanks!"

In his spare time, and McGregor had a fair amount of it since he retired from the United States Marshals Service, he volunteered his services at Dulles International Airport, one of the main gateways to Washington, D.C., assisting travelers with their questions and problems. Being a service-oriented person was not new to him. For years, he'd been dealing with folks who seemed, he felt, to fit into the same categories as travelers: the demanding, "all about me" person; the spacey novice; the "deer in the headlights" individual; the "all about business" personality; or the *laizzez faire* casual. *All in a day's work*, was his usual business-like posture.

As he approached one of the Travelers Aid Information Desks in the main terminal that morning, Bill Hunter and Elizabeth Smallwood were hustling around the desk like they knew exactly what they were doing—and they did!

Maybe they'll know what's going on with the stranded passenger Maria was talking about, he thought.

"Hi, Cam," Elizabeth said. "Our relief is here, Bill!"

"Wow," McGregor commented, "it looks like, from the number of flights arriving, you've had a busy shift! Uhh, the lady sitting in the last row over there—is she the German passenger who's supposedly stranded?"

"Yeah, Cam, her name is Angelika Schafer, and I've already made a couple of phone calls for her—same number, both went to voice mail. Some guy, some place in D.C.. I left a message for him to call us here, but nothing yet. Here's his name and cell phone number. Angelika's been here since three o'clock *yesterday* afternoon."

"Thanks, Elizabeth," McGregor said. "Can you hold the fort for a couple of minutes while I talk to her?"

As he walked toward Angelika, sitting alone in an obscure waiting area, he couldn't help thinking of her as one of those who arrive at airports alone and nameless.

2

Airports are where everyone comes together, but nobody knows your name, he mused.

Over the years, and in many airports, he had observed hugs and kisses of greeting and farewell, and people watching the clock and buying last-minute souvenirs and gifts. On any given day, in airports everywhere, countless travelers arrive and depart—to visit grandma, to close a business deal, to hook up with a lover, to climb a mountain.

What's Angelika's story? he wondered.

At first glance there was nothing unusual about Angelika Schafer, but as he moved closer, he could see more of her. Her white-blonde hair fell in a dead straight curtain to just below her shoulders. Her pale eyebrows arched delicately over eyes which were rimmed with eyelashes so pale as to appear invisible. As she looked up to greet him, he could see the almost opaque quality of her light blue eyes—eyes that gave no hint as to her thoughts.

"*Guten morgen,* young lady! Did I say that right? Are you Angelika Schafer? Are you German? Sorry, but my German is lousy. You can call me Cam. I'm a volunteer with Travelers Aid."

"Yes, I'm Angelika Schafer, and yes, Germany is my home—Berlin to be exact, *Ich komme aus Berlin*—and you said 'good morning' to me. Thank you. The way you spoke had a tinge of Bavarian accent. Have you been to Bavaria?"

"As a matter of fact, I have, but you're just hearing my own native southern accent," he laughed as he sat down beside her. "Ms. Schafer, how about bringing me up to date on your situation—I understand you might be stranded?"

"What do you mean by 'stranded'?" she asked with an apprehensive look on her face.

"I understand your flight from Frankfurt arrived at three o'clock yesterday afternoon, and it's now seven forty-five a.m.," McGregor clarified. "If my math is correct, you've been here in the airport for about sixteen hours. Was someone supposed to be here to meet you?"

"Yes," she said with an anxious look. "I gave the lady over there his name and phone number. She's been trying to contact him for me. My cell phone doesn't work in this country. I'm a high school teacher in Berlin, and I've never been to this country before. *Hier ist mein Reisepass,*" she said, offering her passport to McGregor.

"I met this American man, Mr. Loren Stringer, at a conference in Frankfurt," she continued, "and he invited me to come here for a week and visit his school in Washington, District of Columbia. He said he had *bewilligen,* uh, grant, I believe, money available to pay for my plane tickets and my hotel. I got permission from my *Schulleiter,* oh, sorry, Headmaster, and sent Mr. Stringer the dates I could come. He sent me plane tickets and the name of the hotel where I'd be staying and said he would pick me up at the airport. I have his letter right here."

3

"Did he tell you the name of his school?" McGregor asked as he looked at the letter.

"Just that it was in Washington, District of Columbia."

The whole thing seemed strange to him. *Human trafficking* flickered through his mind.

"Have you had anything to eat since you've been here?" he asked.

"No, I only have a few euros, and they won't take them over there," she said, pointing to a deli a little way down the main walkway.

McGregor reached into his pocket and pulled out a food voucher worth ten dollars. After he signed and dated it, he handed it to her. "Here, take this over to the deli and get some *Frühstück*—am I right? Breakfast?"

"Close enough," she laughed. "Thank you! I'll repay you after I trade some euros for dollars."

"Is this your luggage?" he asked. "I'll get it and walk over to the deli with you, and while you're eating, I'll go back to the desk and see what I can do about reaching your contact person."

McGregor was going to be working the next few hours by himself, and, from the look of the flight arrival screen on the desk computer, he knew he was going to be busy.

He looked at the note that Elizabeth had handed him.

Angelika Schafer--to be picked up by a Loren Stringer @ 202-777-0442

He dialed the number and the call was picked up immediately by voice mail, "You've reached the office of Consular Officer, Loren Stringer. Please leave a message, and I'll return your call as soon as possible."

"Officer Stringer, this is Cameron McGregor with Travelers Aid at Dulles airport. Please call me immediately regarding Angelika Schafer, a guest, perhaps yours, from Germany. My number is 703-444-3000."

As soon as he hung up, McGregor called upstairs to the Travelers Aid office. Bobbie, one of the TA coordinators, answered.

"Good morning, Bobbie, this is Cameron McGregor. I'm working in the main terminal this morning. Can you do a reverse lookup on a phone number for me? The number is 202-777-0442."

"Right away, Cam—I'll call you right back," she promised.

"Excuse me, sir!"

"Hi! Can I help you?"

"Yes!"

"Uhh, can you be more specific, or should we talk about world events— perhaps, say, the stock market?"

"No, no, silly—where do I go?"

"Are you flying out or are you meeting someone?"

4

"Where do planes come from?"

"They travel from all over the world and come down from the sky. Didn't you see the movie 'Airplane'? Are you flying out, or are you meeting someone flying in?"

"Chicago."

"Are you flying to Chicago? Do you have your boarding pass? Nope, that's a ticket confirmation. Have you checked in yet?"

"I only have this."

"Okay, go to the escalator, or, if you prefer, the elevators located directly behind the escalator on the back wall. Go to the United ticket counter upstairs and check in. They'll tell you where to go from there. Feel free to come back if you need more help." *All in a day's work,* he reminded himself.

"Hey, Bobbie, I didn't see you coming! You decided you needed some exercise and walked down to see me?" he smiled.

"I've got the info on the number you gave me, Cam. It's a cell phone, so I couldn't track it, but I asked the airport police to run the number for me and it checks back to the German embassy. What's going on?"

"I've got a stranded passenger," McGregor explained, "and that's her contact number. When you get back upstairs, would you see if you can find me the phone number for the security office at the German embassy?"

"Will do, Cam. I'll call you in a few minutes."

"Thanks, Bobbie! Yes, sir—can I help you?"

"Thank you. Will Air France be on time?"

"If so, it'd be a first," McGregor laughed. "Right now, they're showing on time."

"Why are they never really 'on time'? I've noticed that too."

"I'm not sure," McGregor said, "but I've heard that they often land in Nova Scotia if there's a wine tasting party goin' on."

"Is that true?"

"Just kidding. They'll be here soon—they're about twenty minutes out," he said, looking at his computer screen. "Excuse me, my phone is ringing."

"Hi, Bobbie, that was quick...I've got it, thanks!"

McGregor looked across the hall towards the deli. Angelika had finished her breakfast and was heading his way.

"Angelika—may I call you that? —how was your breakfast?" he asked. "I'll be with you in a few minutes. I'm in the process of tracking down your contact per..."

"Hey, you! Where's number four?"

"Excuse me, Angelika—we'll get interrupted often, I'm afraid. Hold on a minute," McGregor whispered as he gave his attention to the rather officious looking individual shouting at him from across the hallway.

"Door or baggage carousel, sir?" he inquired politely.

"Door!"

"If you'll look at me, sir, I'll point the way!"

"I don't need to look at you to hear you!"

"Okay, it's that way," McGregor responded, without pointing.

"What way?"

"That way!"

"What are you, a smart-ass?"

"Thank you for asking, sir. It's still that way, and—glad I could help!"

Angelika was giggling.

"Sorry about that, Angelika. I meet all kinds of people in the airport, but most are not like that." he said laughingly. "Find a chair and relax; I promise I'll be with you shortly."

McGregor dialed the number Bobbie had given him for security at the German embassy. The man who answered the phone was all business. McGregor hastily explained the situation and asked if one of their people might be able to resolve the issue. The man asked if Angelika was a German citizen, and McGregor affirmed that she was. He was promised a quick return phone call.

"Yes, ma'am, can I help you?" McGregor turned to a woman approaching the desk.

"Thank you. What's the best way to get to National Airport?" she asked.

"Are you catching a flight?"

"Yes, to Spokane."

"What time is your flight?"

"It's at eleven."

"Okay, you've got two and a half hours. Is it just you?"

"My husband is with me—he's in the bathroom. He doesn't travel well and…"

"Okay, because you don't have a whole lot of time," McGregor said, "I think you should take a cab. You'll find the cab stand at the bottom of the ramp at door six. Take the down ramp, look to your right and you'll see the sign for the Washington Flyer Cab. Have a great trip!"

McGregor dialed the non-emergency number for the airport police and asked for Lieutenant Morgan, thinking that Morgan should be aware of the situation with Angelika. He and the lieutenant, a former bodybuilder, now running to portly, had swapped airport stories over coffee a few times since McGregor started volunteering for Travelers Aid. Morgan was away from his desk but told the dispatcher he'd drop by and see McGregor in a few minutes.

"Hi, young man, you look…." McGregor began.

"I'm right here—right here by some desk! There's a desk with an old guy with hideous maroon sport coat on…. hold on, I'll ask! Excuse me, sir, I have my friend on the phone here, and we've been looking for each other for over an hour. He's here somewhere, but I can't find him."

"Is that who you're talking to on your phone?"

"Yes!"

6

"Perhaps if I talk to him, I can help you both figure this out!"

"Here!"

"What's his name?"

"Walter."

"And your name is..."

"Simon."

"Hi, Walter, this is Cameron McGregor with Travelers Aid—the 'old guy with the hideous maroon sport coat.' Look around, please, and tell me what you see...wow, that doesn't sound familiar to me! What else do you see? Oh, you're at a gate? What's the number on the gate? No, it can't be gate 87; we don't have a gate number like that here! No, I believe you, but we don't have a gate with that number at this airport. What else do you see? Again, that doesn't sound familiar to me. Walter, what's the name of the airport you're at? No, I'm *not* kidding; look at your ticket stub and tell me what the name of the airport is, please. Oh, okay, Walter—hold on for a minute. Simon, Walter's at *Dallas-Fort Worth International Airport.*"

"I know that—where is he?"

"All right, Simon, here's your phone back. Let's try this. What airport do you think you're at?"

"I'm at Dallas."

"Here's the problem, Simon. Listen carefully please. You're at *Dulles* Airport and he's at *Dallas* Airport. You're in the Washington, D.C. metropolitan area, and Walter's in the Dallas, Texas metropolitan area. One of you is in the wrong place. You guys will have to work this out. I'll be here for the next couple of hours if you need more help."

Morgan arrived, and, standing next to McGregor, he'd undoubtedly overheard much of the conversation with Simon and his "lost" friend, Walter.

"Hey, Lieutenant, thanks for stopping by. Can you believe that?" McGregor laughed.

"Yep, I can," Morgan said in his usual low-keyed voice. "Couldn't help but eavesdrop—it's my job, you know! I reason that kid's somewhat lacking in geography skills. What I can't believe is that there's any way you're gonna solve his problem *if* he comes back for more help!" he said. "You called my dispatcher—what's up?"

"If you've got a moment, I'd like you to visit with the young lady seated in the corner over there. Her name is Angelika Schafer —she's from Germany," he explained. "She flew in yesterday afternoon and is still waiting for someone to pick her up. I'm trying to locate her connection now. He's with the German Embassy, according to his cell-phone number, and, well, I dunno, something just doesn't feel right to me."

"I'll talk to her," Morgan said as he ambled over to where Angelika was seated. McGregor tagged along, just long enough to assure her that it would be

7

helpful for her to visit with Morgan. A line had formed at his desk by the time he got back.

"Yes, ma'am, can I help you?"

"Where do I catch the 5A bus to Washington?"

"Curb 2E, ma'am—here's a schedule. The bus leaves in fifteen minutes. Take the down ramp at door six, walk across the street to the first curb with a red awning over it, turn left, look up and follow the signs to E. Have a great trip!"

"Can I help you, sir?"

"Yes, thank you. Where can I find my baggage?"

"Where did you fly in from? What airline?

"Los Angeles—United."

"Baggage claim three, sir—that way," McGregor said, pointing.

Morgan returned to the desk. "All right, Cam, I talked to Angelika. Sounds like a communication mix-up to me. Let me know if you can't get in contact with her ride. I have some suspicions, but let's see how this unfolds before I get too interested in it."

"Will do, Lieutenant. Thanks for your assistance! Oh-oh, here comes Simon again! You might want to stick around."

"I'm out of here," Morgan said flatly as he did a military-like about-face and walked away.

"Simon, you're back! Did you and Walter get this worked out?"

"How far is Dallas? Can I walk there?" Simon asked.

"No, sorry—you can't walk there from here! If you were a crow—and you're clearly not—as the crow flies, it's about twelve hundred miles."

"Can I take a cab?"

"In that case, it would be about fourteen hundred miles, and I'm sure you're not going to find a taxi that would go there!"

"What would that cost?"

"If you could find a cab?"

"Yes!"

"I dunno! But a cab ride from here to downtown Washington is about sixty bucks and, again, I don't..."

"So, it'd cost me about two-hundred dollars if I could find a cab—right?"

"Wrong, Simon! Let me see what flights are going from here to Dallas for you—or would you rather just fly home? Where'ya from?"

"Detroit!"

"Okay, Simon, why don't you get yourself a cup of coffee or a soda and give me about fifteen minutes. When you come back, I'll have a list of airlines that have flights going out today or in the morning for both of those destinations. Then you can decide what you wanna do!"

"Howdy, gentlemen, how can I help you?" McGregor inquired as three dark-suited men approached the desk."

8

"Is this Travelers Aid?" one of the men, evidently unable for some reason to see the TA sign boldly posted above their heads, asked in a distinguishing accent. *Perhaps German?* McGregor wondered. "We're looking for someone named 'Cameron McGregor.'"

"That's me, gentlemen. How can I..."

"We're here to pick up a woman named Angelika Schafer," the man interrupted.

"Which one of you is Loren Stringer?" McGregor asked.

"Mr. Stringer is unable to be here," one of the men said in a no-nonsense voice. "We're from the German Embassy. We'll see that she's taken to her destination."

"It takes three of you?" McGregor commented, eyebrows raised, as they quickly flashed identification cards in his face.

"Just a minute, guys," McGregor said as he picked up the phone and dialed airport security. He wanted Morgan to handle this for him. Morgan was there in a flash and quickly whisked the three men away from the desk to a less populated area.

Something I shouldn't hear? McGregor wondered as he glanced over his shoulder and saw that Angelika was dozing.

"Hi, ladies, are those flowers for me?" McGregor asked of the two middle-aged women walking toward the desk.

"No, sorry," one of the ladies giggled. "Our sister is flying in from Phoenix—landing at Terminal C." answered one of the women. "Where can we meet her?"

"Do you know if she'll have checked baggage?"

"No, just a carry-on, we're sure."

"Okay, here's the problem. You can't meet her at Terminal C. She'll come into this terminal either through the door behind me, or a door just like this behind baggage claim twelve. I'd suggest..."

"Why is that?" interrupted the other woman.

"Well, when she gets off the train in the main terminal station, she'll have her choice of two escalators. One will lead her here, and the other one will lead to the doors behind twelve. There's no way to guess which one she'll take, so I suggest you simply split up and cover both entrances. Make sense?"

"What happened to the people mover things?" the first woman asked.

"If she'd landed at Terminal D," McGregor responded, "she'd probably use a people mover to get to the main terminal. That's the only area where people movers are still located, and, to confuse things even more, those folks enter the main terminal through a door behind the oversize baggage carousel located by baggage claim eight. It's been awhile since you've been at the airport, I'm guessing—are you sure those flowers aren't for me?" The women laughed and headed off in different directions.

McGregor glanced toward Morgan and the three men from the German Embassy, who were still tightly huddled just out of McGregor's earshot. Morgan seemed to be agitated about something.

"Hey, Simon, glad you're back," McGregor said, as the hapless young man approached. "Here's a list of airlines that have flights going out today or tomorrow morning for both Dallas, Texas, and Detroit, Michigan. I've also included the phone numbers for Amtrak and Greyhound. If you want to go to either Dallas or Detroit, the airline ticket counters are upstairs. If you want to take a bus or train somewhere, talk to Super Shuttle at the bottom of the ramp at either door six or door two. They can take you to either station. Have a great trip, whatever you decide to do." As Simon walked away, McGregor heaved a sigh—whether of sympathy or relief, he wasn't sure.

He was shaking his head over the Simon situation when he noticed Morgan and the three men he'd been questioning, heading back toward his desk.

"I'm gonna let Angelika go with these fellows," Morgan declared. "Their documentation checks out, and I've got their names for the record. I see no problem," he assured McGregor. "I'll handle things with Angelika," he added as he herded the men toward her.

Angelika appeared willing to go with the men. She finished her coffee and rose to her feet. Slender as a willow, she reached for her scarf and threw it gracefully over her narrow shoulders.

"Thanks, Cam," she said as she walked by with Morgan and the embassy personnel on the way to their car. "I owe you breakfast!"

"Forget it, Angelika," he said. "It was a pleasure meeting you. If there's anything else I can do for you, here's my card. Don't hesitate to call." He knew when he gave her his card he'd probably broken some Travelers Aid rule—the card had his personal phone number on it—but he was still concerned about Angelika's well-being—something just didn't feel right about the whole situation, whatever that might be, he thought.

"Hi, Cam, had a busy morning?"

"Hey, Mort, hi, Sheila! It must be about quittin' time for me! Not too busy, just the usual—mixed, of course, with the typical unusual," he smiled. "Lest I forget, folks, if a young man named Simon comes back—well, he has trouble with both geography and math. But with your combined skills, I'm positive you'll be able to resolve all of his problems."

"And just what are those problems, Cam? I smell a rat here!" said Mort suspiciously.

"Ask Simon—you'll love his answer! Some people should never be allowed to travel; actually, some shouldn't even be allowed to be near an airport," McGregor laughed as he turned to leave the area.

"Excuse me, sir! Can you direct me to the underground walkway to the parking garage?"

"Follow me, young man; I'm heading in that direction!"

10

CHAPTER TWO

McGregor couldn't help thinking about Angelika as he left Dulles and headed for his home in the Bull Run mountains, west of the airport. He had that *what the hell was that all about?* concern—the kind that, over time, he'd learned to mark up to experience, and quickly move on. And, quickly he did, maneuvering his Corvette on a "racer's straight" through the curves of his favorite mountain roads, enjoying the "top down," weather, endless mountain vistas, dark forests and peaceful valleys. He was in no hurry that day—he felt like driving.

Bypassing the turn to his house, he pointed the nose of his car due west toward West Virginia, eventually stopping at one of his favorite "mom and pop" roadside restaurants for a glass of real southern-style sweet tea and whatever their blue plate special was for the day. Even though he was always recognized immediately by the "locals" at Hoppy's Place, he enjoyed sitting by himself and listening to them discuss the weather, the local football team, the demise of the tobacco or coal industry, all in the backwoods drawl of rural West Virginia. In this particular restaurant, conversations were frequently interrupted by coal trucks using their air brakes as they carefully measured their speed down the steep mountain road outside.

As he got out of his car, he glanced back in the direction he'd come from. He'd noticed a car with diplomatic license plates he thought might be following him. *Nowhere in sight*, he noted, shrugged, and opened the well-worn screen door to the restaurant. He knew as he arrived that two things were certain at Hoppy's Place. First, the food would be home-cooked good, and second, there would be at least one old fellow holding court with a number of equally elderly gentlemen recounting various tales from up and down the holler. *Someday soon, but not quite yet, I'll probably be one of them*, he figured. And even though they'd have to pause every few minutes to allow for the sound of a passing coal truck, it amazed him that their patter never missed a beat.

Today might be an exception, he was thinking, as two tough-looking men in dark suits and ties entered the restaurant and purposefully headed for his table.

Yup, with these two thugs in attendance—well—today actually might be an exception. These two dudes are clearly out of place in this environment, he thought to himself. *Must be government workers—extremely boring ties*, McGregor noted.

"Are you McGregor?" one of the suits snapped in a heavily accented voice.

"I am," McGregor snapped back. "Who are you, and did you enjoy your drive? You're lousy at surreptitious tailgating, in case you didn't know. Embassy license plates? —you gotta be kidding!"

11

Thrusting a German embassy security badge at McGregor, the man grunted, "We need to talk to you, if you don't mind."

"I do mind," McGregor said sharply. "I'll be glad to visit with you, gentlemen, but this is neither the time nor the place. I'm gonna have lunch, and if you want to wait for me outside, I'll come out when I'm finished and we can talk," he said quietly.

They defiantly ignored him and pulled out chairs to sit down.

"Look, guys," he said, less quietly this time, "I'm not kidding—you have no authority here, and all of us in this room are either Virginians or West Virginians. This is the United States, the last time I checked, and regardless of the diplomatic license plates on your car, I'm betting the local sheriff is bored and doesn't give a rat's ass about diplomatic immunity. I'm guessing that he, or one of his deputies, is probably running a speed trap or shoveling-up a squished 'possum just around the next corner. Bottom-line," he continued, "I'll meet with you outside, *after* I enjoy my lunch. Now, if you want to sit at that table over there," he pointed, "feel free to do so. The special today is red-flannel hash and fried chicken livers with brown gravy."

The room was silent. No coal trucks were air-braking for the next curve, and the patter had stopped, as the suits got up and left.

"Hey, McGregor," one old-timer laughed, breaking the silence, "You now running moonshine action somewhere around here? Hell, we all knew you'd retired from the cops and robbers business, but you sure sounded like the old McGregor we used to know with those goons. Remember that time you…."

When McGregor finally left the restaurant, the suits and their car were nowhere to be seen. Despite his concerns about what they wanted, his lunch was great, and the patter had refocused from "whatever happened to…" to "remember when ole Franklin ran the still up in Marsh's holler?"

He called Morgan later that day, and Morgan informed him that he was aware of the incident.

"An Embassy spokesperson, somebody by the name of Chardonnay Feathers or something like that, I think, called to apologize for their security personnel's bad judgment regarding the restaurant incident," he said. "I was just about to call you about it! Hope they didn't give you too much trouble. If so, I can scare 'em a bit for you."

"No problem, Lieutenant. It's a dead issue, and I think the person who called you was the embassy's *'Charge d'affairs'*."

"Yep, that's what I said. Have a good evening, Cam!"

Dead issue? Could McGregor be so lucky? Not by a long shot! Two days later, in an early morning phone call to his home, Angelika Schafer, a.k.a "stranded passenger," was once again asking for his help. She was pleading for McGregor to help her get back to Germany ASAP. She claimed she was sick and wanted to go home.

"No one has contacted me at all," she told him. "I've been sightseeing all over the place by myself and…well, I don't know what happened to this Stringer fellow. It seems like I've been dumped here and forgotten. I just want to go home! I've made a mistake, I'm afraid. Please come—take me back to the airport. I'm in Suite 624 at the Marriott Capital."

The morning traffic between his house and the Marriott Capital in the heart of downtown D.C., was a nightmare any day, and this day was no different. It took him almost two hours to get into the District, locate a parking garage, and find his way to Angelika's hotel. He visited with the hotel's concierge and explained that he needed to pick up his friend in Suite 624.

"Her name is Angelika Shafer and she needs a plane ticket to Germany right away. Can you help with that?" McGregor asked.

The concierge said he would work on it, and then volunteered, "That suite's usually reserved for German Embassy dignitaries. It's like, you know, twelve hundred bucks a night—lots of strange things goin' on up there—people comin' and goin' all day and night!"

There was no answer when McGregor knocked, and then banged, on Suite 624's overly ornamental door. He called down to the lobby and asked his new acquaintance, Dane, the concierge, to meet him with a key. Dane arrived quickly. Angelika was gone—her luggage with her—and the room had been cleaned of any trace that anyone at all had been there. When they returned to the lobby, Dane checked with the front desk. They had no record that anyone by the name of Schafer, or anyone else for that matter, had been checked into Suite 624. In fact, they noted, no one by the name of Angelika Schafer had even been a guest at the hotel. McGregor checked his notes—*Marriott Capital Hotel, Suite 624.* He checked the recent calls on his cell phone, found the call from Angelika, and compared that with the phone number in Suite 624—they were the same.

What the fuck, McGregor fumed, as he made his way back to his car. *What the fuck! What kind of game is this? I smell a rat!*

As soon as he reached his car, he called Morgan. After listening to the story, the lieutenant suggested that McGregor come to his office at Dulles.

"I'll make some phone calls—I'm going to get Immigration and Customs involved," he said. "Let's see what they think. I'm betting they'll want to talk to you."

Great, what a waste of time, McGregor thought as he fought traffic on the long haul back to the airport. He'd planned to spend the day at a casino. He'd been on a winning streak, and today he knew he was going to finally hit a jackpot. *Dammit!*

The lights were out in Morgan's office when McGregor arrived, but a note on the door directed him to the airport's diplomatic reception room.

"Cam, come in, grab a chair," Morgan requested

13

"Gentlemen, this is Cameron McGregor. He's a Travelers Aid volunteer and a retired U.S. Marshal. He's got a bit of a situation that I know you have an interest in hearing about. Basically, Cam," he continued while looking at the men seated at the table around him, "we think you may have stumbled into something, and I've taken the liberty of calling in representatives from Immigration and Customs, Homeland Security, and the FBI. You know Randy McCall, Airport Police, and this is Harold Clover and John Robbins, FBI; Glenn Smith, Customs; and Gene Henson, Homeland Security.

"You didn't know," Morgan said, "but we've been monitoring, as a task force, the Angelika Schafer situation, right from the moment she was picked up here at the airport by the German Embassy fellas. We already have more information than you know about. We know exactly what happened this morning, and we know where Schafer is now—we have her in protective custody with some of your buddies from the U.S. Marshal's service."

He glanced around the table, looking smug, and went on. "As soon as she made that call to you this morning, it became a race to see who would get to her first, embassy security or us. You were not part of the race. Unfortunately, we needed you to complete your 'wild goose chase,' as part of our overall plan. I'll fill you in on that in a minute. We're hoping that embassy security think you got to her before they did, and they soon will be, if they're not already, looking for both of you here at the airport. We've got someone manning the security cameras—any questions?"

"You've got to be kidding," McGregor scowled, clearly annoyed. "What the hell is going on, is clearly the question that you fuckin' well have got to be anticipating I'd ask."

"Simply this, McGregor," Morgan went on, "the 'Angelika Schafer' you helped the other day is not the person you might have thought she was. This character, 'Loren Stringer,' the guy whose name Angelika gave Travelers Aid, is, we think, a member of the *security* detail at the German Embassy, and he, along with two other embassy security people, one guy and one gal, are running a high-end prostitution and trafficking , money-laundering and espionage ring that's based in D.C. and services big-money clients all along the east coast. We've been watching them for over a year. We're pretty sure that this activity is confined to just these three security people and that the embassy is probably unaware of their extra-curricular activities, but we're not positive." Nods from the others confirmed what Morgan was saying.

"Schafer's a street-level prostitute who was working out of Berlin when Stringer recruited her with the promise of a free trip to the U.S. and some quick big money. Unfortunately, Stringer has her passport and she is, or was, destined to become a sex slave for their purposes and profit. She knows that now," Morgan revealed.

"Regardless of the passport issue," Morgan continued, "Immigration and Customs and TSA are simply going to deport her within the next few days. The

14

Secret Service and FBI are in the process of trying to gather enough evidence to snatch the three embassy people up as co-conspirators in an espionage ring. Their girls have been shacking up regularly with some pretty high mucky mucks in the federal government."

Morgan paused and then summed up the situation for McGregor.

"Upshot? With your *all in a day's work* ethic, you may have inadvertently thrown a monkey-wrench into the whole works! Want some coffee—or perhaps some of 'Hoppy's red-flannel hash and chicken livers with brown gravy?'" he laughed slyly. "Embassy agents were following you, and we were following them. John, here, was sitting in the parking lot listening to your conversation. Those ol' boys at Hoppy's thought you were some kind of city gangster the way you told off Frick and Frack. You should have heard what they had to say about you the minute you walked out the door!"

"Coffee will be fine. Not that decaf crap though, and I see a box of doughnuts on the table, Morgan. One of those has my name on it," McGregor said grumpily. "And…you should try some of Hoppy's red-flannel hash and chicken livers with brown gravy, some time! Now, about this monkey-wrench thing— what's that all about?"

"Marshal McGregor, my name is Harold Clover. I'm with the FBI."

"Hold on, Clover," McGregor quickly interrupted, "I retired from the U.S. Marshals Service three years ago, turned in my badge and service revolver, and haven't looked back since. My *Marshal* days are behind me!"

"We know that, Cameron," Clover continued, "and we know that you were just doing what you would do for any passenger stuck in the airport, and we know you've done it many times. We're not going to ask you to do anything we wouldn't ask any other good citizen to do. Hell, it's not your fault that you singlehandedly stimulated a hornet's nest by hassling this Stringer character and ultimately connected him to the German Embassy the other day. And, hell, you didn't think for a moment that you might be giving Schafer a 'way out' when you befriended her and slipped her your phone number. Hell, we…"

"Okay, okay Clover, I got it! I'm hearing you—and your facetious act is unimpressive, to say the least."

"Message received?" Clover said.

"Yeah, I heard you," McGregor responded again.

"Moving on then," Clover smiled. "We were listening when Schafer called you this morning, and I'm sure the bad guys were listening as well. Their mistake was that they left the phone lines open on one of the phones in her suite. We picked her up within minutes after you hung up. But, listen— we see this whole situation as more of an opportunity than a setback in our combined investigations if—and that's the operative word—you can help us just a bit more."

He leaned earnestly toward McGregor. "The Embassy guys don't know that we've got Schafer," he said intently. "They think *you* have her! Right now," he continued, " a pair of them are searching the main terminal looking for the two of you. One of them is watching the check-in desks at Lufthansa and United, and the other is roaming. This whole situation puts you squarely in a bargaining position we've not been able to create on our own. However," he continued, "here's the kicker. They're not really looking for Schafer—she's a 'throw-away.' They're looking for the bag of 'toys' we found in her carry-on— 'tools of the trade'," he laughed. "We found a bunch of really close replicas of 'D' batteries in that bag and, after close examination, and the extraction of the negative ends of each battery, we found a hundred grand in thousand-dollar bills cached inside, along with a list of some extremely sensitive government documents they're seeking. We're sure the money was going to be payment in advance for the documents, probably already copied from the originals, and scheduled to be smuggled out of the country—how, we're not sure, and to whom, we don't know yet."

"This looks like, smells like, feels like something right out of a dime store spy novel," McGregor said with a flattened voice and a disgusted look.

"It probably wouldn't be Schafer that does the smuggling," Clover, seemingly unfazed by McGregor's indifferent attitude, continued, "We believe she was intended to become part of the considerable stable of women they already have, who are trying to earn their safe passage back to their respective countries. And, it's probably not Germany seeking the documents—we suspect Syria or Iran. Are you following me so far?"

"Yeah, I'm following you," McGregor said, "but I don't see why you're telling me this, or what you want me to do about it—it's your problem! I just want to go play a poker hand or two at the casino! It looks to me like you have some bad guys on the German security force who have three sidelines—international prostitution, money-laundering, and foreign espionage."

"You're on track," Clover acknowledged. "You pull off what we'd like you to do, and we'll see that you have a few extra bucks to ante-up in whatever game you want." Clover waited for McGregor to react.

McGregor gave him a stone-cold stare. The "extra bucks" suggestion was an insult but not worth rebuttal. In his mind he was busy running various scenarios that he thought might be next in the conversation. This whole scene, even though he was stonewalling the group, was confusing to a certain degree, but a bit stimulating to him. It'd been a while since he'd played "fox and geese" in the world of espionage.

I'm just not sure who's the fox and who's the goose in this game, he wondered, *and, as far as prostitution is involved, well, that's something I...*

"All right," Clover continued, "here's what we'd like for you to do for us. Assuming you agree! Where it leads, we're not sure."

"Well, that certainly makes me feel confident in your ability to protect my ass!" McGregor sniffed.

Clover rolled his eyes at the interruption. "Two things are certain at this point," he continued. "You're here and they're soon going to find out you're onto

16

their scheme. And, you have Schafer and her bag of goodies. You're already in the driver's seat, whether you want to be or not. But now, you have us riding shotgun for you. You found the money and the list, and, well, what do they want to do about it? We want to connect them directly to Schafer, which we've really already done, but we also badly need to connect them directly to the money and the list, and find out all the rest of the, who, what, when and where, info—you know the drill."

McGregor nodded with understanding--he knew the drill all too well.

"We have a Schafer look-alike agent being flown in from Denver," Clover said, looking at his watch, "and she should be here soon— actually my ear-piece is telling me she's arrived. Her name is Maggie Douglas, She's a Deputy U.S. Marshal. The two of you will leave here, with her baggage, go to lunch, and eventually end up at your house. You know you're going to be followed and watched, and you also know we'll be there as well. By the way, you let your gun permit and your 'permit to carry' expire after you left the agency. We've renewed it, and we picked up your SIG Sauer, clips and holster at your house within a few minutes after you left this morning. When you get home, you'll find your dogs locked in the garage. We picked the lock on your gun cabinet and, I promise you, we *did not* damage it. Here's your gun, your gear, and your renewals," he said, passing the items to a nonplussed McGregor.

"Your phone is tapped at the substation," Clover said. "When you get home, here's Stringer's unlisted number. Call him, tell him what you've got, and that you want a piece of the action or…"

"I got it, Clover. No problem."

"I take it you're in, then. Is that SIG a P226 model?"

"This *is* a P226 model," McGregor said as he picked up his gun, popped in a clip, holstered it and hooked it to his belt just above his right buttock. "I'm in."

"Marshal Douglas's here," someone behind him announced.

McGregor turned, smiling, and did a double take.

"Hello, Marshal—Maggie, if that's okay. Glad to meet you. I'm Cam," he said, reaching to shake her hand. "My God, you *do* look just like Angelika! If these guys are finished with us"—they nodded— "let's grab some lunch and talk strategy. Let's make sure the bad guys finger us before we leave the airport. We'll debug my place when we get there."

"Cam, your house, garage, horse barn and shed have already been debugged, and RF blocking equipment has already been updated and reactivated," Clover quickly interjected. "We didn't do the dishes or your laundry, but your barn sure needs mucking out," he laughed. "Here's a secure cell phone for each of you. Use them exclusively to contact me and each other, and keep it turned on so I can track and contact you."

"Maggie, I've often wondered who the bad guys *really* are," McGregor said playfully as he closed the door behind them.

17

"Hold on to my arm, Angelika—and smile," he said as they left the room and instantly became just plain, ordinary, airport pedestrians.

CHAPTER THREE

After a quiet lunch and getting acquainted, without revealing to anyone who might be listening who they really were and what they were doing, they headed toward McGregor's house. No one seemed to be tailing them, at least within rearview mirror sight, but McGregor was confident that embassy security had undoubtedly attached a GPS tracking device somewhere on the frame of his car.

Maggie is actually better looking than Angelika, he thought. *She speaks almost perfect German, and English with a remarkable German accent. And she's got a great...*

"Is this your house?" Maggie exclaimed, using a fake German accent, as they pulled into the long winding driveway to McGregor's garage.

"You have horses? What are they, quarter horses?" she asked. "I've never ridden a quarter horse, but I've read about them. I understand they can stop and turn on, what you say, a dime? Will you let me ride one?"

McGregor's home was in a picturesque setting. He'd taken a neglected farm, nestled in the mountains west of the Washington D.C. metropolitan area, and built it into a place for fleeing the voices of crowds, relentless traffic, and the city lights that hinder the beauty and restfulness of a clear night sky. Surrounded by the colors and cover of both deciduous and non-deciduous forests, he considered his home and land as his "other identity"—his hideaway and escape from day-to-day realism. The loss of Polly, his wife and best friend of thirty-one years, to cancer three years ago had driven him into an almost solitary state of mind and was a large part of his decision to retire.

"The question is not whether I'll let you ride one, but rather *can* you ride one?" McGregor laughed. "They're spirited beasts with minds of their own."

"As am I, *Herr* McGregor!" she smiled with a flirtatious look on her face.

They walked into the house and McGregor retrieved his dogs from the garage where Clover's people had put them. Instantly, they were greeted enthusiastically by Zeus, McGregor's German Shepherd, and Annie, his dog of many varieties. While Zeus offered his paw to Maggie, Annie quickly inspected her pant legs to ascertain where she'd been, who she'd been with, and what she had for lunch. Knowing that the house had been 'debugged', McGregor was now able to speak freely.

"Between the two of them, Maggie, you can be sure no one will get within a hundred yards of this place without our knowing about it. Make yourself comfortable. We can talk openly now. The RF interrupter system the guys have on this house is extremely effective, and any bugs, except those on the phone line,

19

planted by our guys or theirs, are now completely blocked," he said as he opened a small cabinet in the kitchen and flipped a switch.

"Now we're doubly covered," he mentioned, "I have my own blocking and detection system. I'm gonna pour us a drink, and then call Stringer to get this party started. What's your poison?"

After fixing drinks, McGregor picked up the phone.

"Loren Stringer, my new best friend—good to talk to you and not your answering machine. This is Cameron McGregor from Travelers Aid at Dulles Airport. I'm calling because I'm betting you want to talk to me."

"Yeah, you know I do," Stringer said acidly, his tongue tripping over his second language translation difficulties.

"Well, for a moment," McGregor replied calmly, "why don't you just sit back, relax, and listen carefully to what I'm going to say. I'm going to cut directly to the bottom line. First, Stringer, you know I've got Angelika Schafer, and second, I have her luggage, and most important, her carry-on bag. The question for you today is simply, what do you want me to do with the money and the list of documents that were hidden in the D battery cases? I'm guessing that you already know that I retired from the Justice Department a few years ago, and that I'm perfectly capable of putting two and two together, or in this case, a hundred grand and a shopping list, and coming up with the correct answer."

"What do you want? I have no idea what you're talking about," Stringer sputtered.

"Yeah, ya do," McGregor responded. "I want a sizeable piece of the action, or
I turn Schafer, along with her bag of goodies, over to the authorities. I'm sure there would be a sizeable reward from the government, aren't you? Now, what 'piece of the action' am I talking about? I'll let *you* attempt to answer that question yourself. Take some time to think out your next move and call me back at this number—preferably not between nine and ten o'clock this evening—I don't want to miss *CSI-Miami*! So, Springer, the ball's clearly in your court, at least for the next few hours, and then it's my turn. I look forward to hearing from you."

As McGregor hung up the phone, he could almost hear agents from both camps simultaneously declaring, "game's on!"

"You okay with that, Maggie? What I said?"

Dead silence. He turned, and Maggie was nowhere in sight. "Where are you?" he hollered.

Dead silence. He drew his gun and slowly made his way down the hallway to the bedroom wing of his house, checking out each room on his way. When he reached the master bedroom, he saw Maggie's clothes strewn across the bed. The rear sliding door to the deck was slightly open and the cover on his hot tub was off. He holstered his gun, opened the door the rest of the way, and announced his presence.

"You missed a good conversation, Maggie!" *She should have been there to hear what transpired,* McGregor thought. "Have you ever been involved in something like this?" he asked.

"Come closer, I'm having trouble hearing you," she said.

As McGregor moved to the edge of the hot tub, it was evident that Maggie was soaking in the buff. *Great body,* he noted. "I said, have you been involved in anything like this assignment before?"

"No," she laughed, slowly moving from one area of the hot tub to another. "I like this tub. After I left the military, ten years in active duty, I joined the Marshal's service. After training, I was assigned to the federal courthouse in Denver—been there six years now—did I mention that I really like this hot tub?" she asked while slowly guiding small waves of water over and around her curves. "Men love to watch water glide over a woman's skin, I'm told," she spoke in a sensual tone in rhythm with her hand motions.

This show could be a spontaneous thirty second tease or a planned-out, full speed ahead, performance. Either way, McGregor forced himself to concede, *the tease is great, but the performance will have to wait. Business first.*

"Any agency commendations?" McGregor continued.

"Four to date— three major incidents, and I had to drop a perp last year. It wasn't pretty, but unfortunately, very necessary. I heard his bullet whiz by my right ear before it slammed into a marble wall. I've still got a few chips embedded in the back of my shoulder."

"Ouch," McGregor reacted. "Look, I want you to go over to the safe house where we're holding Schafer. It's only about twenty minutes away in Middleburg. She needs to be questioned about everything that took place, starting in Germany. I want to know as much as possible about the people who picked her up at the airport and delivered her to the hotel, and I want to know as much as possible about her. Take my camera and get a picture of her. Be careful about what's behind or beside her when you snap the picture. We don't want to give anyone we might show her picture to a hint as to where she is. You need to do this today. I've given a proposal— ultimatum, if you wish— to the bad guys and I expect some action any time now. I need the Schafer stuff ASAP."

"No problem," Maggie said, popping out of the water and exposing herself fully to McGregor. "Toss me a towel, would you?"

While she was dressing, McGregor walked out to his barn, where, along with his horses, he kept a sizeable collection of cars, trucks and a couple of all-terrain vehicles.

Why did she laugh, he wondered, *when I asked her if she'd been involved in anything like this assignment before?*

After punching the coordinates to the safe house into the GPS system of one of his cars—a vehicle that had been scanned for any kind of tracking device— he sent Maggie, wearing dark sunglasses, and one of his own cowboy hats, on her way.

21

"Be careful, Maggie, watch your tail!" he advised her.

"Thought you'd already done that," she retorted with a sly smile.

After she'd gone, he notified Clover about what she was doing, and asked him to fax him a picture that included the cash, the list, partially obscured, and the opened batteries.

An hour later, Maggie rang McGregor's cell phone.

"You're ridin' a wild mustang, cowboy," Maggie said quietly. "You've got a mole in your pasture, according to the info I got from our girl. Get Clover on the phone as soon as I hang up and tell him to limit any knowledge of our activities from now on to just you, me, and him. I think I know who the mole is, but I'm also thinking there may be more than one in range; this situation goes much deeper than we thought. My new friend is doing fine and she's safe here for the time being—but she lied to you about why she was here in the first place, and then again when she told you why she wanted out—she's sorry about that," she said. "I'm on my way back now, and we'll talk more about the rodeo when I get there," she said as she hung up the phone.

McGregor used the cell phone to call Clover again and told him to limit his contacts to just him and Maggie. He mentioned the word "mole." He knew Clover would know exactly what he was conveying. He'd no sooner hung up when his regular phone rang. It was Stringer. "Listen carefully, McGregor," he said. "I want to meet with you as soon as possible. We need to talk. I can come to your house if you wish. Or we can meet…"

McGregor cut him off mid-sentence. "I'll meet you at eight a.m. sharp, tomorrow morning at Hoppy's Place" he said. I know that you know where that is. I'll be sitting at the old picnic table outside and just to the left of the place. You need some fresh air, and the view is spectacular. It'll be just me and my dog. If you feel you need company, leave 'em in the car. It's just you and me, Stringer, and this is the only opportunity you're gonna have to cut a deal with me—make it a   good   one."

"There's something familiar about Stringer's voice," he muttered to himself. "Hey, Zeus, wanna go for a ride in the car in the morning?" Zeus wagged agreeably.

Twenty minutes later, Maggie returned from her meeting with Schafer. While McGregor started a fire in the patio grill, she filled him in on what she'd learned from Schafer.

"Contrary to what she told you," Maggie began. "Angelika Schafer is not, and never has been, a high school teacher. She's a high-class call girl slash escort with clientele all over the world. She's been traveling between Berlin and Washington for almost ten years, she told me, but this is the first time, she claims, that her pimps—she calls them her 'bookers'— have used her as a *mule* for the espionage side of their business. When she found out she had no clients waiting for her services this trip and was carrying concealed contraband, she *raised one hell of a stink with her handlers*—her words. Her booker, Loren Stringer, was on his way to *punish* her, she said, when she called you. She also said she didn't know at that point that she was carrying the stuff we found in what she called her *tool kit*."

"Okay," McGregor interrupted. "Two questions, Maggie. How do you want your steak, and, how much of what you just told me do you believe?"

"Medium well," she said, "and, I think Schafer did a really good job of fooling you, starting right at the airport. She realized she was being 'dumped' by her handlers—I'm going to call them the 'syndicate'—and used you to put some pressure on them. I don't think she knew what was stashed in her carry-on, and I think one of the 'bad guys' goofed when it wasn't confiscated in customs. The guy that fucked up is a customs agent who works at Dulles and is on the syndicate's payroll."

"That's not good," McGregor frowned.

"The two agents from the German embassy who picked her up are also part of the syndicate," Maggie continued, "and your good friend Morgan—the airport authority cop—might be, in fact, the Stringer guy you've been dealing with. I may be wrong, but I'm feeling that he might actually be the head man in this whole game."

"Damn!" McGregor exclaimed incredulously.

"So, here's what I'm thinking at this point," Maggie said. "Stringer's syndicate has latched onto one or more customs agents, one or more TSA folks, at least two or three employees of the German embassy, and who knows how many Airport Authority cops—maybe even FBI people."

McGregor was shocked and angry at what he was hearing. "You've gotta be kidding," he said vehemently.

"By connecting Schafer with the embassy, you suddenly became a major fly in their ointment, Cam. They need to get rid of you, but not before they get the evidence you've got against them out of your hands. I don't know why," she hesitated, "but, well, I've got a feeling that we're dealing with just the tip of an iceberg. Clearly, we have some things to think about, but in the meantime, I saw salad makings in your fridge, and I'm going to throw a couple of those potatoes lying on your kitchen counter in the microwave—you know, the ones you've been saving for this 'special' occasion. Slow the steaks down a bit, partner, and show a little excitement. You're back in the saddle, cowboy—whether you wanna be or not!" She turned and headed toward the kitchen. "Come on, pooches, follow along; you can help me wash the potatoes while your master plays chuck-wagon chef. We've all had a long day!"

After dinner, Maggie excused herself, took a shower and curled up on the couch in McGregor's den to watch some TV. She was asleep in minutes, McGregor noted as he walked by on the way to his office.

Something's wrong with this whole Schafer/syndicate picture, he thought to himself while waiting for his computer to power up. He had an uneasy feeling that the next day was going to be full of surprises.

After checking his e-mail and posting a few responses, he grabbed a blanket from the linen closet and walked to the den. He gently placed the blanket over Maggie in case she spent the night on the couch. He couldn't help but notice her Colorado State University *Go Rams!* midriff tee-shirt that had either shrunk tight over time or was specifically designed to allow full exposure of any female wearer's upper body endowments and whatever she decided to wear or not from the belly-button down. In Maggie's case, he noted, it was bikini panties highlighted by a strategically placed CSU mascot's head. He checked to see if her gun was within her reach if she needed it, turned off the TV and lights, and invited Zeus and Annie to take a short walk with him.

"Brisk mountain air or a cold shower—I need one or the other, maybe both, my canine friends," he commented to them as they crisscrossed the yard, noses down, searching for who-knows-what.

Stabs of worry woke McGregor from a fitful slumber often that night. Replays of the events of the last few days were running through his head like a runaway train. Foremost, he was thinking about just how he got involved in this challenge and about his concerns for the unknowns that are often inherent in this kind of situation. At the same time, he couldn't help thinking about the woman who'd come into his life and was sleeping just down the hall—a woman who had willfully or unwittingly aroused some feelings that he hadn't experienced since Polly died.

He was jolted awake by his phone signaling that it was time to get the day underway. He'd set it at 6:00 a.m., knowing it would take him a few minutes to shower and get dressed and thirty minutes to get to Hoppy's Place, leaving plenty of time for a cup of coffee and one of Hoppy's overly greasy, but incredibly delicious, Western omelets.

Hoppy Purcell cooked his omelets quickly—lightly browned on the outside and a bit runny on the inside, with fillings and special touches that McGregor had never been able to figure out.

Maybe today I'll put some pressure on him and just simply ask him. On the other hand, maybe I'm better off not knowing, he chuckled to himself as he headed toward the den to wake Maggie up.

She was still sleeping as he sat down on the edge of the coffee table. The blanket that he'd gently placed over her last night had fallen to the floor. For a moment he just sat there and looked at the tightness of her tummy, the smoothness of her skin and the silkiness of her uncombed hair.

"Good morning, Maggie," he said softly, placing his hand gently on her shoulder. "Time for me to get rollin'. I'll call you on my way back, which should be around nine-thirty or so. I'm taking Zeus with me for backup. I'd rather take you, but, well…anyway, any problems, call; I'm only thirty minutes out," he advised her as he reached to pick up the fallen blanket.

"Be careful, Cam," she said as she sat up and put her arms around his neck. "These are not nice people you're dealing with!"

24

McGregor whistled up Zeus. "Annie, guard Maggie and the house; I'll be back soon. The F150, Zeus—we need the truck to fit in with the locals at Hoppy's this morning."

He ejected, carefully checked, and reinserted the ammunition clip in his gun as he walked toward the truck. Zeus was already there, waiting anxiously for McGregor to open the passenger door.

As McGregor and Zeus arrived, the parking lot at Hoppy's was masked with early morning mountain fog and was almost full of pick-up trucks—all sizes, brands, and colors.

"My kind of folks, Zeus, my kind of folks, and every one of those trucks has a shotgun wedged behind the driver's seat," he observed as he parked, got out, and walked up the well-worn wooden steps to the front porch and door.

"Stay here, Zeus. You know I'll bring you a treat."

McGregor looked at his watch. 7:25. "Coffee—black, and a Western to go" he called out to Mary Beth, Hoppy's wife and chief waitress.

"Hadn't seen you for a while, Cam," she said. "But twice in the same week? Are you back on the job again, or you just got the hots for me?" she laughed as she poured his coffee.

"Why, Mary Beth, you know it's you, the coffee, and the Western," he retorted with a grin. "Tell me what's in the filling that Hoppy puts in his Westerns, and I'll double your tip this morning."

"What the hell am I goin' to buy for fifty cents? Make it fifty dollars and we might talk! You know all too well that it's an international secret!"

McGregor had only taken a few sips of coffee before Mary Beth plopped two Styrofoam containers, a plastic fork, knife, and three carefully folded paper napkins in front of him.

"The smaller one is for Zeus. He's been lettin' everyone pet him as they come and go. I'll bet someone would lose a finger if they tried to leash him up, huh?"

"A finger would be just an appetizer for him, Mary Beth; he loves elbows," McGregor joked, as he laid a ten spot on the counter, smiled, and left. "Come on, Zeus, I've got breakfast—we'll be dining at our usual picnic table."

He looked at his watch—7:40. Before he sat down, he found a stick and walked Zeus to a spot between the table and the parking lot. He stuck the stick in the ground as Zeus watched. "No one gets closer to me than this stick, Zeus, unless I tell you okay. Got it? —let's eat," McGregor said as he walked back to the table and took a seat where he had a clear view of the parking lot. As he ate, he carefully eyed the areas around the grounds for anything unusual or out of place. He'd eaten at that picnic table many times in the past—he knew the area well.

At 8:00 sharp, a Mercedes, noticeably unembellished with diplomatic plates, pulled into the parking lot, and a well-dressed woman got out of the rear passenger side door. She was carrying a large purse and wearing a below-the-

25

waist sport jacket, he noted, as she headed straight towards him. When she approached the stick, Zeus let out a low growl.

"It's okay, Zeus," McGregor assured him, while unsnapping the strap that was keeping his gun safely holstered. "It's okay."

"May I join you, *Herr* McGregor?" the woman asked with a noticeable German accent. "What a beautiful dog, native to my homeland. May I call you Cameron? I studied your profile and picture last night. I feel as if I've known you for years. You had quite a distinguished career with your government. My name is Birdie Steiner; I'm a security officer with the German embassy."

"Sit down, please, *Frau* or *Fraulein* Steiner. I'll just call you Birdie if you don't mind—feel free to call me Cam. Please place your purse on the table along with both hands. Can't be too cautious, you know. Are you armed? Both hands on the table please," he reminded her. "If you're armed, where are you carrying your weapon, and where's Stringer?"

"My gun is in my purse," she said, sitting down across the table from McGregor. "*Herr* Stringer couldn't make it this morning, so he asked me to speak on his behalf."

"Why am I not surprised? Let me see your embassy ID please. I know our every word is being heard and recorded by your two friends in the car, so let's keep this brief and to the point," McGregor said, as he took a phone picture of Steiner's ID. "For five-hundred grand," he continued, "I'll see that Angelika Schafer is well paid, that her U.S. green card and visa is cancelled permanently, and that she's unceremoniously deported back to Germany. In addition, upon receipt of the money, I'll arrange for the transfer of the list you'd like to have. The hundred grand the authorities found in the batteries…well, you can consider that money a gift of friendship to this country's peace officer's benevolent fund. There's more. I want an additional two-hundred-fifty grand deposited in a bank account in my name on January fifteenth of each year, for the next ten years, just to keep my mouth shut about your prostitution enterprise and anything else you've got going."

"Can you show me proof of what you have in your possession?" she asked. "And," she continued, "how much time will you give me to discuss this with Mr. Stringer, and get back to you?"

"Here are pictures of what I have. Your time is up immediately. I'm reckoning that Stringer's on the line eavesdropping in the car with your buddies as we speak, and that you're undoubtedly wired. This is not a game, Birdie and company; this is rock bottom, hard-ass business. We either make a deal today, right now, or I go authority hunting."

I must have said the magic word, McGregor guessed. Looking past Steiner, he could see two men from the Mercedes get out of the front seat of the car and start walking toward him.

He nodded a silent signal to Zeus.

26

By the time the men got five steps from their car, Zeus was at the pre-placed twig showing both guys the bone-polished whites of every tooth in his mouth, and McGregor was displaying his gun.

"Stop right there, gentlemen. If you draw your weapons," McGregor shouted, "Zeus will disarm one of you, and I'll put a bullet between the eyes of whoever Zeus decides to leave for me. I promise, guys, it'll be Washington Post front page bloody mess fodder!"

Thinking this might be a good time to disarm Birdie, and still focused on the two men, he opened Steiner's purse with his free hand and removed her gun. It was a Browning BDM. Out of the corner of his eye and across the table, he could see Steiner mouthing words to him.

"Take the clip out. Read the note inside. Later. Get out of here. Now. Trust me!"

After ejecting the clip, he laid her gun on the table, and dropped the clip into his pocket.

"Nice meeting you, Birdie," McGregor said, his eyes still focused on the two men, "sorry we couldn't do business."

He motioned to Zeus, "Okay, Zeus, let them pass! Gentlemen! Walk toward me slowly. I want to see your IDs. Put them on the table in front of me, step back and keep your hands where Zeus and I can see them. There's only one wrong move between living or kissing your old friend Hitler in Hell."

The men moved cautiously forward and placed their IDs down as McGregor had commanded—again he used his phone to snap images for posterity.

"Okay, take your IDs, gentlemen. Birdie, take your gun, and the three of you get out of here. *Gehen Sie jetzt*," he said sharply. "Zeus and I will walk you part way to your car...And," he declared just short of reaching their car, "be sure to tell Stringer that *his* ass is definitely *mine* now!"

"Good job, Zeus!" he said as the Mercedes disappeared around the bend and headed down the mountain. "Good job, my great friend. Let's vamoose!"

"Good job yourself there, partner—you sure know how to make enemies," a voice behind him declared.

Startled, he spun around hurriedly and saw Maggie and Annie sitting on Hoppy's front porch. Maggie must have found where he'd placed the contents of his wife's closet after her death, he quickly deduced. She was wearing Polly's favorite cowgirl hat, one of her western style shirts, a pair of her riding boots, and one of the many wigs she had needed during her long and frequent chemotherapy treatments. He didn't recognize the tight-fitting jeans.

"What the hell are you doing here?" he snapped. "Annie doesn't ride well in the car! She always..."

"Annie and I had you covered, cowboy. It was Annie's idea to come, and she only barfed once on the way here. She thought we should cover your back,

27

you know, just in case. We felt it was our job, didn't we, Annie?" Annie agreed, wagging her tail emphatically.

"How'd you know how to get here...which car did you drive?" he asked.

"I knew the name of the place here, and I have a GPS on my phone," Maggie grinned, "and I just love that delightful little miniature Corvette I concealed over there behind those dump trucks—runs just like a real one. Gonna buy me breakfast?"

"I'll make you breakfast when we get home," he grumped. "I hate to say it, but a red wig under that Stetson. It makes you look like a fuckin' circus clown. And," he continued with a stern look on his face, "that Corvette you're driving is an original 'Vette, a 1953, 138Z, convertible, auction valued at a mere two hundred and sixty grand. You put a scratch on that car or leave a speck of dog barf on the upholstery and..."

"See ya there, Cam...wanna race? Come on, Annie, let's go home. My tummy's growlin' and I'll bet yours is too," Maggie giggled as she and Annie disappeared into the dump truck parking area. "We'll be right behind you," she yelled, "covering your back."

"I think that's a first for both of us," McGregor said to Zeus as they climbed into his truck and started home. "Maggie had my back and Annie had yours. Both are real firecrackers, don't you think?"

As he pulled out onto the highway, he patted Zeus on the back. "You did a great job this morning, my friend. Thank you! Keep a keen eye on the road for a possible surprise from the bad guys—you never know what's just around the next corner."

After arriving home and fixing the promised breakfast for Maggie, McGregor opened the clip Steiner had wanted him to pocket, and, just as she'd said, he found her note, carefully rolled up and placed between the fourth and sixth cartridges in the clip.

"Well, crap! This is written in German," he exclaimed.

"Let me see it," Maggie said. "I was born in Frankenmuth, Michigan. Two-thirds of my friends spoke German as a first language. My minor at CSU was in Germanic languages, and I was stationed in Frankfurt for three years. I might be able to decipher it. Got a pencil?"

It didn't take her long. In five minutes or less, Maggie put down her pencil and handed her translation to McGregor.

"Cam, we're in deeper than we thought," she said softly.

To whom this may concern: My name is Bridget (Birdie) Steiner; I am a security officer with the German embassy stationed in Washington, DC. I am a German citizen. I hold a US Green card. I want to turn witness for you. I am requesting amnesty. I'm asking you to arrest me, place me in protective custody, and I will reveal all the details regarding the espionage

28

I've been forced to be involved in with the spies we employ. To prove my sincerity, recheck Schafer's baggage. You probably don't have the real inventory of documents ordered. There is fake one in the batteries. The real one is embedded in glans area of pink dildo. I stuck a list of everybody involved under the picnic table at the meeting this date with McGregor. Please help me.

Sorry I don't write good English.

Without saying a word, McGregor picked up the phone and punched in a number.

"Roberto," he said, "I know it's short notice, but I have some tree work that needs to be done immediately......Can you come up to my place with your chainsaw and help me?.....Bring a friend or two if you can?.....Great! Thank you."

"Maggie, please take Zeus in my truck and get that note from under the picnic table at Hoppy's. Be careful and get back here as fast as you can. You'll probably be followed when you leave here—just be aware. We're going to bring this to a head, right now."

Maggie knew the drill, and she'd developed enough confidence in McGregor to follow his lead. She checked her clip, grabbed a couple of extra ones from her duffle bag, and headed out the door.

"Come on, Zeus, let's go have some fun." She looked at McGregor over her shoulder. "Cam, tell me your conversation with this so-called Roberto was a call for reinforcements."

"Big time, Maggie—again, be careful," he said, as she raced Zeus to the truck.

By the time Maggie returned with the retrieved note, entering the house cautiously through the back door to the kitchen, four men had joined McGregor and were sitting around his dining room table discussing, Maggie surmised, the current situation. McGregor's words, *we're going to bring this to a head, right now*, rushed through her mind.

McGregor got up from the table and walked into the kitchen to greet Maggie and Zeus. Annie left the men in the dining room as well, to invite Zeus to come and join her in checking pants legs for evidence. Zeus, as might be expected, gladly accepted the invitation.

"Was there a note? Did you find it?" McGregor asked impatiently.

"There was, and I did," Maggie said. "I've got it right..."

"Come and meet these guys," McGregor interrupted her. "I want you to know your new best friends. All four of these beat-up, scarred, and semi-ugly pirates are retired U.S. Marshals. We all mustered out at the same time, but over the years, the five of us raised major havoc, and broke more than a few rules in the process," he laughed.

29

"Gentlemen, this is Maggie Douglas. She's one of us, although far from being retired."

All four men stood up to greet Maggie and introduce themselves—Clardy English, Andrew (Andy) Bristow, Harvey Daniels, and Roberto Gonzalez.

"I've brought them up-to-date, Maggie," McGregor announced, "just waiting for any new info you found in Steiner's note. What did she use, gum?"

"No," Maggie said, "she used a simple push pin. You know, it's interesting. You had your eyes on her the entire time, from the moment she left the car, to when she sat down. And remember? You had her keep her hands on the table all the time she was with you. I'm thinking that, as soon as Stringer or Morgan or whatever his name is, contacted her about meeting you in his place, she did a lot of planning about this whole thing, drove herself out to Hoppy's Place the night before the meeting, and pinned this note under the table. Zeus and I think she hammered the pin in with a rock or something, because I ruined a perfectly good nail file getting it out of that old wood. It was also covered in plastic wrap to protect it from the elements. How she knew you'd be sitting at that table is a mystery to me."

"Good analysis, Maggie," McGregor said, "but she must have planted it while she was there with me. Don't know how or when. Must have been part of her sitting down movements. You're right, pre-planned for sure!"

"Nevertheless," Maggie continued, "here's her note—it's short, but with info we need," she said as she handed it to McGregor. "I translated it while I was still at Hoppy's, in case I needed to contact you immediately."

To whom it may concern. This is a list of people, including me, who are part of a group referring to itself as 'Mirror-Dot 699'. MD 699 is actively involved in the trading of classified United States documents to foreign buyers, mostly Iranian and other Middle East for cash-only payments. Our method of contact, trading, delivering and collection is entirely through use of a stable of female escorts. Escorts gather information from clients, you call 'Johns.' I know where the list of escorts is, and who their clients and contacts are. Too many to include now.
Please, I want to turn witness and seek amnesty. Please help me.

"And here," Maggie said as soon as McGregor finished reading the note, "is what we need the most right now. Here's her list of names. Hold on to your hat!"

McGregor quickly passed Steiner's note to his colleagues, while he looked at the list of names Maggie handed him.

Lorenzo Stringer Morgan, Washington Airport Polizei Department (MD 699 Leader)

30

Randolph Joseph McCall, Washington Airport Polizei Department
Harold Robert Clover, Federal Bureau of Investigation (FBI) (MD 699 Leader)
John Robert Robbins, Federal Bureau of Investigation (FBI)
Larry Glenn Smith, USA Zoll (Customs)
Richard Raymond Rodway, USA Zoll (Customs)
Eugene Allen Henson, Transportation Security Administration (TSA)
William Penn Grün, Transportation Security Administration (TSA)
Burkhard Dieter, Security Officer, Deutsche Botschaft, Wash., D.C. (MD 699 Leader)
Bridget Steiner, Security Officer, Deutsche Botschaft, Washington, D.C.
Dirk Franze, Security Officer, Deutsche Botschaft, Washington, D.C.
Hans Joachim, Security Officer, Deutsche Botschaft, Washington, D.C.

"Son of a bitch," McGregor exclaimed. "Maggie, these are some of the same guys that were in that meeting with Morgan slash Stringer," he said, pointing to the names of McCall, Clover, Robbins, Smith, and Henson. "I thought it was Clover who called you into this, wasn't it?"

"No," she responded sharply. "I got an order directly from headquarters—can't remember her name."

"They *were* trying to set us up!" McGregor said hotly. "You were absolutely right, Maggie. When Customs screwed up on Angelika Schafer's goodies, and she took my card and called me, I became, along with her and her 'tool kit', a big problem for them. Well, their problem just got bigger," McGregor announced as he shared the list around the table.

"Roberto, toss me your cell phone—all of mine are being monitored, and the direct line to Clover is, well, clearly out of service. I'm going to call in some favors! Maggie, did you get the names of the two marshals that are guarding Schafer at the safe house?"

"Red and Brad," Maggie recalled. "I didn't get their last names."

"Good enough—both dependable guys." McGregor said. "Maggie," he continued, "I want you and Andy to hightail it over to the safe house and warn Red and Brad to be especially alert. Bring them up to date, and tell them not to release Schafer to anyone, including those with badges, warrants, anything, without checking with me first. Leave Schafer enough clothing and necessities to make it through a couple more days, and then bring the entire suitcase and its contents and her carry-on bag and its contents back here. Let's see if they missed anything else. You know what we're looking for, so make sure Schafer hasn't hidden it somewhere in the house. We need any evidence! Don't be hesitant to get tough with Schafer if you need to. She's no longer a 'guest' in this country as far as I'm concerned— she's a foreign agent."

As they prepared to leave, McGregor asked Andy if had a gun with him. "If not, hit my firearm locker in the mud room as you leave. Ammunition is in the bottom drawer."

As soon as Maggie and Andy had gone, McGregor checked the phone directory in his laptop, picked up Roberto's cell and punched in a number. After giving a code alert to the secretary who answered his call, he was connected to the head of the FBI office in Phoenix, Arizona. Allen Beck, special agent in charge assigned to the Southwest territory for the FBI, answered the phone. Beck and McGregor had worked together on several high-profile cases in the past and had become trusted colleagues and close friends over the years. Beck had given the eulogy at Polly McGregor's funeral. McGregor knew he could be unquestioningly trusted to help him get safely in touch with someone far up the FBI's chain of command in D.C., and someone who, like him, hated cops and agents who had, in the vernacular, "gone over to the dark side."

After McGregor quickly explained the situation, Beck took the lead.

"I'm going to set up a conference call," he said, "between you, me, and Lawrence Brody. Brody is currently serving as an assistant director at the FBI headquarters in D.C. He's a trusted friend and the most honest cop I've ever known, next to you of course," he laughed. "I'll call you in just a few minutes at the number that's showing up on my caller ID—glad to see you've got Roberto Gonzalez back working with you. You two make a dangerous pair. I'll never forget…" he started to laugh, "but, not now— that's for another time. By the way, Brody is a take-charge and a totally bottom-line guy. Be prepared!"

While waiting for the conference call, McGregor sent English and Daniels on a reconnaissance excursion to the wooded areas surrounding his house.

"See if you can spot anyone out there keeping tabs on the house," he suggested. "There's a small cutback just off the main road on the north side of my property, just big enough to park one car. Check to see if anyone's parked there and, if so, disable the car. If you can, pop the trunk, and if you find any weapons or ammo, confiscate them and bring them back here. I'm not trusting anyone with or without a badge right now."

McGregor pointed in the direction of his barn. "There are two all-terrain vehicles out there. They're gassed up and ready to go. Use them, make a quick sweep, and be back here in forty-five minutes if you can. Be careful, be safe, and if you spot anybody, just pretend you didn't see them and ride on by. They may be good guys for all I know."

Within seconds after English and Daniels left, Gonzalez's cell phone rang. "That'll be Beck and Brody," McGregor noted. "Roberto, I'm going to put this on speaker phone so you're in the loop. You are in, aren't you?"

"I wouldn't miss it," Roberto assured him. "Feels like old times!"

"McGregor here," he announced on the phone. "Roberto Gonzalez, U.S. Marshal, retired, is also listening."

"Marshals McGregor and Gonzalez, this is Special Agent Lawrence Brody speaking. I'm Assistant Director, headquarters, FBI. Special Agent Allen Beck from our Phoenix office is also on the line. Agent Beck brought me up to date—sounds like you've scored a bull's-eye," he said.

"We've been marginally aware of Mirror-Dot 699," Brody continued, "and have been trying to gather evidence on them for almost three years. We've *just* managed to get one of our own on the inside, but he's not been able to get us enough evidence yet to make arrests and shut this national security leak down. Tell me you've got such evidence—evidence, mind you, that we can use to legally put these bastards out of business, and I'll bring the full force of my office down on their heads."

"I have a question, Agent Brody. Has your 'insider' identified himself as an FBI agent to the leadership of MD 699?"

"Oh, yeah, McGregor, he's playing the role of a turncoat—at least he's supposed to be! What's up?"

"Do you feel free to tell me his name?" McGregor asked.

"Not at this time, I don't," Brody quickly responded.

"Cam, what's going on," Beck interrupted, "why do you..."

"Agent Brody," McGregor snapped. "I don't have the time, the patience, or, to be honest, enough firepower to play games. According to my informant, you've got *two* FBI agents inside MD 699. They're *both* on my kill list if that becomes necessary. If either of them walks up the path to my door in the next few minutes, which one's ass do you want me to spare—FBI Agent/insider Harold Robert Clover, or FBI Agent/insider John Robert Robbins?"

"Clover's our man on the inside," Brody relented. "I don't know Robbins. He's not working out of my office nor has he anything to do with our investigation of MD 699."

"Give me your FAX number, Agent Brody—yours as well, Agent Beck. I need the three of us looking at the same documents I have in front of me. The two items I'm going to send you are from Bridget Steiner, a security officer with the German embassy in D.C. One is a list of names, and the other is a note that was attached to the list. The note's been translated into English by U.S. Marshal Maggie Douglas. I'm putting you on hold while I send these."

"Andy and Maggie are coming up the driveway," Roberto said, as McGregor was faxing the documents to Brody and Beck.

"I hope they found the evidence we need," McGregor grunted. "Okay, Agents Brody and Beck, you should have the documents by now. I think the situation needs to be acted upon now rather than later—your thoughts?"

After taking a moment to look over the documents, Brody reacted assertively, "I'm going to take the lead here, gentlemen. My deputy is on his way to get premise-search and arrest warrants for everybody on the list—including my people. The word 'leader' beside Clover's name has me thinking. Every time I've met with him about MD 699, I've kinda felt as if I were getting the runaround.

33

The kind of runaround you might expect from a possible double agent. I hope I'm wrong. Regardless, as soon as my deputy signals me that he has the proper warrants in hand, we're going to execute sweep-arrests immediately— I'm guessing within the next hour. In the meantime, I want you folks to just sit..."

"Sir," McGregor interrupted. "My people and I, under the leadership of Marshal Douglas, who, at present, is the only one of us with active law enforcement status, want to pick up Bridget Steiner— she's on the list— before she's formally arrested. We owe her a favor, and to be honest, I'd like to question her, with Marshal Douglas present, about where we might find the files she mentioned in her note. Steiner risked her life getting those notes to me, and I'd like to at least thank her. We also have the person who got me involved in this situation in protective custody. She's not on the list, but we want to hold her for at least another day before we turn her over to your office. Her name is Angelika Schafer, and U.S. Marshals have her in protective custody at one of our safe houses in Virginia."

"No problem, McGregor," Brody responded.

"I'm finished here, gentlemen," Beck said. "Cam, good work! Keep your head down, and I promise to visit with you sometime in the near future. You know where I am if you need more assistance."

"Thanks, Allen," McGregor said.

"Yes, ditto that," Brody interjected. "Contact me directly, McGregor, if anything I need to know comes up; I'm going to enjoy this upcoming party! Oh," he continued, "call me when you want us to pick up Steiner and Schafer."

"Will do—it's been a pleasure working with you on this," McGregor said as he punched 'end' on Gonzalez's cell phone. *So far*, he noted to himself.

"Maggie, did you find the inventory of documents Steiner mentioned?" McGregor asked.

"Right where she said it would be," she said laughing. "I thought poor Andy was going to have a heart attack and run us into a ditch when he saw me dissecting a pink penis-looking thing on our way back. His eyes were practically falling out of their sockets when he asked me what I was doing. I told him this is what I do to men I don't like!"

"Shame on you, Maggie," McGregor grinned.

"Okay all, this is when I start acting like a person in charge...a.k.a... asshole," McGregor announced with a toothy smile. "Roberto, please FAX that list to Brody right away. Maggie, gather up all the evidence we've collected and put it on the bed in the master bedroom—here are a couple of evidence envelopes. I'll be back to put them in my safe in just a minute. Clardy and Harvey just got back and I need to talk to them, so I'll be in the barn for a few minutes. Andy, use the house phone, and order us five large pizzas. The number for the pizza place is lying right beside the phone."

"Hey, McGregor! You can send us anywhere, anytime, with these ATVs—they're great!" Harvey yelled as McGregor approached the barn and watched him carefully back his ride into an empty stall.

"And, as you can see, Cam, we did quite well on our excursion," Clardy boasted, pointing to the carrier mounted on the front of his ATV. "We spotted only two guys in the woods, and we determined from the contents of their car that they are both U.S. Marshals. Thinking that they are both most likely on our side, we didn't disable their car—just popped the trunk. By the way, you *were* right; they were parked in your 'cutback' just off the main road on the north side of your property. But, as you can see," he said, as he pointed at the carrier, "we did requisition a few things from their trunk—namely, these two M4s and enough ammunition to mount a small war. You can see by the service markings that these rifles belong to a U.S. Marshals unit. Feels really good," he said as he snapped a clip into one of the M4s, stretched the sling open, and slung the rifle over his shoulder and across his chest. "Yup, feels really good and makes me feel pretty damn young again."

"You still look like an old fart," Harvey snorted, as he slung the other rifle over his shoulder. "Cam," he added, "there are two cars and four guys at the entrance to the road leading up to your house. Want us to mosey on down and pay them a visit?"

"Not unless they attempt to highjack the pizza delivery guy who's due to come up the road in just a few minutes," McGregor smiled. "Come on in— we need to catch a bite to eat and, I'm sorry to say, we've got a few more loose ends to tie up before we call it a day. Good work, guys!"

While they all chowed down on their pizzas, Maggie and McGregor visited quietly away from the hyped-up personalities of English, Bristow, Daniels and Gonzalez putting their thoughts together in a frenzied rehash of past conquests.

"Maggie," McGregor whispered, "right now, the atmosphere in my dining room is like Hoppy's place on steroids!" They both laughed. "But," he continued, "we still have work to do tonight."

"Okay, folks," McGregor said in a loud enough voice to get everyone's attention, "we have just a bit more work to do yet tonight. Here, in a nutshell, is what we need to do after we finish our pizza. Andy, stop feeding Annie the crusts unless you want to sleep with her tonight—she's goin' have incredible gas!"

"Right now, folks," he continued. "the FBI is in the process of doing a sweep and arresting all of the perps on the list we provided for them. Maggie, Roberto, and I are going to track down and pick up Bridget Steiner and bring her here for questioning—Andy, damn it! Stop with the crust. That dog will explode!"

"Clardy, Andy and Harvey, I want you three to stay here. When the boys down the road and in the woods see us leave, they're liable to want to get in the house and look for evidence. They won't find any, because you guys are not, under any circumstances, going to let them come anywhere near here." He stopped as a noxious odor wafted up from under the table.

"Annie! Go outside! Andy! See what I mean?"

"Man!" Clardy interrupted, "that little dog really does put out a stink!"

"Outside, Annie!" McGregor barked.

Maggie was already at her laptop looking up possible addresses for Steiner. "She's got an apartment in old town Alexandria, Cam. It's now seven o'clock—she should be home by now, I would think."

"Let's roll!" McGregor said. "Clardy, give Roberto your M4—just in case. Load up the shotgun in my gun safe; you'll feel more at home with that than with a M4 anyway. Zeus, guard the house! We'll be back as soon as we can. Andy, there's some Pepto-Bismol in my medicine cabinet if Annie needs some. Be safe everyone!"

McGregor was already in his truck by the time the others caught up with him and was punching Steiner's address into his GPS while Maggie and Roberto were buckling up their seatbelts.

"Yeah, those are FBI cars sittin' there," Roberto noted as they sped by. "Big tires, cheap-ass hub caps, need to be washed," he mumbled.

In less than forty-five minutes, they were circling the block where Steiner's townhouse was located.

"Those don't look like any of our guys," Roberto said, as they passed a parked car with three men inside.

"Looks like they're watching her house," Maggie noted. "Drop me off here, and I'll walk back and keep them occupied while you go in and grab Steiner," she said, as she checked the clip in her gun. "I noticed a walkway between her house and the next row of townhouses. I'll be waiting for you in the alley behind her place in about—whaddya think—ten minutes?"

"Yeah, we'll crash the door, if she doesn't answer our knock pretty quickly," McGregor said. "With these guys out front, we're gonna come in through her back door, so we'll just park in the alley and all of us can head out from there. Be careful folks," he said, as he turned into the alley behind Steiner's house and parked.

Steiner was waiting just inside her back door.

"I watched you circle, Marshal McGregor," she said, sounding relieved. "I recognized your truck from this morning. I've been keeping an eye on those guys parked out front. Are you arresting me?"

"Not right now, Ms. Steiner," McGregor assured her. "You've got five minutes to grab whatever you need, and then we're taking you to a safe place. We need to talk!"

"Call me Birdie, please. I've got everything I need in my backpack," she said, throwing it over her shoulder. "I was already thinking I might need to get out of here anyway."

36

"Birdie, I need your service revolver, please. Any other weapons on you or in your backpack?" McGregor asked, as Steiner handed him her gun and then reached down and removed another one from her ankle holster.

"That's all," she said. "We'd better get out of here!"

"Maggie's at the truck," Gonzalez said, as the three of them made their way through Steiner's back yard. "I'll check Ms. Steiner's backpack when we're back on the road."

"They were our guys," Maggie said, as she climbed into McGregor's truck. "No problem—we can slow down now. They've got the entire list in custody and on their way to arraignment." Extending her hand to the other woman, she said, "Hi, Ms. Steiner, I'm Maggie. Is there anything else in your house you want to take with you?"

After shaking hands with Maggie and shaking her head in the negative, Steiner approached McGregor.

"Uh...Marshal McGregor? Could you and I step away from your truck for a moment? I need to talk to you, in private, if we can."

"What is it, Birdie?" McGregor asked when they were out of earshot of the others.

"My car is there," she pointed, as she handed him a slip of paper and a ring of keys. "All the keys you're going to need are on this ring. Please take my car and go to this address on South Capitol Street, downtown, D.C. It's a store front office, with a sign on the wall outside the front door. It says it's a private school for special needs children, but it's not. We have a lady who works full time there placing girls with clients. I think you call her a 'Madam?' It's closed at night. It's where Clover has his private hideaway. Upstairs, in the first room to your right, you'll find a...I think you call it a Murphy *Bett* –no! Something else? I don't know—one that folds up in the wall?"

"A Murphy bed?" McGregor asked.

"*Ja*, yes," Steiner sighed, "it kind of looks like a wardrobe cabinet. But when you open it and fold the bed down, there's another wall behind that unlocks and lifts. Do that, and you'll find a bookcase with all the records, names, dates, you know—things you need to get right now so that someone else doesn't find them before you and destroy them. Please go now. Here's the key to the front door—the address is 1270 South Capitol Street. I wrote it on the slip, there. This is the key to the upstairs room, and this is the key to open the Murphy. This key will open the wall directly behind the mattress. Bring all the records to me, and I'll gladly explain each record to you."

McGregor, after making a lightning fast decision, returned to the truck with Birdie Steiner in hand.

"Roberto, Maggie. Take Birdie with you, and I'll meet you at the house in a couple of hours. Roberto, tell the guys thanks, and send them home. Can you wait until I get home before you leave? I'm gonna take a little side trip in Birdie's car. I'll see ya in a couple of hours. Hand me the flashlight in the center console, will you Maggie?"

"Consider it done," Roberto said as he slid behind the wheel of McGregor's truck. Maggie, after handing McGregor a flashlight, sat with Steiner in the back seat.

South Capitol Street was not the safest place to be after dark, McGregor knew, as he wheeled Steiner's car out of her parking place and onto the street that would take him the quickest way into D.C. At least, with the junker he was driving, he felt somewhat assured that, wherever he parked, the car would still be there, with all its wheels still on when he got ready to leave.

"Shit, I've got the accelerator to the floorboard and I'm going all of thirty miles an hour. It's gonna be a long trip home in this thing!" McGregor shouted at the dashboard.

After circling the block, McGregor pulled to the curb and parked, without any problem, right in front of 1270. The place was completely dark, and the buildings on both sides were boarded up. The sidewalk was badly torn up, and trash was everywhere. A homeless person was curled up in one of the doorways.

A completely dead neighborhood, McGregor noted, as he glanced up and down the deserted street.

He reached back, felt his gun, and picked up the flashlight lying on the seat beside him. *Which one of these is the front door key?* He tried to remember what Steiner had told him as he approached the door.

He stopped for a moment to peer through the dusty display window. With the light from a practically full moon outside, he could see a desk with a dated telephone sitting on it, a chair, and two cheap four-drawer file cabinets. After fumbling with the keys, he quietly opened the front door with his left hand. In his right hand he'd pulled his gun from its holster and, with the flashlight tucked in his armpit, he stepped inside the building. He stood completely still for a moment, listening for any sounds. He heard none.

This place smells like my grandmother's attic, he thought as he swiped his hand across the top of the desk. *No dust,* he noted as he picked up the phone receiver. *No dial tone. Whoever uses this desk uses a laptop computer and cell phone,* he surmised as he gently opened each of the file cabinet drawers. *Yep, empty. This place is a front, and whoever works here takes the computer and cell home with him or her each night and locks the files and records upstairs. I need to find out from Steiner if she knows the name of the 'madam' who works out of here,* he noted mentally, as he approached the stairway that led to the second floor.

One step at a time, McGregor, one step at a time— keep your head up and forward, swing the beam of your light to the left and to the right of the opening at the top of the stairs. One step at a time. How many times have I delivered that message to rookies over the years?

38

Steiner was exacting in her directions, he observed as he reached the top of the stairs and, again, fumbled with the keys she'd given him to unlock the door to the room. As he opened the door, he switched off his flashlight. *Enough light,* he reasoned. The light from a streetlight outside was beaming through a heavily weathered and dirty window, illuminating the entire room including, *as advertised,* he noted, the Murphy bed installation in the wall.

He opened the bed and, just as Steiner had told him, he was confronted with a solid wall. He switched on his flashlight and found the lock mechanism just a few inches above the badly stained and worn mattress on the right side of the bed. He located the only key he hadn't used so far and shoved it in the keyhole. He felt the lock turn and the wall, evidently spring-loaded, opened out and upward, exposing a large bookcase packed with ledger books, office supplies, and carefully bundled packets of cash.

For a moment he was overwhelmed with the amount of stuff he was going to have to remove from the shelves and transport to the car, but then he remembered some U.S. Postal Service canvas bags crumpled up and stuffed behind the main entrance downstairs.

As he turned to go back downstairs, he heard the front door being rattled. Looking cautiously out the window, he could see a D.C. police cruiser parked behind Steiner's car on the street below. He figured that the cops were wondering why a car was parked here at that time of the evening, and that they were checking for unlocked structures.

Be cool, McGregor; they'll leave in a moment, his inner voice told him as he froze in place. He fervently hoped that Birdie didn't have any outstanding parking tickets. All he'd need was for the cops to decide to tow her car!

As he waited, silently, for the police car to leave, he wondered about the history of the old building and decided that the whole block would be a good candidate for demolition.

Man, this place stinks! Crap! There's gotta be rats in here. No fun for me or the homeless guy outside—I'm not built to stay still this long! C'mon, cops—beat it, will ya?

Growing tired of waiting, he punched the speed dial button pre-designated "home" on his cell phone. Andy Bristow answered.

"Andy, McGregor here," he whispered. "Use the FBI cell and call the D.C. 911 number. Report a burglary in progress, shots fired, at 1600 South Capitol Street. Do it now!"

Within seconds, it seemed, McGregor heard a car door slam shut and the screech of tires and, as he looked carefully out the window, he saw flashing blue and red lights streaking away from 1270. Wasting no time, he dashed down the stairs, grabbed the mail bags he'd spotted earlier, and was quickly back in front of the now exposed bookshelves. It didn't much take time for him to scoop each shelf's contents into two of the bags—the files in one and the money and office supplies in the other.

They won't need the office supplies—but, I can always use them. Man, there's a ton of money here, he observed as he closed the bags, threw them over his shoulder, and headed downstairs and back to the car. He checked the street carefully and placed both bags in the trunk of the car— when, seemingly out of nowhere, he felt a tap on his shoulder.

"I didn't tell the cops you were in there," a raspy voice said. McGregor reached for his gun and spun around to find an obviously homeless man grinning at him through a mouthful of a lot of missing, broken teeth.

"Thank you, friend, I appreciate that," McGregor smiled as he slipped his gun back into his holster, reached into his pocket and slapped a five-dollar bill into the man's hand.

"Have a good night," he said, as he sped off towards home, stopping only briefly to pick up a couple of buckets of Colonel Sanders "crispy please" fried chicken to feed whoever was still at his house.

As McGregor drove up the road to his house an hour later, thankful that Steiner's car had made it, he noticed the lack of other vehicles—particularly the kind that, on the way out, Gonzalez had so perfectly identified and creatively described as belonging to the FBI. He drove into a shed next to his barn—a shed that could be locked tight for the night and was easily seen from the house.

"The stuff in the trunk can wait 'til morning. I need to get everyone fed," he muttered to himself, loading his arms with Colonel Sanders buckets. He walked into the kitchen and plopped the buckets on the table.

"Anyone else hungry but me?" he hollered. Maggie and Steiner were deep in conversation and, for the moment, didn't respond.

"I sure as hell am," Gonzalez yelled from the den. "Got any more beer stashed somewhere?"

"Check the garage refrigerator—there's plenty unless the three musketeers drank it all while we were out braving the unknown, fighting back the evils of society, and tipping a really malodorous homeless guy five bucks for keeping his mouth shut."

"You're a cheap-assed bastard, McGregor! Back in the old days, that tip would have been at least five-fifty," Gonzalez laughed as he walked through the kitchen, grabbed a piece of chicken and headed to the garage to find a beer. "Malodorous? What language is that?" he smirked. "If you don't need me any more tonight, boss, I'm gonna head out. I'll come back in the morning if you want. Just call."

McGregor walked Gonzales to his car and gave him an appreciative pat on the shoulder.

"Thanks for all you did today, Roberto, getting the guys together and taking orders from me. We'll always be brothers, and we'll always be a team to reckon with. I'm gonna take you out to dinner next weekend. That's a promise!"

"More of a threat, McGregor! I know the restaurants and the food you like. Midwestern tasteless," Gonzalez said as he jumped into his car. "The guns we borrowed from the Marshal's car trunk are stacked, locked and loaded, in your dining room," he said, letting his car slowly coast down the driveway. "They'll need to be unloaded!"

McGregor returned to the kitchen, where Maggie and Steiner had already started eating. "I got you a plate and napkin," Maggie announced. "Get something to drink and join us. I put Birdie's stuff in the bedroom next to mine. Is that all right?"

"No problem," McGregor said, reaching across the table and snatching a sizeable piece of chicken. "Birdie, we'll go through the ledgers with you in the morning, then you and I and Maggie are gonna make some plans concerning what's next in your life. Okay? So, Ms. Birdie Steiner, tell me about your life in Germany—do you know Bavaria very well? Do you know the secret for making great weinerschnitzel? Pass me the chicken bucket, will you please?"

They'd all had a very long day by the time they finished dinner, and the next day was destined to be the same. McGregor excused himself from the table to take the dogs for a walk and check the area from around the house to the edge of the woods.

"Come on, guys," McGregor called. "Time for our evening walk."

"Me too, Cam, I need the exercise," Maggie said as she finished carrying the plates and silverware to the sink.

"I'll load the dishwasher, and then I'm going to take shower," Steiner said.

"Thanks, Birdie. There are towels and washcloths in the hall linen closet—first door on your left," McGregor said as he followed Annie and Zeus to the door.

"You know I'm going to have to arrest her when we're finished with her tomorrow," Maggie said softly as she and McGregor started on their walk. "I've already made arrangements for U.S. Marshals to pick her up, along with their missing firearms, at six p.m. tomorrow."

"I know, I know, Maggie, and I'll be making a call first thing in the morning to the FBI to have the records, ledgers and a transcript of the information she's going to give us, picked up—probably six p.m. as well."

"Beautiful sky out here tonight," Maggie said softly as she tucked her hand around McGregor's arm. "Just smell that fresh air. You have quite a hideaway here. Could you and I get up early in the morning and go for a horseback ride? I'd love to see more of your property. We don't have to worry about Steiner— she's not going anywhere. She's terrified she's going to be hurt by other members of MD 699—ones that we may not know about yet, I suppose."

"Is Annie invited to go with us? Zeus would have to stay with Steiner," McGregor asked.

"I wouldn't have it any other way," Maggie laughed.

41

"Seven a.m. it is, then. If you need them, you'll find some riding clothes in my storage closet," McGregor advised.

"As opposed to nude, *ala* Lady Godiva," Maggie laughed. "Yuck! What did I just step in?" she suddenly yelled. "What the hell! What is this foul-smelling stuff all over my shoe?"

"Welcome to the woods of Northern Virginia, Maggie," McGregor grinned. "You've just been personally greeted by the unusually large, and extremely fresh, excrement of a black bear. It's called *scat* for you urban folk. I'll clean that off for you when we get back to the house. In the meantime, please walk at least ten feet behind us. And don't worry, mama bear won't come anywhere near us with Zeus in her line of sight."

On the way back to the house, McGregor detoured Maggie to the barn. Grabbing some fresh straw from a feed trough, and dampening it with some water, he carefully scraped, scrubbed, and washed the bear poop from Maggie's shoe.

"That's how we do it here in ol' Virginny," McGregor explained, to Maggie's amazement.

"Steiner's fast asleep in the guest room," Maggie noted when they got back to the house. "I'm going to take a shower, unless there's more work to do tonight."

"Nope, we've done our chores for the day," McGregor said. "Please save some hot water for me."

As McGregor carefully unloaded the Marshals' guns that Gonzales had stacked in the dining room, he could hear the guest bathroom shower running and then stop. He turned off the lights in the dining room and headed for the master bedroom. His shower that night felt especially good—and so did Maggie, who was sitting on the edge of McGregor's bed when he stepped out of the shower.

He picked up his Marshal's Service acknowledgement plaque lying on the coffee table beside him. It was steadily gathering dust, unceremoniously waiting to be hung.

Yup, I'm formally retired, he silently proclaimed while making a feeble effort to puff the dust away.

Looking back, I am reminded that I was informed by one of my high school counselors that with my magnetic personality, he laughed audibly, *I could become a super salesman. She suggested used car sales. If I'd been a little more mature, a little more schooled in common sense and the theories regarding leadership, I would have told her that mine was not a magnetic personality, but rather, at age 17, just a fantastically glib tongue. Commenting on my ability to make friends and influence people in my life was simply flattery. But then, at that age and time in my life, I really had no clue where life would take me anyway, and hell, I'm not sure I cared much. Hot cars and sexy girls were my canon of life,* he chuckled to himself.

I was smart enough however, to realize that my future would probably be decided by me and others—not necessarily somebody associated with high school counseling. Life to me has always been about discovering who I am—not what others think I should be. Becoming a leader in life, was synonymous with becoming myself. It was precisely that simple and it is also that difficult and regularly hampered by the unexpected forces of happenstance! Sorta like now— again?

"Deep thinking?" Maggie asked as she came around the corner from the dining room where she'd been questioning Steiner for the last few hours. "I need a break," she said, plopping down on the couch in the den beside McGregor.

"I'll throw some hotdogs on the grill in a few minutes. How's that sound for lunch?" McGregor asked. "It'll be just you and me after Birdie is picked up this evening. How 'bout we go out for dinner? I don't have…"

"Going out will be just fine," Maggie agreed. "I'm a lousy cook anyway. I got a text message from my boss a little while ago. I've gotta return to Denver tomorrow morning; my flight is at ten-forty. Will you take me to the airport?"

"That soon, huh?" McGregor mumbled. "Yes, of course, I'll take you. How much more do you have to do with Birdie?" he asked, quickly changing the subject. "Any new info?"

"I'll finish up with Birdie after lunch— about mid-afternoon, I'm guessing. She's pin-pointed several high-ranking government officials who, I'm positive, the FBI will want to investigate. I can see a pattern of activity for at least four officials who I think have been supplying the syndicate with lots of little, but important, stuff over a fairly long period of time. I've included a list of documents or information they've allegedly, at least by the ledger entries, supplied to foreign interests over the last two years. I'm just giving the FBI 'heads-up' information and an index of materials they need to more closely examine. I do see some headlines coming down the pike—a few heads are going to roll," she laughed. "We did good work, Cam!"

"Yeah, we did," McGregor responded in an "of course" manner. "I'm gonna go fire up the grill," he said. *Happenstance* was still fresh in his mind.

At six o'clock sharp, a black Suburban entered the driveway leading to McGregor's house. Two boxes of carefully sorted and indexed materials sealed with reinforced packing tape with McGregor's signature scrawled across the bottom and top seams were ready to be picked-up. After a show of FBI badges, and the exchange of the appropriate codewords, the car disappeared down the road with what McGregor hoped would result in the arrest of more members of the syndicate and close the case with convictions of all involved.

A few minutes later, a second black Suburban showed up.

"Hey, McGregor! You've been keeping us kinda busy the past couple of days. Still up to your old tricks, I'm told. Did you really steal some weapons from us?" Marshal Brian Woolsey, an old friend of McGregor's, said as he stepped from the car.

"They just suddenly appeared at my front door," McGregor said feigning innocence while exchanging a handshake with Woolsey.

"Your agents' wheels would have gone missing as well, except for the fact that you're still assigning junkers to field officers. Your weapons are in the dining room."

He nodded toward Douglas and Steiner,

"This is Marshal Maggie Douglas, from your Denver office, and this is Bridget Steiner, or, as she likes to be called, Birdie."

Immediately, as McGregor expected, standard procedures kicked in. Birdie was placed under arrest and given her Miranda rights. At McGregor's request, she was not handcuffed.

"Thank you, Birdie," McGregor said as he gave her a hug. "I hope everything works out for you."

"I'll be putting in a good word for you, Birdie," Maggie added, as the Marshals prepared to leave.

"And, Marshal Maggie Douglas, I'll be putting in a good word for you as well," McGregor smiled as he watched the Suburban drive away. "Let's go find some dinner."

"This is a really nice restaurant, Cam." Maggie observed, an hour later as they were looking over their menus. "I have two questions: One, do you eat here often, and two, will I see you again after tomorrow?"

"Yes," McGregor answered. "I eat dinner here quite often. This is, by far, the best Italian restaurant around these parts. I highly recommend the *penne alla puttanesca*! As to your second question, Maggie—to be honest, I'm not ready for a long-term, not to mention a long-distance relationship, right now," he said earnestly. "I like you, and I could easily fall in love with you, but I'm not in a good place in my life right now. My wife's illness and eventual death took a lot out of me. I'm sorry, but I need more time to get my life in order."

"No need to be sorry, Cam," Maggie said sympathetically, "I wish it could be different, but I understand—I really do. Now," she said, looking at the menu, "I think I'll just have spaghetti *bolognese*—mainly because I can't even come close to pronouncing that *penne alla* thing."

Later that night, they sat by McGregor's fireplace, drinking wine until almost daybreak, simply enjoying each other's company, holding each other close as the world outside melted into oblivion, and they became, it seemed to them, the only two people on the face of the earth.

CHAPTER FIVE

Within a few days, the *Washington Post* was headlining the fact that the FBI had broken up a Washington, D.C. based "spy ring."

It was interesting, McGregor felt, to read about a case in which he'd played a substantial part in closing. He thought, with a certain amount of chagrin, about how the true facts of a case are so often skipped over or misinterpreted by the news media. He laughed out loud, thinking, *as usual, not even close! Now, I wonder if another story is in the making about the prostitution ring.*

He finished his morning coffee, took care of his animals and headed out for a shift at the airport, still shaking his head over the newspaper's handling of the "spy" story.

"Hi! Can I help you, ma'am?" McGregor asked, leaning across the Travelers Aid counter to catch the attention of a women who appeared to be turning *prima ballerina pirouettes* in the middle of the hallway.

"Oh! Yes, please. My husband's waiting for me in the cell phone lot, and he's not answering his phone. It just goes to voice mail!"

"Let me try—what's the number?" He dialed, waited, and then said, "well, you're right—I'm getting voice mail."

"What should I do?" she asked in a worried tone, again twirling around in a circle.

"Let me page him to see if by chance he's looking for you here in the main terminal. What's his name?"

"Oh, he'd be upset if I did that."

"Okay, then, here are your options as I see them. Keep calling every few minutes or take a taxi over to the cell phone lot and see if he's there. *Quarter circle*, he noted. Call home and see if he's there, or call someone you know and ask them to come and pick you up. *Another quarter circle!* Or you can forget all the aforementioned, and just take a cab or shuttle home." *A third quarter circle!*

"I'm going to kill him!!" *Full circle movement completed*!

"Let me try his number one more time for you......Hi, this is Cameron McGregor from Travelers Aid...your wife is looking to kill you—I'll put her on the phone. Here, ma'am. I have him on the phone! You can stop circling the airport now and land," he smiled as he handed her the phone.

"Yes, sir, how can I help you?"

"I'm supposed to meet my friend here. Her flight landed over two hours ago, and I can't find her."

"Does she have a cell phone?"

"Yes, but it doesn't work in the United States. She's from Croatia— landed in New York. She's flying here from La Guardia."

"Let me page her for you! Write down her name for me, please."

"Her name is Lararunastalsia Orinthropers."

McGregor blinked, cleared his throat and said in an even tone, "Okay, thank you. Please write that down for me."

"That I will gladly do for you," he smiled, clearly understanding McGregor's request.

"*TRAVELERS AID PAGING LARA-RUN-ASTAL-SEEYA ORIN-THROPERS.*
LARA-RUN-ASTAL-SEEYA ORIN-THROPERS,
PLEASE MEET YOUR PARTY AT THE TRAVELERS
AID INFORMATION DESK BY BAGGAGE CLAIM SIX.
***LARA-RUN-ASTAL-SEEYA ORIN-THROPERS.*"**

"How'd I do?" McGregor asked.

"Very good sir, thank you! Oh! There she is now!! I see her coming this way! Thank you! Thank you!"

I'm just thankful that she didn't have a middle name, McGregor thought as he reached for his cell phone. He'd heard his phone ring and vibrate against his leg several times during the preceding hour, but he hadn't had time to answer until now. "Cameron!" A voice barked in his ear. "This is Lawrence Brody. We need to talk. Lunch today at your favorite hideout in the boondocks? Hoppy's, isn't it? We have some new developments in the MD 699 situation you might find interesting. Do you have time—would one o'clock work for you?"

"One o'clock at Hoppy's Place sounds good to me. Leave your tie in your car! How do you know about Hoppy's?" McGregor asked curiously.

Brody chuckled. "The FBI told me."

After wrapping up his shift at Dulles, McGregor arrived at Hoppy's a few minutes late. He'd never met face to face with Brody, but a fit looking man wearing a dark pinstriped business suit, crisp white shirt with no tie, and sitting alone, with his back to the wall in a back corner of the restaurant, looked like a sure probability to McGregor.

He smiled at Mary Beth as he paused at the counter where she was busy reading a copy of *National Enquirer*.

"I see you're *deeply* into superficiality, envy, cattiness, mockery, and melodrama today, huh? I think I'll have sweet tea and pastrami on rye today, please, Mary Beth."

He walked over to the table and reached to shake hands with the man sitting there. "Lawrence Brody, I'm guessing," he said. "I'm Cam McGregor— have you ordered yet? Want a menu?"

49

"Yes and no," Brody answered. "Mary Beth and I had a delightful chat before you got here, and she convinced me that an order of chipped beef on toast was what my stomach was crying out for. How often, for God's sake, do I find a place that serves *SOS* in downtown D.C.?"

After a few minutes of getting acquainted, Brody quickly got down to business. "Cam, I'm going to ask you a few questions. None of these need to be answered—I already have the answers, and I'll answer them for you along the way. I just want you to listen to the questions. Okay?"

"No problem, Lawrence. Fire away," McGregor said as he took a bite from his pastrami sandwich. "Man, this is great! I love this place!"

"Let's talk about Maggie Douglas," Brody began. "Who brought her into the picture? You were in a meeting with airport cops Morgan and McCall, FBI agents Clover and Robbins, Smith from Customs, and Henson from the TSA, when you first heard Douglas's name mentioned. Who called her in on the situation in the first place? You might have thought it was Morgan, and you were right. However, Morgan had contacted Douglas simply to inform her of the situation with you and Angelika Schafer. She, Douglas, originally thought that Morgan and the others could put a lid on your activities and deep-six this whole thing. When she learned you weren't just going to lie back and forget about Schafer's dilemma, she flew here with a mission much different than you thought, and far different from what the rest of the people in that meeting could imagine."

Brody ignored the look of consternation on McGregor's face and continued. "Her goal was to shield, from this particular incident, a much broader syndicate than we expected, and, if necessary, entirely sacrifice this arm of the organization—dump them into the hands of the Justice Department. Think about that for a moment, please—my chipped beef is getting cold." He stopped to take a few bites. "Oh, and Birdie Steiner was instructed by Douglas to expose the people she put on her list. Douglas dictated the list; Birdie just copied it down...my God, this is incredibly delicious white sauce!"

"Are you telling me," McGregor queried in disgust, "that Maggie Douglas is one of the people behind this espionage syndicate, supposedly MD 699? She told me that someone at headquarters had called her in."

"Uh, huh," Brody mumbled and nodded. "I gotta have this white sauce recipe!"

"Well, it's simply butter, flour, and milk with a pinch of salt and pepper," McGregor said wryly. "No matter—Hoppy wants you to keep comin' back! You're telling me that I've been double screwed by Douglas?"

"Can't speak to that," Brody said, without missing a gulp. "But I can tell you this. When we informed Birdie Steiner that we weren't going to give her full amnesty, she started naming names all over the place. She was found dead—poisoned, apparently, in her cell last night—damned D.C. jail."

McGregor sat in stunned silence. He was being barraged with information he never would have anticipated, but, as a veteran law enforcement officer, he probably shouldn't have been surprised.

"We have fresh pumpkin pie!" Mary Beth hollered from behind the counter. "Hot from the oven."

"Two with whipped cream, if it's the real stuff, please," Brody hollered back at her, and continued, "Cam, I want you to consider doing some work for us, and, before I forget, you know that money you confiscated from the syndicate office stash? Where do you think it is now? I know you probably haven't had time to distribute it yet."

"It's still locked in the trunk of Steiner's car—parked in a locked shed at my place," McGregor replied. "Why do you ask?"

"Who else knew where it was?" Brody pressed.

"I'm not sure whether I mentioned it to anyone, Lawence, other than you—well, on second thought, perhaps I told Douglas."

"Did you ever count the money?" Brody asked.

"Not to the dollar," McGregor said. "It was in stacks of twenties. I think I estimated between seven-hundred to eight-hundred thousand total, but I'm not sure."

"You're estimate is pretty close," Brody affirmed. "I'm betting that if you look for that money when you get home today, it'll be long gone from your shed. We think it was just deposited in a bank account in Key West under the name of Douglas's brother, Thomas Girafalco."

"Oh, come on, Lawrence! Maggie didn't have room for all that cash in her duffle bag. Besides, I carried her bag from the house to my car the morning she left. That amount of money is heavy, and I would have noticed."

"No, she didn't take it," Brody continued. "She probably made contact with someone who got it right after you left to take her to the airport—that would be my guess. Anyway, I'm betting it's no longer in the trunk of Birdie's car."

"Ouch! Triple screwed," McGregor winced. "All right, I'm getting pretty damned angry. What do you need my help on?"

"First things first—we'll pick up Steiner's car from your place tomorrow, take it to our impound lot and go over it with the proverbial fine-toothed comb… and," Brody went on, "I'm sending a courier out to your place tonight to deliver a package of files I want you to look over. The files contain our most current information regarding the particulpar MD 699 syndicate that included this D.C. group. You gonna be home?"

"Yeah," McGregor responded. "Then what?"

"Well, it depends on you," Brody answered. "After you review the files, the question that only you can answer is simply this: are you ready and willing to carry a second badge again, along with your reactivated Marshal's?—this time, an FBI badge with a Special Agent in Charge rank? That's a rank higher than you held with the Marshals Service. You'd be reporting directly to me.

51

"Why do I need you in particular?" he leaned toward McGregor and continued. "It's simple. First, your law enforcement record speaks for itself, and second, this MD 699 syndicate has systematically burrowed itself inside of just about every law enforcement division on the books. I'm totally frustrated by the fact that I can't trust anyone—even my own agents—to shut down an extensive transatlantic espionage network that's working through, while hiding behind, an equally extensive high dollar prostitution, money laundering, and perhaps drug smuggling ring, headquartered in Florida. I think you'll find, after reading the files, that we know an awful lot about this organization; however, we've not been able to get enough solid proof concerning their obvious illicit activities to make arrests and shut them down. This D.C. bust we just wrapped up was made possible solely on happenstance, created when you inadvertently stumbled into a problem with a pissed-off German prostitute at Dulles Airport—that, of course being Angelika Schafer—along with a local syndicate boss who was too dumb to cover up his mistakes and blew their cover. It's no wonder Douglas threw him and his organization to the wolves!"

"And I was just trying to be a nice guy," McGregor broke in. "How'd I get so lucky?"

"Yeah, and by the way, Steiner, during questioning, gave up the name of the woman who managed the ledgers for the syndicate," Brody continued. "We arrested her and searched her apartment. The ledgers you found at the Capital Street address were just the tip of the iceberg. We found a bunch more that incriminate at least a dozen or so high and middle ranking U.S. government people. We're getting indictments on those folks within the next few weeks...My God!" he exclaimed, "this pumpkin pie is something to write home about. I can clearly see why you're a regular here."

As the two men finished their meal, they agreed that McGregor would think seriously about Brody's proposal and would get back to him promptly. They shook hands again and went their separate ways. McGregor was still feeling a bit "shell-shocked," if not betrayed, by what he'd just learned. He drove the mountain roads back to his place, hardly aware of where he was. As soon as he returned home, he checked Birdie's car, and, just as Brody had surmised, the trunk lock had been punched out and the contents of the trunk removed. Angry, but not surprised at this discovery, he called Roberto Gonzalez and asked him to join him to look over the files Brody had provided.

"It looks to me," Gonzalez concluded, "that there are two main bosses running this MD 699 ring. One is Douglas's brother—this Thomas Girafalco character in Miami—and the other they've identified as Alard De Smet, head of some kind of a Belgian Mafia outfit working out of Brussels. Both are quite wealthy so-called businessmen—both have thick FBI folders with lots of suspicions, but no indictments. Have you looked at Douglas's folder yet?"

"Not yet," McGregor answered. "If you've looked at it, talk to me."

52

"Well," Gonzalez began, "Margaret Elaine Girafalco Douglas has been married three times—each ending in divorce. She has a sterling record with the military, but a spotty record as a U.S. Marshal. She came to the FBI's attention a few years back in an incident where an extremely important federal witness she was transporting from St. Louis to a court hearing in Denver suddenly went missing and has never been found. Whatever happened, the FBI suspects that she disposed of him to keep him from testifying in a case where the defendants were alleged to be involved in some kind of espionage scheme. The case eventually collapsed. The FBI later discovered that her brother was one of the potential defendants. Interesting, huh?"

Gonzales flipped the file and continued, "Okay, let's see—what else is here? Oh, she has a condo in Key West and makes frequent trips to an apartment in Miami. Nothing else of importance, but you might want to look this over to see if I missed anything."

"You know, I don't know whether I want to get involved in this thing at all," McGregor said impatiently, tossing the file he was reading on the table. "If I do, I'd want the ability to create my own plan, my own strategies, and, if you can slip away for a month or two, I'd like you to go with me. But really, I'm just not sure...." McGregor paused. "What is it, Zeus? Roberto, Zeus thinks we have company—are you armed?"

"I am." Gonzalez acknowledged.

"Zeus, come with me," McGregor commanded. "I'm gonna let Zeus out the back door," he said to Gonzales. "You and I are going out the front door. Zeus will alert us—big time, if anyone's out back."

As McGregor turned the corner from his kitchen to the back door, a shot rang out and a bullet crashed through the back-door window and slammed into the woodwork next to McGregor's head. He ducked back around the corner.

"Party time! Damn! I just had that molding painted," McGregor shouted as Gonzales ran past him and opened the back door.

Zeus was outside in a flash, followed by both men, guns drawn. Two more shots were fired before Zeus could be heard attacking someone just outside the reach of the security lights on McGregor's house. Cautiously following the sounds of someone screaming in pain, McGregor and Gonzales found a man pinned to the ground by Zeus, with the sounds of another person running through the woods away from them. With a sharp command from McGregor, Zeus was fast in pursuit of the second person, McGregor racing behind, leaving Gonzales to hold the man Zeus had downed. He slowed when he heard a distinctive bark from Zeus, letting him know that the perpetrator had been cornered or treed.

"Let's see now," McGregor shouted at the man who was clinging to a large oak branch, "I can shoot you down from up there or, better yet, I can leave you there until you get so tired and hungry you fall from the tree and meet my dog face to face as your partner did. Actually," McGregor snarled, "you could just drop your gun and tell me who sent you here, and I'll consider letting you climb down peacefully. Your choice, mister!"

"You can have my gun, but I ain't tellin' you nothing!" the man said, dropping his gun to the ground at McGregor's feet.

With just the light from a half-moon illuminating the area, McGregor raised his gun and fired a shot just above the man's head, shattering a branch and showering him with bark and wood chips. "My next shot is going to add a little bit of you to the debris," McGregor shouted.

"Go to hell! You won't shoot an unarmed man!"

McGregor could hear the wail of sirens coming up the mountain and heading his way. "Stay with him, Zeus, and if he comes down you know what to do," he ordered. "Zeus is not your friend, stranger," he yelled, as he walked back to where Gonzales was holding the other man.

"I called for police and an ambulance," Gonzales said, as McGregor approached. "This guy's in pretty bad shape—you really need to feed your dog more often," Gonzales laughed. "Where you goin'?" he asked, as McGregor walked back toward his barn.

"Chain saw," McGregor answered. "A back-woods lawman's best friend!"

The sirens were getting closer as McGregor worked his way back to where Zeus was holding court. By the time he got there, he'd already given the pull cord on his chain saw a few swift yanks, and, by the time he reached the treed man, his saw was running loudly, smoothly, and at almost full throttle. Without saying a word, he laid the blade of the saw tightly against the tree's trunk, squinted his eyes to protect them from sawdust, and triggered the throttle to full speed. Within minutes, the tree started to lean. If there had been any objections or last minute "I'll tell you" pleas from above, McGregor wouldn't have been able to hear them. Zeus was on the man almost before the tree had completely reached the ground, and, with his leg pinned between the thick branch he was sitting on and the ground it now rested on, the man was easy pickings, and Zeus was on him immediately.

"Hold, Zeus!" McGregor commanded, turning off the chainsaw. "Who sent you, mister?"

"Fuck you and the horse you rode in on!"

"Actually, asshole, in case you didn't notice, I rode a mean and angry dog in," McGregor remarked. "You like the smell of his breath? Wanna get closer to him? Zeus! Go, boy!"

With that command, Zeus tore into the man's free leg, ripping his pants leg away, along with some flesh.

"Hold, Zeus! Wanna tell me who sent you yet?" McGregor snarled.

"I don't know who it is! It's one of my bosses," the man cried. "I don't know any real names, just code names. The caller ID is still on my cell phone. Call off your fuckin' dog! I need a doctor, damn it!"

54

"Toss me your cell phone. I'll send the medics up here as soon as they've finished with your partner," McGregor snapped as restarted his chain saw. "I'm gonna cut and release that limb on your leg—don't move! Back off, Zeus!"

After McGregor and Gonzales finished talking to the police, McGregor called Brody and reported the incident, advising him that local police had the two perps in custody. "I'm sending you seven phone numbers I need traced and faxed back to me ASAP. We may have a lead here."

"So, Roberto, are you thinking we should get more involved in this situation?" McGregor asked, as he carefully dug the bullet that was meant for him out of the molding directly across from the smashed back door window.

"Damn, man," Roberto laughed, "I think the bad guys just gave us an engraved—perhaps, at this moment, the better word is embedded—invitation to join the fun!" Examining the mutilated piece of lead McGregor handed him, he said, "I'll give this bullet to the police on my way out. I've gotta get back to my place. I need to check my wardrobe to see if I have any Florida-type clothes. I'm thinkin' Bermuda shorts, knee-high dark dress socks and sandals, topped off with Hawaiian shirts, a straw hat and cheap sunglasses." He grinned impudently.

"I'm thinkin' you're gonna be a prime candidate for deportation dressed like that!" McGregor snorted, as he reached into his pocket to answer his cell phone. "Hold on a minute, Roberto, it's Brody calling."

After silently listening to Brody for a moment, McGregor's response was simply, "That's interesting. I'll call you back later. I might have a proposal for you."

"Roberto, one of the recent calls to our perps was from a desk phone located within the confines of the Denver Federal Court House." He said as he hung up the phone. "Wanna venture a guess who ordered the attempted takedown we were just involved in?"

"No question in my mind!" Gonzales quickly responded. "Anyway, let me know what you decide and when we're leaving—I'll be ready. FYI, I just took 'not very smart Maggie' off my Chri

Within the next few days, McGregor had cut a deal with Brody. He'd left his house in the hands of a good man he'd hired on a trial basis, with the possibility of keeping him on permanently. Zeus and Annie were staying with Gonzales' daughter, Lucia.

With some up-front expense money, fictitious identities and documentation and two previously seized luxury cars with New Mexico tags, he and Gonzales convoyed their way south from the D.C. area to the beaches of South Florida. What was normally a day and a half trip by car turned into a leisurely three-day drive for them as they hit more than a few beaches, bars, and clubs along the way. They knew nobody was waiting at trip's end to meet them, and, at this point they were more interested in logistics than tactics. They clearly understood what their ultimate goal was, and that the means and methods for achieving that goal were entirely in their hands and in their own time.

CHAPTER SIX

After settling in at their South Beach hotel, McGregor put his duffel bag on the bed and opened it. Inside was a black leather case which he carefully held the steady while gently unzipping the cover. He pulled aside the sheepskin inner lining to reveal the cold, compelling, gunmetal-blue steel of his SIG Sauer pistol. He knew he had to follow through with his commitment to Brody, but he was unusually uneasy, and more than a bit apprehensive about this specific assignment.

Something's still bothering me about the whole situation, he worried. He took *temporary* comfort from his SIG, and considerable satisfaction and *enjoyment* from the fact that they'd be starting their investigation in vibrant South Beach in Miami—a party playground for the rich and famous, with streets lined with great cafes and colorful historic art deco buildings. *Still...*

Every crazy man's dream has been identified and soon the be fulfilled, he thought as Gonzales came bouncing into the room.

"I'm ready when you are," Gonzales announced gleefully. "I'm gonna go sink my butt in the sand, concentrate on some serious tannage, and contemplate which of the red-hot clubs we should hit this evening. Like my new 'flip-flops'?"

"They make your feet look pretty ugly—but then you have ugly feet anyway!" McGregor observed mildly.

"No problem, then. Despite your aging pecs and my feet, the chicks can still admire our other, more important attributes," Gonzales grinned.

In what they hoped would quickly become a morning ritual, McGregor and Gonzales picked up folding beach chairs, towels and bottles of water in the lobby, and with their ever-present duty bags (weapons, badges, and sun screen) slung over their shoulders, they strolled across Ocean Drive, followed a path through the sand dunes, and staked out a plot of beach as close to the water as possible.

"I may never go home," Gonzales said, dreamily, as he and McGregor bobbed up and down with the never-ending ocean swells. "Warm water, white sand beaches, topless bikini-clad chicks parading the shoreline pretending to be seashell collectors—what more can a guy ask for?"

"Oh," McGregor laughed, "perhaps a cold beer and a pastrami sandwich?"

"You've been coming down here for years," Gonzales remarked. "I've only been here a few hours, and I think I can see why. This is where people come to see the weird, excessive side of life and live to tell about it, I'm thinkin'."

"You've hit the proverbial nail on the head, my friend." McGregor agreed. "When I discovered this place in 1986, it was a collection of run-down

57

hotels and neighborhood shops. Back then, the place was populated mostly with Mariel boatlift refugees and elderly retirees. Hell, you could buy a one-bedroom oceanfront condo for less than forty thousand. Today? —well over a million bucks, I'd bet. Welcome to the new, and greatly improved, South Beach, home of Hedonism Lite!"

That night, while Gonzales explored some of the local clubs, McGregor sat under the cover of a grove of palm trees on the patio of a local restaurant, drinking iced tea and carefully mapping out an action plan, while enjoying the gentle breeze coming off the ocean.

Douglas will soon learn, he kept repeating to himself, *"that the man, Cameron McGregor, she worked and toyed with just a while ago, has another side to him—a side that is as cold, hard, and brutal as the steel barrel of his gun—a man with a heart of stone to anyone who betrays him.*

McGregor flagged down a waiter, ordered another iced tea, and continued his pondering. He concentrated on figuring out who he knew in Miami who might be able to give him some insight into the Thomas Girafalco organization, and who he could trust not to blow his cover. He needed, at least for now, to remain undercover, and he needed someone who might recognize his face, but not remember his name.

The first name he added to his mental list was that of Calisto Estrada, who, a few years ago, had provided McGregor with a first-class tour of his restaurant in Little Havana. *A mouth-watering lesson in authentic Cuban cuisine,* he recalled. Estrada had bragged, at the time, that every gangster and public official in Miami loved his restaurant so much that he never had to worry about anybody horning in on his territory.

He also thought of Stella Daniels, a Miami local he'd met while admiring her Rhodesian Ridgeback dog one afternoon while walking on Ocean Drive in South Beach. *I wonder if crazy Stella, the cigar-smoking chick who used Old Spice as perfume, is still roaming around in Miami? What a character! She got dumped by some big shot Miami politician and really wanted to hook up with...*

"Marshal McGregor! Good to see you! I'm Thomas Girafalco. You've met my sister, Maggie, and I understand you're looking to meet me! Well, here I am." A stocky, well-dressed man sporting a neatly trimmed mustache, a Van Dyke beard and a well-oiled pompadour sat down across the table from McGregor and leaned back as if he owned the place.

"I'm sorry," McGregor responded, quickly turning his notes over, "you're mistaken, my name is ..."

"Aliases ain't good for nothing in my business, Marshal, only cold hard cash! And, there ain't no secrets in my town," Girafalco declared, leaning forward aggressively. "Right now, Federal Marshal Cameron McGregor is sittin' at a table in the courtyard at the News Cafe in South Beach, with a Sauer in his man-purse and a guy named Girafalco sitting across from him getting ready to order a Cuban mojito. Your sidekick, Roberto Gonzales, has already tossed back five boiler-makers and is getting a lap dance from some honey at Cookie's Cabaret."

McGregor stared at him, stony-faced—saying nothing.

"Waiter," Girafalco yelled, "two mojitos, extra lime! *Rapido, por favor!*"

Still no reaction from McGregor.

"Now, Marshal, I've got a proposition for you. You can hear it here, or I'll clear my guys out of the limo that's parked at the curb and we can talk there. Your call! By the way, one of them, at least, has you in his sights if you reach for your piece! Thought you should know that," he sat back and smiled, still waiting for McGregor's reaction.

What the fuck, McGregor thought to himself. *Two can play at this game!*

"Your call," Girafalco repeated, as he overpaid the waiter who placed two drinks on the table.

"I can stick anything you want to say—your so-called 'proposition'— up your ass just as easy here as I can in your car," McGregor said, as he quickly surveyed the courtyard. He needed to know how many people might get hurt if he physically challenged Girafalco, and he needed an escape route if he decided to make a quick exit.

"Talk to me, Girafalco. I'm listening! And knock off the stupid Sicilian mafia boss threats! I'm not a bit impressed!"

"Good," Girafalco said smugly. "I think you're gonna find what I have to say quite interesting, and I'm bettin' you'll find it pretty lucrative as well. Here," he said, as he pushed a mojito across the table toward McGregor. "Let's drink a toast to my sister, our only mutual acquaintance so far. She was a good fuck, wasn't she, Marshal McGregor?"

With that, McGregor abruptly stood up, pushed and tilted the table toward Girafalco as hard as he could, knocking him to the ground, with the table and its contents landing squarely on Girafalco's chest. Within seconds, and assuming he was going to be pursued by Girafalco's goons, McGregor worked his way between buildings toward the alley behind the restaurant. He quickly retrieved the badge from his bag and ducked in the backdoor of the restaurant's kitchen area. Briefly flashing his badge, he announced himself as a health inspector. After lifting a thermometer from one of the cooks, he pretended to check for safe anti-bacterial temperature levels of various orders about to be served. Moving to an isolated part of the kitchen, he called Gonzales' cellphone as he checked quickly for his pursuers.

"Roberto! Don't ask questions, just listen. You're in harm's way. We've been compromised. Girafalco's people are all around you. You've got to get out of there. Meet me back at the Miami Beach Marina, Monty's Bar, main deck, ASAP! Kiss the lovelorn chick I hear in the background goodbye, unpack your heat, pull the fire alarm to create some confusion, and haul ass. Be careful, brother!"

Making his way through the kitchen and back out to the restaurant, McGregor found a seat at the bar where he could watch the patio area. Girafalco was nowhere in sight, but his limo was still parked at the curb. Since the front seat appeared to be empty, McGregor figured he was huddled up in the backseat waiting for his entourage to return from their unsuccessful pursuit.

Soon, one by one, he could see Girafalco's men returning, and the limo slowly pulled away and disappeared into the night. McGregor looked at his watch. Ten-fifteen—he'd called Roberto a little after ten. "I'd better get the hell out of here," he thought. As he started to get up, he felt a hand on his shoulder.

"Where are we going?" a familiar voice behind him asked. "We need to talk." It was Maggie. "No, you don't need that," she said as she discreetly blocked his hand from reaching his gun. "I'm unarmed and, believe it or not, I'm here to play on your team. Please, take a walk on the beach with me so I can explain. I've taken care of the damages with the manager and you'll be welcomed back tomorrow." She tugged on his arm invitingly. "Come on, follow me," she said. "I promise you that you'll get to listen to the music of the surf, get some sand between your toes, and, if you're lucky, get to see a sea turtle or two."

"Maggie, I'm meeting someone in about fifteen minutes." McGregor said.

"Is it a woman?" she asked.

"No, it's…"

"Gonzales can wait. You can call him. You need to hear what I have to say, and why I'm here. You need to trust me."

"Maggie, I did trust you …."

"I know, and I led you down a pretty precarious road. But, well, it's different now. You're doing the leading and I want to follow. And, for your information, I didn't place the call from the Denver Courthouse that set up the ambush at your house, but I know who did."

"Bullshit," McGregor exploded, yanking his arm away. "You expect me to believe you now? I'm outta here!"

"Come on," she wheedled, "I know I'm in trouble, but at least give me an opportunity to make things right with you, and, hopefully, better for me."

"How'd you know I'd be here tonight?" McGregor grunted.

"My brother was eating dinner, as he always does, on the patio of Lario's—Gloria Estefan's restaurant, next door—and must have recognized you from a picture or something. I flew into Miami a couple of days ago. I didn't know you were here until Tommy called me about thirty minutes ago and told me you were at the News Cafe. I have an apartment just around the corner from here—but," Maggie continued, "I didn't know he was planning to confront you. I arrived just as you dumped him out there on the patio. You've got to know, embarrassing him like that in public—soiling his tailored clothes—well, it's not sitting well with him right now. You're on his turf. But then, I know, you couldn't give a rat's ass! Anyway, don't worry about him returning tonight; knowing him, he's taking his frustrations out on some cheap trick, snorting dope, and drowning his sorrows in one of his clubs as we speak. Come on," she said, grabbing his hand.

They crossed the street to the sand dunes separating Ocean Avenue from the ocean. A full moon was casting a blue, almost mystical glow on the beach that lay ahead of them, and the gaudy neon lights and noises from the South Beach strip seemed to be carried away by the warm and gentle Gulf Stream breezes blowing onshore from the Atlantic.

Despite his anger with Maggie, McGregor still found the beach to be a place of calming sameness. Clockwork cycles are at the core of the shore, he felt. A comforting repetition of all that has come before and will come again: the ceaseless metronome of waves, the daily pulse of tides, an endless array of shorebirds, tee-shirt, beach chair, and soft drink vendors, sea breezes and tan lines.

"I really want to live and die here someday," Maggie sighed. "Life is so different here. Time doesn't seem to move from hour to hour," she said as she took off her high heels and skipped away from McGregor, "but from mood to moment. People here live by the currents, plan by the tides, and follow the sun," she said as she tossed her purse to McGregor. "Go ahead, open it and check inside. I know you've been thinking I have a gun in there. I wasn't kidding, Cam; I want to help you bring down my brother and every part of his evil enterprise. I want to be free from him and start my life over as soon as possible, and…I want you in it!" she exclaimed.

Does Maggie think I'm buying this crap? She was right about one thing though, McGregor thought to himself as he opened her purse. *I've been eyeing this purse since the moment she approached me at the bar.* Okay, no gun, no knife, he noted—no vials of poison, no sticks of dynamite or hand grenades—just two hand-rolled Cuban cigars and a lighter.

While Maggie continued her "moon-dance," which had now taken her, ankle deep, into the ocean, McGregor made a quick "change of plans" call to Roberto. He took off his shoes and socks, stripped off his shirt, and laid it carefully on the sand to sit on. Once seated, he bit off the head of one of the Cubans and gently rotated and warmed it for a few seconds with the flame from the lighter. Placing the cigar in his mouth, he brought the flame nearer the foot, still not allowing it to touch the cigar, and gently puffed with quick shallow breaths while slowly rotating it between his lips to ignite it as evenly as possible.

Well done, McGregor, he said to himself. *Well done,* he repeated while closely examining the lit cigar. *I'm gonna play Maggie's game for a while and see where it leads me. Her "I want to be free from him and start my life over as soon as possible" declaration is a total crock!*

"Light the other one for me, please," Maggie said as she approached, pulled her dress off over her head, spread it on the sand, and sat down beside McGregor. "You really know how to light a cigar. I was getting turned on just watching you. Where in the world did you learn how to do that?"

61

"What? Light a good cigar or turn a woman on?" McGregor coolly asked.

"Both," Maggie laughed.

"Cuba!" McGregor said tersely. "Look, Maggie, I don't mean to sound harsh—*like hell I don't!* —but no more philosophical bullshit like your 'I want to live and die here' pronouncement. Right now—just bottom-line stuff. What do you want from me? Clearly you know, or have guessed, why I'm here. And as far as trust is concerned…well, tell me, how do you see yourself fitting into my agenda?"

"Look, Cam," she said resolutely. "I know I'm gonna get busted when this is over. I've pretty well screwed up my career in law enforcement, and I'm probably gonna have to do some hard time. Bottom line…I can stretch out the amount of time before my brother's syndicate explodes, and I eventually get indicted as a co-conspirator…or, I can speed the process along, become an informant, plead for a Justice Department deal, and eventually be free to start over. My brother is an agent for any number of foreign interests, and, as you know, has been actively involved in MD 699 espionage and other criminal activities. What you don't know is that he's also involved in illegally procuring and shipping weapons overseas, and has murdered, or has had murdered, at least a dozen people that I know of. He owns more politicians than you can imagine, has business interests all over the country, and has people like me under both his thumb and his gun. His base of operation is here in Miami. And, because he considers me one of his chief troubleshooters and sends me out whenever there's a problem, I know where all the action is. And, because I'm family, I know where he keeps all of his records."

"Yeah, you're family, Maggie. That's my problem!"

"My mother was family too, McGregor," she angrily snapped. "She died last year begging me to get away from him—get a new life—get…"

She stopped abruptly. The moonlight was reflecting off the tears streaming down her cheeks. Whether they were real or just part of her façade, McGregor couldn't tell.

"Is it true, Ms. Douglas," McGregor leaned forward and asked, "that sharks frequent the waters by this beach after dark?"

"I dunno," she said, wiping her face with her arm. "I'll find out for you." She jumped up and ran toward the ocean, waded in up to her knees and dove through the first wave that dared push her back toward the shoreline.

McGregor wasn't ready, by far, to trust Maggie. He had a job to do, and Maggie was certainly involved, and, to his mind, particularly dangerous at this point. He called Roberto.

"Meet me in the morning, nine o'clock…yeah, the Marina will be fine…yeah, Monty's."

"Come on in, Cam! No sharks to worry about…just me!" Maggie yelled from the water.

On the other hand, McGregor laughed to himself as he stripped off his pants. Although it was not completely waterproof, he intentionally left his extra service revolver strapped to his ankle, and a sustained eye on the beach was clearly warranted.

"Don't you just love the warm water of the Gulf Stream," Maggie said, as McGregor swam out to where she was standing on a sandbar, her practically naked body silhouetted by the backlight of the moon.

"Make love to me, Cam," she whispered as he reached the sandbar.

CHAPTER SEVEN

"Last night was…well… inspiring," Roberto said looking over the breakfast blackboard at Monty's.

"I'll have *chilis rellenos* and eggs, over easy, and hash browns, please," he smiled at the waitress. "What about you, Cam? I couldn't figure out from your phone calls what the hell you were up to. One minute I hear dishes clanking in the background…the next, sea gulls. What…."

"Two eggs, over easy, rye toast, and orange juice for me, Miss." Thank you, McGregor said, as he handed her his menu. "Just a short visit with Thomas Girafalco and his sister, the infamous Marshal Maggie. Girafalco was cool when I met him, hot as hell when I left. Maggie was…well…hot and hotter! One thing for sure, we need to go deep undercover, starting now."

"Speaking of old pals, guess who I saw on stage at Cookie's last night," Roberto remarked off-handedly.

"Gosh, Roberto, I'm guessing I know 'what' you saw at Cookie's last night, but 'who' you saw would be a mystery to me." McGregor said, raising one eyebrow quizzically.

Roberto leaned across the table. "Angelika Schafer," he declared.

"I should be surprised," McGregor said disgustedly, "but…unfortunately, I'm not. Girafalco seems to have Customs and Immigration in his pocket…Roberto, my God! How can you eat that stuff?" McGregor snorted, causing the waitress to giggle as she placed a large concoction—a mixture of green, white, brown and a touch of red—in front of Gonzales.

"*Es en mi sangre, Señor McGregor*," Gonzales replied laughingly as he tossed a napkin over his lap. "It's in my blood!"

"Listen, my friend," McGregor continued seriously, "as I said, we need to go undercover, and at the very least, we need to find a place to stay where we can be…well…unobtrusive, might be a good word."

"We should relocate our base of operations to an area just north of here," Gonzales quickly suggested. "It's the only place in this area that Girafalco has very few, if any, connections. In fact, he's a number one pain in the ass to the small, but rapidly growing, Mexican community. The number two pain they have is with the Cuban community, who think all Mexicans are blue-collar day laborers and should stay that way."

"And you know this how?" McGregor asked.

"Let's just say I have connections," Gonzales smiled slyly. "Want me to make a call?"

"Go for it!" McGregor prompted.

After a highly animated conversation, mostly in Spanish and interrupted by mouthfuls of *chilis rellenos* and eggs—occasionally punctuated by muffled belches—Gonzales settled down to business. *"Gracias*, Armando! *Eres un gran amigo*," he said, finally laying down his phone. "All right, Cam, we've got a three-bedroom furnished house in Bay Front—about ten minutes from here. We can move in this afternoon. The keys will be in the flowerpot to the left of the front door. It's a gated community, and I've got our password code in my phone. In addition," Gonzales added, "we've got a meeting in Hallandale at the Cactus Moon Cantina tonight with a few Mexican community leaders to talk about their relations with our mutual *enemigo*, Thomas Girafalco—they call him '*El Falcon*! I hope you like Mexican cuisine."

"I'm not trying to solve a mystery here, my friends," McGregor said to the group gathered later that evening in a back room at the Cactus Moon. "I already know what Girafalco's alleged crimes are; I just need enough hard, fast evidence to bring him down, and bring him in. I'm not a detective, and working undercover has proven fruitless. I'm a man-hunter—a U.S. Marshal on special assignment for the FBI— who doesn't have a judge in his pocket to issue search warrants or subpoenas and, to be honest, a guy who doesn't know whom to trust in the law enforcement community here in Miami-Dade County."

He paused briefly and glanced around at the assembled men who were giving him a gratifying amount of attention.

"As you probably know, Girafalco has his meat hooks into so many things, and has connections in so many places, that the only advances I can make have to contain a high element of surprise. The kind of 'flash-bang' designed to make him so angry he starts making rash decisions and stupid mistakes. I need to 'turn' some of his key people so that I have qualified witnesses who, for certain benefits, will testify against him and his syndicate in court. And…as I said, I need hard, fast evidence—evidence that clearly covers all, not just parts and pieces, of his syndicate's illegal activities. I welcome your advice, counsel, and *any* assistance you can give my partner, Roberto, and me in bringing *El Falcon* to justice."

As they had entered the Cantina, Gonzales had asked each man invited to the dinner for his cell phone number, just in case he or McGregor needed to contact them directly in the future. He had then excused himself while McGregor was speaking to the group and located a private spot on the restaurant's patio. From there he forwarded the list of phone numbers to Washington headquarters and asked for an immediate forty-eight-hour tracker to be placed on each number. He had a hunch that at least one person in the meeting that evening, although supposedly "trusted," might be connected to Girafalco and might call him immediately after the meeting.

"Are these Mexican cigars they gave us at dinner?' McGregor asked Gonzales, as they shared a lighter on the traditional smoking patio almost always found at authentic Mexican restaurants.

"I assure you they're not Mexican," Gonzales replied. "Other than that, who cares! You think all Latinos are cigar experts? You're a dumb-ass, profiling cracker cop at heart—you really are! And, to make things worse, you're a—hold on, hold on! — my bobber just went under water; I've got a fish on the line." Gonzales stared at the screen on his smartphone. "I was right, Cam—absolutely right. I got a matching 305 area code number that just completed a call to Girafalco's cell. We've got ourselves a double agent— our first possible stool pigeon! Let's go get…"

"If you don't mind, I'll finish my beer and this cigar, whatever it is, while you work on getting an address and matching up the number with a name," McGregor said in a deliberate manner. "I'm on a partial, as you say, *vacacion!*"

"Already done," Gonzales said, as he took another puff on his own cigar. "By the way, these *are* authentic hand-rolled Cuban cigars! I guarantee these were hand-rolled on the thigh of a Cuban virgin with big knockers and four kids," he cracked. "Now, getting back to business, our snitch is that little weasel-faced dude with the God-awful comb-over— Elián Sánchez. He's the one that was sporting an expensive white tweed fedora when he came in. We need to go after him ASAP."

"How 'bout another beer first?" McGregor said casually.

Later that evening, McGregor and Gonzales parked their car in front of Sanchez's house in an exclusive area of Spanish-style mansions just northwest of Miami. The driveway gate was closed, the house was dark.

"Call his cell number, Roberto, and see if he's home. If he is, see if you can get him to come out to our car. Tell him we have some important information for him," McGregor said.

Gonzales dialed, then spoke briefly to the person who answered.

"He's on his way out now, Cam. When he gets here, I'll put him in the back seat with me and check him for weapons."

McGregor nodded in agreement.

"Good evening again, *Señor* Sánchez, let's sit in the rear seat," Gonzales said as Sánchez approached the car.

"*No problema*," Sánchez replied as he slid into the back seat with Gonzales.

"Clean!" Gonzales said as he finished searching Sánchez.

"Nice house, Mister Sánchez—you live alone?" McGregor asked.

"Oh, no," Sánchez exclaimed. "I have three maids and a gardener—all living on the property."

"The house market here must be in pretty good shape for you to afford all this. You did tell me at dinner you're a realtor?"

"I own fourteen agencies in South Florida, Señor McGregor. I also own a mortgage company and I do some new construction work as well—never renovation, just new stuff, you know—here's my card. Need a house?"

"Sánchez, you and I are going to become best friends— *amigos,* you might say— but not for the reasons you might think. We're going to become *amigos* in our combined efforts to keep you from going to prison for a very long time. Your phone call to Girafalco right after our dinner meeting tonight is just enough co-conspirator evidence for Gonzales and me to bust your ass all the way from here to a federal penitentiary."

"I didn't…"

"Bullshit!" McGregor turned around in his seat and snatched the white fedora from Sánchez's head. "Listen, if you want to continue to smell the flowers in your garden and play footsy with your maids, then don't even think of playing dumb with us. You need to listen to what Gonzales and I have to say. Do you understand me, or does Roberto need to translate? Bottom line, Sánchez — you've been busted and are about to lose everything you have, including your freedom, not to mention your standing in the Miami Mexican community— possibly your life! However, if you fully, and I do mean *fully*, cooperate with us, starting now, we can and will make your phone call to Girafalco disappear, and this meeting with us tonight disappear. Or, we can make you disappear right now. We'll simply dump you in jail somewhere or…"

"Hell, Sánchez," Gonzales interrupted, "we could even put a bullet through your weasel head and dump you in Biscayne Bay."

"One way or another," McGregor continued, "you're not leaving this car without making a decision. The ball's in your court. You need to make a choice. Talk to Roberto— I need some fresh air," McGregor said as he opened his door. "I'll be waiting outside the car for your decision."

Maggie's left six messages on my phone today, McGregor noted to himself as he forwarded the Caller ID number from the last message she left. He was sending the number to his Washington contact to secure an address.

Perhaps I'll pay Maggie an unexpected visit later tonight, he was thinking, when he heard the unmistakable sounds of a physical struggle between Gonzales and Sánchez taking place in the back seat of the car.

He knew from experience that Gonzales could easily subdue an uncooperative subject, and if it was necessary for Gonzales to use lethal force, he would. Since the windows were all heavily darkened, he couldn't risk getting in the line of fire if Gonzales had to use his weapon. All he could do was duck, cover, and wait.

Within seconds, the back door on the passenger side of the car opened, and Sánchez, propelled by one of Gonzales' size 14 shoes, flew out the door and landed face down on the grassy strip between the sidewalk and the curb. Gonzales, bleeding slightly from a shoulder wound, leaned over the seat to grab

67

the keys from the car's ignition and headed immediately for the trunk, while McGregor ran over to examine Sánchez, who was lying very still.

"He pulled a fuckin' knife! My fault—damn it!" Gonzales groaned. "I missed it when I searched him."

"He's dead, Roberto. Looks like you crushed his larynx and—what is that in his hand? A switchblade stiletto?"

"Get him in the trunk, Cam. We need to get out of here!"

"Do you need to go to the hospital, Roberto?"

"No, it's just a flesh wound—that little bastard," Roberto mumbled. "Let's just get out of here! I want to dump his body on Girafalco's doorstep, wherever that is. I'm gonna stuff Sánchez's cell phone down his fuckin' throat so Girafalco knows what's going to happen to his people."

McGregor had seen Gonzales angry before, but this time it was different. He'd made a mistake, and he was taking it personally.

"Damn it," Gonzales continued his rant. "I wanted Sánchez alive and squealing like a stuck pig. Now, thanks to my stupidity, he's nothin' but a fuckin' dead pig! Drive, McGregor, damn it! Drive!"

After a quick stop at an all-night grocery store for a couple of gallons of bleach and some plastic trash bags, McGregor pulled into an alley behind what looked to be a machine shop of some kind.

"Stay in the car, my friend, while I dump Sánchez," McGregor said as he reached across Gonzales, opened the glove compartment and pulled out a flashlight. He carefully removed Sánchez's body from the trunk and removed his wallet, some papers in his pocket, and his cell phone. He removed Sánchez's clothing to eliminate any traces of Gonzales' DNA from the stab wound and carefully emptied an entire gallon of bleach over Sánchez's limp and naked body. Collecting the clothing, along with the empty bleach bottle, he placed them in a plastic bag and tossed them in the trunk.

"Here, before you do anything else, Roberto, disengage the GPS on Sánchez's cell phone and download his address book to your phone," McGregor said as he opened the driver's side door, slid behind the steering wheel and drove slowly away from the alley, leaving Sanchez's body behind.

"Wipe down the phone completely, and we'll toss it off the bridge on MacArthur Causeway—checking his wallet and papers can wait. How's your shoulder?"

"I'm fine, Cam. Sorry about the screw-up!"

"If you'll recall, my friend," McGregor assured him, "some of my final words to Sánchez were, 'One way or another, you're not leaving this car without making a decision.' And I told him he needed to make a choice. Well…he did. Dead issue—end of story!"

McGregor purposely took a circuitous path back to Bay Front, looking for a place to inconspicuously dump the bag of clothes he'd removed from Sánchez. After finding a suitable dumpster, he emptied the remaining gallon of bleach directly into the bag and wiped any traces of fingerprints from the bleach container before discarding it. On the way back to Bay Front, Sánchez's information- drained cell phone became turtle food.

"Man, I needed that shower," Gonzales later hollered from the bathroom. "Find anything in Sánchez's stuff?"

"Just the usual billfold paraphernalia," McGregor responded. "However, he was carrying about twenty grand in cash and an invitation to a poker party on Girafalco's yacht tomorrow night. Wanna go?"

"Got a date with a cookie from Cookie's," Gonzales answered, "unless, of course, you need me."

"Take tomorrow off," McGregor said, smiling. "At your age, you'll need all your strength tomorrow night. Besides, I've seen you play poker and, to be honest, you're a lousy bluffer! Here," McGregor offered, "here's ten grand. You can pretend you won it at poker, or…well, you could just consider it 'blood money.'"

After Gonzales had left to go barhopping, McGregor returned Maggie's call. She'd stopped by his condo earlier in the evening and was upset after the manager told her he'd moved out.

"Where are you?" she asked, in a somewhat demanding voice. "How come you didn't…"

"I felt it would be best if I went dark for a while," McGregor said bluntly.

"I've been trying to call you all day, Cam, and…"

"I've been on the job, Maggie. Just leave it there!"

"How about tomorrow night?" she asked. "You could come here…no, wait, sorry, I've got a meeting tomorrow night. How about…"

"I'll call you Maggie, I promise—just as soon as I have time."

"I thought we were going to be a team, Cam!"

"Not yet, Maggie—perhaps soon. I'll call you," McGregor said, as he hung up the phone.

Poker party, Girafalco's yacht, tomorrow night—that sounds intriguing, McGregor thought as he turned out the light beside his bed.

Hell, since Girafalco paid me an unexpected visit at the News Café the other night, perhaps I should do the same. I've got an invitation, I know where his yacht is moored, Sánchez gifted me ten grand, and I can easily round up a white dinner jacket. So…why not!

69

CHAPTER EIGHT

Girafalco's yacht, a one-hundred-foot-long "Baia Supreme," sat magnificently calm in the water, basking in the remaining hints of a picture-perfect sunset. Using Sánchez's invitation to gain access to the dock area, McGregor approached the yacht's gangway with caution. He'd purposely arrived late, hoping that the gangway would be unguarded, and that there would be a large enough crowd so he could easily blend in. He was lucky. His purpose in attending was simple. He wanted to let Girafalco know, in no uncertain terms, that law enforcement was in his face—no longer in his pocket or on his payroll—and that McGregor was the new "Dirty Harry" in town and not open for intimidation.

"Hey, bro, howya doing? Don't remember me, do ya?" McGregor felt a hand on his shoulder and a voice behind him from someone who evidently had just ingested a heavy dose of garlic. "I'm one of the guys you apparently didn't want to meet the other evening at the News Cafe. Where'd you disappear to anyway? Never mind, come on, I think the boss will want to talk to you."

"Listen carefully, bro," McGregor responded without turning around. "I just got here, don't have a drink yet, and the *hors d'oeuvres* are calling my name. Feel free, however, to let Girafalco know that McGregor's on board."

"I've got a gun that says now!" the voice countered.

"Mine says tomorrow at high noon at the central fish-cleaning dock," McGregor retorted, as he made his way through the crowd toward the bar. "Bring a friend to carry your grungy remains away, and—for God's sake—do something about your breath! Bourbon please, bartender—on the rocks."

The unseen owner of the threatening voice and the garlic breath didn't follow, and McGregor guessed that he was hustling to tip off his boss.

As McGregor made his way around the various decks, he wondered what the connection was between the apparently wealthy partygoers and Thomas Girafalco. He guessed that most of them only knew him as a successful business owner and were unaware of his side businesses. As he reached the top of the stairs leading to the third deck, he spotted Maggie being closely attended to by what she would probably describe as "a real hunk."

I guess this was the 'meeting' she was supposed to be at, McGregor laughed to himself, as he positioned himself in just the right place for Maggie to notice him. She made startled eye contact with him before he quickly disappeared back down the stairs. He figured Girafalco knew by now that he was on board, and that Girafalco was choosing to avoid a confrontation by simply ignoring him.

"Where can I find the poker tables? McGregor asked a passing steward.

"The central lounge below the main deck," was his fleeting answer.

My God! Is there anything on this boat that isn't gold plated, he thought, as he traded five thousand in cash for the same in poker chips and entered the lounge.

"And Mr. Girafalco's table is where?" he asked the cashier.

"*Centro de extremo lejano,*" she pointed. *Far end center,* he translated.

"Sorry, sir, this table is reserved and, as you can see, full," the dealer said, as McGregor pulled a chair from another table and sat down.

"These guys don't look very reserved to me, and you're absolutely right, the table is now full."

After a subtle nod from an obviously surprised Girafalco, the dealer called for antes and expertly dealt the next hand. Including McGregor, there were seven players at the table, with each anteing one hundred dollars to start the round. The game was "Texas Hold-em," one of McGregor's favorites. By rule, the dealer dealt two cards, face down, to each player. McGregor looked at his cards. *Junk,* he noted to himself, but he would bluff by raising the pot by five hundred dollars. Three players, including Girafalco matched his bet, while the remainder folded. After the dealer dealt the three "flop" cards, face up in the center of the table, all but McGregor and Girafalco folded. McGregor slid another five hundred dollars in chips toward the dealer. Girafalco answered McGregor's bet with the same. After matching bets on the "turn" and "river" cards, McGregor quickly declared "all in" and pushed his remaining chips into the pot. Girafalco, now visibly angry and red in the face, threw his cards in the direction of the dealer and folded.

"Thank you, gentlemen," McGregor drawled, as he pulled the pot towards himself. "And…thank you, Tommy baby, for inviting me here this evening," he laughed as he made his way toward the cashier.

Nothing beats trapping a man on his own turf, he thought smugly, as he walked down the gangway to the dock. *I bluffed my way into the party; bluffed my cards, resulting in a nice win; embarrassed the hell out of Girafalco in his home court; and probably embarrassed Maggie as well—job well done, McGregor, job well done.*

"Have a great evening, guys," he called to some of Girafalco's security detail who were idly swapping stories on the dock. "You're clearly working for the wrong side—so, I'm quite sure we'll meet again."

Early the next morning, McGregor got a call from Agent Brody. Some new developments had occurred, and Brody was flying in later that day to bring him up to date.

"Good morning! Mmm, I smell coffee! Want me to fix you some eggs? Roberto's still sleeping. I guess I kinda wore him out last night," a feminine voice giggled over McGregor's shoulder. "I'm Cindy, Cindy Flores," she said, walking around the kitchen table and extending her hand. "You must be Roberto's friend. I hope we didn't keep you awake last night. Roberto was having waaay too much fun," she giggled again as she opened a cabinet door and reached for a cup.

"Oh, hi, I'm Cam. Can I get you a robe or shirt or something? It's a bit chilly this morning."

"It's Florida, Cam. If your briefs are good enough for you, then my thong is enough for me. Am I embarrassing you?"

"Oh, no, not at all," he smiled, swallowing hard.

"I'll see if there're any eggs in the fridge," she said

They say that preparation is the key to gourmet cooking and Flores was clearly into preparation, McGregor thought, as he watched Flores twirl around the kitchen like a pole dancer slowly performing her act, evidently for the sizzling eggs on the stove.

"You want one or two pieces of toast?" she sang. "Butter or jelly? Let me freshen your coffee."

"One with butter will do, thank you."

"Oh, Cam, one is never enough for me. Just ask Roberto," she giggled and snaked around the table. "Don't I have pretty feet?" she asked, in a quirky non-sequitur, as she slid fried eggs and toast onto two plates and brought them to the table.

"Hadn't really noticed," McGregor said warily, as Flores sat down beside him, and proceeded to caress his thigh. *Sheesh, what next,* he wondered.

"Buenos días, todos," Gonzales groaned as he made his way toward the coffee pot. "Sorry, I wasn't in time to join you for breakfast." He looked as if he'd been run over by a Sherman tank.

"Here, Roberto, take my chair," McGregor said, as he reached down and gently removed Flores' hand from his thigh. "Cindy makes a great breakfast. I've got to get dressed. We have a visitor from the 'main office' comin' in, and I need to pick him up for a meeting. I'll bring you up to speed later."

McGregor was waiting when Brody's government plane arrived at Miami International. Brody was accompanied by two other agents.

Something's/. up, McGregor assumed, as they drove to a nearby restaurant where he'd arranged a private room so they could have an uninterrupted lunch meeting.

"We got a call about three o'clock this morning from a guy named Almossawi," Brody began. "Clevis Almossawi to be exact. He said he was Thomas Girafalco's attorney. The agent who took the call forwarded it to me at home immediately. I dispatched four agents from my office to Almossawi's home and office after he told me that if he and his family 'got protection', he was willing to 'spill the beans' on Girafalco's organization."

Brody took a bite of the Cuban sandwich he'd ordered, and continued, "Almossawi said that a very agitated Girafalco had just called him and told him that you'd likely killed one of his associates and were threatening him—said you showed up at a poker party he hosted last night. Girafalco wanted him to order up a 'hit' on you and Gonzales."

McGregor sat, calmly regarding Brody and his agents, as Brody went on. "Now, I know that the Miami office got wind of some guy the police found dumped in an alley. He'd been doused with chlorine of some kind. They've seen a security tape of some guy purchasing what looked to be a couple gallons of bleach at a local grocery store shortly before or after, according to the coroner's report, the guy was killed. 'Couldn't see his face,' they said, 'because the possible perp was wearing a fedora hat and seemed to know exactly where the store security cameras were.' You don't know anything about that do you?"

"How do you think I'd look in a fedora?" McGregor asked blandly. "They're pretty common around here, you know. I was thinking that I'd get…"

"With that face, you must have done pretty well at poker last night!" Brody retorted. "Look, here's what we're going to do. First, based on what we learned from Almossawi this morning, we're going to round up Girafalco and Douglas, and, to be safe, we're going to transport them back to D.C. for arraignment. We've got federal search warrants in hand for both of their properties and any other holdings we might find interesting. In addition, we've got a federal arrest warrant being wired to Belgium, asking authorities there to detain this Alard De Smet, the Belgian Mafia gang leader slash Godfather, and to seize and search his properties."

Brody took a minute to work on his sandwich and then continued, "Now, as far as Clevis Almossawi is concerned, he and his family are going to be placed in a witness protection program and are going to disappear for a while. Bottom line…good work, McGregor. Before you pack up and say goodbye to Miami, enjoy a little vacation at our expense. It may not seem to you that you've done much, but whatever you did, you managed to flush out and turn a key witness for us. That was more than enough— Girafalco is officially 'out of business,' as far as I'm concerned. As soon as we've finished eating, we'll be on our way to arrest him. We've contacted Gonzales. He's on his way over and should be joining us in a few minutes. You guys want in on the bust?"

"I can't speak for Roberto, but I wouldn't miss it for the world," McGregor said, just as Gonzales appeared in the doorway.

"Would you really *want* the world? Really now, McGregor, that's an awful lot of responsibility even for a superhero wanna-be like you!" Gonzales hooted, as he introduced himself and shook hands with Brody and the other agents and sat down across the table from McGregor. "And, Agent Brody, McGregor and I will be glad to have *you* and *your* people backing us up as Cam and I present *ourselves* to Mr. Girafalco. I think we've earned the right to *personally* confront his miserable ass and present him with a customized pair of steel bracelets. You agree, don't ya?"

"I couldn't agree more, Roberto—Miss, I think we're ready for refills on our coffee over here," Brody said catching the waitress's eye.

About halfway through lunch, and seemingly out of nowhere, Brody asked McGregor why he'd decided to take early retirement from the Marshal's Service.

"I've been thinking about my own future," Brody confessed. "Some days I envy guys like you—guys who got out before the job got them. Other days—hell, I just don't know."

"I know what you're feelin'," McGregor acknowledged. "You know—as a 'good guy', a cop, I spent my days and many, many nights driving around crappy neighborhoods, talking to stupid people, drinking cold coffee, and looking for bad guys. I spent most of my time experiencing the seamy side of life that most people don't see. Eventually I found myself judging the world from an extremely limited perspective, and I started to see everything with a jaundiced eye—my whole existence began to be in a world of criminals and idiots," McGregor explained.

"After the death of my wife," he continued. "I just woke up one morning and realized that I badly needed to rebalance my life. Police work lacks balance. A doctor loses a patient today but brings a baby into the world tomorrow. Most jobs have a healthy balance; the good things are mixed with the bad. Not so in the kind of police work I did. On call after call, case after case, I'd only see criminals or people making fools of themselves. It's like I've never been called to a party when everyone is behaving well. Cops are called when some dude gets drunk and decides he can whip anyone around. When we make an arrest, we only see the man at that moment, *not* when he's working hard for his or her family. I found myself thinking that ninety-eight percent of the people in the world are no good—and the two percent who *are* good—well, they carry badges, and even then…well… that's not right—but that's where my mind was when I decided to bow out. Make sense to you?"

"Yeah, unfortunately it does," Brody conceded. "You've described exactly the road I'm starting to travel down. I was telling my wife just the other day that about the only friends I have any more are cops."

"You ought to come out and volunteer at the airport like me," McGregor suggested lightly as Brody checked a message on his phone. "You'll immediately find a whole new world of law-abiding citizens— a world where ninety-eight percent of the population are good folks just passing through."

"It's a thought, McGregor—it's a thought," Brody responded rather dismissively as he looked around the table. "Okay, I think we're ready," he proclaimed. "Time to go."

As they walked toward the restaurant's parking lot, Brody took McGregor aside for a moment.

"In case there was any doubt in your mind, my friend, we've learned that Maggie is in this just as deeply as her brother—perhaps, in some aspects of her relationship with the MD 699 syndicate, even deeper."

74

"Surveillance has both perps in their apartments, boss!" one of Brody's agents announced. "They live in the same high-rise, with Girafalco on the fourteenth floor—Douglas on the twelfth. We have agents ready to secure the building as soon as you give them the word."

"How far away are we?" Brody turned and asked McGregor.

"Ten minutes, max." McGregor said.

"Tell them to wait five minutes and then secure the grounds and lobby," Brody directed. "Saddle up, folks, let's roll—think smart—be safe! McGregor, you and Gonzales can lead the strike on the fourteenth floor, other agents will take care of the twelfth floor, and I'll call the shots, as necessary, from the lobby."

By the time they reached the building, Brody had radioed ahead a complete action plan for all his agents and the other law enforcement agencies involved. Those involved in the final takedown would take the elevator to the twelfth floor, disembark and take the stairs to their final destinations.

"You up for mounting a two-story staircase?" McGregor grinned and whispered to Gonzales as they approached the lobby area of the complex.

"That's about all I can get up for after last night and this morning," Gonzales groaned. "God, Cindy's relentless!"

All the teams Brody had set up moved in quickly and simultaneously. "Hit 'em hard and fast—I don't want them to know we're coming," he advised.

When McGregor and Gonzales finally reached Girafalco's apartment, Gonzales' knock on the door and his thick Spanish-accented announcement that he was from maintenance, was readily answered by one of Girafalco's security men.

"Who else is here?" Gonzales asked, while quickly grabbing the man's shirt front and placing the muzzle of his gun between the man's eyebrows.

"Just Mr. Girafalco and me—he's taking a shower," the man said as McGregor checked him for weapons.

"Come with me, punk," Gonzales ordered as he led the man through the door leading to the staircase he and McGregor had just climbed. After handing him off to another agent, he quickly rejoined McGregor in the doorway to Girafalco's apartment. Moving cautiously through the apartment, they concluded that the security man was telling the truth—Girafalco was in the shower completely oblivious to what was going on around him. While Gonzales grabbed a bathrobe, McGregor casually sat down on the toilet, reached around and pressed the flush handle down.

"God damn it," Girafalco yelled as McGregor held the handle in the down position. "Steven, how many times have I told you not to flush the john when I'm taking a shower! Damn it! Hand me my bathrobe, you asshole!"

When McGregor flung open the shower door, releasing a cloud of steam, he and Gonzales stood face to face with Girafalco, their guns drawn and pointed directly at him.

75

"Your bathrobe, sir," Gonzales announced. "Would you perhaps like me to powder your balls for you?"

"Step out, Girafalco," McGregor ordered. "You're goin' with us."

"What the hell? Where do you think you're taking me?" Girafalco protested hotly.

"To the lobby, *El Falcon,* to be arrested of course—the party's over," McGregor informed him as he placed him in cuffs.

"At least let me get dressed!" Girafalco demanded to deaf ears. However, not deaf enough to drown out the sirens they could hear emanating from the street below them.

"It's an ambulance, Cam. I hope it's not coming for one of our people. I didn't hear any gunshots," Gonzales said as they left the apartment and headed toward the elevator, man-handling a robed and still damp Girafalco along between them.

All entry points below the twelfth floor had been secured by agents, so the ride down was quick and easy for the three of them. After reading a sullen Girafalco his rights, McGregor turned to Brody to give him a "thumbs up" and ask about any injuries to agents.

"Pretty clean operation," Brody responded in a flattened tone as he pulled McGregor and Gonzales aside. "Maggie's dead, guys. She took a twelve-story swan dive through the window of her bedroom when our guys broke through her door. It's not pretty. She supposedly had a girlfriend up there with her, but nobody else was in the apartment, according to my agents. We're sealing off both apartments now, waiting for the evidence and forensics teams." He sighed in frustration at losing a key figure in their investigation.

"Medics and some of our guys are cleaning up the mess outside. The coroner's here now, and the mayor of Miami is pissed off because I didn't give him any advance info about the takedown. All this because you tried to help a stranded passenger at Dulles Airport—who'da thunk! Anyway, thanks, guys, your work is done—get out of here—go have fun," he told them.

"You okay, partner?" Gonzales asked McGregor as they relocated back to their cars.

"If you're talking about Maggie," McGregor responded dismissively, "she was *not*, as I heard you say to—what's her name—Cindy, as I got dressed this morning, 'the sun in my day, the wind in my sky, the waves in my ocean and the beat in my heart.' So—how 'bout shrimp at Monty's tonight, and then we can hit a casino or two—that's assuming, of course, that you can handle an evening *without* a lap dance?"

CHAPTER NINE

As McGregor pulled his car into the main parking lot at Dulles, he was hoping that his volunteer work at the airport would help him take the edge off the feelings and events of the past few weeks. He needed to put himself beyond what he labeled the "Angelika and Maggie fiasco" and the follow-up events in Florida, and he was more than ready to enjoy the kinder side of life for a while.

Please be nice to me today, folks. I just wanna be a friendly face and answer simple questions, he thought, as he put on his Travelers Aid badge and sport coat. He knew full well that, regardless of his wishes, half of what he'd be doing for the next three hours or so would be hand holding, and even though he'd get a lot of the same questions over and over from various travelers, he knew that he needed to keep reminding himself that what seemed old to him was new to them.

"Welcome back, Cam, you working this post today? Man, where'd you get that suntan?" Brad Fuller, another volunteer asked.

"I've been in Florida—on vacation," McGregor replied. "I'll be here for this shift. Anything I need to know?"

"Nope, pretty quiet so far—except for the guy who's 'seeking Jesus.' I put him in contact with the airport chaplain and, well...who knows? Hey, if he doesn't get the assistance he needs from the Chaplain and comes back here, I'm sure you'll be able to set him on a righteous path," Fuller teased. "Be forewarned, however, he's pretty obnoxious."

"Thanks a lot, Brad. Have a great rest of the day." McGregor turned and greeted his first "lost soul" of the day. "Yes, ma'am, how can I help you?" he asked as he leaned across the counter.

"Oh, thank you very much. Where can I find my baggage?"

"Where did you fly in from? What airline?" he asked

"Charlotte—US Air."

"Baggage claim twelve, ma'am—that way," McGregor pointed.

"Restrooms?"

"Right behind you," he said. "And, how can I help you sir?"

"Where do I catch the bus to the green parking lot?"

"Go to door six," McGregor indicated. "Go down the center ramp and out the door at the bottom. Your 'green lot' bus will be waiting for you, or on its way. Have a great day!"

McGregor couldn't help noticing the three scantily dressed and heavily made-up young women parading toward him.

"Excuse us, sir, there's supposed to be a limo waiting here for us somewhere. We're from the Wild Stallion Brothel in Parks Station, Nevada and…"

"Your driver eagerly awaits your arrival," McGregor observed, "I saw him just a few minutes ago at door two. That way," McGregor pointed. "Have fun!"

"Thank you, honey, you can bet on it! The next time you're out our way, look me up! I'm Emerald Tonight. Here, my card will get you a free drink," she said, as she and her friends paraded towards door seven.

It's a good thing Gonzales is still in Miami, McGregor thought amusedly, looking at Emerald's card before putting it in his pocket. He remembered the comment that Lucia, Gonzales' daughter, had made when he returned home from Miami and stopped by her house to pick up his dogs. When he told her that her father was extending his stay in Miami and that, "no, he didn't have a clue as to when he might return," she'd remarked that her father "really needs to find a good woman!" McGregor just smiled.

Emerald Tonight
At the
World Famous Wild
Parks Station, Nevada
555-473-2222

The rest of McGregor's shift that day, as he'd hoped, was blessedly mundane, and, as usual, it didn't take him long to regain the "do good, feel good" sentiment that he always got from helping someone. As he walked toward the airport exit that would ultimately lead him to his car, he was approached by a man who looked distraught.

"Can you help me, sir?" the man asked anxiously.

"Sure, my friend," McGregor smiled. "What do you need?"

"I need to find Jesus! I've been looking for him here for hours. Can you help me find him?"

"Didn't we put you in touch with the airport chaplain? Wasn't he able to help you?" McGregor asked.

"Yeah, I talked to him. He's a fake and mother-fuckin' asshole. I told him so to his butt-ugly face, and you want to know what that anti-Christ bastard said then? He told me…"

"You wanna know where Jesus is at this very moment?" McGregor immediately interrupted.

"I told you I did! You deaf?" the man shouted.

"Here, take this card!" McGregor offered. "There's a phone number on the front. Mind you, I'm not sure, but I think Emerald may be able to help you," he said with more than a hint of sarcasm in his voice as he walked away.

McGregor laughed as he reached his car. *Sometimes doing something really, really bad can make you feel really, really good as well. This was one of those sometimes!*

His plans for the remainder of the day would put him on his tractor, mowing at least part of the grounds surrounding his house. Virginia had received its fair share of rain while he was in Florida, and it was clear from the sheer height of the grass that—*well,* he thought, *the grass never sleeps.*

As he turned the key to start his tractor, he was reminded of what his Zen-practicing father used to say to him to get him to mow the yard. He preached that, "not only does mowing offer the *pleasure_*of visible accomplishment in a life often strikingly without it—it sets the mind free to release those bigger thoughts that lurk just beneath the surface."

His motive and word play, McGregor knew, was not based in anything Zen-like, but simply a carefully crafted ploy to convince McGregor that *he alone* was the one in the family who *needed* this kind of *pleasurable escape.* Regardless, McGregor always found peace in the sweet smell of freshly cut grass and order in the lines of his tire tracks.

As he finished his mowing, at least for that day, he purposely detoured away from his barn and headed his tractor down the road to his mailbox. His mail was, as usual, an almost overwhelming pile of material he did not seek from persons and places he didn't even know.

Hardly worth the trip, he grumbled to himself, as he stepped down from his tractor after returning to the barn, and ambled toward the house. Stopping by the trash container in his garage, he carefully sorted the mail into three distinct categories: junk, bills, and a couple of letters. One letter looked like an expense check from the federal government, and the other was from a person whose name sounded vaguely familiar.

Stacy Dalcour—why does that name ring a bell? he wondered as he opened the letter.

Dear Marshal McGregor,

I don't know if you remember me, but I was arrested by you and another agent about five years ago, as an alleged member of an organization that was involved in a money-laundering operation based in Tucson, Arizona. My father is Robert Dalcour, who is now serving twenty-five years in federal prison. You were the only one, other than my attorney, who understood that I was merely the daughter of one of the main operatives and not at all involved, much less had knowledge of their activities.

I want to take this opportunity to thank you for your testimony on my behalf in that case. Without you, I would probably be in prison as well. Since then, I finished college, got my degree in public affairs, and have recently been promoted to Director of Public Information for a major non-profit organization headquartered in Washington, D.C.

I knew that your home was in this area, and I'd been thinking about you, so I looked up your address so I could personally thank

you by inviting you to be my escort at a reception and dinner we're sponsoring for the International Green Earth Foundation, which will include in attendance both Robert Redford, Actor/Director, and, HRH Prince Charles, as well as many other notable environmentalists from around the world. This promises to be a great event.

Please consider allowing me the opportunity to express my gratitude to you for your kindness. I promise you a wonderful evening.

I've enclosed my <u>e-mail, my office direct phone number, and my home phone number.</u> I don't want you to have an excuse for not returning a positive response to my invitation.

Sincerely,
Stacy Dalcour

On a more personal note, and please excuse me for being so direct, I just must confess that since I saw you at my trial, I've had this crush on you. You were so calm, collected, and caring—even under the unpleasant circumstances surrounding my ordeal.

Hmmm..., *if I remember correctly, Stacy is a very attractive woman,* McGregor reminded himself as he looked at his calendar and compared it to the formal invitation that accompanied Dalcour's letter. *No excuses here,* he thought as he e-mailed an acceptance note to Dalcour. *Why not?*

Stacy:
Let me know the time and place to pick you up.
It'll be a pleasure to see you again under much better circumstances.
Cam

"Come on, Zeus, let's get cleaned up! *You* can be my date tonight for dinner at Hoppy's."

An hour later, after leaving a sad-faced Annie to guard the house, McGregor, with Zeus sitting tall in the passenger seat, drove west on Route 50 and meandered through Aldie, Middleburg, and Upperville, heading in the general direction of Hoppy's.

"You know, Zeus, there's hardly a town or village along this route I wouldn't live in; not a hill I wouldn't like to climb, or a hollow that doesn't invite me to relax under a tree. How 'bout you, boy?"

80

Zeus—while he was a fine listener—as usual, opted not to comment. McGregor knew full well what was foremost in Zeus's mind; he was busy searching the air for the distinctive open-flame barbeque smell that always signaled that Hoppy's was just around the next bend in the road.

"Hi, Mary Beth," McGregor called through the screen door of the restaurant as he parked Zeus on the front porch next to a dish of water.

"How 'bout you, Cameron, you want water as well?"

"Of course, Mary Beth, but put some hops and barley in it please," McGregor winked as he sat down at the counter. "And how is Hoppy doin'?" he asked.

"Oh, he's all right," Mary Beth said, forcing a smile. "He's really worried, however, about some group that's trying to get us to sell our property. They want our land, all four hundred plus acres of it, I understand, to build a hotel and casino on. Some outfit up north in Pennsylvania or New York. They've been getting pretty nasty with Hoppy—threatening to put us out of business if he won't sell to them...whaddya want for dinner?"

"Pulled pork sandwich and coleslaw will do it for me tonight." McGregor replied.

"And, a side dish of pulled pork for Zeus, I imagine," Mary Beth speculated laughingly. "Want some to take back for your other dog—Annie, isn't it?"

At McGregor's nod, she went on,

"You know, Cameron, Hoppy and I have owned this place for almost thirty years now. Our plan has always been to retire right here, on the job, and in the same house we built down the road when we first came here. All our friends are here, and we've got at least three generations of regulars that walk through that screen door every day. We employ eleven people who count on us to help house and feed their families—and Lord knows how many truckers crossin' over the mountain count on us for quick stopovers to cool their brakes and satisfy their never-ending need for coffee, snacks and gossip. Cameron, we're not interested in selling, no matter what the price is!"

"Does Hoppy have someone to help him with these 'up north' guys? You know, like a lawyer?" McGregor asked.

"Yeah, best we can afford," Mary Beth answered grimly. "But we have a hunch our lawyer might be playing both ends against the middle and is getting some money from the folks up north, who think he can help them pull off a deal. More money, we guess, than we can pay him for honestly representing us."

"Ask Hoppy if I can come back to the kitchen and talk to him about this after I finish my dinner," McGregor said. "Assuming, that is, I don't have a heart attack and die after eating all this rich food!"

"We've got coconut cream cake tonight!" Mary Beth tempted. "Want a slice?"

"Might as well put the last nail in my coffin, Mary Beth" McGregor sighed. "If I'm gonna die, it might as well be because of something to die for!"

Hoppy's is a great 'Mayberry' place to eat; he was observing silently when he felt his cell phone vibrate in his pocket. *Kind of a laid back 'country cooking' restaurant, with great food and great prices and your coffee cup never goes empty—it really would be a shame to lose this place.* His phone's caller ID was displaying Gonzales' number.

"Roberto, you cigar-smokin', chick-chasing, tequila-soaked beach bum— how ya doin'? You caught me about to eat dinner at Hoppy's—you 'bout ready to come home?" McGregor exclaimed.

"No, no, Cam, I'm just getting started down here," Gonzales hastily replied. "That's why I'm calling you. I've been busy as hell since you left. I put together a bunch of my old contacts from the Latino *comunidad*, and we managed to pick up some of the businesses and real estate that our mutual friend Girafalco owned. One of the places that closed immediately after we took him down was Cookie's. I now own the building, and Cookie's will reopen big time in two weeks! Yeah, I can guess what you're thinking, but I really want to do this. I'm going to make this the best and hottest adult entertainment joint in the country. I'm going to bring in some new talent, provide a real show business atmosphere, and open a restaurant inside the club!"

"You've got to be kidding," McGregor said, knowing full well from the excitement in Gonzales' voice that he wasn't.

"I'll be sending you a formal invitation for the grand re-opening," Gonzales shouted. "I'd love for you to attend! Gotta go now! Enjoy your dining experience," he laughed as he hung up.

My God, McGregor mused. *The whole idea of Roberto operating a strip joint is ridiculous. But then again...*"

"Thank you, Mary Beth," he said as she placed his dinner on the table in front of him. "Looks great!"

"You're welcome, Cam. I took care of Zeus, and he gave me a smooch. Hoppy wants to visit with you out here. He'll join you in about ten minutes or so. Okay?"

"I'll be right here," McGregor answered.

Their situation is simple on the surface, McGregor thought, as Hoppy Purcell carefully explained that they'd been contacted by a resort and gaming organization named Cren-Able Enterprises located in northeast Pennsylvania. Hoppy's Place and their nearby home sat on just over five of the 431 acres of heavily forested land that they owned free and clear. Cren-Able wanted the whole tract and offered Hoppy a flat $1200 per acre including the house and business. While Hoppy thought a $517,200 package deal was a lot of money, he wasn't ready to give up their home and business, much less the many friends they enjoyed chatting with each day. Neither he nor Mary Beth was ready to retire, didn't want to abandon their employees, and Hoppy felt strongly that working boosted his health and kept him active and sharp.

"You know, McGregor," he proclaimed, "when yer retired, hell, you get up in the mornin' with nuttin' to do and go to bed at night havin' only done half of it. I'm *jest not* gonna do that!"

"Let me ask you this, Hoppy," McGregor interrupted. "If you were able to keep your house and business, plus about forty or so acres around them, and if I were able to get you $6000 per acre, would that be of interest to you? If my math is correct," he continued, "that would let you keep your house and your restaurant, and walk away from the deal with over $2.3 million to put in that swimming pool you've always wanted behind your house, and expand your restaurant and parking lot to handle the new business that a resort and casino would bring your way—not to mention that honeymoon trip to Italy you've been promising Mary Beth for as long as I've been coming here."

"Don't need no swimmin' pool—got a lake jest outside my back door," Hoppy mumbled. "But...well, this place could use some sprucin' up, I guess. How much you say?" he asked, as he reached for the napkin McGregor had been scribbling on. "Is that number right? $2,346,000? Mary Beth," Hoppy shouted. "Come over for a minute, would you? Take my chair and listen to what Marshal McGregor is sayin'—I'll handle your customers for a few minutes."

Later that day, as McGregor headed back down the mountain from Hoppy's, he wondered what he'd gotten himself into. The Purcells—Hoppy and Mary Beth—had agreed to let him try to make a deal with Cren-Able at the price he'd proposed to them earlier. Hoppy was scheduled to meet again with the Cren-Able folks in just a few days.

"This time, Zeus, I'll be sitting at the table with Hoppy, along with an attorney of my own, a comprehensive contract to lay on the table, and only two goals in mind—keep Hoppy and Mary Beth housed on a generous tract of land, and keep Hoppy's Place open for all to enjoy—especially me! I can do this, Zeus, I can do this—don't you think?" McGregor crowed, reminding Zeus that he was the only one who truly appreciated the special genius of his master's exploits.

Back at his place, he parked the truck in front of his barn and opened the door so Zeus could stretch his legs and chase a couple of marauding squirrels up a tree, then took a moment to check a text message he'd just received from Stacy Dalcour.

"2120 O Street N.W.," he read to himself. *Dupont Circle area. Pretty classy neighborhood,* he noted. *"I'll be ready to go at 7:00 p.m.,"* she'd written.

"I'll be there!" he quickly texted back.

"Come on, Zeus, you've gotta help me pick out a tie and something besides sweat socks for tomorrow night!"

McGregor spent the next day working on the Purcell's situation. Along with making contacts and checking the credentials and past business practices of

Cren-Able, he set up a meeting with an attorney, a realtor, and a land appraiser. He also hired a surveyor to check property records and past surveys to determine the exact amount of land that Hoppy and Mary Beth owned. Bottom line: he wasn't going to be able to really help them without a solid foundation of facts and issues, and—he was going to have all he needed before he met with Cren-Able.

But all that can wait, he thought that evening as he gingerly accelerated his Corvette through the mountain roads leading to the flatlands below. He'd cross the Potomac River on the Roosevelt Bridge, take a quick left on 18th Street, and head toward O Street. *Stacy said she'd be ready to go at seven o'clock p.m. and I'll be there,* McGregor smiled. *2120 O Street N.W... Dupont Circle area,* he reminded himself, as he lucked into a temporary parking space, activated his flashers, and hurried to ring her doorbell. As he waited for her to answer the door, he wondered if the guy at the airport—the dude that was seeking Jesus— got any help from Emerald!

CHAPTER TEN

Stacy's even more attractive than I remembered, McGregor noticed, as he reached to shake her hand. She insisted on an embrace, and he was more than happy to oblige.

She was slender and pale, with raven-black hair cascading down her back, and beautiful sapphire eyes that beamed with warmth at seeing him again. She moved gracefully around her apartment gathering up a few last-minute things she needed for the reception. Each time she looked at McGregor, it seemed to him that she could see right into his mind and knew exactly what he was thinking. By the time they arrived at the reception, he could easily see why she'd been selected as Director of Public Information for a major Washington D.C. organization.

"You look as handsome as I remember you," Dalcour remarked, as they walked from the parking garage to the hotel ballroom where the reception was being held. "Right after dinner," she continued, "my work here will be done, and we will have been well wined and dined. Unless you want to—I'm guessing you won't—we don't have to stay around for the ego-fed politics and good ol' boy claptrap that usually follow one of these things. I know a club where we can sit back, relax, and get to know each other better" she continued. "It used to be my husband's and my favorite hide-away."

McGregor was caught off guard for a moment. "Your husband? I didn't…"

"I kept my maiden name! Don, my husband, was an incredible man," she declared. "But one night eight months ago, he suddenly died. We'd gone to a club that night. When we got home, we finished off our 'date' with a passionate late evening in the bedroom. I got up and went to the bathroom, and when I returned to bed, I found him on the floor. I miss him terribly…oh, good evening, Walt, I'm so glad you could make it. This is my friend, Cameron McGregor. Susan, oh, Susan, so nice to see you again; this is my friend, Cameron McGregor…"

After making the rounds and greeting what seemed like a never-ending parade of Green Earth Foundation invitees—all while helping himself to an on-the-rocks bourbon and an occasional *hors d'ouvre,* McGregor followed Dalcour to their table. Following a rather typical banquet dinner and a remarkably short run of presentations, McGregor, as was usual for him in these kinds of situations, found himself in his typical, "I came, I saw, I conquered," mind frame and was more than ready to leave. When he shot a head nod and telling wink in the direction of the door to Dalcour, he was quickly, but politely and silently reminded that they hadn't put in an acceptable amount of face time.

Got the message, he smiled.

So, with another drink, another couple of conversations and some working of the room, they stayed for what he assumed Dalcour considered a socially acceptable amount of time before escaping into the night. What she'd promised to be "a great event" was, at least in McGregor's mind, *a rather dull evening in a ballroom full of effete central characters chatting and backslapping with ludicrously stilted dialogue, coupled with the usual irritating overuse of flashbacks that all seemed to start with "what did you think about…"*

"I made a lot of women jealous tonight, Cam," Dalcour said, in a sultry voice as she offered her hand to lead him in the direction of a nearby exit. "Did you see the looks I got when I introduced you? You stirred up a lot of warm tingly reactions for a lot of love-starved women in that room tonight—me included!"

"You didn't do so bad yourself, Stacy," McGregor returned.

"We can walk to the club from here. It's a short walk and a gorgeous evening," Dalcour said softly. "I don't know how you'll feel about this place I'm taking you to, Cam, but I've always pictured you as the adventurous type. Bellarmine's Cabinet is basically like any other kind of club where people are trying to pick each other up. The only difference is that it's with sets of two instead of singles, and if everyone is feeling a good vibe, you eventually make your way upstairs. Bell's is a swingers' club, and, as unlikely as it may seem," she continued, "some of the members have become some of my closest friends."

At first glance, Bellarmine's Cabinet was simply a discreet door at the end of a long corridor in a nondescript office building, with a small sign next to it marked "Private. Members Only." Inside, the décor was—well—*interesting*, McGregor noted. *Red and purple walls, velvet couches, lots of big screen TVs with myriad undulating bodies in various forms of sexual escapades—holy crap! —clearly not ESPN! —this place is much bigger than one might imagine!*

McGregor quickly scanned the vast main room and noticed that the highly diverse crowd seemed to be in their late 30s to late 70s. There were toned, tanned business types and plump, relaxed retiree types; whites, blacks, Hispanics, and Asians; there were couples playing volleyball in the indoor pool, a few more drinking in the hot tub, and a few men hovering around a supersized grill on a patio seen through some sliding doors. Men and women were talking quietly at the bar.

"Stacy," McGregor exclaimed with a laugh. "Only about half of the people here are wearing clothes!"

"Keen observation, lawman," she giggled, "If you didn't know that a few couples have wandered upstairs — where no clothes are allowed, period — to have sex with one another, it might seem like a backyard barbecue with a few nudists." Noticing a couple that she knew, she gave a shout out,

"Hi, Mark, hi, Karen!" and they returned her wave. "Mark and Karen," Dalcour explained, "are in their 50s, and have been coming here for more than ten years."

Mark's slicked-back dark hair matched his closely cropped beard, and his white, buttoned-down shirt was undone to his sternum, revealing a large dragon medallion. Karen, a short, shapely blond, had on a sheer, white Guinevere-style dress with a slit up the side. She was walking with a silver-handled cane.

"Horse riding accident, Cam," Dalcour explained. "What's your pleasure—bourbon on the rocks?" she asked as they sidled up to the bar.

"Just so you know how I got into this scene," she continued, "my husband and I were introduced to this alternative party lifestyle— the most common term used to describe swinger culture — about three years before he died. We began by 'soft-swapping' — where I would engage other women and he'd just watch. In the beginning, we'd swing only with single women. But after a while there was a guy or two that I felt like going all the way with, so we began 'full-swapping.' Although both my husband and I were afraid we'd get jealous, when we finally crossed that line, we were surprised that neither of us felt territorial. The interaction was just so—well—titillating to watch. Jealousy," she smiled, "is just thinly veiled insecurity. Bring your drink and I'll take you on a tour," she said.

Every room in the place was a new and strange adventure for McGregor. He'd thought he'd seen it all, but this place, he marveled, was almost overwhelming to his eyes and senses. The lights were just low enough that his imagination was going crazy, and his vision was so overloaded, he repeatedly found himself wondering, *did I really see that?*

"Stacy," he laughed nervously, "this has got to be one of the wildest places that I've ever visited!"

"How's your comfort level, Cam?" she asked. "Are you feeling that you'd rather go back to my place for a refill on that drink?"

"Yeah, I think…"

"I completely understand," she smiled. "Will you put the top down on your 'Vette," she coaxed, "and take me on a short cruise around the mall? This late at night, when the crowds and traffic are low, the floodlit memorials are really spectacular."

"Why not?" McGregor answered, a bit relieved that they would be leaving. "I enjoy seeing them myself and the fresh air will feel good."

In spite of the physical attraction that seemed to be building between the two of them, McGregor was not particularly interested in seeking what was beginning to look like a sexual payoff at the end of the evening; there was something about Stacy Dalcour that just didn't seem right to him. He couldn't quite put his finger on it, but it…

His train of thought quickly vaulted to the car that appeared to be following them as they pulled out of the parking garage. He'd noticed a guy with a Bluetooth-style earpiece rather indiscreetly watching them as he and Dalcour walked to their car. He couldn't help but wonder if there was a connection between the car whose headlights were clearly visible in his rear-view mirror, and the fellow in the parking garage.

"You know, Cam, I really miss my father," Stacy announced. Even though her conversation was disrupting McGregor's thoughts, he kept monitoring the headlights in his rear-view mirror. "My mother dumped him right after the trial and quickly married some bum she'd been shacking up with for years. They're going through her and my father's money like wildfire. She's breaking my father's heart."

"It's not your problem, Stacy. You just take care of yourself. Its looks to me like you've got a great job, good friends, and you're destined to move up the ladder," McGregor said kindly, still keeping a close eye on the car that, regardless of the number of circuitous sightseeing turns he taken around the Washington mall, was still on his tail.

"Please take me home, Cam. It's been a long day. May I give you a rain check on that drink? Maybe we can get together again? Soon?"

"Sure, Stacy. I'm gonna be busy for the next couple of weeks, but I'll give you a call as soon as I get some free time. Fair enough?"

"Fair enough," she agreed, as they pulled up and parked in front of her apartment. The car that had been following them drove on by and pulled into a parking place about half a block down the street. McGregor counted two people in the dark-colored sedan as they passed.

"Cam? Can I kiss you goodnight? My daddy used to always get annoyed when I tried to kiss him good night."

"Sure," McGregor said, opening his arms for what suddenly seemed to be a little girl who was needy for a father's attention.

"Sweet dreams, Stacy," he whispered.

The words *father figure* flashed through his mind as he headed away from the lights of the city and back toward his moonlit mountain retreat, with the same dark sedan's headlights still obvious in his rear-view mirror. He knew from experience that they weren't professional investigators, who, whether governmental or private, rarely conduct a surveillance using a single unit. The risk of getting burned is just too great.

It's about time for this cat and mouse game to come to a screeching halt, he told himself. *When we get farther out in the sticks where there's less traffic, if they're still behind me—well, it's been quite a while since I attempted what we used to call a 'bootleggers' turn, but I'm guessing that whoever these guys are, they've not seen a Corvette change its direction 180 degrees, without stopping, within the width of a two lane road.* He laughed in anticipation of his upcoming maneuver.

As he got farther from the city, the road narrowed. The vehicular traffic, at that hour of the night, was replaced by an occasional deer or opossum, which, for many unknown reasons, always seemed to want to cross the road under the watchful eyes of his headlights.

88

McGregor looked at his speedometer and, slowing to about thirty m.p.h., quickly cranked his steering wheel about a quarter turn to the left and, at the exact same time, pulled up on his emergency brake as hard as he could. He waited for his car to skid into an anticipated ninety-degree angle, released the emergency brake, stepped on the gas and straightened out the steering wheel as he sped by his pursuers in the opposite direction. Quickly repeating the same actions, he wound up right where he wanted to be—with himself in *their* rearview mirror, rather than him in theirs.

He quickly memorized their license plate number as he let them distance themselves with as much horsepower as they could muster. He wasn't interested in catching them; he had what he needed, but he'd spend what few hours were left that night wondering who they were and why they were so interested in him.

Did Stacy Dalcour or her father have any part in this? he wondered. As soon as he got home, he called in the license plate number and got a name and address. *Maybe they were just poorly trained law enforcement people,* McGregor speculated, as he pulled his car into the garage. *I wonder if, somehow, I'm still involved in something regarding Girafalco and his organization.*

The light on his answering machine was blinking as he entered his house. Two messages, McGregor noted.

"Mr. McGregor, this is Stu Cully from Beta Land Surveyors. Please call me as soon as possible to discuss the Purcell property. There's no problem with the survey— it's done—but I walked the property and I've discovered something interesting that you might want to know," was the first message. The second message was from Dalcour thanking him for the "delightful evening."

Ambivalent feelings about the evening rushed into his head.

Delightful was not the word I would have used. It was more like...well...yeah, it was just plain weird. Walking around with her in that Balla-whatever joint, I felt about as safe as a tap dancer on a floor full of dynamite caps, McGregor thought, with a bit of a shudder.

As soon as he'd received the information regarding the plate number from the State Police, he sent a text to Brody with a brief description of what had occurred that evening. He included Stacy Dalcour as a possible connection. He wondered, he told Brody, if there might still be unfinished business with the Girafalco organization and if Dalcour, either father or daughter, might somehow be involved. He'd wait for his answer. *No hurry*, he realized. He'd return Cully's call first thing in the morning. *This guy,* McGregor amusingly forecasted, *probably found an active still hidden back there in the woods or... maybe... an acre or two of Indian hemp waiting to be harvested and processed for the street,* he laughed as he turned out his bedroom light.

"Good night, Annie! Good night, Zeus!"

CHAPTER ELEVEN

McGregor pressed the numbers that would return the phone call from Beta Land Surveyors' Stu Cully. Cully confirmed what Hoppy and Mary Beth had told McGregor about their property—that their restaurant and home sat on just over five of 431 acres of heavily forested land—land that they owned free of debt and clear of title.

"I finished the formal survey, and that specific paperwork will be ready Monday," Cully said. "I set new markers to clearly show the property lines, as well as the designation of the Purcell's house, shed, garage, and their restaurant and parking facilities within a forty-acre tract of the land, not to be sold, as you requested. Now, be advised that, in addition, I took the liberty of including a separate thirty-five-acre tract— again, not to be sold— directly behind and attached to the original 'not to be sold' tract—a total of seventy-five acres not for sale. Now, I hear you asking, why am you recommending this?"

"Yeah, why?" McGregor quickly interrupted. "Hoppy doesn't need that much extra acreage around his buildings and in-use grounds. He just wants…."

"Let's see if you still think that after I tell you what I uncovered," Cully interrupted him, then continued with his finding.

"Supposedly there are no gemstones in West Virginia—at least that's what geologists generally think. However, I hasten to point out that opals have been found at Coopers Rock, and the third largest diamond found in the United States, the so-called Punch Jones diamond, was found in the southern part of the state. I've studied gemology, and I'm certified in colored stones and diamonds through the Gemological Institute of America, the GIA, and I can tell you that there are diamonds to be found on at *least* thirty-five acres of the Purcell's holdings."

"You're kidding!" McGregor interjected. "Diamonds?"

"I'm not kidding," continued Cully. "Within the thirty-five acres I'm referring to, I found glacially formed *tailings*, meaning that the materials on this portion of the Purcell land are not indigenous to West Virginia, but were carried along miles and miles of territory, centuries ago, by a glacier that covered a small part of the area I surveyed. Over the years, these tailing piles were covered by topsoil. In a little less than an hour, I picked up four raw diamonds."

McGregor was astounded. "Are you suggesting that Hoppy could make money from mining that particular area? Is thirty-five acres enough land to warrant a full-scale mining operation?"

"Oh, no," Cully responded. "I like to call something like this 'hobby land'—a place where Hoppy and his friends can get really dirty for pocket money whenever they have the urge. Kinda like playing 'finders, keepers', with a small Bobcat-type back-hoe, shovels and a case of beer."

"So, you're serious about them keeping this extra thirty-five acres?" McGregor asked. "Are you mentioning your find, or your rationale for adding this extra land, in your report?"

"I'm dead serious, Mr. McGregor. And, you hired me to survey the property for real estate purposes, that's all—you didn't hire me as a gemologist. This conversation is between you, me and your clients. There's nothing in my report about this particular thirty-five-acre tract, other than the fact that I've attached it to the original forty-acre tract leaving 356 acres for possible sale. Anyway, I'll put all the survey information in the mail to you Monday morning. It's up to the owners and you to decide what you want to do. If you want a gemologist's report, I'll be glad to recommend someone for you."

"Fair enough, Mr. Cully, and thanks for your services. Send me your bill," McGregor said, as he hung up the phone. He'd wait for the land appraiser's report before scheduling a strategy meeting with Hoppy and Mary Beth.

"Come on, Zeus—you too, Annie! Let's go throw a saddle on Shadow and take a run in the woods—I need to clear my mind!"

Being in control of a majestic, powerful horse is a real turn on, especially when you can ride it through beautiful woodland like I have here, he reflected as he saddled his favorite quarter horse.

Horses, including Shadow, McGregor felt, *are projections of peoples' dreams about themselves - strong, powerful, beautiful - and they have the capability of giving us escape from our mundane existence. And, with my magnificent pooches leading the way, —well...* "Come on gang! Let's race to the edge of the woods," he commanded. *When you're on a great horse, you have the best seat you'll ever have.*

Later that day, McGregor got a return call from Brody regarding his inquiry about being tailed after dropping off Stacy Dalcour. Brody's agents had followed up on McGregor's phone call, and they'd talked to the owner of record of the car—Sergio Vargas.

"Vargas admitted, without hesitation," Brody reported, "that he was the driver last night and was simply 'on the job' for Robert Dalcour, Stacy's father. His company, 'Beltway Investigations, Inc.', has a contract with Robert Dalcour for a 24-7 tail on both Stacy and her mother, and reports on their activities on a weekly basis directly to his attorney.

"My agents also talked to Stacy Dalcour at her apartment," Brody continued, "and they believe that she really had no idea that her father was checking up on her activities. According to the agent who questioned her, she was very upset when she learned that she and her mother were being tailed, and even more upset that she'd involved you. As far as any connection with Girafalco, you

91

can relax. Girafalco's quickly fading organization had nothing to do with this situation. So, tell me, did you have a good time on your date?" he laughed.

"Ever been to Bellarmine's Cabinet?" McGregor asked flatly.

"Oh, my God," Brody yelped. "I don't want to hear about it! When I was a rookie cop with the D.C. Police Department, that place used to get raided at least once a month—I've heard stories! Did you...."

"Have a great day, Larry…and thanks for checking my tailgaters out for me," McGregor broke in, "I owe you a beer or two," he promised as he hung up the phone.

Later, sitting at his desk with a yellow legal pad, he began listing the recommendations he would present to Hoppy and Mary Beth Purcell. In the deal he'd suggest:

> ✓ *The Purcells would keep seventy-five acres instead of the original forty acres.*
> ✓ *The Purcells would then sell the remaining 356 acres at $6500 per acre rather than the $6000 he'd originally proposed, which would equal a $2,314,000 net gain rather than $2,346,000.*

Close enough, McGregor surmised. Bottom line:

> ✓ *The Purcells would present Cren-Able with an asking price of $7,200 per acre to start, and accept any total figure above $2,314,000, with all attorney and closing costs to be paid by Cren-Able.*
> ✓ *McGregor would negotiate a "finder's fee" for himself directly with Cren-Able, separate and aside from any proceeds that would be paid to Hoppy and Mary Beth Purcell.*

He felt a flush of satisfaction over the deal that he felt would work out beautifully for his friends, the Purcell's, as well as the physical effects of a long day, as he parked his car in his usual spot at Dulles that evening.

I wonder how Gonzales is doing in his Miami venture—I sure hope he knows what he's doing! McGregor was thinking as he arrived at his airport desk.

"Good evening, sir, how can I help you?" McGregor asked an elderly gentleman who approached the desk. He noted that the old guy looked tired, and a year older than dirt. His hands were shaking, his skin was coarse and the color of a well-worn leather jacket. Worst of all, he didn't look happy.

"We're here to escort our daughter to her plane. She's flying to Frankfurt, Germany tonight. How do we get to her gate?"

"How old is your daughter, sir?"

"What does that matter?" the man snapped, "She's 43."

"Does she have her boarding pass?"

"Of course, she does," he snapped again.

"And, you and your wife also have boarding passes?" McGregor continued his query.

"Are you dumb or something?" the old man angrily asked. "We've not flying anywhere; we're just going to go with her to her gate. I simply asked you how we *get* to her gate!"

"I understand that, sir, but here's the problem. You can't get through security without a boarding pass, so…"

"She has a boarding pass! I told you that already. How do we get to her gate?" the man yelled.

"Through those doors right there, the ones marked 'To All Gates'," McGregor pointed, while trying to maintain his patience. He knew full well that security would abruptly stop them and tell them exactly what he'd been attempting to explain. "Have a great trip!"

"Yep, partner," he said to Loraine Pelliter, who was working the desk with him, "it's starting to look as if it's going to be a long evening for us. How's your family? Did you get your son off to…"?

"Can you help me, sir?"

"I'll certainly try," McGregor smiled at the young lady whose head barely reached the top of the counter at his desk.

"I'm here to pick up my boyfriend who's coming from Phoenix, and I don't see his flight listed on the board over there. He's supposed to land at 8:00."

"What airline is he flying on, and do you have his flight number?" McGregor inquired.

"Southwest, flight number 251," she answered in a tone of voice that suggested to McGregor that she thought she was in good hands and was anticipating that he was going to give her the information she wanted.

"Cam?" His partner looked over the top of her glasses at him.

"I know, just let me double check," McGregor mumbled as he fiddled with the computer.

"All right, young lady." McGregor leaned over the counter towards her. "Southwest 251 will be arriving on time—eight o'clock. That's the good news. However, it's now six-forty-five, so you have an hour and fifteen minutes to get to Reagan National, where he'll be landing. I'm sorry, but you're at the wrong airport. Can I help you with directions to Reagan?"

"But he told me DCA," she said, showing him a cell phone message.

"I can see that, but this is IAD. But look, you're not the only one that makes that error," McGregor said in a soothing voice. "Do you need directions to Reagan? If you leave now, you'll make it there easily, with even a few minutes to spare!"

"I know the way. Thank you. It's just that…well, anyway, thank you—you've been most helpful," she said as she walked away—noticeably steeling herself for the unanticipated drive.

"Damn," McGregor grumbled to himself. "I hate it when that happens."

"No one delivers bad news better than you do, Cam," Loraine said. "Remember that lady, and I use the term 'lady' lightly, who almost tore your head off when you tried to tell her that Alaskan Airlines didn't land at Dulles, and that her plane was boarding right then at Reagan, and that she needed to rebook herself on another flight as soon as she could. I swear, she was about to…. Yes, ma'am, can I help you?"

The evening continued to be busy, with myriad glitches presented and problems solved. The elderly folks who were struggling to escort their daughter to her gate where she was catching her plane to Frankfurt, Germany returned to the desk and apologized for their impatience.

"We just didn't understand," they admitted.

A few minutes before closing time, while Loraine was still busy helping people, McGregor started systematically shutting down the Travelers Aid desk for the night. Loraine's voice caught his attention as he carefully worked his way from cabinet to cabinet, stowing equipment and locking doors.

"Cam, this young lady is looking for you," his partner announced.

"Stacy, what are you doing here?" he questioned with a surprised tone. "Are you traveling somewhere?"

"Just here," she said. "I know it's getting late, but I'm thinking that you probably haven't had dinner yet, and since I haven't either, how about joining me? I'd really like to…"

"Sounds good to me—give me a minute to close up and I'll be glad to go with you. Did you bring your escorts with you?" McGregor teased.

"Yup, I did! However, to be honest, the last time I saw them they were being pulled over. I called the airport police right after I picked up my parking lot ticket and told them I was being sexually harassed by someone in a black Suburban with DC plates," Dalcour laughed. "Did I do good?"

"You did!" McGregor agreed.

After a late dinner and an energetic conversation, and as the night grew long, McGregor began to realize that Stacy Dalcour was perhaps one of the most exquisitely beautiful women he'd ever met. In spite of his mixed feelings about their first date and her admitted history as a "swinger," she radiated an inner beauty that really attracted him. She seemed so comfortable in her own skin and displayed a deep sensual appreciation of life and love. Suddenly, seemingly out of nowhere, she leaned forward and whispered, "Cam, make love to me verbally, will you?"

"Stacy," McGregor said, after a moment of surprise and quick thinking, "you certainly have a way of getting a guy's attention, don't you? You know, over

94

the years I've been asked, occasionally coerced, to perform various tasks, deeds of valor or otherwise. Some I've elected to fulfill, others not, for reasons ranging from personal preference to circumstantial inability. Never, though, have I been asked, until this evening at least, to—excuse the expression— fuck someone verbally. That isn't to say I can't, or that I don't wish to—it's…well…it's simply a *dramatically* unusual request. Wouldn't you rather just come home with me and spend the night? We can pick up your car in the…"

"Well," she observed. "Since you're clearly not one of that hard-core, grunt and slobber faction of men I usually see—you know—those to whom sex is little more than an animalistic rutting between like-minded pinheads, actions which fully undermine, if not totally negate the intrinsic beauty of the female form—then, of course, my answer is yes. Check, please!"

Totally weird, but…what the hell…, McGregor thought. He pondered for a split second: *What's with: "animalistic rutting between like-minded pinhead's thing? OMG, does anybody ever have little moments where life and existence feel strange and you're thinking: "What on earth is this all about, what am I, why am I, and why is everything?" and your familiar surroundings suddenly feel and look different,"* he giggled to himself.

Later that night, Dalcour was able to inspire McGregor's *animalistic wonderment* and put his *moments* back in order. When he returned Dalcour to the airport the next morning, the black Suburban with DC plates was still waiting to escort her to her next destination. McGregor made sure they knew he'd spotted them.

Over the next few weeks, McGregor, with the help of an attorney friend, was able to help the Purcells close the deal on their property with Cren-Able. They walked away from the bargaining table with their restaurant and house intact, seventy-five acres to live, work, and play on, and a hefty check for $2,314,000. Almost immediately, they were making plans for the renovation and expansion of the restaurant. McGregor, with a feeling of accomplishment, walked away with a hearty pat on the back, a promise of chipped beef on toast whenever he wanted, and a check from Cren-Able for a tidy $100,000.

"Hey guys," he exulted to Zeus and Annie as he returned home that day. "We really pulled off a good deal for Hoppy and Mary Beth today. Tomorrow let's go celebrate by shopping for a new collar for each of you. You're beginning to look just a bit ragged and clearly behind the style curve! Annie, you can get your nails done as well—Zeus, a good tooth brushing may properly be in store for you!"

CHAPTER TWELVE

The fireplace in McGregor's family room always provided him with a restful and, at times, romantic retreat—a place to escape daily stresses and recharge his batteries. Fall had begun to change the color of the leaves on the mountain, and a wintery chill called for a fire in the fireplace that evening. He couldn't help recalling the many evenings that he and Polly sat wordlessly mesmerized by the crackling embers of a fire, with Zeus and Annie guarding the hearth. It'd been three years since Polly died after her dreadful bout with cancer. Sitting quietly by the fire helped McGregor kept the memories of her alive.

She was brave to the end, McGregor thought sadly as he reread a passage from a note Polly had written him the day before she died.

> *Learn from yesterday, Cam. Live for today, plant seeds for tomorrow, live a life worth living. Your philosophy of life has always been, and should continue to be, to make the most of it, enjoy the happy moments and accept the challenges thrown at you. Every gift, whether it warms your spirit or brings you disappointment, is a blessing. Please continue to see your life in a positive light—please continue to think of me...and us in a very special way.*
> *I love you,*
> *Polly.*

McGregor was asleep in his chair, the fireplace was cold, and Zeus and Annie had moved from the hearth to his feet, when his phone abruptly signaled an incoming e-mail.

"4:17 a.m.," he groused.

At that hour, he knew it had to be either bad news or an invitation for him to send money to some dude in Ethiopia who, in turn, would make him an instant millionaire. For a moment he debated whether to answer or to just let it lie unretrieved until daylight.

"Well, hell, time doesn't make news any worse or better," he growled as he checked the e-mail inbox on his phone. It was from the Miami, Florida police. The message simply read:

Marshal McGregor—sorry to give you the news this way but thought you might want to see the attached dispatch regarding Roberto

Gonzales. We have no leads at this time—his daughter has been notified.

It'd been sent by police detective Hans Mueller, with whom he had become acquainted during the Girafalco situation. McGregor's body stiffened as he quickly opened and read the attachment.

MIAMI SHORES, FL. For the third day in a row, police have found more body parts floating in Biscayne Bay, and police believe they all belong to the same man.

Early Friday morning, a kayaker in Miami Shores spotted something wrapped in plastic floating in the water, roped it in, and brought it to a pier near 96th Street and called police. A part of a human torso was found inside. Now investigators are waiting to find out if the remains are connected to the grisly murder of a Miami businessman, 57-year-old Roberto Gonzales.

This marks the sixth such find in three days. The gruesome discoveries began on Wednesday morning, when more remains wrapped in plastic were found near the waters of North Bay Village. The following day, a local resident found a bag of bloody clothes near the shore in Pompano Beach, which police believed were related to the body parts. Soon after the clothes were found, police found two more sites with body parts: a leg in the water near Northwest 36th Street and an arm in the water off Bicentennial Park in Downtown Miami.

"Only DNA will confirm whether these body parts are all from the same man," Miami Police Detective Hans Mueller said. Police believe these discoveries are all related to the murder of Gonzales, owner of a Miami nightclub. Gonzales was last seen at his club, *Cookie's Cabaret,* in the City of Miami, early Sunday morning. Police said they expect to find more body parts in the coming days.

McGregor sat in stunned silence. His immediate emotions ranged from absolute grief to icy horror to intense rage. Gonzales was a *best friend*—a rare title McGregor bestowed on very few others over his lifetime. Their friendship had been born of shared history, shared values, and ten thousand laughs. He'd become part of McGregor's chosen family, and after Polly died, Roberto Gonzales became his go-to backup; the first person he'd call to share a joy, and the one he'd call at two o'clock a.m. in times of stress.

Looking for the comforting they were always willing to give, he reached down to pat Zeus and Annie, who had both silently relocated at his feet, close together, now warming their master's toes. As he ran his hand over Zeus' hind quarters, he felt the stem of what he thought might be a large thorn. Zeus, usually alert to any kind of bodily touch, didn't move.

Has he been drugged or poisoned? McGregor worried, as he immediately dropped to the floor to check Zeus' vital signs and quickly yank out what he instantly recognized as a dart-like projectile. Before he could check Annie, he heard a voice behind him.

"You're next, asshole!"

The sound of a gunshot was all McGregor heard before a bullet tore into his shoulder from the back. He turned and managed to pull the gun from his ankle holster and fire at a shadowy figure partly obscured by the darkness of the room. The barely visible gunman slowly slid to the floor, trembled for a minute, and then flattened out like a leaf in a pool of water. McGregor was able to see the man grab his chest just before he died, as if he didn't like the way it hurt. And then—he looked like he didn't care.

Thank God, Zeus and Annie are both breathing, McGregor sensed in relief, as he dialed 911 moments before he passed out from the pain of his shoulder wound.

He was rudely awakened by the acrid smell of an ammonia capsule being swiped under his nose. Even though his eyes were still clouded, he could see police and medics examining the body of his unwelcome visitor. Zeus and Annie were staggering around the room trying to shake off whatever it was that had knocked them cold. Both were being aided in their struggles. He tried to stand, but it wasn't easy. Finally, he made his way to the body of an unidentified guy splayed on his back, eyes open, looking surprised. He had a scar that ran across his forehead that dug deep into his hairline.

"This was one ugly dude with a forehead so low he must've had to look down to see his hairline," McGregor mumbled as medics quickly escorted him to a gurney, and under red lights and siren, rushed him to the hospital. He'd lost a lot of blood and the painkillers he was given were making his head feel like an overinflated basketball.

"This shit just got real," he remembered telling the medic. He couldn't recall the rest of the ride.

"Good morning, Cameron," FBI Agent Brody said in a sing-song voice. "Five minutes more and it'll be good afternoon," he laughed. "How ya feelin'? You know that in addition to carrying some lead, you also had a collapsed lung when they hauled you in here—you should be feelin' pretty lucky! Rest assured that I'm working with some of your nurses to assist them in coping with you. They're saying that they'd greatly benefit if you'd agree to 'aggressive euthanasia' for your obnoxious disposition!"

"Yeah, right," McGregor grunted. "I feel like I'm hanging by my thumbs in a musty jail cell with electrical wires attached to my testicles. It's like a bad dream where this large woman with a mustache sits in the corner of my cell with the other end of the wires attached to an old telephone crank rotor. Every time I resist her sexual advances, she sends forty amps of current through my 'nads! But I'm not going to whine or complain." He stopped to take a sip of the water, grunting again as he turned to grasp the glass beside his bed.

"I may be hurtin', and I may grunt, but you won't hear me groan," McGregor boasted with a grimace. "Every muscle in my body aches, but I'm not going to admit it. Blood pressure 120/80, respiration 16, CBC and Chem Panels normal. Got a cigarette on you?" he asked. "I know for a fact that I must be okay because my name is not in today's obituaries. So, basically, I'm just happy to be above ground, thank you! Who called you? Why are you here? Where's my cigarette? You got a name on that ugly piece of crap that messed up my house? How are my dogs?" He collapsed back against his pillow—worn out from his tirade.

"Zeus and Annie are recovering well; they're in the capable hands of your veterinarian friend Steve Willingham. They both took a heavy dose of ketamine from your assailant—enough, I understand, to knock down an elephant. It's a wonder that little Annie wasn't any worse off than she was," Brody said. "You're on oxygen, idiot. No cigarette!" he said sharply.

"Knowing you were a United States Marshal," he continued, "your county police called the Service first. They, in turn, called us. Your visitor's name is, or should I say, was, Alfred Cripps, aka 'Al'. Last known affiliation—wait for this—the Girafalco organization. But, there's more…he was working for Beltway Investigations, Inc., and he was one of the ones that we questioned after your incident with Stacy Dalcour. Cripps was one of the bodyguards hired by her father, Robert Dalcour, for a 24-7 tail on his daughter. We've hauled in everyone from Beltway for questioning. I'm being kept up to date."

"So, there *was* a Girafalco connection, if only coincidentally!" McGregor exclaimed in amazement. "Tell me, Larry" he said, "what do *you* think is goin' on? Any ideas?"

"I've got more questions than theories," Brody quickly responded. "After the Miami raid, we had Thomas Girafalco in secure custody—still do—but I neglected to check out his sister's body. She, the supposed Douglas chick, was pretty torn up—the glass window, you know— and, well, she landed headfirst in the parking lot. Like I said, it wasn't pretty. Did you check out her body when you got down there?"

"Nope. After talking with you, Roberto and I went straight to our car and hit the road. We left it to you and the Miami Police to clean up the mess, write the reports, file the paperwork. The last time I saw Maggie Douglas was…. "

"Remember when we entered the lobby of the apartment building," Brody interrupted, "you were with me, and I asked the concierge guy if Girafalco and Douglas had anybody else in their apartments? Remember, he told us that Girafalco had a butler or bodyguard with him, and that Douglas had a live-in girlfriend who hardly ever went out. You remember that?"

"Vaguely," McGregor said, an inquisitive look on his face. "You're not thinkin'..."

"It's the first thing I thought about when I got the news about Gonzales' death. I spent most of the day yesterday talking to Miami Police Detective Mueller, our FBI guys in Miami, and the Miami Coroner's office."

"Whaddya mean yesterday? I just got the news this morning!" McGregor barked.

"You got the news the same time I did—day before yesterday. All day yesterday, while I worked my ass off on this, you were flying high on drugs while the doctors here patched you back together—as best they could. And, just so you know, the Miami Coroner's office is exhuming the dead women's body to get some DNA, and we'll know in the next few days whether my guess is right on this thing."

"And you're guessing what?" McGregor asked, pretty sure he already knew the answer.

"I'm guessing we may have screwed up big time!" Brody said in a disgusted tone. "I think it was Maggie Douglas's girlfriend who was lying in the parking lot, not Maggie. I think she threw her girlfriend out the window, hid somewhere in her apartment, and that she's very much alive and has taken over her brother's organization, or what's left of it. I believe we did a poor job of sweeping Douglas's apartment, and I'm guessing the coroner did a wham-bang job in identifying the woman's body. I think Douglas fingered Gonzales, and you, for a hit, and I think that Al, your visitor. was your designated executioner. On top of that," Brody stopped for a moment to catch his breath, "Belgian authorities released Alard De Smet, the so-called Belgian Mafia Godfather—lack of evidence, they said. Final thought! I think Douglas and De Smet are still in business and running the MD 699 syndicate. Wanna put some money on my thinking?"

"Well, I'll be damned!" McGregor exclaimed. "Shit just keeps pilin' on and pilin' on—is Stacy Dalcour involved in this?"

"We're looking at everything and everybody," Brody said in a well-practiced professional tone. "You want back in the game? You do look great in a fedora and your Miami Beach tan is fading!"

"Let's see what you find out, Larry. Then, ask me again," McGregor said quietly. "I need time to think, and time to heal. I'm hurting in several different ways. Thanks for stopping by. You really think that Douglas..."

"I really do." Brody said with his eyebrows raised.

"I think we screwed up!" they both agreed.

CHAPTER THIRTEEN

It's downright chilly this morning, McGregor thought as he unsaddled Shadow after a brisk morning ride. He'd needed to do some heavy thinking and getting out in the fresh air with Shadow provided the solitude he craved.

He couldn't help thinking about the news he'd gotten from Brody a few weeks ago. He'd been dead right in his speculation that Maggie Douglas was still alive, Alard De Smet was still in action, and that they were in back in business. After fixing himself some breakfast and skimming the Washington Post, he flopped down in an easy chair in his den and clicked on the TV. After just a few minutes of uneasy channel surfing he'd had enough.

"Zeus, Annie, damn it! We can't just lounge around here another day watching talking heads debate soap opera scenarios! I need to...." McGregor stopped himself in mid-sentence. Although part of him cried out to go immediately to Florida, or wherever necessary, to avenge Gonzales' death, the other part of him knew he should wait for Brody's agents to do their work.

It won't take much to track down Douglas, he felt, and, although he knew just how good she was at hiding, often in plain sight, he also knew that Brody's agents were, at this point in McGregor's life, a lot sharper in their investigation skills than he probably ever was.

She's still in Florida, McGregor figured. *She likes that kind of setting with its brilliant sunsets, swamps with alligators, and million-dollar yachts.*

"All right," he sighed. "Come on, Zeus; let's leave Florida for the mosquitos, not us! Let's take a drive and see if we can get our GPS lost, kick up some dust along the way, and find some lunch in small-town USA. Annie, guard the house!"

They hadn't gotten far before their drive was interrupted by his car's Bluetooth phone connection. It was Brody calling.

"Hans Mueller has Maggie Douglas in custody," he announced, in an authoritative tone. "She was discovered on a yacht moored in Key Largo. She refuses to talk to him about the Gonzales situation, but says she has some information she'll *only* share with you. If you want to talk to her, I'll make the arrangements. I think we've got enough on her relationship with her brother's organization to hold her for arraignment, but she could 'lawyer up' on us if we press her on Gonzales. She's being held in Miami Central Lockup."

"I'll fly down and talk to her tomorrow," McGregor said. "Good work, Larry!"

The next afternoon, as he walked through the well-worn front door of Miami Central Lockup, he couldn't help but feel a hint of concern for Douglas.

This is one of the places, as a U.S. Marshal, I've hauled people in and out of for years in the past, he reminisced with a bit of apprehension.

She's finding out that this lockup is far from a pretty place and definitely doesn't offer the up-scale comforts this woman's been accustomed to—no fluffed pillows, no down comforters, no perfumed candles. She's confined to a six by eight cell in this sunbaked joint, with a bunk bed bolted to the wall, a toilet with a sink connected to the top, and, if she's lucky, a makeshift desk. Her view of the world is limited to a one by one window looking out on rooftops and sky with no way to judge where she is within a facility that was strategically designed so that inmates couldn't determine their location within the building. She'd better get used to it!

"I need to see your papers or badge," a rather robust woman, with an equally robust and confrontational voice, demanded as McGregor entered the building.

"I'm Cameron McGreg...," he started to say.

"Not important!" the woman snapped, "I know who you are! I need to see your papers or badge."

"I'm supposed to meet Detective Mueller from the Miami Police..."

"Again, not important," she snapped again. "I need to see your papers or badge."

"I don't have whatever papers you're asking for, but here's my badge," McGregor said, forcing a smile.

"And your name is Cameron McGregor?" she snapped.

"Yes, but you already knew that! And your name is Alice Felton?" he retorted after looking at her name tag.

"Sergeant Felton to you, Agent McGregor!" she hissed. "Detective Mueller is waiting for you in Interview Room 330. Third floor, turn right. Leave your armaments, clips out, barrels cleared, with the clerk at the desk. The elevators are straight ahead. Have a good day."

"Thank you," McGregor said. "You're certainly a..."

"Move on, Marshal! Leave your armaments, clips out, barrels cleared, with the clerk at the desk. The elevators are straight ahead."

Wow, sweet little thing! Nothing like a warm welcome for a fellow law enforcement officer, he thought as he proceeded, as ordered, to the elevator and to Interview Room 330. He couldn't help looking back over his shoulder to see if Sergeant Felton was monitoring his progress.

"I am!" McGregor heard her say.

"Hans Mueller! Good to see you again," McGregor said as he opened the door to room 330.

"Hey, Cam! Congratulations! You made it past lovely Alice, the county jail's elite champion female wrestler and wanna-be football lineman! She's somethin' else, isn't she?"

102

"Well-behaved women rarely make history," McGregor responded wryly. "What's the story with Douglas?"

"She lawyered up yesterday afternoon, so we're finished asking her any questions about her involvement in her brother's enterprise. We've got enough on her, anyway, to hold her for a while, at least. I don't know if we have enough to get an indictment though—that's out of my hands. When we asked about the Gonzales situation, she said she had information, but that she'd only share it with you. You have history with her?"

"You could say that. Do you have any new leads on the Gonzales murder?"

"Not a one," Mueller answered. "We're completely stymied and just waiting for some kind of a break. What kind of history do you..."?

"Do you think Douglas or her organization had anything to do with it?" McGregor interrupted.

"Just don't know—just can't connect the dots," Mueller said, looking down to check his notes. "My sources tell me that some Cuban businessmen have quickly appeared out of nowhere and taken over Gonzales' joint. Now then, you want me to get Douglas in here?"

"Yeah, let's do that," McGregor said. "However, be advised, she's pretty smooth at wool-pulling."

"That she is," Mueller conceded. "She also pretty keen on trying to cut deals—I think that's what she's going to try to do with you."

It took quite a while for Mueller to return to the interrogation room with Douglas.

Waiting time is dead time, McGregor groused to himself. *Come on, cop— get the lead out of your ass. Gonzales is calling out from his grave for results, results, results—or at least, damn it, progress."*

"Hello, Cam," Maggie said, in her usual seductive voice. "Thanks for coming down. You're lookin' good. I've missed you!"

"Wish I could say the same about you, Maggie...I mean the looking good part. You look awfully bedraggled in your jail duds and, well...I won't mention your hair! Are you being treated okay?"

"Doing the best I can. They really don't have much of a case against me; I'll be out of here in no time. Listen, I'm really sorry about Roberto. I have some information you need to hear, but...." she glanced at Detective Mueller.

"It's alright, Hans," McGregor said. "I'll handle this alone, if you don't mind."

"I'll be right outside if you need me," Mueller said, closing the door behind him.

"Maggie, I think it's fair to warn you, even though you probably know this—our conversation is being observed and recorded. I don't have any control over that—so be aware that anything you say can ..."

"I know that, Cam. It really makes no difference, because I know that anybody I finger here today is going to be at your mercy by tomorrow. And I know you well enough to know that they probably won't even be around by day after tomorrow," she stated darkly. "Gonzales was a good man, and didn't deserve…" She stopped abruptly and reached for a pad and pencil lying on the table. Tearing off a sheet, she carefully folded the paper and began tearing off small squares.

Is she making paper wads or, perhaps she's thinkin' flick football?" McGregor was sarcastically wondering.

"As soon as I heard about Gonzales' death," Maggie said, ignoring McGregor's snide looks, "I knew you'd think it was me or someone connected to me. I had nothing to do with it. What I know is that he somehow pissed off…" she stopped for a minute and scribbled a name on one of the small pieces of paper she'd created and pushed it toward McGregor.

"Evidently," she continued, "Roberto had started to organize and fund some of his Mexican friends, and they were beginning to encroach on someone else's territory. Miami is all about cultural territory, and Roberto's organization had started to, let's say, overreach!"

Again, she scribbled something on a piece of paper and pushed it in the direction of McGregor. By writing notes, Maggie was protecting herself from anyone other than McGregor knowing who she was naming. After thirty minutes or so, McGregor still didn't have any better idea about what had happened to Gonzales and why, except for the scant information he'd gotten from Douglas, which, to McGregor, was suspect from the start. "Nice seeing you again, Cam," she murmured coolly. "We're finished here. See you on the outside—probably much sooner than you expect."

McGregor waited as Mueller escorted Douglas back to her cell.

"Any good?" Mueller asked as he returned to the interrogation room and closed the door. "She sure played the system; I got very little good audio from outside. I hope the notes she gave you will give us some good leads."

"Don't know yet," McGregor said. "I'll be staying here in Miami for a few days; I'll let you know. Gonzales is your case."

"You gonna share the notes she gave you? I'd like…"

"Like I said, it's your case, but…the notes? Not quite yet. I wanna study them a bit. Okay?"

"No, but I can use a partner on this," Mueller said. "Let's close this case together."

"Talk with you later," McGregor said as they walked out into the notorious midday Miami humidity. "I'm staying at the Hard Rock."

"That's cougar hunting ground," Mueller laughed. "Be careful."

McGregor crossed the street to a small coffee shop, ordered an iced mocha cappuccino, and found himself a secluded corner table. He unfolded the few scraps of paper Douglas had given him, and carefully transferred the

104

information to his cell phone. She'd given him the name "Arturo Camilo," the name of his business, "Camilo Plásticos," and the words "drug smuggling." Perhaps, he hoped, she had given him enough information—assuming she'd leveled with him—to avenge, one way or another, Gonzales' death.

Was she really being truthful with me? —was still a big question in his mind. *She didn't ask for anything in return for the information. Regardless,* he thought, *"crede sed proba"—trust but verify,* as he headed for the men's room to flush Douglas's quickly scribbled notes down the toilet. On his way out, he typed the words *"Cookie's Cabaret"* into the GPS on his phone.

"I'm looking for Angelika Schafer," McGregor said to one of the girls who approached him as he walked into Cookie's.

"Oh," she remarked, "I'm much better than she is! What are you looking for? Lunch, a dance? How about a private champagne party upstairs—just you and me?"

"Perhaps some other time," McGregor said politely. "What's your name, so I can ask for you? In the meantime, here's fifty dollars for you to find Angelika for me. Okay?"

"I'm Cherry, and I'm here every day except Monday. And I promise you...."

"Angelika?" McGregor firmly interrupted.

"Oh, okay," Cherry frowned, "I'll go ask around. Wait at the bar."

Not a bad lookin' place, McGregor thought as he found a seat at the bar. *I'm thinkin' Gonzales was aiming for an upscale clientele.*

The place was clean and comfortable, with plush chairs, plenty of polished brass, acres of carpeting, lots of mirrors, and two stages with poles.

I don't spend a lot of time in places like this, he laughed to himself, *but the usual endless parade of ghetto dancers seems to have been replaced by friendlier, somewhat cleaner looking girls. Yeah, McGregor, they're still strippers, but at least tattoos aren't covering their entire bodies.*

"She's working at our other place," Cherry announced, interrupting McGregor's silent critique of his surroundings. "She's at our private club in Pompano Beach. Here's the address. Remember, my name is Cherry and I'm here every day except..."

"Monday, thank you" McGregor said as he headed for the door.

Cookie's Private Club was located at the end of a beach area strip mall, next to a Laundromat and a dollar store, and across the street from a staid-looking synagogue. The only hint of what went on beyond the front door was a worn sign leaning against a pole near the parking lot. It read,

Cookie's Private Club, Members Only
Press Button for Service

There's no neon sign flashing HOT, ILLICIT SEX, McGregor observed silently, as he parked his car. *The only bit of flair on the building itself is a few pink tiles over the front entrance,* he noted as he pushed the "Members Only" button to the right of the door. *How did Gonzales get involved in all this stuff in such a short time?* he marveled to himself, as a voice from a speaker-box asked for his member number.

"I'm a guest," McGregor answered, "I have an appointment with…"

Buzz, click, the door automatically unlocked. A madam, he assumed, greeted him immediately. Somewhere north of fifty, she was conservatively dressed, bleached-blond hair dangled down her back, and was adorned with skin that looked as if she'd jumped out of a tanning bed just moments before she opened the front door. The foyer looked like the lobby area in a 70's-era hotel, with glistening black tile and plush benches. The assumed madam led him into what she called the "living room"—a room that would fit right into a Polaroid snapshot from 1978, he noted. There was a disco ball, a wooden bar adorned with Christmas lights, vinyl chairs situated around a few Formica tables, and a parquet dance floor furnished with a single brass pole. There were twenty or so people, nearly all between forty and sixty years old, scattered about the room, talking, drinking…

"And who did you have an appointment with?" the Madam asked in an accommodating voice.

"Angelika," McGregor responded.

"Ah, yes, the German girl!" the madam said, as she handed McGregor a glossy brochure along with an "erotic menu" describing what the employees of the club would and would not be willing to do.

"Have a seat; she's with a member right now. Would you like something from the bar? It's on the house," she said, again in that same accommodating tone.

"Bourbon on the rocks sounds good right now," McGregor said nodding his thanks. *She's with a 'member' right now,* sounded funny to him.

"All right, in a minute I'll bring out the ladies. They'll introduce themselves. You take your pick and she'll give you a tour of the house."

"I'll just sit here and wait if you don't mind," McGregor said. "I don't…"

Ignoring him, she continued with her patter. "Or, if you would prefer, you can head straight to her room. Each lady has her own room with a large bed, an HDTV," she emphasized, "and a private bathroom and shower. Remember, the tour is free," the madam said as the bartender placed a drink on the table in front of McGregor.

"You're not obligated to have sex if you don't want to, but you can't discuss prices or what you're looking for until you're behind closed doors. This is the rule," she stressed.

Before McGregor could process her words, much less the *carte du jour*, the madam stepped into an adjoining room and returned with a dozen scantily clad women.

106

Oh my God! McGregor thought. *My brain just shot a jolt of culture-shock down my spine.* He smiled nervously and tried to avoid eye contact while attempting to maintain some semblance of calm.

Stay cool, he told himself as the urge to flee hit. *"Remember, you're a professional! Hell, McGregor, if you've survived as long as you have already, you can clearly handle a dozen women who would love to drain both your genitals and your bank account,* he laughed to himself.

Most of the ladies, as the madam called them, were in their twenties. A few had a natural, co-ed look about them, while the rest resembled porn stars, with lots of breast augmentation, collagen lips and Botox-injected cheeks.

Oh my God, there's one that looks as if she's endured more than her fair share of plastic surgery. She looks like a buxom space alien!

"Thank you, ladies. Nice to meet you all, but I'm waiting for someone," McGregor announced, still feeling out of his element.

As they pouted out, he couldn't help but notice the looks in their eyes— looks that seemed to range from quiet desperation to a hungry twinkle worthy of a Wall Street stockbroker about to unleash a Ponzi scheme on a client. He also noticed that he'd somehow gulped down his drink in the last few minutes. He looked over at the bartender and held up his glass. The bartender was standing in front of the bottles on display behind him which seemed, from the lighting, to glow red like the dying embers of a campfire in hell.

Gonzales invested in all of this. I'm beginning to think I didn't know as much about this guy as I thought. What was he…?

"You look familiar sir; do I know you? I'm Angelika," a heavily accented, somewhat hesitant voice whispered over his shoulder.

"Angelika Schafer." McGregor turned and smiled at her. "We met at Dulles Airport a while back."

Schafer gasped and started to back away.

"You're not in trouble," McGregor assured her. "I'm not interested in your immigration status. I just need for you to sit down for a moment and visit with me about Roberto Gonzales. Okay?"

"I'm not allowed to visit out here," she whispered, looking over her shoulder at the madam. "Come to my room, please. I don't want to get in trouble," she said as she led McGregor down a narrow hallway to her room. A plush bed took up most of the interior, leaving only a little space for a long dresser. McGregor didn't want to be in there, but he took the only seat in the room available to him…a seat next to her on the bed. He struggled to get down to the nitty-gritty.

"Let's talk about Roberto Gonzales," McGregor began. "I'm looking for any information you can give me regarding his death."

"So, what kind of a budget are you working with?" Schafer interrupted. "The lowest I can go is $300, and that would be for the first fifteen minutes. Thirty minutes runs $500. For $1500, anything goes. Hot tubs, playing doctor, anal, toys…. you name it. This is probably your first time in a brothel, right?" she observed, accurately as it happened.

We're in the middle of a recession, but this woman can still make $1500 in a few hours of getting kinky, McGregor thought in amazement.

"Look, Angelika," he said sharply. "I'll pay you for your time, but I'm here for only one purpose. I want anything you can tell me about Roberto Gonzales' death."

Even though he was getting nowhere fast, it seemed to McGregor that Schafer was willing to keep chatting, and she ultimately launched into a history lesson on both her relationship with Gonzales and her work at Cookie's. It was clear that she had a head on her shoulders and was anything but a bimbo—plus, she knew only too well that McGregor knew of her immigration status.

"You need to talk to Cindy Flores, Roberto's live-in girlfriend," Schafer suggested in heavily accented English. 'I think she knows a lot about what happened. I know nothing. She's afraid, as well she should be, that the Balseros are going to kill her as well."

He was surprised at her use of the derogatory term. "'Balseros'? You think it was Cubans that killed Gonzales?" McGregor asked. "Do you have some names? Where can I find this Cindy Flores?"

"I don't have any names, but I have her cell phone number and I'll call her. Can you help her if I bring her to you?"

"Yes, of course," McGregor responded. "I can protect her and find her a safe place, *if* I can talk with her. Can you hook me up with her today?"

"I work a twelve hour shift out here," Schafer said. "Three days a week. Other days I dance at the Cabaret. I'm considered an independent contractor. Where are you staying? I'll bring her to you late tonight. Say, about eleven-thirty or so. Okay?"

"I'll meet you both in the casino bar at the Hard Rock Hotel," McGregor said. "Here's $500 now and another $500 will be waiting for you tonight. Fair enough, I think. Tell me, Angelika, why do you do this for a living...prostitution, I mean," he asked. "Really, you're smart enough…"

"You know what? Before this, I *really was* a mathematics teacher in Berlin. I probably don't need to tell you that I make a *lot* more money working for people like Girafalco's syndicate and then Gonzales' people than I did back there," she explained. "I pick the hours I work, and it's much more fun than having to deal with parents and rotten kids pissed off about grades and lukewarm wiener schnitzel." She stopped and glanced at McGregor to see if he was following her explanation.

"I like sex and I like having sex," she continued. "I can turn away any customer I want. If I don't like the look of someone or I feel uncomfortable, I graciously escort them back to the living room, where they can find another girl and end up leaving satisfied anyway."

McGregor shrugged and thanked Schafer for her time. "That's all right," she said, leading him back to the hellishly illuminated bar.

"I want to help you, *Herr* McGregor, I really do. I'll be there tonight—with Cindy Flores—I promise," she whispered, as she gave him a kiss on the cheek.

McGregor felt as if his emotional investment in Roberto Gonzales was starting to crack as he drove to his hotel. He wondered what the hell Gonzales was doing or not doing to get himself killed? Was his demise the result of their having put Girafalco behind bars? Or, as Maggie suggested, had Gonzales simply gotten "too big for his pants" and crossed a prohibited cultural business line in either the Cuban or the Mexican business communities—or both?

Maybe I should just write Gonzales off and leave this whole thing to local law enforcement? Hell, I thought I retired from all this crap! The trouble with retirement, it seems, is that you never get a day off. He knew that someone had to be the "bad guy" in this lust and money-driven scenario, but he seemed to be dealing with two distinct social and business groups—Gonzales' Mexican colleagues and the South Florida Cuban element. Aside from that, he was still finding traces of Girafalco's organization, MD 699—apparently, now, in the hands of Maggie Douglas—possibly still embedded in the action.

Who ordered the attempted "hit" on me and why? Does Stacy Dalcour or her father have anything to do with this whole situation? If the roles were reversed, and I got bumped off, would Roberto be here doing what I'm attempting to do right now? "Yeah, he would!" McGregor growled, and hit the steering wheel of his rental car with his fist. "Yeah, he would."

After checking into the hotel and finding his room, McGregor called Lucia Gonzales.

"Just calling to see how you're doing and to let you know I'm in Miami looking into what happened to your father," he began. After about thirty minutes of conversation, McGregor was satisfied that Lucia had little to no information regarding her father's activities or, most important, his death.

"Take care of yourself—I'll keep you informed," he promised as he hung up the phone, double-locked the door to his room and dialed room service for a club sandwich.

After checking both his weapons and strategically placing them where he could easily reach them if needed, he headed for the shower. By now, he figured that the word was out that he was in town looking for Gonzales' killers. He needed to be careful. He hoped to be able to call Detective Mueller in the morning with some new information and possible leads after his meeting tonight with Angelika Schafer and Cindy Flores.

I wonder if Cindy remembers me, he chuckled as he turned on the shower. *Hell, she should at least remember my right thigh which she caressed so adeptly while Roberto was asleep, and while I attempted to eat the breakfast she fixed for me the morning I first met her—quite a women! I wonder how Angelika will feel if she doesn't follow through on her promise to appear with Cindy this evening and I end up having to drag her to jail, sans toys, in her negligee?*

McGregor was relaxed as he sat at the bar waiting for Angelika and Cindy. He'd purposely picked the bar in the Hard Rock Casino because of its location right in the middle of the gaming area—an area carefully patrolled by security and entirely under the 24-7 eyes of security cameras. Besides, he liked the constant rhythm of a casino where everything seemed to happen at regular intervals. Dice are rolled. Cards are dealt. Wheels are spun. Bets are placed. And then it happens again—and again. He often thought that the constant barrage of noise from slot machine spins, games dinging, the pinging sounds of fake coins hitting fake metal, mixed with the constant patter of croupiers' urging voices and gamblers' shouts of success or failure, were all there to give customers some kind of false sense of hope.

With all that noise going on and all those bells ringing and dinging, the would-be gamblers must think that somebody must be winning something, he laughed to himself.

Eleven-thirty came and passed, and by midnight McGregor was beginning to think his deal with Schafer had tanked.

If she doesn't follow through on her promise, I'm going to ship her shapely ass back to Germany in a ...

"Help me with Cindy," a voice behind him cried out. It was Schafer. "She's very drunk and not happy to be here. It'll take me a month to get the smell of vomit out of my Porsche," Schafer complained as she forced Flores into a chair next to McGregor. "When I called her, she was hiding at her sister's house, scared to death."

"Hey there, Cindy, remember me?" McGregor asked. "Roberto's friend!"

Flores swayed alarmingly to one side but caught herself on the edge of the table. Her eyes wandered around the room, then fixed on McGregor's face.

"Me mandaron su pene en una caja de zapatos!" she cried out as her voice suddenly trailed off, and for an instant, her eyes blazed clear. Then, she crumpled slowly to the floor—eyes blank, and a wide, stupid smile on her, at this point, highly unattractive face.

"Let's get her upstairs to my room," McGregor said to Schafer, as they lifted Flores from the floor and made their way through the crowded casino. When they got to his room, they stripped Flores' clothes off and forced her into the shower. While Schafer steadied her, McGregor started a pot of coffee and pulled a hotel bathrobe from the closet.

"What is that '*me mandaron su pene*' business, she yelled out downstairs in the bar?" McGregor asked Schafer.

"How would I know?" Schafer snapped. "I have enough problems with understanding and speaking English. I don't think that's English she's speaking!"

"No, it's Spanish," McGregor snapped back. "But I..."

110

"I said that they sent me his penis in a shoe box," Flores sobbed, as she came back into the room. "I need some coffee and a whole bottle of aspirin. My head is pounding and I'm freezing to death. Turn off the fuckin' cold water and gimmee that damn bathrobe," she demanded between sobs. "You *do* understand English, don't you!"

It took a while for Flores to sober up and calm down enough to talk to McGregor. *Getting Cindy Flores to calm down was like trying to bathe a cat*, he said to himself as he thanked Schafer and handed her the additional $500 he'd promised.

"I'm going to keep Cindy here with me tonight and put her into protective custody tomorrow," he said, as he escorted Schafer to the door. "Be careful—I'll be in touch," he advised her as he closed and locked the door.

"All right, Cindy, you're going to help me find Roberto's killers," he said, as he poured her another cup of coffee. "You're safe here with me! I have several questions I need you to answer for me, but first, let's talk about this shoebox package you got. Where is that package now?"

"They sent me my Roberto's penis in a ..."

"I understand that, Cindy, and I'm very sorry, but I need to know what you did with the package!" McGregor said forcefully.

"I left it where I found it, right on the front entry porch of our house. Then I ran away to my sister's house to hide. Oh, I remember that I kicked the shoebox into the bushes to the left of the entry before I left. I've been so damned scared..."

"This is the porch of the house where you and Roberto were living?" McGregor queried. "What's the address?"

"It's the same house where I met you—on Bay Front. 14753," Flores answered.

"Hold on a minute, Cindy," McGregor said, as he punched in Detective Mueller's cell phone number. "Hans, McGregor here. Sorry about the time, but I need for you to dispatch a forensics team to 14753 Bay Front Drive—right now. Send a..."

"That's where Gonzales was living," Mueller interrupted. "Sorry to tell you this, Cam, but it burned to the ground about two hours ago. Investigators haven't filed their report yet, but they're suspecting arson."

"Still," McGregor insisted, "send forensics anyway, and send a cadaver dog as well. They'll be looking for a shoebox containing human remains in the bushes beside the front porch. If they can recover it, they may find prints. This could be a major break for you in the Gonzales case."

"Fortunately," Mueller said, "if I remember right, the house was brick and stucco, so the exterior walls are probably still intact--don't know about the shrubbery though. I'll send a team right now. When can we talk? I'd like to know..."

"I'll call you when I can," McGregor snarled. "Find us a fingerprint!" he barked as he hung up.

111

"Okay, Cindy," McGregor said focusing in on her again. "Let's get down to some of Roberto's activities. But first, who do you think killed him?"

"I don't think, I know," Flores glared. "The 'Balseros', the Cuban guys. They were threatening Roberto because he wouldn't give them a piece of his action. Since he started remodeling the Cabaret and put in a classy restaurant, he was making a fortune from both the Cabaret and the Private Club. He was even talking about opening a Cabaret in Tampa. But what really pissed them off was that he and his Mexican community buddies were in the process of trying to close a deal on a big chunk of land right in the middle of all the big Cuban restaurants in the town center of 'Little Havana.' Roberto had a hunch that the Balseros must be working with or for the Girafalco organization, especially after two guys came to our house one night. They said that Ms. Maggie—is that her name? — sent them to tell him, in no uncertain terms, that 'wetbacks' were not welcome in Little Havana. Roberto lost his temper when one of them called me 'La Tota!' He beat the crap out of both of them and threw them out. You need to look for a guy with a half a front tooth. He left the other half in our foyer."

Flores needed to talk. She was clearly shaken up by Gonzales' death and McGregor was a good listener. After about thirty minutes of listening to Flores vent her anger and heartbreak, they were interrupted by McGregor's phone ringing in his pocket.

"I won't ask what 'La Tota' means," he said wryly, as he reached into his pocket.

"It means 'little pussy,'" Flores scowled and screamed "mi coño es justo"as McGregor answered the phone. It was Mueller.

"I'm at the Bay Front address with our people and equipment from forensics. We found the shoebox and we processed it on the scene. We found a print which belongs to Francesco Perez-Alonso, aka, 'El Guajiro', which, in English, means 'the hick.' He's a petty thief and a small-time drug dealer who hangs around, for the most part, down in the Miami River area. His rap sheet is full of nuisance crap. I put an APB out on him. It won't take long for him to be picked up by some routine patrol in that area. We know where he hangs out. I'll let you know when we pull him in."

"Great work, Hans!" McGregor said with satisfaction. "How'd you get all that info so fast?"

"We're Miami cops, that's how! And, by the way," Mueller continued, "we didn't find any actual human remains out here, but our c-dogs paid a lot of attention to that shoebox. What were we supposed to find?"

"I really don't want to say right now," McGregor answered. "Just put Gonzales and Lorena Bobbitt together in your mind. In the meantime, keep your forensic folks looking at that shoebox for any traces of human remains—we need some DNA! Call me as soon as you pick up the Alonso perp. Again, really good work," he reiterated as he ended Mueller's call.

"Cindy, do you know a guy named Alonso? They call him 'El Guajiro?'"

"Yeah, I know him," she said in a disgusted voice. "Dirty little slimy Cuban guy who was a runner for Girafalco. He hangs around Cookie's a lot, looking for a free ride from any of the girls. He may have even done some work for Roberto—I don't know...he didn't have anything to do with...?"

"The police are looking for him right now. I'll let you know as soon as I find out anything," McGregor said. "Why don't you get some sleep? You're safe here with me tonight, and in the morning we're going to find someplace even safer for you."

"Okay—thanks, *Señor* McGregor. I *do* feel safe with you," she said gratefully.

Two-thirty a.m., he noted. *This is going to be a long night of old movies.* He turned on the television, cranked the sound down for Cindy's sake, and checked the on-line TV Guide.

'The Treasure of the Sierra Madre,'1948—just started—channel 102— why not? I can't remember whether I've seen it.

The actor playing El Bandido had just finished growling the line, "Badges? We ain't got no badges! We don't need no badges! I don't have to show you any stinking badges!" when McGregor, muffling his laughter at El Bandido's proclamation, thought he heard the sound of an apparatus being used to test the latch on the door to his room. Flores was sleeping soundly as McGregor pulled his SIG from his belt holster, released the safety and carefully approached the door. Through the door's peephole he could see the upper torso and head of a man with in-ear headphones hooked to an iPod in his shirt pocket, looking down at the door's locking mechanism.

"I'll put your iPod up your ass and put it on shuffle with my fucking fist," McGregor said sharply, as he flung open the door and pushed the intruder against the wall on the opposite side of the hallway.

"And every time your iPod plays something that I don't like, which, by the way, will be every time that something comes on, I will skip to the next track by crushing your balls! Who are you and what do you want?" he demanded, forcing his gun beneath the stranger's chin.

"I—I'm with hotel maintenance," the man stuttered. "I thought the room was—was unoccupied. I've got a—got a work order for your toilet!"

"Yeah, right," McGregor said, pushing his gun deeper into the stranger's chin. "Try again, asshole. See if you can convince me that the gun under your shirt's a plumber's helper. You know, you oughta see a dentist about that broken front tooth—don't you need a license to be that ugly?" he snarled as he removed the man's gun. "And if you tell me it got broken by eatin' hard candy, the next thing you'll taste is your tongue and your pea-sized brain as they both splatter up the ceiling. Get your ass into the room!" McGregor spun the man around, pushed him through the door and cuffed him to a handicap grab bar in the bathroom.

"You're a dead man!" the stranger yelled.

"If I agreed with you, we'd both be wrong," McGregor returned grimly.

113

In spite of the noise, Flores was still sleeping off her hangover. But then, again, it was four-thirty in the morning. McGregor put his hand softly on her cheek. "Cindy! Wake up! I need to talk to you!"

"Oh! Your hand is ice cold," she purred as she threw back the covers, her body glistening in the early morning light. "Come on, I'll warm you up," she said, grabbing McGregor's hand and pulling him toward her.

Gently wresting his hand away, he sat down on the bed. "We had a visitor a few minutes ago," McGregor announced. "Not to worry—I've got him cuffed in the bathroom. Slip your robe on and see if you know this guy, will you?"

Flores recognized him immediately as one of the men who had come to their house.

"That's the one that called me *La Tota*," she said, kicking him in the leg. "*La Tota*?" she snarled. "*You'll* never know, you...you fuckin' bastard! I found your tooth! Did you kill my Roberto?" she yelled and kicked him again. "Did you?"

"Okay, Cindy, that's enough," McGregor said as he dragged her out of the bathroom. "Let me handle this, Okay?"

"I gotta pee," she cried. "I gotta pee and I hurt my foot, damn it!"

"I'll move him out here," McGregor said calmly, "so you can use the bathroom. Get yourself dressed, and get prettier than you already are; meanwhile, I'm gonna have this asshole taken down to the precinct for interrogation. Then you and I are gonna go to the lobby, see if we can get some breakfast, and talk about your future."

After contacting Mueller to have "half-tooth" picked up for booking and questioning about both the attempted break-in of McGregor's room, and anything having to do with Gonzales' demise, McGregor set up a meeting with him for later in the day. Mueller informed him that they'd picked up Francesco Perez-Alonso, aka, "El Guajiro," aka, the "hick," and that he was talking up a storm.

"His vocabulary is significantly increasing by the hour," he laughed. "He's afraid he'll be 'raped' if we put him in a general population jail, and he admitted," Mueller continued, "that he delivered the package to Gonzales' girlfriend and told us who gave it to him. By the way," he announced, "Maggie Douglas was released on bail late yesterday afternoon—thought you'd find that interesting."

"Or not," McGregor said dismissively. "I'll see you this afternoon."

114

CHAPTER FOURTEEN

With Cindy Flores temporarily stashed at a safe house, and with the scanty information he'd gotten from Schafer and Douglas, McGregor was eager to find out what Detective Mueller had learned from the interrogation of "half-tooth" and the "hick."

Half-Tooth and the Hick? —sounds like a helluva good name for a grade B movie, McGregor thought as he made his way to Mueller's office through a maze of cubicles on the third floor of the Miami Central Police Station.

Whew! Smells like everyone who works on this floor is addicted to microwaved popcorn and burnt coffee, he noted as he opened the door to Mueller's office.

"Hey, Cameron! Come on in—find a chair," Mueller said, waving him into the room.

"Kinda looks like you've been living in here," McGregor remarked as he sat down next to an overflowing pile of paper and folders on Mueller's desk.

"Yeah, I know. I'm a messy housekeeper. How do you take your coffee?" Mueller asked, handing McGregor an extremely fat folder.

"Black, no sugar, and preferably so strong that it's trying to climb out of the cup," McGregor said.

"Got it! Start looking through that folder. We need to fill in some blanks," Mueller suggested and hurriedly left the room.

This is going to be a long meeting, McGregor surmised as he started leafing through Mueller's collection of material.

"Look," Mueller said, closing the door and offering McGregor his coffee. "I know you're really *only* interested in who killed Gonzales, but there's more here than either of us bargained for. I've got enough to call for international arrest warrants for Gonzales' murder, but I'd like to hold off on that for just a little while to see if we can cast a wider net. Here's the situation as I see it. First, we can eliminate anything having to do with the *original* Girafalco organization— that's a dead issue, and Maggie Douglas doesn't seem to be involved. Her problems are from past issues, not this one. Brody concurs."

"I'm not sure I agree with that assumption," McGregor interrupted.

"Okay," Mueller continued, "but I really think we can eliminate anything regarding Stacey Dalcour and her father—there's nothing there that I can find— dead issue."

"I think I'll reserve judgment on that as well. At least for the time being. I'm not sure I trust anyone who has appeared on my radar in the past few weeks. No offense, but I'm not even willing to fully accept any of your findings or assumptions at this point. I've been badly burned." said McGregor.

"In light of recent events, I can understand your point of view," Mueller said as he took a big drink of coffee and grimaced. "God, this is terrible stuff. Sorry 'bout that! I drink so much of this crap that Juan Valdez is gonna name his donkey after me. Anyway, you remember this Alard De Smet character—the Belgian Mafia Godfather who was in tight with Girafalco? He's been calling the same shots since we took Girafalco out of the picture. Same game—prostitution, drugs and espionage—but," Mueller hesitated, "a different cast of characters. I wasn't privy to any of the behind-the-scenes, Brody-led, investigation that you were involved with in Washington, or even some of the stuff here in Miami that led to Girafalco and at least part of the MD 699 being taken out of the picture. But you were there, you know the…"

"Alard De Smet, the mystery man," McGregor interrupted. "I really don't know anything about him at all, other than that he had some kind of affiliation with Girafalco. And," he continued, "I know zilch about this Belgian Mafia gang stuff. The folks in Washington had the lead on him, and I don't have a clue as to whether any charges were filed in Belgium, or if the feds are simply waiting for him to set foot in this country so they can collar him. I just don't know."

McGregor paused to gingerly sip at his cup of horrendous coffee.

"As far as letting the remnants of the Girafalco organization and Maggie Douglas off the hook…well, I'm not quite sure I'm ready to do that. I'll let it sit inactive for a while. Now, are you saying that De Smet is the one responsible for Gonzales' death? That he ordered the hit? I was thinking more like it was Cubans retaliating for Roberto moving into their territory—at least that's the impression I got from Gonzales' girlfriend."

"Hold on for a minute and listen," Mueller continued. "Alonso, 'the hick', and the other guy you caught trying to break into your hotel room—his name is Lisandro Molinero, by the way—small time thug with a short record of assault and battery kind of stuff—have *both* fingered three guys, by name, in Gonzales' murder and have given us information about where they stayed, and who their main contact was in Miami. None of the three they named showed up in any of our databases, but, on a hunch, I contacted Homeland Security and got copies of their current passport information and mug shots. And even if they don't currently appear on TSA's No-Fly List, I was told that all three appear on their 'Watch List' as members of the Belgian Mafia movement, and that they *are* connected in one way or another to De Smet's organization. That's where, I think, De Smet enters the picture. It's interesting that all three arrived here from Belgium two days before Gonzales' death and left the U.S. right after we started pulling the remains of…"

"Who'd they finger as their Miami contact…the guys from Belgium, I mean…anyone we know?" McGregor interrupted.

"Arturo Camilo, a Mexican immigrant who's made it big in the plastics industry. Both the FBI and the Miami Police have watched this dude for a long time. We suspect he's involved in unlawful activity, but we've never been able to

116

find any tangible evidence. He's a major player in the Mexican community and is often at odds with the Cubans and some of the South American expats. He's on the board of the Service Employees South Florida Union, SESFU, and he's openly targeted companies that have under-the-table policies of only hiring Mexican workers for menial and low-paying jobs. If Mexican workers go on strike anywhere in this region, you can bet he's behind it."

"That's the same guy that Douglas fingered as well. But really, that makes no sense when it comes to Roberto Gonzales' murder. I mean…they're both Mexican!" McGregor scoffed.

"Doesn't seem to, does it? But, if Camilo's taking orders from De Smet and is running a Mafia gang or branch for him here, an ordered hit is just that…nothing to do with race, creed, culture, or sex… just plain business as usual. I think you and I need to take a trip out to Camilo's office and have a chat with him," Mueller said. "Before we go, though, why don't you make contact with your boss in Washington, and see what the deal is with this De Smet character and if they know anything about a Belgian underground operating here in Miami?"

McGregor shook his head as if in denial.

"Hans, I'm retired, remember? I was brought back into action just for the Girafalco game, through a hodgepodge of circumstances. I don't have a 'boss,' as you call him. Let's just say I have friends in high places who, if I make that call, are probably going to put the screws to me to come back to the game, full blown, when all I want to do is find out who killed Gonzales, bring him or them in, and just go home—leaving you, of course, to do the shitwork." He smiled grimly and finished his cup of coffee. *Now stone cold but considerably better tasting,* he noted wordlessly.

"Yeah, right, make the call! Enough BS!" Mueller ordered. "I think we know who killed him, and I also think you *really* want to follow through on this thing. Just see if you can get your 'friend in high places' on the phone while I get the car. I'll pick you up out front! I promised my wife I'd be home for dinner at six!"

Assistant FBI Director Brody was in a meeting when McGregor called, but returned his call just as Mueller and McGregor pulled into the parking lot at the SESFU building where Arturo Camilo's office was located. Directly across the street was a block-long industrial building with railroad tracks running along the street side and the Miami River flowing towards Biscayne Bay on the back side. A large sign, "Camilo Plástico" identified the place as the factory for Camilo Plastics.

"I'm informed that, if you get hungry after you talk to Camilo," Brody said, "there's a great Tex-Mex restaurant about two blocks from where you are right now. You might want to check it out!"

"How the hell did you know about Camilo?" McGregor burst out. "Not to mention that we're on his doorstep as we speak!"

"Peace, brother! I've had two trusted agents from my office—Bob Wilson, who grew up in Miami and knows the territory well, and Dan Conroy, originally from our Kansas City office—on your tail ever since you had your encounter with Police Sergeant Alice Felton. She works undercover for us and cued us in on your arrival! She's a real sweetheart, isn't she? Hope she didn't give you much trouble. She's been known to do that," he laughed. "Anyway, we've had Camilo in our sights for a long time—mainly on suspicion of drug smuggling and, more recently, as a possible underling of Alard DeSmet. When my guys realized where you were heading just now, they called me—just before I called you back—and I faxed them some notes they need to share with you."

"How did I not notice we had a tail? These guys must be really good!" McGregor exclaimed.

"Of course they're good! They're *my* guys! I think you and Detective Mueller will find them interesting, and I suggest you meet up with them *before* you talk to Camilo. He's slicker than snot on a glass doorknob. After you read the stuff they share with you, I'm betting you'll know what to do. Ask Mueller if he'll add my two men to your team. Have fun, play safe, catch a big fish for us…gotta go."

"And? What's up?" Mueller asked as McGregor hung up.

"A slight change of plans, Hans," McGregor said. "There's a Tex-Mex restaurant somewhere close to us. Let's go have coffee and do some planning. Do you know where it is?"

"Just down the street that runs parallel to the railroad track about two blocks. A left turn across the tracks and the restaurant I think you're talking about is right on the river front—the Sabroso Tex-Mex Palace," Mueller said as he pulled out of the parking lot.

"Good," McGregor said. "We need to wait until tomorrow to confront Camilo, and we need to hook up with the two FBI agents who've been on my tail since you and I met at the Miami Central lockup. They're now on your tail. If you spot their car, don't try to lose them; they have some information we need. Let them follow us to the restaurant. By now they've been alerted that we've been told about them. They're not local FBI but hand-picked headquarters guys. Best part about this sudden change of plans? —you'll be home by six o'clock for dinner," he laughed.

As they headed toward the restaurant, McGregor could clearly see the car that had been following them.

"They're good," McGregor thought again. *"They've managed to follow me all over town without me spotting them. Damn good...or perhaps I'm just getting old."*

"Hans, what kind of bags were used to hold Gonzales' body parts?" McGregor casually asked as they drove past Camilo Plastics' main entrance. "Are we talking common Hefty-type trash or leaf bags here, or what?"

"I'll have to check the forensic report to be certain," Mueller answered, "but I'm pretty sure they weren't bags, but rather that type of wrap that you see people paying big bucks for having their luggage wrapped in airports. You know, you've seen them—those spinny-thing machines—Secure Wrap, I think they call them. They use some kind of industrial-strength clear wrap. I'll call forensics in the morning. What are you thinking?"

"I'm thinking iced tea with a lime twist instead of coffee—this humidity is getting' to me!" McGregor said. "I'm also thinking I'd like to know what kind of packaging machines they use at Camilo Plastics. Do you think you could get a search warrant for Camilo's plant? I know it's a stretch, but I'd like to have a crack forensics team go into his plant, armed with Blue Star, Luminol, and Florescence particle finders; find any and all plastic wrap machines, and go over them for latent drug residue, traces of gun powder, and latent blood splatters—the latter being the main reason for the search warrant, but be sure to include drugs and gunpowder as well, when you request a warrant."

"Interesting! I see where you're going," Mueller said as he pulled the car into a spot in front of the Sabroso Tex-Mex Palace. "If I can get the search warrant," he continued while writing down the particulars McGregor requested, "we'll want to go with the forensic folks. I'll set that up now," he said, reaching for his phone. "Perhaps we should do the search *before* we interview Camilo— shake him up a bit?"

McGregor shook his head. "I'm thinkin' both at the same time. We don't want Camilo to be tipped off by the search and maybe skip out on us!"

Agents Bob Wilson and Dan Conroy, the agents who'd been tailing McGregor, pulled up next to Mueller's car, got out and walked over to introduce themselves. They described themselves as seasoned agents, specializing in arms trafficking, money laundering, and drug smuggling going to and from the United States in the so-called "tri-border" area between Argentina, Brazil and Paraguay.

All four men went into the restaurant, found a table, and ordered iced tea before getting down to business. Wilson told McGregor and Mueller that they suspected Camilo was the local "Godfather" for the Alard De Smet organization, which included the Belgian Mafia *and* MD 699.

"De Smet calls the shots, gives the orders, and Camilo, like Girafalco, gets rich—even though he has to subordinate himself entirely to De Smet, who gets a *huge* cut of all proceeds," explained Wilson. "For some unknown reason, members of De Smet's various Belgian affiliated gangs demonstrate fierce loyalty toward their local Godfathers— which, in the end, causes us *incredible* difficulties in penetrating them, much less recruiting informants."

"Looks like we have a job to do," Mueller said. "Can I assume that you two will be joining us? Good," he continued, acknowledging their nods of agreement. "I think our best approach is to base all of our immediate actions on one main goal—to find out who killed Roberto Gonzales. Using *that* goal as the *legal* platform for all our moves, we may also be able to bring down Camilo's part of the organization in the process. And…surprise, surprise, we have a search warrant, gentlemen," Mueller announced as he checked his text messages. "We also have a forensics team lined up and ready to go. My department is at its best today!" he bragged.

"Let's hit Camilo's office and his plant simultaneously tomorrow," he continued. "That will give me some time to make sure all my people are on the same page. Let's call it a day and meet at my office at eight o'clock tomorrow morning."

"I didn't have much breakfast today, Hans, and the restaurant at the Hard Rock doesn't appeal to me right now, so I'm going to stay and have lunch here," McGregor said. "Some of the entrees on the Sabroso Palace's menu intrigue my usually cast-iron stomach. I'll take a taxi back to Miami Central and pick up my car, and I'll see you in the morning. Tomorrow's going to be an interesting day," he said, as he attracted the attention of a waitress.

"Gracias, Anita," McGregor said, reading her name tag as she handed him a menu. "I'll be staying for lunch. What would you recommend?"

She smiled at him in a friendly manner. "Oh, *Señor*, that will be my pleasure. You'll love our *Pollo Encacahuatado*—that's chicken in peanut sauce, with *camote*—that's sweet potatoes," she explained. "*Bolillos*—our famous Mexican rolls, and for dessert you must have our Creamy Flan—and that's custard in a caramel sauce. Sound okay? What would you like to drink?"

"Sounds wonderful," McGregor remarked. "And thank you for translating for me. A refill on my iced tea would be great, and a shot of tequila is definitely called for."

Anita quickly brought his drinks, and, with a smile, went back to the kitchen to turn in his order.

"Here's to you, Roberto, my dear friend and colleague," McGregor whispered as he lifted the glass of tequila, first in a salute, and then in a one gulp swallow.

Only for you, Roberto, only for you would I ever drink this horrible stuff that tastes like burning piss. Payback, my friend, is just around the corner!

"Thank you, Anita," McGregor said as she served his lunch. "I see that the screen door at the back of this room leads to a deck and what looks to be a docking area. Do you get many people coming by boat to your restaurant?"

"Oh, my, yes, *Señor*. Our dock is full almost every night and all day on the weekends. We also get our seafood deliveries there, and we have a good take-out business up and down the river. We have our own delivery boat, and there are lots and lots of businesses and factories that call us."

"That's really cool," McGregor remarked. "By the way, this food looks and smells wonderful. Tell me", he laughed, "are you the captain of the delivery boat?"

"Oh no, *Señor*, I tried to pilot a boat once, my brother's, but I kept crashing it into every dock I struggled to moor at. Marcos Martinon-Torres is our delivery man. He's been working here since this place opened almost thirty years ago. When he's not delivering, he tends to the dock and patio area, trims bushes and so forth. He's a good man!"

"I love boats and being on the water," McGregor fibbed. "Is he here today? Could I perhaps visit with him after I finish eating?"

"Marcos is always here, when he's not on a delivery. Remind me when you're finished, and I'll find him for you. He loves to talk about *his* river."

As promised, after lunch, Anita took McGregor to the dock to meet Marcos.

"Be forewarned, *Señor*," she whispered. "Nothing pleases an old salt like Marcos more than a story with the boys on the dock. If you're not careful, he'll talk your head right off!"

Anita led McGregor to a boat moored next to a short ladder from the patio loading area to a small dock below. Torres was busy loading what looked to be pizza boxes into a warming apparatus attached to the deck of the boat.

"Marcos! This gentleman would like to visit with you about the river. Can I send him down?"

"You bet, pretty Anita, rose of my heart, lily of my soul! Watch your step, mister, that ladder will grab you and throw you into the river if you're not careful!"

"Whaddya loadin' there, Mr. Torres?" McGregor yelled down at him.

"Mexicana Pizza!" Torres yelled back. "Party going on up the river a bit, ordered eleven of these things. They're popular, but I don't eat 'em—they give me big time hiccups! Again, watch your step! Bonita, my baby, will get you if you fall in!"

"And 'Bonita' is?" McGregor inquired.

"Look down the river toward Biscayne Bay," Torres said, pointing. "See that flock of sea gulls fishing? That's saltwater! Now look up the river! No sea gulls. Where you're standing is about where the fresh water from the Everglades starts to turn brackish. Alligators don't take to saltwater much, but Bonita, my 'pet' 'gator and her babies, nest here, under the dock, year-round," he explained while making a clicking sound with his mouth. She's our resident garbage disposal unit," he laughed, "always turned on and ready to go!"

It only took a few additional 'clicks' from Torres before Bonita soundlessly glided into view from under the dock. Torres greeted her with a chunk of bread and resumed loading pizzas aboard his boat.

"Permission to come aboard, Captain?" McGregor asked, glancing warily at Bonita.

"Come on," Torres answered.

"Never heard of 'Mexicana' pizza before—what's that all about?" McGregor asked as he carefully stepped over the rail and onto the heavily varnished deck of Torres' boat, while Bonita watched his every move.

121

"Just the usual cheese pizza," Torres said, "except the toppings are chorizo, jalapeño pepper slices, grilled onions, tomato, chile, hominy, shrimp, avocado, and sometimes beef, bell peppers, *tripas* or scallops. All the ingredients for sure-fire stomach aches. And, like I said, they give me hiccups—I don't eat 'em," he repeated. "They'll give you a sample up at the restaurant if you ask! I gotta deliver these now, upriver a bit. You can ride along if you want," he said as he started his engine.

"I'd love to," McGregor shouted over the roar of the engine. "I'm Cameron, by the way... call me Cam," he said as the boat pulled slowly away from the dock and headed upriver. Bonita slipped like a ghost back under the dock

"This won't take long," Torres said. "We're just going up two miles or so to a dock by a public park. Not much to see up this way—mostly terminals and other businesses that use cargo shipping. They were moved farther upstream, away from Miami, about twelve years ago because of crooked shipping activities. Going down the river from this point you'd see nothing but renovation and offices, hotels, and condos as we get closer to the bay."

"What's that building over there?" McGregor asked as they passed Camilo Plástico

"Just what the sign says," Torres responded. "They make plastic things, I guess. Ship mostly out the front by railroad or trucks. Not much else on that dock during the day, but lots of small boats real early in the morning and late at night. The watermen are not local, so I really don't know any of them, and don't want to. They're not friendly at all. Nobody there ever orders carry-out, so I don't know what's inside the place. Don't think I want to—I hear rumors."

"What kind of rumors?" McGregor asked, immediately alert.

"Well, some of the local watermen think it's a smuggled goods gathering point—you know, illegal drugs, illegal aliens, guns, that kind of stuff. I mind my own business. By the way," Torres quickly changed the subject. "Did you know that the earliest known inhabitants of the area around the river were the Tequestas? I don't know anything about them, but they built mounds along the river further up and they're still there—the mounds I mean. Pullin' in here to deliver—sit tight for a minute."

On the way back to the restaurant's dock, Torres continued to bombard McGregor with all the facts he'd ever need if he wanted to launch an exploratory mission to rediscover or revive the Miami River.

"What's with the wrecked boat over there on the shoreline?" McGregor asked, interrupting Torres' chatter for a moment. "One of your friends have a little too much tequila and run ashore?" he laughed.

"Well, it's not like that *never* happened before," Torres acknowledged, "but not that one. That boat belonged to my brother Ferdinand, and one night, about four, maybe six weeks ago, it got swiped from his dock and whoever did it hit a submerged log or something and left it listing and rotting there. It's got a hole in the hull and a broken drive shaft. Ferdinand's got insurance, so he got a new boat. That one now belongs to his insurance company and, hell, it's probably gonna be sittin' there until the next big storm hits and sinks it. I strung a line from the boat to the mile marker post to keep it from floating out into the main channel. I looked the boat over to see if there was anything worth salvaging, but there wasn't. I wonder if anybody but me noticed the mess on the deck. Ferdinand, despite his other shortcomings, always kept a clean rig!"

"What kind of a mess?" McGregor quickly asked.

"Well, to be honest," Torres said with a grimace. "It looks like whoever took it slaughtered a sheep or goat on the deck—it's a disaster! I know Ferdinand didn't leave it like that— he took real good care of that boat. Maybe some kind of a religious cult took it—I've heard about stuff like that—hell, I dunno! Whoever ditched it, tried to set it on fire, didn't burn much I guess."

"Did your brother file a police report? You know, stolen boat and all that?" McGregor queried.

"My brother and the Miami police don't get along too well, but that's another story," Torres said as he maneuvered his boat up to the restaurant's dock. "He might have called the Coast Guard, but they don't come this far up the river very often. I'm guessin' he just called his insurance company, and they came out and looked at it and wrote him a check. I really don't know—didn't ask him."

As Torres dropped him off, McGregor thanked him and, in parting, lightheartedly recited a line from "The Waterman's Song."

"Oh, waterman, waterman, how good is your boat?" he quoted.

To his surprise, Torres immediately responded with the next line in the poem, "My boat is as good as my own two hands," he recited.

"You're a good waterman, Mr. Torres. A good waterman!" McGregor smiled. "Better you than treasure should come home," McGregor hollered over his shoulder as he headed into the restaurant to call for a cab. He could still hear Torres laughing as he walked inside.

While waiting for the cab, McGregor called Agent Wilson and asked him to contact his Miami office and have the abandoned boat, lying wrecked and tethered at mile marker 3 on the Miami River, picked up immediately and placed on a barge for evidence preservation, and taken in for processing.

"Have them consider it an active crime scene," he said, "and note the possible human blood and any traces of remains on the deck. I want a complete comb job," he requested.

As his cab pulled up to the curb, McGregor could still hear Torres boisterously reciting parts of "The Waterman's Song." *A good man,* McGregor concluded.

123

CHAPTER FIFTEEN

Mueller walked into the Miami Central Station conference room at eight o'clock sharp the next morning. McGregor, Wilson and Conroy were already there, sipping lethal-looking cups of coffee and pecking at yesterday's leftover donuts.

"Good morning, Cam, Bob, Dan. Hey, Cam! Did you play any poker last night? I hear the Hard Rock just opened a new first-class poker room. Oh, and how was lunch at the Palace?"

"Lunch was fantastic! Afterwards, as Bob and Dan are aware, I took a short boat ride up the Miami River on the restaurant's delivery boat, and then later I hit a couple of high dollar slot machines at the Rock, and turned in early," McGregor answered.

"How about you guys?" Mueller asked Wilson and Conroy. "Hell, you had the afternoon and night off from tailing McGregor all over the place—did you find some Miami night life?"

"You might say that," Wilson scoffed. "We spent a good part of the night cruising on the river ourselves, courtesy of McGregor and the Miami Harbor Patrol. Beautiful city you've got here, Hans! We were following up on a…"

"All right, guys, hold up a minute on the story-telling," Mueller interrupted. "Sounds like fun, but I've gotta get serious for a moment."

"I got word," he began, "when I got to the office this morning that both Francesco Perez-Alonso, the 'hick', and Lisandro Molinero, the one McGregor calls 'half-tooth', died this morning at Miami lock-up. It looks like they were both poisoned this morning at breakfast. Guards believe someone slipped something into their food. I've ordered an autopsy on both perps, and we're conducting an evidence-gathering lock-down. Bottom line—we've lost two key witnesses. Anybody got any good news? Please?" he said as he sank into a chair at the table.

"Son of a bitch," McGregor growled. "Even though they weren't the strongest of witnesses, they were the only connection we had linking Camilo to Gonzales."

Mueller sighed. "We're looking for whoever served up the poison for breakfast this morning. Slim chance of finding anyone though," he said, his voice trailing off.

"That makes three witnesses that have died by poison since I started dealing with MD 699." McGregor observed angrily. "I'm beginning to think that's their method—MD 699, that is—of silencing people who might turn on them."

"Hey! We're far from finished," Conroy quickly broke in, sensing the momentary doomsday attitude. "Thanks to McGregor's after-lunch foray up the river yesterday, we may have another lead. He'll have to fill us in on the complete details of his mile marker three discovery, but, well, we think he may have located the boat that transported and scattered Gonzales' body parts in Biscayne Bay. We'll know for sure when our lab finishes DNA testing, promised by noon today."

"So that's what you guys were talking about a moment ago! Let's have it!" Mueller exclaimed.

"Along with the obvious blood from the boat's deck and bulkheads," Conroy continued, "our investigators found shreds of imported shrink wrap, also with trace blood splatters, caught on a cleat inside the boat. They also found some wound around the boats' propeller and shaft. We've already processed the shrink wrap—pretty easy to do since it's embossed every twelve running inches with the manufacturer's logo, 'CGPM.' That designates it as a shrink wrap made exclusively by, and for 'Chang Guang Packing Machinery Co.' machines—and that, my friends is one of the things we're looking for at Camilo Plastics—A CG packing machine. I've got our Miami office checking to see what other companies in the area might also be using Chang Guang machines."

"Good work!" both Mueller and McGregor exclaimed at the same time.

"Were you able to determine the owner of the boat for sure?" McGregor asked.

"Ferdinand Martinon-Torres *is* your source's brother, just as he said," Wilson confirmed. "We ran his name—been arrested a number of times for public intoxication, held one time for *suspicion* of smuggling illegal immigrants into the U.S., and has been fined three times for 'maintaining a public nuisance'—using his boat as a floating whore-house." He laughed, and then complained, "Man, I gotta tell ya the mosquitos were *unbelievable* on that river last night. I can only hope that this Torres character provides mosquito lotion for his clients! I've got bites in places on my body I didn't even know existed!"

"Sounds like you three had a busy, and, I should add, fruitful afternoon and evening," Mueller smiled. "Our search warrant is here and signed by a judge," he advised, "and there's some hydro-cortisone in the top drawer of my desk, Agent Wilson. I've scheduled some marked cars from the Miami Police to meet us at the main entrance of Camilo Plastics at exactly ten o'clock. Check your weapons, gentlemen, and let's roll!"

Man, this is one extraordinary team I'm working with. Brody sure knows how to pick the rising stars of law enforcement for his office, and Mueller...well...I like his style, McGregor thought as he and his fellow lawmen headed toward their individual cars. *I can hardly believe that Wilson and Conroy worked all night on this case and are still up and at 'em this morning. Oh, to be young again!* he lamented inwardly.

125

The Camilo Plastics plant was running at full throttle when they were besieged by marked and unmarked police cars at ten o'clock that morning. Mueller, using a plant guard's radio that he'd confiscated, summoned the plant's manager to the main gate, handed him the search warrant, and asked him to accompany them as they entered the plant.

McGregor estimated the plant to be about 45,000 square feet, and he could see what looked to be huge indoor silo-type structures at the far end of the facility.

"Hans," McGregor called, catching Mueller's attention. "While you guys check out the plant, I'm going over to see if I can catch Camilo in his office."

"Be nice, McGregor, be nice!" Mueller replied.

The building across the street, where Arturo Camilo's office was located, was a two-story, Art-Deco building, typical of this part of Florida. The Union offices were located on the first floor, and an exposed steel staircase led upstairs. On the second-floor landing, McGregor opened a door marked "Camilo Plásticos," and entered an elegantly decorated reception area where he was greeted by a secretary. Sitting at a table in the corner of the room were three men playing dominos, all wearing tailored suits over their open-collar tropical shirts. One man was just hanging up a phone when McGregor entered.

"Hello…uh, Betty," he said, noticing the name plate on her desk. "My name is Cameron McGregor; I'd like to visit with Arturo Camilo."

"He's just been called to go across the street to the plant. Do you have an appointment? He may want you to wait."

"Has he left his office yet?"

"No, he's on the phone with…"

"Is that the door to his office behind you?" McGregor asked.

"If you'll have a seat, I'll tell him you're here, just as soon as he gets off the…"

"That won't be necessary," McGregor said, flashing his badge as he walked around her desk.

"Don't get up, gentlemen," he said firmly to the three men as he pulled his gun from his holster. "This is law enforcement business! Feel free to finish your domino game, though, and…listen, guys…try to allow yourself more than one option each time you place your tile," he said with feigned expertise as he reached for the door knob to what he guessed was Camilo's office. It was.

Camilo hung up his phone, stood up, and walked around his highly ornate desk to greet McGregor as calmly as if he'd been expecting him.

"Cameron McGregor, I've heard so much about you! It's a pleasure to meet you. Please come and sit with me so you can tell me what's going on across the street in my plant. I just got off the phone with my attorney, and he said you fellas have a search warrant. Perhaps I can help you find whatever it is you're 'searching' for?"

"Probably not," McGregor said dismissively. "But you can tell me what those silos are inside your facility. That'll give you a little more time to come up with a good reason why I shouldn't put a bullet in your forehead on behalf of Roberto Gonzales."

Camilo didn't bat an eye. Instead he launched into an explanation of what McGregor had called silos.

"Those, Cameron... may I call you Cameron?... are fifty-foot-tall resin flow towers—I call them silos, as well—that I personally designed and built to meet the diverse needs of my customers. I set up my manufacturing facility with a *superb* flow process in mind. My resin is shipped to me via railcar from resin-producing countries in South America. Each railcar can hold up to ten tons of resin. Buying in bulk costs me less and saves the customer money. Resin is conveyed pneumatically from the railcar into one of my 200,000-pound capacity resin silos. From the silos, it's conveyed to blenders at each extrusion line. Am I boring you yet?"

McGregor just stared at him coldly. Camilo's braggadocio was clearly salesman-polished claptrap, he noted.

"By blending different resins," Camilo continued, "I can achieve different physical properties or results, depending on what my customers' requirements are. The manufacturing flow process continues through my plant to either my shipping docks or warehouse storage. For your information," he hesitated, "I speak often at schools in Miami and Dade County. The presentation I just gave you was designed for third graders. *You* probably have questions," he said in the same snide tone that McGregor had used earlier.

"Listen, let's get down to why I'm here," McGregor snapped. "I..."

"Let me get this phone call first; it's my plant manager," Camilo said coolly.

After a moment of listening to his plant manager's panicked voice, Camilo said firmly, "All right, settle down, no big deal, we'll get it all worked out. Close the plant, send my workers home—tell them they'll get paid for the day. Call my suppliers and stop all deliveries in and out. Then just sit tight until I call you back!"

Camilo was no longer calm and collected.

"You've closed off all of my packaging area, McGregor! I must shut down my entire plant. You know what this is going to cost me? It'll take days, maybe weeks, for us to catch up on our orders. Hell, I'm gonna have to..."

"I couldn't care less about that, Camilo! Right now, you and I are simply going to have a chat. I'm going to place a deal on the table that's going to be well worth your while. Unless, of course, you're thinkin' about lawyering up, in which case, as you know, any deal is off. So, I suggest you hear me out, cut your losses here and now, and get on with your life, one way or another. Right now, I hold all the cards. Deal or no deal? Your call!"

127

"Look, I didn't have anything to do with Gonzales' death, if that's what you're thinking. He and I were just getting…"

"Stop whining! I'll do the talking, you listen. That way, there will be less bullshit for your low-paid amigos to clean up." McGregor could see him starting to crack.

"I pay my people very well, you…"

"Name-calling is beneath your dignity, Mr. Camilo," McGregor interrupted. "After all, *you* consider yourself a leader in the Mexican community—but I doubt if the community *really* does! And the *infamous* Alard De Smet has given you the grand title of area 'Godfather' for your chicken-shit Belgian Mafia gang. Hell, in case you haven't realized it, you're nothing but a Mexican migrant worker to him."

"I need to get over to my plant. It's gonna be a mess," Camilo insisted. He was starting to sweat heavily, and continually mopped his forehead with a large flowery handkerchief. "Please just tell me what you want!"

"First," McGregor began. "I'll tell you what I think: I think you were afraid Roberto Gonzales was starting to get too much attention in the Mexican community and was going to cut into what *you* think are your interests in the community. Second, I think you mentioned your concerns to De Smet. I think De Smet had had enough of the inconvenience Gonzales and I had caused for him in the Girafalco situation, and your complaint was the last straw. He ordered a hit on me and Gonzales. I survived the attempt; Roberto didn't. Third, I think we're going to find Gonzales' DNA on one or more of your CG packing machines and plenty of CGPM supplies in your stockroom. That's what we're looking for across the street right now. Finally, we know the names of Roberto's murderers, and we know that you arranged accommodations for them while they were here. So, when you say you didn't kill him—well, maybe you didn't do it personally, but you're certainly connected to his murder, if only indirectly. If you give us De Smet, you can probably keep your plant in operation, even while you're in prison for a lesser charge than murder. Keep quiet and you lose everything you've got, plus you'll spend the rest of your life in prison, because we'll consider that you killed Gonzales all on your own initiative."

Camilo feigned shock at McGregor's words. "Are you telling me that Roberto Gonzales was killed in my plant?"

"Do you know a Ferdinand Martinon-Torres?" McGregor asked.

"Never heard of him! Did *he* say that Gonzales was killed in my plant?"

"No, but if my hunch is right," McGregor said, "his boat will!"

"Let's get my plant manager over here right now. I wanna talk to him about this whole thing," demanded Camilo. "I smell a rat!" His bravado seemed to be making a reappearance—his sniveling of a few moments before was now changing to righteous indignation.

128

"We're probably talking to your plant manager right now; no need for you to assist us. But, Camilo, if you're going to try to make a patsy out of him, forget it." McGregor warned.

"Patsy? No, I don't think I have to. I think you're absolutely right about your theory on who ordered the hit on Gonzales, but, McGregor, you've got the *wrong* middleman, and I'm not saying another thing to you without my lawyer! So, unless you're going to charge me with some cockamamie, trumped-up crap, get the hell out of my office!"

"Thank you for the chit-chat, Mr. Camilo, and the deal's now *off* the table," McGregor said flatly. "Keep your head down and hope we don't find something illegal or suspicious across the street!"

The area in front of Camilo Plastics was crowded with police cars, vans, and mobile labs, as McGregor worked his way across the street and into the plant. It took him some looking around, but he finally spotted Mueller fully engaged in a heated exchange with someone he thought might be the plant manager. By the time he worked his way around and through a maze of machinery, the person Mueller had been talking to was in handcuffs and being led away by a uniformed officer.

"How we doin' over here?" McGregor asked as he approached a noticeably red-faced and angry Mueller. "Is that the plant manager who's still managing to give you the finger despite his hands being handcuffed behind his back? I like that kind of spunk in a guy, don't you?" he laughed while blocking Mueller's path.

"I'll break off his finger and stuff it down his fuckin' throat," Mueller said, trying to sidestep McGregor.

"Settle down, super-cop, your day will come—just not right now. Come on, bring me up to date," McGregor said.

"I've got to get an engineer in here to explain a whole lot of stuff that doesn't make sense to me," Mueller complained. "I mean, I can readily see what they manufacture. Mostly gadgets, fittings, bottles and containers, and a variety of what looks to be party supplies. I need an auditor to look over orders, invoices, *et cetera,* but what I really need is somebody to explain to me what the hell an extrusion line is all about. Everything made here is supposedly formed by forcing semisoft resin through a specially shaped mold or nozzle. The resin comes from those big silos over there at the far end of the building. For all I know those silos could be holding moonshine or drugs or who knows what?" He paced angrily back and forth as he paused in his tirade. "Right now, I'm pretty frustrated," he continued. "So far, things around here just don't add up and that fuckin' plant manager wasn't in an explaining mood. I know that the only reason we're here is to check out the packaging machines, and we're doing that now. But I really wanted to hit pay dirt. Yeah, I want to solve the Gonzales murder...but, damn it, I know that Camilo isn't making the kind of money he flaunts around Miami with the stuff he's producing here. There's got to be something else! Camilo has to have something that's making money in order to keep Alard De Smet interested in him, just like Girafalco did with his little enterprise. There's something else going on here. McGregor, I can smell it!"

"I can too," McGregor said, "but I think it's the resin in those silos. Somebody's turned off the industrial exhaust fans, and this place is getting toxic. I'm going to see if I can find the main electrical control panel and get some fresh air in here. I'm betting it's somewhere near the plant manager's office. Where's that at?"

"At the end of that hallway, underneath the stairway to the catwalk above us," Mueller nodded to indicate the direction. "I'll be over with my people investigating the packaging area. Holler if you need me! God, I'd love to wring that plant manager's neck!"

Working his way through the maze of equipment on the factory floor, McGregor spotted one of the plant's security guards sitting on a stack of empty pallets, looking distressed.

"Excuse me, sir," McGregor said as he approached the man. "Can you help me get the exhaust fans turned on? Got any idea where the switch is?"

"Yeah, follow me." the guard said. He turned a worried face toward McGregor.

"Am I gonna lose my job, mister? I've got a family, and this is a *good* job. I don't understand what you all are doin'—shuttin' down the plant like this. What's goin' on?"

"What's your name, my friend?" McGregor asked as the man led him down a hall to a room marked "Electrical Control Room."

"I'm Martin Pena," he answered over his shoulder as he stuck a key in the locked door, opened it and turned on the lights. "I've worked here for almost eight years now—started pushin' a broom, moved to assembly line, worked for a while with the plant engineer, and been in plant security for about a year and a half. I don't know who turned off the fans. They're supposed to be on all the time," he said, pushing a bank of buttons and listening for the sounds of the exhaust system kicking in. "Okay, they're on, mister! I better get back to the main entrance. I dunno what I'm supposed to put in the log about today— never had anything like this before."

"Martin, I'm Cameron McGregor. Call me Cam and, yes, I'm a cop. We're investigating a murder that someone in this plant may know something about, and I'm betting you don't have a clue as to what we're looking for. So, relax and tell me how you knew exactly where the exhaust system breakers were located—I mean, this room is full of breakers, switches, flashing lights and I guess those are timers of some kind? What's through that door over there?"

"That's a whole 'nuther control room," Pena said with authority. "Once a week, always Thursday, a crew comes in to do something with the number three resin flow tower. They come in at seven o'clock in the evening and are finished and gone by the time the plant opens in the morning. None of us on the day shift knows what that's all about, or even who the workers are. They come, they do their thing, and then they leave. Come back out in the hallway, and I'll show you where they work. Actually, I can only show you the door—none of us has a key. I don't have a key to their electrical control room either. But in answer to your question about how I knew where the breakers for the exhaust system were? Like I told you, I spent some time working with the plant engineer. When's the plant gonna reopen, you think?"

"Give us a few days, Martin," McGregor hedged. "Nobody that you know of has a key to either this room or the separate control room?"

"Maybe Mr. Camilo or one of his men? I dunno!"

"Thanks, Martin. Go do your report now and thanks for your time— you're a good man!" McGregor said as he walked Martin back to the main floor of the factory. Mueller, Wilson and Conroy were gathered by the front door comparing notes as McGregor approached them.

"Looks like our work here is done," Mueller was saying. "The lab folks are hard at work and nothing seems to be here except what, I guess, is *supposed* to be here. They do use CG packing machines however! We're going to keep this plant closed through tomorrow, at least. I've got an engineer, who's supposed to be an expert in whatever they do here, flying down from Kentucky tonight, and I'm gonna bring him here tomorrow to give this place a good look-see."

"All right," McGregor interrupted, "but we have one more bit of work to do before we call it a day. Which one of you can pick a lock?"

"Show me the lock," Conroy said. "Today may be your lucky day!"

"What did I miss?" Mueller quickly asked.

"Two rooms," McGregor responded. "One inside the electrical control room and one further down the hall from the manager's office. Both locked, and the keys are with a group of people that seem to appear only on Thursday nights after the plant's closed for the day. Remember that 'paydirt' you wanted to find?" he asked, looking at Mueller.

"Let's take a look at that lock," Mueller demanded as he hastily walked toward the hallway.

After about fifteen minutes of what resembled a scene involving the Three Stooges plus one, it was mutually decided that no one on the team was really a locksmith, and that the dangers involved in trying to shoot the lock out were, well, just that—too dangerous.

"We're going to have to post a guard at that door tonight," Mueller said as they walked up the hall to the factory floor.

"Perhaps not," McGregor said astutely as he headed toward a forklift parked near one of the riverside loading docks. Before anyone could say anything, McGregor had climbed into the seat of the machine, turned the key and was heading down the hall, occasionally scraping one or both sides of the passageway until he reached the locked door. He stopped briefly to raise the forks

131

just high enough to be even with the locking mechanism on the door. With a quick release of the forklift's clutch, the machine lurched forward, plowing through the door with ease and smashing into some kind of shelving just inside the door. Realizing, after the dust cleared, that no one could get past the forklift to get into the room, he crammed the machine in reverse, and gingerly backed it down the hall, again taking bits of wallboard with him, to its original parking place.

"Now, where were we?" he said with a satisfied grin as he hopped down from the forklift's seat and brushed plasterboard dust off his clothes. "I didn't like the color of those walls anyway—far too Miami pastel for my taste! Gentlemen, please, be my guests," he invited, pointing down the hallway to a brutally smashed door and what was left of the frame.

Mueller was already in the room by the time others made it down the hall. He'd found the light switch and discovered even more equipment that he couldn't relate to, as well as rows of shelves with bricks of cocaine worth an eye-ball estimate of at least a $30,000 each, stacked in batches of twenty.

"Worth over a half a million dollars on the street," he estimated. "Gentlemen, we've hit paydirt big time!" he continued. "I'm calling in the DEA folks right now, and McGregor, you and I are going to pay that bastard Camilo a visit. Bob and Dan, you get to look after this stuff until the DEA shows up. Be careful, though, you're sitting on somebody's very valuable cache."

After checking on the progress the technicians were making on their examination of the packaging machines and the areas around them, Mueller and McGregor headed across the street to Camilo's office. On the way, Mueller called for a backup. He needed to apprehend and arrest Camilo, but at the same time he needed to secure Camilo's office and files for other investigators he was going to call in to assist.

"This is a major operation we're about to shut down, and repercussions will reach all the way to South America, I'm guessing, and Belgium, for sure," Mueller said as they climbed the stairs to Camilo's office.

"Today, we'll arrest him for the drug smuggling and distribution. Within the next few days, I'm hoping, as I know you are, that we're going to able to charge him with murder. You take the lead, McGregor."

It was a few minutes before one o'clock, as McGregor and Mueller opened Camilo's office door. Missing were the domino players at the table, but his secretary was still at her desk.

"Hello, Betty, I'm back," McGregor announced. "And just like before, I've come to visit with your boss."

"I'm sorry, Mr..... oh, sorry, I can't remember your name. Anyway, he left about an hour ago. I'm closing the office now; you'll have to see him tomorrow."

"That's all right, Betty, you can leave now," McGregor said. "Perhaps you should hurry," he advised, "because this place is going to be flooded with cops any minute now. Please leave the file cabinets unlocked as well as your desk. Leave your computer on and signed in."

"Oh. I don't think I can do that," she protested.

"Well, then, I'll have no choice but to arrest you and handcuff you to your desk until uniformed police arrive and escort you to jail. You really don't want that, do you?"

"I'm leaving now," she said, hurrying out the door. "My computers logged in and my keys are in the top drawer of my desk."

"I'm sure you'll want to talk to her later," McGregor said as he turned to Mueller. "In the meantime, I doubt if she's the kind to play 'run and hide.' Shit! I should have figured that Camilo would skip as soon as I left him earlier! Do you know where he lives? I'm thinkin' maybe we should go see if he's home, don't you?"

"Oh, indeed, we should! — and you'll love his house—or should I say, *palace*," Mueller said as he and McGregor hurried out to Mueller's car.

"When I was a beat cop," Mueller said, "Camilo was building his house in the zone my partner and I were assigned to patrol. We stopped one day, before they fenced it in, and looked around the joint. His house sits on about four acres of Star Island, with a formidable gated entry and numerous security goons. We estimated about 28,000 square feet of living space looking out on Biscayne Bay. I don't know how many bedrooms it was destined to have, but we were able to identify an extravagant grand ballroom, a living room, library, dining room, and gourmet kitchen with a family room."

"Do you think…?" McGregor interrupted.

"Hold on, I'm not finished yet!" Mueller said as he started across the gated bridge connecting mainland Miami to Star Island. "Hell, the place has a screening room, a game room and fitness center with what appeared to us to be a Roman-inspired indoor pool, spa, and wet and dry saunas. We counted eleven fireplaces. It even has what they call a 'grand motor court' for at least forty cars. But the most important thing for us, at this moment, is simply that I know the location of a well-hidden entrance to a service driveway, which is probably not as well guarded as the main entrance."

"It'll be interesting," McGregor commented, as he watched Mueller flash his badge toward the bridge-gate guard, "to watch the fight between various local, state, and federal agencies over the seizure of Camilo's property and its contents if it turns out this place was bought with drug money."

As they approached the house McGregor turned to Mueller and asked with a purposely questioning tone.

"Have you thought about going into real estate sales when you retire?" he joked. "I mean, you literally just sold me this house!"

"One guard," Mueller announced as they drove slowly down the back-estate service road on the Camilo property. "You can't afford the outhouse," he countered pointblank. "He sees us— he's on the phone. Head down, I'm going to crash the gate! I want Camilo to have as little advance notice of our arrival as possible."

He turned on the concealed police lights on his unmarked car while pushing its accelerator pedal to the floor.

"If he shoots at us, he's yours, McGregor! He's seen my lights—he's fair game," Mueller shouted above the roar of the car's engine and the sound of metal on metal when the car hit the gate, imbedding it solidly in the car's grill and carrying it all the way to a pea gravel roundabout directly in front of Camilo's highly ornate front door.

"That was fun," McGregor said sarcastically as he opened his passenger side door and got out, using the car as a shield between himself and the house. "My God, this pea gravel dust is terrible!" he said, coughing.

Before sliding across to exit the car the same way, Mueller handed McGregor the microphone to the car's PA system and then hit the button to mechanically pop the trunk lid open.

As he carefully made his way to the rear of the car to unload some heavier weapons from the trunk, he shouted, "Try talking Camilo out, McGregor. I'll call for backup. If we have to go inside this place to find him, we'll need help."

"Better make it fast," McGregor said in a "take-charge" voice. "We've got people filing out the front door— probably the house staff people. I need you to cover the front. There're gate guards coming up the main entrance road in a golf cart. The guard at the service gate jumped into the bushes as we flew by him, so we need to keep an eye out for him as well."

"Hell, I think that's Wilson and Conroy in the golf cart. Yep, it is!" Mueller announced. "The DEA folks must have arrived earlier than I anticipated. Looks like our guys must have taken out the front security when they got here— we've got help coming!"

"All right folks, please keep your hands where we can see them and walk toward the grassy area in the middle of the roundabout," McGregor said over the squad car's intercom system. **"Arturo Camilo! I want you and anyone else who's with you to come out now with your hands on your head."**

"Señor Camilo no es casa," a frantic women's voice shouted from the group assembling in the middle of the roundabout. *"Por favor, no dañar la casa! Interior de nadie, estamos todos aquí! Prometo! Dejó!"*

"Damn it! What's she hollering?" McGregor shouted, turning to Mueller as Wilson and Conroy took positions on the other side of the house.

"She said that 'he's not there—don't mess up the house,'" Mueller chuckled. "Sit tight here and keep me covered. I'm gonna try to get her and bring her over here where we can talk to her."

"Wait! There's somebody still in the house. Wait for a minute." McGregor warned. "I saw somebody in the second-floor window just above the front portico. Hand me that rifle with the scope."

134

"Come out of the house with your hands on your head—final warning," McGregor hollered on the intercom. "Final warning!"

Seconds later, there was the sound of glass breaking from the same window, and a shot grazed the edge of the passenger side door standing open beside McGregor.

"Now, that pissed me off!" McGregor said angrily as he advanced a shell in the chamber of the rifle Mueller had handed him. Quickly adjusting the rifle's sight on the broken window, he took a deep breath and waited. The recoil from the 30.6 rifle caused the gun's stock to bang hard into McGregor's shoulder as he fired and hit the person in the window. A pistol flew out of the window as the man fell backwards into the room.

"There may be two more," McGregor shouted as he remembered that there were three men playing dominos in Camilo's office that morning. "Damn," he said, glancing at Mueller, "I'd forgotten how punishing a round can be shot from a 30.6 that isn't 'customized' for the shooter. My shoulder's gonna be sore for a week!"

"*Oh mi, haces daño la casa*," McGregor heard the same lady's voice screeching from behind him.

"What's she yelling now?" McGregor frowned.

"She's not happy with you at all," Mueller chuckled. "You're hurting her house! Uh, oh! The shooting gallery's still active," he shouted as a second face appeared in the same window.

Before McGregor could raise his rifle, he heard the loud report of a shotgun being fired. Conroy had taken out the second man, along with both shutters and the window's frame, and was running toward the front door. Wilson signaled that he was going in with him. Within minutes, they came back out the front door with the third man in custody.

Yep, one of the domino players, McGregor noted to himself over the continued screeching and the tribal-like gyrations of the frenzied woman in the driveway.

He must have heard my advice—to allow himself more than one option—and he did. He chose to place his tile on life! Smart man.

"Camilo left here about forty minutes ago, heading for his private plane hangered in Fort Lauderdale," Wilson yelled from the portico, while he and Conroy escorted their prisoner down the steps toward McGregor and Mueller.

"I called my office, and they've sent agents to out to see if they can stop him before he flees. We should hear back from them within the hour! We still need to search the house!"

"Don't hurt *la casa*!" The same lady was still screeching at them. "*Por favor, comencemos a limpiar el desastre que hizo!*

"She wants us to go in the house to clean up the mess *you* made," Mueller translated. "I'll go talk to her and the others. I'm probably going to send the lot of them home, or at least, away from here. I'm going to place some of my people

135

here tonight. We'll go over every nook and cranny in the house with a fine-toothed comb, and then lock the whole place down in the morning. Oh, wait, we've got a message from forensics," he said and paused to read the message.

"Well, they found no human blood or tissue on the plant's wrapping machines or on any of the wrapping supplies—none on the floor around the machines or on any of the loading areas or docks. They did get a match on Gonzales' DNA in the boat however! They're asking if we want them to check any other places?"

McGregor frowned. "No, that's it. Tell 'em to pack up and thank them for their efforts!" he said as he walked toward the edge of one of the mansions' gardens.

So where are we now? he asked himself as he sat down hard on a well-weathered bench beneath the long, relaxed branches of a timeworn willow tree. McGregor had good reason to frown. He'd come to Miami to avenge the murder of his best friend, but it was looking more and more like a not-enough-evidence dead end. *Whatta we have?* he mused.

He started going over in his mind the leads and pieces of evidence they had to work with so far. They had Gonzales' remains and his DNA confirmed on the deck of an abandoned boat owned by Ferdinand Martinon-Torres—a boat which had been allegedly stolen by some alleged guys from Belgium allegedly sent by De Smet. They had hearsay, non-evidence from Maggie Douglas, Angelika Schafer, and Cindy Flores. They had two dead prisoners—Francesco "the hick" Perez-Alonso, and Lisandro "half-tooth" Molinero—poisoned, before they could testify, by someone unknown.

Hell, after all this, I'm still not convinced that Douglas is in the clear on any of this.

He realized that they really had nothing definitive leading to the person or persons who called the hit on Gonzales, or the attempted hit on him, and still had nothing to directly connect Camilo to Gonzales' murder. *Lots of alleged, hearsay, and non-evidence,* he groaned in frustration. He wanted this case closed! He yearned to be back on his mountain, walking the dogs in the crisp autumn air, encouraging Shadow's forward motion to be free, energetic and rhythmic to the rein, discovering that the leaves were nearly gone and bracing himself for the first cold winter wind howling through the woods.

I want to talk to this Ferdinand Martinon-Torres character, and, if they catch up with Arturo Camilo, I want a second crack at him, for sure.

"The FBI got him—Wilson and Conroy's boys got him! Camilo, that is! Are you hearing me?" Mueller leaned over the back of the bench and waved his hand in front of McGregor's face.

"Just clearing my mind," McGregor said. "I heard you. What's next on our agenda, partner? I'm feelin' pretty depressed about…"

"Yep, they cornered him on the runway. Scared the crap out of him. Fell down trying to run to his plane and scraped his knee. Conroy told me his agents

136

said that Camilo cried like a baby! For security, they're gonna jail him in the federal courthouse for at least tonight. Man, what a bust we've made! Whaddya mean, you're feelin' depressed? We just...oh, you mean about Gonzales. Sorry, Cam, I got carried away."

"Listen, Hans! You start the paperwork on Camilo. Wilson and Conroy need to be in on that—you've got both police and FBI business there. You also need to oversee the securing of all of Camilo's property, his bank accounts, his...hell, you know what to do! I need to find this Ferdinand Martinon-Torres guy. There's something fishy about the boat story and, well, I think I'd like to play lone wolf for a couple of days. Okay?"

"I understand. I do! I'll have one of my men take you back to your car. You know where I am if you need me!" Mueller said in a sympathetic tone that McGregor had not heard from him before. "I'll be spending some time with Camilo in the morning," he continued. "As soon I wind up my questions regarding the drug situation and his various connections, I'll push him on the Gonzales situation—see if I can't get him, at least, on 'conspiracy murder.' "

"You do that, Detective Hans Mueller, you do that!" McGregor said as he headed back toward the roundabout, checking his gun's ammunition clip as he walked. "My shoulder's still sore as hell from that piece of crap 30.6 you gave me!" he yelled.

"Think worker's compensation," Mueller retorted. "And you best keep your distance from Camilo's head housekeeper, or you'll be hurting even more."

CHAPTER SIXTEEN

McGregor's stomach was telling him that it was almost dinner time as he picked up his car at the police station and headed back toward the Miami River area where the Sabroso Tex-Mex Palace was located. It'd been a long day, but cops' days often spill over into the night. His agenda—a good dinner, and perhaps Ferdinand Martinon-Torres could be persuaded to join him for dessert.

"*Hola, Señorita* Anita! "McGregor called out as he walked in the front door of the Palace. "It's a beautiful evening; may I sit on the back patio for dinner?"

"Certainly, *Señor* McGregor, nice to see you back so soon, Marcos will be happy to see you. You left him yesterday with, how shall I say, a song in his heart! I just wish he had a better singing voice," she giggled as she handed him a menu. "Find a table anywhere you want out there—Maria will be your server."

Marcos' boat was gone—he was out on a delivery, McGregor supposed as he found a table and sat down. Questioning him about his brother Ferdinand would have to wait. Maria appeared within minutes and took his drink order.

"How 'bout a margarita, Maria, and the special looks great for dinner!" he said.

"It *is* very good, *Señor,*" Maria agreed as she left to place his order and get his drink. "I'm sure you will enjoy it!"

McGregor was on his second margarita, when he noticed Marcos' boat chugging up to the dock.

"Drinking on an empty stomach will kill you, my friend" Marcos called out as he docked his boat. "Good to see you back. Here to help me with my deliveries tonight?" he asked jokingly.

"Sounds like fun, but really I'd like to talk to your brother Ferdinand about a deal I might have for him! Can you whistle him up for me?"

"Let me deposit this money in the cash register, and I'll call him and see if he can come up the river and meet you. He's a good man, just a little wild at times—just warning you!" Marcos whispered. "He's good to Anita though! She doesn't know about a lot of the stuff he does."

"What's that mean—he's good to Anita?" McGregor queried.

"She's his wife—my sister-in-law," Marcos said softly as he headed inside to the cash register.

It was almost twenty minutes later, and McGregor had finished eating, before Marcos reappeared on the patio.

"He's on his boat with a customer and doesn't expect to be back until very late," he said. "But I told him it was important. He said he'd meet you here at nine o'clock tomorrow morning. I said okay. Is it okay? I can call him back if..."

"No, that's fine." McGregor said. "That'll work. I'll come back in the morning."

"I don't come to work until eleven, but breakfast here is good! Hope you'll like my brother. He's just..."

"Don't worry about it," McGregor said as he picked up his dinner check and headed toward the cash register. "Thanks for calling him and making arrangements for me to meet him. Have a great evening, waterman!"

As he was getting in his car to leave, his phone announced that he had a text message. It was from Mueller and read:

> **"Just to bring you up-to-date. Found interesting papers
> and files at the house. Got an engineer coming in the morning
> to check out the plant. Camilo implicated his plant
> foreman and assistant foreman in the Gonzales murder.
> I have them both under arrest and am taking them to the
> plant to meet with the engineer to see if I can convince
> them to assist themselves by coming clean.... more later.**

McGregor replied back:

> **"Had a great dinner. Meeting with Martinon-Torres
> in the morning. Taking the rest of the night off!"**

Early the next morning, McGregor took a walk along the beach at South Pointe, the southernmost tip of South Beach, Miami. He knew that the area had once been the home to a broken-down collection of police horse stables, a police intelligence unit warehouse and a training area, but now it had been transformed into a beautiful park and an ideal spot to enjoy a sunrise.

So, what is the symbolic meaning of a sunrise? he asked himself. *Does it represent new beginnings? Maybe it represents perseverance because the cycle continues no matter what happens? I wish I knew....*

McGregor brought his thoughts back to the real world as he noticed the time and headed back to his car. The drive to the Palace for his meeting with Torres was longer than anticipated.

Morning traffic in Miami? Like D.C., he swore.

"Two eggs over easy, bacon, but no salsa or green chile. Just a plain ol' gringo breakfast, okay, *Señorita*?" he ordered, smiling as he took a sip of the coffee she'd set on the table in front of him.

"Okay, but you don't know what you're missing, *Señor* McGregor!" the waitress replied teasingly. "I'm Rosa! Marcos left me a note saying you'd be here this morning for breakfast, and I should treat you as his friend and feed you well!"

"Why do you think *I'm* the guy Marcos is talkin' about?" he asked curiously.

"Look around you, *Señor*," she smiled. "To use your term, do you see any other 'gringos' in here? And, *Señor*, McGregor is *not* a common Hispanic name. Two eggs over easy, bacon, but no salsa or green chile comin' up. *Dos huevos más fáciles, tocino, pero no hay salsa o chile verde subiendo,*" she said to the cook as she bustled back to the kitchen.

Ferdinand Martinon-Torres arrived late. It was close to nine forty-five when he pulled his boat up to the dock and climbed the ladder to the patio where McGregor was enjoying the cigar Marcos had left for him at the cash register.

"Good morning, *Señor* Torres," McGregor said in a business-like manner. "Come sit with me while I finish my smoke, and then I want to go for a ride on the beautiful boat you're piloting. I have a proposition for you you're gonna want to consider! While you're waiting, think about a place where we can park your boat, go ashore and talk where nobody can eavesdrop."

"No problem, *Señor* McGregor. No problem at all. Hey, Rosa, Rosa baby," he hollered, "bring me a beer, will ya?"

"Nice boat you've got here," McGregor said a little later as he climbed down the ladder to the dock. "What's below?" he asked.

"A bedroom, a full galley, and a head—storage for life vests and fishin' stuff on the main deck here, some small equipment storage up in the wheelhouse—lots of mahogany, brass and triple-strength fiberglass," Torres bragged. "Two 450 horsepower Gray-Marine diesel engines make it ocean safe— only use one here on the river and most parts of the bay. Had a little party on board last night—little messy in the hold right now. Come on up to the wheel with me, and we'll head up the river a bit. I got a place where we can talk business...or pleasure, if that's your business," he laughed.

It wasn't long before the warehouses and tall trees disappeared, and the land around the river looked more and more like Everglades country. Torres' boat was leaving a trail of muddy water as he pulled it up to a small dock.

"We're on Seminole land now," Torres said. "A short walk and we'll be in an open grove with some picnic tables. They hold native ceremonies like the Stomp Dance and the Green Corn Ritual back there. The only things that will be able to hear us are 'gators and maybe a few 'possums—those that the 'gators don't catch and eat," he laughed. "Here, we can sit at this table. What's the proposition you said you had for me?"

"It's really very simple. You talk, I listen, and..." McGregor stopped talking long enough to reach under his shirt, pull out his gun and point it straight at Torres' forehead, pulling the hammer back far enough for Torres to hear it click into place—"and, you live or you die." Flashing his badge, he continued, "I'm a United States Marshal and a special agent for the FBI, but you can ignore that for the moment. Right now, I'm either your worst deadly nightmare or, if you choose right, your new best friend. If you choose wrong, I'm going to put my first shot square in your crotch, watch you roll on the ground for a long while, and then put my second shot right in the center of your forehead. Your choice—talk to me straight or die right here—now—right now! No more boat, no more parties, no more Anita!"

"Tell me what you want, McGregor. I don't want to die! I'm a good Christian, I'm not…"

"All right, let's talk about your boat. If you lie to me, I'll know it, and that first bullet is going to hurt like hell," McGregor warned. "Now, you know exactly what happened to your *old* boat, and we'll get to that later. What I want to know is, who paid for your new boat? —and you can forget the insurance story. Somebody bought that boat for you because you helped them out with the use of your old boat. Who was it?" McGregor asked as he purposely took a silencer out of his pants pocket, examined it candidly, and slowly threaded it onto the barrel of his SIG. "Who was it?"

"They'll kill me and all of my family if I tell you," Torres cried.

"I'll kill you and sell your wife and any kids you have to South American sex slave traders—your choice!" McGregor quickly retorted, shoving his gun closer to Torres' forehead.

"I never met the woman— it was two guys," Torres blurted. "One worked for her, he told me, and the other is the foreman at the plastics plant on the river back there," he said as he pointed down the river. "They came to me and wanted me to pick them up in my boat at that plastics plant dock and take them out on the bay. They really scared me," Torres whimpered, "they acted real cold. They said they'd have to destroy my boat after I picked them up, but that a new one would be waiting for me, clear title and all, in my name, at the Bella Flora Marina within the next few days after I did what they wanted. They showed me a picture of the new boat," he said, his voice rising, "and they said they would kill Anita if I didn't help them and, to…to keep my mouth shut. I didn't know what they were doing, I really didn't! I think they would have killed me if I didn't do what they wanted!" He sat with his head in his hands, trembling and sniffing noisily.

"What happened next?" McGregor asked less forcefully. "Remember, you're doing this for you and Anita. I mean, talkin' to me now."

"They told me what night they wanted me go with them. It was like three o'clock in the morning. One came to my house, and we left in my boat. The other guy was waiting for us on the plastics plant dock. They loaded a dead guy and a big roll of something that looked like plastic drop cloth stuff—you know, like painters use—into my boat and told me to drive slowly to the bay. They got some of my fishing gear out of the hold and pretended to be fishing until we hit the bay. I looked back at them a couple of times, and they were doing something to the dead guy. I was scared! It was dark and I couldn't really see much, but when we hit the bay they started throwing stuff overboard, and then they told me to turn around and head back up the river."

141

"Tell, me, Torres," McGregor interrupted. "Are you sure the guy they dumped in the bay was dead when they put him on your boat?"

"Oh, yes, *Señor*, very dead, I'm sure."

"Keep talkin', Torres, I'm still listening."

"They got one of my minnow-keeper cans," Torres continued, "and they were trying to wash down the deck. They got more water on them than on my deck, and they were cussing and laughing at each other. When we got back to the plastics plant dock, another guy was there to meet them. Just as I was positioning my boat to pull up to the dock, they threw that big roll of drop cloth stuff overboard, and it hit my prop and broke the shaft. I had to shut my engine down and coast to the dock. They told me to sit at the wheel while they talked. The guy who worked at the plant, the foreman guy, left, and the other two tried to clean up my boat. Then they told me to walk home. That's all I know except that I got a call from Bella Flora Marina the very next day telling me I could come and pick up my new boat. I wasn't angry or scared anymore after that. But now I'm scared again. I just did what they wanted because they would have killed me. Like I'm doing for you right now! I don't like guns—please, I didn't..."

"Torres, here's my deal," McGregor interrupted him sternly. "We're gonna go back to the restaurant, and you're going to tell your Anita that I've hired you for a couple of days to show me around the Everglades, the Indian reservation, whatever works for you, and then I'm going to take you to the Miami police department where you're gonna retell your story—and it better be the same story," he warned. "We're gonna keep you there for a couple of days while we check out everything you've told us. If you've been truthful, we're gonna let you go if you promise that you'll testify against any of the people we arrest. Are we clear on that?"

"Oh, *Señor* I'm telling the truth! Honest! I just don't want trouble for me and my Anita!" Torres blurted.

"Okay, Torres, don't mess with us on this! The guy they dumped in the bay— Roberto Gonzales was his name, by the way—was murdered and slaughtered like a pig. He was a former law enforcement officer and a personal friend of mine. If we tie you into this thing and we label you as a cop-killer, you'll never see the outside of prison walls again. Cooperate and tell the truth and you'll go home. Mess with us in any way and I promise, I'll bring your ass back out here and feed you to the alligators myself. Now, hand me your cellphone... you won't need it for a few days. Are the papers for your boat on board or at your house? Sales receipt, title... you know!"

"They're all on my boat," Torres said with the sound of relief in his voice. "Here's my phone. I want to cooperate! Oh, and I have a rifle in my wheelhouse."

"Let's head back down the river, slowly," McGregor said as he got up from the bench and directed Torres back to the boat. "I'm in no hurry, and you're sweating like a... anyway, you need to cool off a bit before we talk to Anita.

142

We're not going to upset her, are we?" he said sternly as he unloaded Torres's rifle.

McGregor and Torres docked and found a table on the Palace's patio where they could sit and wait for Torres' wife, Anita, to report for work. As they slowly emptied a pitcher of beer, McGregor looked over the boat papers Torres had given to him.

Son of a bitch! McGregor thought angrily. *Son of a ... The woman who paid for the boat signed the check herself. The boat dealer photocopied it and probably didn't realize that he or she included it in this packet of papers. Margaret Douglas signed the check for the boat! Maggie, you bitch, you just made the mistake of your life!*

McGregor looked up from the stack of papers in front of him. "*Señor* Torres! Are you aware that the person who paid for your boat wrote a check in an amount of over ninety thousand dollars? Never mind, Anita just arrived. Go talk to her, and let's get this show on the road. You've got a very important life or death date. I'll wait for you in my car. Think about an immediate and horrible death if you even consider running!"

As soon as McGregor got to his car, he called Mueller and told him that he was bringing in a witness in the Gonzales case. He asked him to either arrange a line-up with the Camilo plant foreman included or, if he had a head shot of the foreman, to set up a photo array for the witness to look over.

Mueller informed him that they were just finishing up with the consultant engineer at Camilo's plant, and were heading back to the station with the plant foreman and his assistant—still under arrest, handcuffed and sitting uncomfortably in the back seat of one of his squad cars.

"They don't know they been fingered by Camilo, and they're bitching like hell, but, man, I gotta tell you...."

"Later," McGregor interrupted him. "I'm betting you found out some interesting stuff about the plant, but right now I'm completely focused on the Gonzales murder and heading for your office with some new information you need to hear from my witness."

He asked Mueller if he'd get in touch with Wilson and Conroy and request them to come to his office as well. He also asked him to find a current address on Maggie Douglas, the make and model of her car, and current license tag information. He knew that Mueller could access that information from his squad car and have it ready for him by the time he reached Mueller's office.

McGregor took a deep breath as he and Torres pulled out of the Palace's parking lot and headed for Miami Central Police Station. He was boiling mad—mad at himself and livid that, once more, he'd been "taken for a ride" by Maggie Douglas.

CHAPTER SEVENTEEN

Wilson and Conroy had already arrived at the Miami Central Police Station by the time McGregor arrived with Ferdinand Martinon-Torres in tow. He placed Torres in a lockable interview room and got him a cold drink before he made his way to Mueller's office.

"Hans should be with us shortly," Conroy said. "We've got a major bust on our hands, and he's got the engineer he flew in talking with a police stenographer downstairs. Camilo and his number one foreman had quite a cocaine distribution business. Mueller's taking care of all the Miami stuff and we've got our major case squad filling in the blanks regarding Camilo's network."

"In short," Wilson added, "we hit paydirt on cocaine suppliers and distributors throughout the United States, plus we've got major leads on Camilo's suppliers in Brazil, as well as a couple of other South American countries. Huge shipments of cocaine were arriving each Thursday morning via a special over-the-road tanker transporting plastic resin. The bricks of coke were hidden in the resin and pumped into that ominous third silo in Camilo's plant. That particular silo had a huge crane-operated strainer that captured each brick as the resin was sucked out of the tanker and deposited in the silo. Then, each Thursday night, a crew came in after the plant closed for the day, emptied the strainer, cleaned the resin off each brick and shipped them out that night by boat."

"I had a feeling there was something going on with those silos—just a hunch," McGregor broke in.

"Mueller's people are still working at rounding up the night crew, and our agents are in the process of attempting to identify the people involved in the night transportation network," Wilson continued. "All of us will be overemployed for the next month or so with this bust!"

"Cam, you left too soon," Conroy chimed in. "You missed all the fun after our agents pulled Camilo out of the cockpit of his plane. I heard he actually peed his pants, he was so scared," he said as they all laughed. "He's still in lock-up—we need to talk with him some more, but he's going to be an easy mark. He's going to spend the rest of his days and nights in prison. We're going to use prison placement choice—you know, 'Hey, Camilo! You want country club or Hell?' —as our enticement for him to tell all."

"Yeah," Wilson continued, "you disappeared without even thanking us after we came in riding high in a commandeered golf cart to save your and Mueller's sorry asses. Hell, we…"

"Well," McGregor said off-handedly as he casually leaned back in his chair, "I took a leisurely cruise up the Miami river in a ninety thousand dollar boat, drank my share of imported beer, enjoyed the food at the Palace and found out who ordered the attempted hit on me, the kill on Gonzales, and who just might be the company store that owns Camilo's soul."

"What's that?" Mueller asked as he walked into his office and plopped down in his chair. "You were saying"?

"I was sayin' that you look like shit warmed over. When's the last time you slept?" McGregor asked sternly. "Have you got the info on Douglas for me?"

"Yeah, I got it, no problem," Mueller grunted. "I also got you the address on her place in the Keys as well. What's up with that?"

"Simple, I think!" McGregor began. "Maggie Douglas is good at burying truths real deep and playing dirty games so far behind the scenes she always seems to come out unscathed and looking innocent. But this time she made a dumb and ultimately fatal mistake, and I'm going to bring her in for you for conspiracy in the murder of Roberto Gonzales. And, after you get through questioning Ferdinand Martinon-Torres—who, by the way, is waiting to talk to you in interrogation room three— you can add an 'accessory to murder' charge to Camilo's foreman as well. Now, here's the kicker—and right now it's just another hunch— but I think Camilo answers directly to Douglas, and I think she's taken her brother's place as head of MD 699 and is working directly with Alard De Smet. Hell, maybe she's been working directly with him all along and her brother was just a pawn. I don't know, but I'm going to find out."

"You want us to get search warrants for her house here and in Key West?" Wilson asked. "If she's in with De Smet, that's federal business, and we want to look for anything connecting her with interstate or intercontinental commerce."

"Go for it, gentlemen." McGregor said flatly. "As far as Miami Police are concerned, I've got her for calling the shots on Gonzales' murder, and since it's your case, Detective Mueller, I'll be bringing her to you *personally,* as soon as I track her pretty ass down.

"Now, Hans, we need to talk about Ferdinand Martinon-Torres," McGregor continued as he got up and beckoned Mueller to follow him. "And you golf cart jockeys, get those search warrants as soon as possible, but hold off executing them until I bring Douglas in. Depending on where I find her, it could be a day or so. I'll let you know. Okay?"

"He sure gives a lot of orders for a retired old fart," Conroy said under his breath, but just loudly enough to crack up the room.

"Look, Hans. When you've finished talking to Torres," McGregor said softly, "get his statement on record, send a copy to my phone, and hold him here until I get back to you, confirming that the story he told me is the same as the one he's promised to tell you. If they line up, I've promised him that he can go free, if he agrees to testify. Get him a ride back to the Palace where his boat is moored. Is there a copy machine close?"

"Yeah, right over there" Mueller pointed.

146

"You'll want a copy of this check as he tells his story. You'll quickly see the connection and why I'm going after Douglas," McGregor said, handing him a copy of the document. "You won't have to scare this dude into talking. I've taken care of that for you," McGregor said bluntly.

After McGregor introduced Mueller to Torres, he forcefully reminded him about what he expected from his visit with Mueller.

"Remember, Señor Torres, I'll be reading everything you have to say to Detective Mueller, and it had better damn well match what you told me," McGregor said, as he headed out the door and to his car.

Douglas' penthouse condo was on the eighteenth floor of an opulent high rise on the far south end of South Beach.

She's stepped up a bit from the place she used to have over by the marina, he thought as he parked his car and waited for a security guard to open the door allowing him access to an opulent atrium and lobby. Showing the guard his badge through the glass door, he was allowed to enter. McGregor noticed the guard was instantly on his radio calling a supervisor.

"How can I help you, Officer?" the supervisor, who seemed to appear from nowhere, asked in an accommodating voice.

"You can start by telling me what professional football team you played for before you took this job," McGregor exclaimed incredulously. "What are you? I'm guessing—what? —Six foot ten, two-twenty-five?"

"Not even, close—sorry, no cigar, officer. Again, how can I help you?" the supervisor asked politely while intentionally examining McGregor's badge and identification closely. "Federal Marshal, huh?"

"Are those real sharks in that tank over there?" McGregor asked. "I'm here to talk to Maggie Douglas. Eighteenth floor, I believe."

"Yep, those are real sharks—nurse sharks, I think! Official or personal business?" the supervisor asked, maintaining his accommodating manner.

"A little of both," McGregor responded quickly.

"Ms. Douglas is not in residence," said the officer who was still standing by. "She's at her home in Key West—left yesterday morning. I helped her move suitcases to her car. She didn't say when she'd be returning."

"Is there anything else we can do for you, Marshal McGregor?" asked the supervisor.

"Yes, you can take me up to her apartment, so I can verify that she is, indeed, not here. Just a matter of protocol, that's all—you understand. If you desire, I can call for a search warrant to be delivered by a marked Miami police car with sirens and red lights activated to alert residents to police activity in the building, but ..."

"I'll take him up, officer; you remain at your post," the supervisor said firmly to the door sentry. "Come with me, Marshal—you'll love the view."

It didn't take long for McGregor to verify that Douglas wasn't in her penthouse condo, and, as promised, the views of the Atlantic Ocean and Miami's beaches were spectacular.

Thanking the guard and his supervisor for their cooperation, and advising them that any contact they might decide to make with Douglas could result in charges for interfering with a police investigation, he quickly hit Route 1 south to the Florida Keys and ultimately Key West.

It always feels to me like I've never made this trip before, McGregor mused as the mile markers whizzed by him on the Overseas Highway, destined, he knew, to count down to zero at the tip of Key West. He knew from experience that it was one of the most beautiful and relaxing drives he'd ever made. He enjoyed cruising through the small towns on small islands every now and then along the way, and at the end of the road finding the jewel of the trip—Key West— which, for him, always evoked clear blue-green waters, coral reef islands, lots of pirate stories, great food and spectacular sunrises and sunsets.

It was late afternoon when he finished checking into a small motel within walking distance of Key West's Duval Street activities and Mallory Square, home to some of the best restaurants and entertainment in the area. From his room, he called Mueller with an update on his location.

The motel was well-located, and he knew exactly which back streets would lead him to the fisherman's docks, to Pirate Dustin's Diner, and the best boiled shrimp dinner in town. He was in no hurry that evening, and if Douglas was in town, she'd probably still be around in the morning.

My God, this place is busy this evening. Must be, from all the fake Hawaiian shirts I'm seeing, that some cruise ship is docked at Mallory Square, he thought as he ordered dinner, took a number that would be called when his food was ready, waited a minute for the beer he ordered to be drawn, and looked for a place to sit. He could only see one seat available, at a table for two just outside a side door on the deck. An attractive woman—late forties, he guessed—was sitting by herself at the table picking at a plate of conch fritters.

"I started the day admiring the sunrise in Miami Beach and now I'm doing the same at sunset in Key West," McGregor said to the woman sitting across the table from the empty chair. "Pretty spectacular way to start and end a day, but it would be so much better if I could sit here with you since it's the only chair in the house. Do you mind?"

She glanced around to see if he was telling the truth.

"Sit down if you wish. I don't need any conversation though!"

"Fair enough, and thank you," McGregor said as he sat down and took a drink from his glass of beer. "Great lookin'…is that conch you've got there? This place has the best…"

"No conversation, I said!"

"Oops, sorry, officer," McGregor said with a smile.

148

After a moment or so, the lady looked at him and asked, "What's with the 'officer' stuff?"

"Either you're a woman who simply carries a gun for protection," McGregor answered, "or, you're a law enforcement officer of some kind. Your gun bump is showing! Are you local?"

"Only a cop would notice that!" she said, as she pulled her badge case from her purse and shoved it toward McGregor. "I'm a U.S. Marshal, here to process a federal escapee who was captured here yesterday by the Coast Guard. What's your story?"

"They just called my number; don't drink my beer while I'm gone!" McGregor warned jokingly, as he got up and headed for the pick-up counter.

"Marshal Joan Taminelli," he commented as he returned to his chair, "I gotta tell ya, they've got the best seafood in town here! I always come back to this place whenever I'm in Key West—which, unfortunately, isn't very often anymore. I'm Cameron McGregor, but please call me Cam."

"I asked you what your story was?" Taminelli insisted.

"Didn't you tell me, in no uncertain terms, something like, 'Sit down if you wish—I don't need any conversation?'" McGregor pointed out as he slid his badge case across the table. "Don't get any conch juice on that, I'd smell like something dead for the next two weeks."

"Well, I'll be damned! You're a Marshal as well—with a gold badge even. I've never, in my four years in the service, seen a gold badge like this. What does that signify?" Taminelli asked. "And, what are you doing here— vacation perhaps, or are you spying on me?"

"Neither," McGregor smiled. "I'm on the job, even though the gold badge says I'm retired. After dinner, if you wanna take a walk over to Mallory Square, I'll fill you in—if you have time."

"This conch fritter is wonderful, "she said," and I have all the time in the world, until, I'm sorry to say, tomorrow morning—wharf sixteen, at daybreak. Do you like conch?"

"Tastes like rubber bands to me," McGregor grunted, washing down a giant shrimp with his beer.

After topping off their dinner with an obligatory slice of Key West's decadent Key Lime pie, the two marshals wandered narrow backstreets from the restaurant to Mallory Square. It was after sunset, so most of the street entertainers and the crowds they attract were gone.

"Gee, I'm sorry, Cam," Taminelli said, with mild sarcasm, "we've surely missed the ever-present silly statue man. But the snack stands with their cute touristy things to buy are still open and beckoning to us," she continued, with faked enthusiasm. "I suppose you already know that the sunset from here really is amazing. But did you know that the little porpoise key chain they sell in that cart over there actually glows in the dark, and that you can create your own personal blobs and interblobs from the silly putty they sell at that one over there?"

149

"Blobs and interblobs?" McGregor asked. "What the hell are blobs and interblobs?"

"Oh, it's just something I used to play around with before I decided to join the Marshals Service," Taminelli explained. "In my other life I was a high school science teacher who simply got tired of kids' parents telling me it was my entire fault that their near-perfect children were failing eleventh grade biology. Blobs, for your information and crossword prowess if you wish, are sections of the visual cortex where groups of neurons that are sensitive to color assemble in cylindrical shapes. ON the other hand, interblobs are areas between blobs which receive the same input, but are sensitive to orientation instead of color. Now, aren't you sooo glad you asked—kinda saves you from having to ask me that same old tired question, 'What did you do before you became a Marshal?'"

She smiled, picked up a piece of popcorn from the deck and tossed it in the air.

"It'll be gone before it hits the ground, I'll bet," she said as a sea gull swooped in and grabbed it, proving her right. "This is my fourth year with the Service, and, in spite of being on the low end of the totem pole, I love it! Your story? —you promised!"

"I retired three years ago from the Service, live just outside of Washington, D.C., and recently, I was called back…no, actually, I fell into it, a nasty little job partnering with the FBI. I was temporarily re-commissioned, and, well, here I am. I hope to make an arrest tomorrow and be home-free again."

"Wanna tell me about your case?" Taminelli asked.

McGregor hesitated a moment before answering.

"Not really. It's a long and complicated story with so much strange stuff in it you'd be too agitated to sleep a wink tonight. I'm hoping to arrest the final actor in this deadly soap opera tomorrow, transport her to jail here in Key West, before we haul her back to Miami where she'll be introduced to the defendant side of the federal court system. My warrant for her starts at 'conspiracy to murder,' and my counterparts in Miami and Washington will add a few more counts, I'm sure, down the road. It's been a difficult case," he sighed. "Come on, I'll walk you to your hotel, thank you for sharing your table with me earlier this evening and beg you for your phone number before I leave. *CSI Miami* is on at nine, and I'm hoping to pick up a few new tricks," he laughed.

The Key West Police Department's major case squad and a few extras were waiting for McGregor at their headquarters at six o'clock sharp the next morning. Mueller had briefed the Chief of Police by phone the night before and had asked that McGregor be provided support in the apprehension and arrest of Maggie Douglas. A copy of her arrest warrant and a search warrant for her home had been faxed to the chief just prior to McGregor's arrival.

150

Hopefully, McGregor thought as he walked into the station, *we can pull Maggie's arrest off without any major glitches. I don't want her to get away this time.*

Looking at his watch, he was reminded that Marshal Taminelli had probably finished her sunrise meeting on wharf sixteen, picked up her prisoner, and was on her way to the airport. He planned to call her in a few days and see if they could get together.

Hell, she lives just outside of Philadelphia—what's a two-and-a-half-hour drive to see...

"Good morning, Marshal McGregor?"

"Yes— are you the Chief?" McGregor asked.

"I'm Chief of Police, Purvis Porter," he said, extending his hand. "My squad is waiting for you in the room over there. If you hurry, you might still be able to grab a doughnut and a cup of coffee. My folks have done their homework and have a plan for you to consider. The squad leader's name is Smith—Detective Reginald Smith!"

As the Chief had indicated, Detective Smith and his squad had surveilled Douglas's high rise, had clearly marked entrances and exits, had pinpointed the location of her condo, and had verified that she was in residence, by herself, still asleep and snoring up a storm as they met.

Oh, she does snore! McGregor almost admitted knowing but caught himself in mid-thought.

They would surround the place in unmarked cars, while McGregor and one of the squad members, Jimmy-Joe Johns, went inside to get her. They suggested that McGregor call her from the lobby phone and ask her to meet him in the lobby. Johns would watch the lobby guard while they waited. If this didn't work, and they couldn't arrest Douglas peacefully, then Plan B would immediately go into effect, and the entire squad would mount an assault on her apartment and arrest her by force. McGregor hoped that Plan B wouldn't be necessary, and that he could talk her down to the lobby.

Within the hour, McGregor found himself walking into the condo complex with Detective Johns, while other members of the squad covered all the escape routes Douglas might try to use if she decided to bolt the scene.

When they entered the lobby, Johns quietly removed the guard from the immediate area and had him sit on a couch next to the biggest TV screen McGregor had ever seen. *The Today Show* was on and interviewing someone McGregor didn't recognize.

McGregor took a seat at the guard's desk and picked up the phone.

"Good morning, Maggie," he said. "This is a voice from your *immediate* past—Cameron McGregor, on duty, and sitting down here in your lobby with a huge TV screen entertaining me with nonsense. I'd like for you to come down here and visit with me."

151

He listened to her response and continued, "Yes, Maggie, it's really me! I'm here with the major case squad from the Key West Police Department and I'm hoping—as are they—that you'll just simply come down so they don't have to trash your place and bring you out kickin' and screamin.' Let's just make it you and me. Okay? I need you back in Miami as soon as possible. The show's over! Come on down. You've got five minutes, otherwise we come up! Let's do this peacefully."

After a short pause, McGregor continued, "I'll be waiting for you, Maggie, five minutes from the time I hang up. No, not now," he responded to her request for additional information. "I'll tell you what's happening as soon as you join me in the lobby. Come on, you know the routine!" He hung up and prepared himself for whichever scenario Maggie chose to follow.

"This could go either way," McGregor warned Johns. "Radio the squad, please," he quickly continued, "and tell them to close in on the perimeter now, then bring the guard back over here and cuff him to the desk. I'll unplug his desk phone; you hold his cell. If she comes down on her own, the minute she opens the elevator door, draw your weapon and watch my back; she's sharp as a tack, and quick."

It seemed to McGregor that this five-minute span took a long time, but finally the elevator doors opened, and Maggie was standing in the doorway. He'd never seen her as pale as she was at that moment. She was, incongruously, dressed in her Marshal's uniform, no badge showing, and with an empty holster strapped to her side. She walked toward him holding a pill bottle out for him to see.

"I knew you were coming," she slurred her words, "got a call last night— from Porter —saw cars surround the place just a little while ago. I'm sorry, Cam, I called the hit on Roberto. I'm so sorry," she said as she slumped to the floor.

"Call 911 for rescue," McGregor barked at Johns, as checked her for any hidden weapons and snatched the pill bottle.

"God damn it," he yelled, looking at the bottle, "she's poisoned herself! Tell them to bring a stomach pump!" He frantically searched for her pulse. "Her hearts stopped," he said, after putting his ear to her chest. He was still giving her CPR when the rescue squad arrived.

"She's dead, officer," was still ringing in his ears as he arrived back at the police station with Detective Johns.

Poison again? Seems to be a pattern here, McGregor thought. *Could it be that she was...?*

As they stepped out of the squad car at the station, Johns asked McGregor, "Are you going to tell anyone about what Douglas told us before...."

"Not yet, Detective Johns. Other things to consider first," McGregor said as he slammed the car door and headed toward the station.

"Let's make some fresh coffee, Marshal McGregor," Johns said as they arrived at the squad room. "I'll need your help in making out my report. The

Chief and Detective Smith are sticklers for accuracy and spelling and, honestly, my spelling stinks almost as bad as the cheap coffee they supply us with. But, hey, it goes with the job!"

Just then, Chief Porter entered the room, glad-handing everyone with, "Good work, folks. Glad you all got back safely. Congratulations."

"I'll say the same to you, Chief, but not before you find out the identity of the snitch in your house," McGregor said quietly. "Douglas was tipped off that we were coming, and she told me by whom. Now, go back to your office and play politics while you still can. We have work to do here, and we need to file a report so you can brag about your work to the press."

Porter's lips began to move, but no sound came out. He turned abruptly and left the room, looking nervously back over his shoulder as he went.

Nothing like seeing a cheap politician struggle to cover his ass—God, retirement has so many wonderful "don't give a damn" benefits, McGregor thought as he plunked himself down in a chair. "Where's the coffee, and where's that senseless report form?" he said in an aggressive voice. "My newest partner, Johns, and I are going to make all of us in this room stars. Hell, I see movie roles for you all in the very near future," McGregor said facetiously as the room lightened up with tired laughter. Quickly returning to a more somber tone, he added, "And, if you have one, I also need a death bed declaration form."

While Johns worked on the mandatory incident report, McGregor thumbed through the department's "Official Book of Forms," looking for something that he could use to record Douglas's dying declarations— some of the words of which were still lying heavily on his mind. *"I'm sorry, Cam, I called the hit on Roberto. I'm so sorry…"*

"All right, this will do," he said out loud, selecting one of the forms. "Detectives Smith and Johns, we need to find a private place to discuss Douglas's declarations."

Finding an unused room, they all sat down at a small table. "Gentlemen, here's my problem," McGregor explained quietly. "Johns and I <u>both</u> heard Douglas's dying declarations. There were two. Her exact words were, first, 'I knew you were coming— got a call last night—from Porter —saw cars surround the place just a little while ago,' and, second, she said, 'I'm sorry, Cam, I called the hit on Roberto. I'm so sorry.'"

"What the fuck!" Smith mumbled. "That son of a…"

"I'll bury it if you want me to," McGregor interrupted, "but…"

"Hell, no, you won't," both Smith and Johns responded in unison.

"You've got two witnesses, both yourself and Johns," Smith said strongly. "Write it up just as you heard it—both declarations. When you get ready to sign it, let me know, and I'll get a notary in here to attest to your signatures. I'm going to make an appointment to meet with the district attorney right away. I want him to decide what he wants to do about the Porter thing."

153

Johns looked at Smith, one eyebrow raised. "You already know what he'll do, and so do I. He'll issue an arrest warrant for Porter—obstruction of justice, I'm guessing—and the Chief will be gone tomorrow. Wanna bet?"

"It's your call, detectives," McGregor said with assurance, "and, I venture to say, probably the right and only call. Consider it done. I'll find you when we need a notary."

"Detective Smith, Marshal McGregor has a visitor in the lobby, a Marshal Taminelli, sir," Smith's radio crackled.

"Ten-four—did you hear the call, Marshal?"

"I did. I'll go out and talk to the Marshal, and then I'll finish up both my reports with Johns, get 'em notarized, make copies for myself, and then, gentlemen, I'm outta here for lunch and …the road back to Miami!"

McGregor hurried to the lobby—a bit surprised at how pleased he was to see his "visitor."

"Joan, I thought you'd be on a flight back to…uh…"

"Philadelphia— the flight out of here to Tampa was delayed. My prisoner is locked up here until 3:30. I took a chance you might be here. Are you finished with your arrest? Got time for lunch?"

"Lunch sounds great! Give me about fifteen minutes or so, and I'll be finished. There's coffee in the squad room over there, if you have a cast iron stomach."

"You got it, Mr. Gold Badge," she said, as she walked toward the squad room.

It didn't take long for McGregor to finish his reports. Johns had done a good job on the incident report, and McGregor quickly added his declaration report to the short pile of documents that needed to be notarized. Smith found the notary, and it was "case closed" for McGregor, and a trip to the District Attorney for Smith. After thanking as many of the Major Case Squad folks he could find, McGregor picked up Taminelli and, after a short walk, settled on a small patio restaurant off of Duval Street.

"Joan, I have to tell you that you that you don't look anything like any of the science teachers I ever had in high school," McGregor said, as he held the chair for her.

"Thank you, Cameron—I think! And I must tell you that, right now, you look just like almost every high school boy I ever had in any of my classes. I guess it must be that slightly lecherous twinkle in your eyes. Keep that up and I may have to send you to the principal's office! How'd your arrest go?"

"Maggie Douglas was her name—big in a whole lot of stuff going on in Miami and, at one time, in Washington. Mafia-style business interests, you name it," McGregor began. "I helped take down her brother and his syndicate, MD 699, not too long ago, and Maggie just kinda stepped in and opened her own shop of horrors, in his wake, I guess. Bottom line, she ordered a successful hit on a good friend of mine, and, although I didn't know her involvement at the time, I

154

stumbled into a major drug bust working with the Miami FBI and police—just when I was at a dead end with my friend's murder investigation.

Taminelli nodded, with a "been-there, done-that" expression on her face.

"Suddenly Maggie's name came up, and I was able to get a 'conspiracy to murder' case going against her," McGregor went on. "That's what the arrest was all about, although she took a dose of poison before we could arrest her, and she's dead and down the street at the morgue. I have a death bed declaration, witnessed by myself and a local cop, admitting that she called for the hit on my friend. Case closed. Job done, goin' home to my horses, my dogs, and my back-country mountain friends. Goin' back to my volunteer work with Travelers Aid at Dulles International. Goin' back to chipped beef on toast and liver and onions at Hoppy's Place in the Blue Ridge Mountains, and goin back…oh, crap," McGregor interrupted himself, "I'm really unloading on you, aren't I? I'm sorry, Joan, I'm just…"

"You're just hungry, Cameron. Shut up for a minute," she said, "take a deep breath, and order. I'd recommend a Cuban sandwich. They're authentic here—salty, smoky, tangy, creamy and utterly delicious—a big, in-your-face taste. Be advised, however, that you have to order a hefty beer to balance everything out."

"Sounds good to me," McGregor said. "I'll whistle up a waiter for us. What are you going to have?"

"Same thing," she said. "Now, I have to tell you that I'd already heard of Maggie Douglas. She had quite a name down here for both her gay and her straight parties. She was in with all the Key West politicians and big wigs. The latest gossip is that she'd been hooking up with the Chief of Police here in Key West. A few months ago, it was a state representative from Orlando. She got around a bit, I understand."

"I wish I'd known that last night," McGregor remarked. "It was the Chief of Police who warned her I was coming to arrest her this morning. I'm betting that the next time you're down here, there'll be a different person heading up the police department. Chief Purvis Porter? He'll be gone, I'm betting. Now, about those blobs and interblobs, please tell me more. My life *without* that specific knowledge is surely going to handicap my social discourse, not to mention, of course, my crossword puzzle prowess."

"Don't forget 'Jeopardy' she added. "You won't even have a chance to appear as a competitor!"

They both laughed as they dug into the perfect Cuban sandwiches that had just been positioned before them.

As he made his way back to the Hard Rock Hotel in Miami, McGregor was impressed, again, and as he always was, by the one-hundred-thirteen miles and forty-two bridges of the Overseas Highway linking the Florida Keys to the Mainland. What looked to him to be impossible expanses of water stretched out

155

on either side of the highway, with the Atlantic on his right and the Gulf to his left.

Wow, sensory overload coming and going—tidal flats, teal waters dotted by distant islands, lots of kitschy gift shops peddling seashell necklaces, along with all kinds of burger stands advertising that their burgers and fries are much better than any others along the route. Man, I should take up diving! I'm missing a whole world lurking just beneath the ocean surface—vividly colored fish, mermaids, coral reefs, mermaids, wrecked ships with gold flowing from their rotting bows, mermaids... His silent rhetoric was interrupted by the Bluetooth connection to his cell phone. It was a call from Hans Mueller asking him how things were going.

"Sorry, Hans," McGregor responded. "To be honest, I was so busy, I forgot to call you. Douglas's dead," he continued, "but I got a dying declaration that she's the one who ordered the hit on Gonzales.......No, she got a tip I was coming after her and, get this—she poisoned herself! Sound familiar? What does that tell you about my ability to attract women? No, I'm not kidding! No, really! So, how are things on your end?"

Mueller quickly brought him up to date.

"That's good news, Hans" McGregor replied. "I'm on my way back now. Yep! Tomorrow morning with you and our FBI partners—ten o'clock, your office will work for me—I'll be there! Then, my friend, I'm heading back to Virginia. My job is finished, and you better damn well agree! Gotta go now, there's a mermaid flapping her tail at me in the middle of the road—I think she's trying to flag me down!"

"You can only hope," Mueller laughed as he hung up.

After dinner, a few hands of poker at the Hard Rock, and a good night's sleep, McGregor made his way the next morning to Mueller's office. He hoped it would be the last time. Detective Mueller and FBI agents Wilson and Conroy were huddled together, looking over one of many sheaves of folders strewn every which way around a table in the corner of Mueller's cluttered office.

"Started without me, I see!" McGregor said from the doorway, getting their attention.

"No, Marshal, just the opposite," Wilson said as he looked up from the paper he was reading. "We're going *finish* without you. Hans said you were ready to go home. Now, if you want…"

"Where's the coffee? Same place?" McGregor interrupted. "I'm gonna drink one more cup of that nasty cop-slop, turn in my car, and you're gonna get me to Miami International in time to catch my flight outta here this afternoon."

"Your coffee's right there on the corner of the table—just got it for you," Conroy pointed. "Black, no sugar, and preferably so strong that it's trying to climb out of the cup, as I've been told."

156

"You've got that right!" McGregor laughed as he shook hands with the three of them.

"All right, gentlemen, find a chair," Mueller said. "I'm going to bring us all up to date, and then the City of Miami is going to treat us all to lunch!"

"Now, for all practical purposes," he continued, "we're done. Cameron, after our phone conversation yesterday, I checked in with the Key West police and, as a courtesy, they faxed me copies of the reports regarding Douglas. She's now out of the picture, so that's the end of that story. Sounds like you also took the Key West Police Chief out of the picture as well," he said dryly.

"For the record, Dan and Bob," he explained, "Douglas poisoned herself—seems like the standard method of death for MD 699 members—but Cam got a confession to Gonzales' murder out of her before she croaked. I'll fill you in at lunch about the Key West Police Chief situation. And, you were right, Cam, about their rationale for getting rid of Gonzales. Arturo Camilo called Douglas, and they agreed that Gonzales was getting too much attention in the Mexican community and was starting to cut into their territory. Douglas contacted De Smet, and he sent some of his goons over here do the dirty work under the direction of Douglas, Camilo, and two of Camilo's foremen."

"At the same time," Conroy interrupted, "De Smet, for whatever reason, hired a Washington local goon to try to polish you off, McGregor. Stacy Dalcour's in the clear—she had nothing to do with the attempted hit on you. It was De Smet who made that call."

"By the way," Wilson interjected, "just FYI, Dalcour's no longer in Washington; she got canned for some reason. Our office in D.C. said she left to go back to Arizona to live with her mother, who, we understand, is in the middle of a messy divorce. Don't you have a history with Dalcour's father? Weren't you the arresting officer in something he was involved in?"

"Yep." McGregor replied. "No comment!"

"Moving on, gentlemen," Mueller prodded, "here are the indictments we got late yesterday afternoon from the grand jury. Camilo—drug smuggling, distribution of controlled substance, money laundering, and conspiracy to commit murder. Camilo's head foreman and his assistant—drug smuggling, distribution of controlled substance, conspiracy to commit murder, and second-degree murder. Camilo's plastics plant and his home are shuttered, by the way, and Ferdinand Martinon-Torres is back on his new boat, happily doing his thing, on the Miami River. He did a good job for us, testifying in the grand jury proceedings. And, Cam, his wife says 'thank you' and sends you her very best."

"I can only hope it includes a carry-out plate of her *Pollo Encacahuatado*," McGregor sighed. "Man, that is good stuff!"

"The D.E.A.," Wilson said, "is backtracking all of the delivery and distribution information we collected from Camilo's house and office, and they're busting people right and left along the way. My partner, Dan, managed to get an international arrest warrant issued for Alard De Smet and his two monkeys for first degree murder in Gonzales' death, and attempted first degree murder in De Smet's failed hit on you."

"We're watching him," Conroy added. "He'll make a mistake and, well, we'll get him eventually. Now, it's almost noon—who called this meeting? I'm hungry!"

"Yeah, we should go," Mueller said. "I've got a meeting with the Chief of Police at one-forty-five today. I suspect he's going to want to kiss my feet for…"

"I suspect he's going to tell you that you're going to be promoted to Assistant Chief. At least that's what I heard," Wilson hinted.

"Bullshit! And you heard that where?" Mueller quickly asked.

"Police Commissioner Hartley and my father were cops together twenty years ago. Later, after my dad died, he became kind of a father figure for me when I was a 'wet behind the ears' police rookie before I joined the FBI. The other night I had a few beers with him, and it's amazing what a bit of alcohol will do to a politician's tongue! Now, what was your question?"

"I'm not even going to ask— I'm too hungry," Mueller said stubbornly. "Let's go! We're finished here. Good work, everyone!"

About halfway through lunch, McGregor noticed Mueller eyeing Wilson.

Here it comes, McGregor predicted.

"All right, Wilson, what did the Commissioner tell you?"

"I don't want to spoil your lunch," Wilson said piously as he took another bite of his sandwich and waited for Mueller to take the bait.

And waited.

"I have a plane to catch!" McGregor groused.

"I've gotta take him to the airport!" Conroy complained.

"Tell you what, Detective Mueller," Wilson finally said. "If you'll promise never *ever* to *even harbor* a negative thought about the FBI interfering with…"

"Not on your life," Mueller blustered. "You guys think you're hot…"

"Okay, okay," Wilson relented. "Just for your information, Detective Mueller, Commissioner Hartley, my drinking buddy, will be at your meeting with the Chief today. Congratulations, in advance, Assistant Chief Mueller. And…. this conversation I'm having with you, with the other guys at this table listening—well, this conversation never took place and these guys are deaf," he exclaimed as he extended a congratulatory hand. "How's your lunch lookin' to you now?"

Mueller looked dumbfounded as Conroy and McGregor both reached across the table to shake his hand.

Great group of guys to work with, McGregor thought as he headed down the ramp to his gate at Miami International Airport after Conroy dropped him off. *I'll be glad to get home. Tomorrow, I need to call Gonzales' daughter. She needs closure on her father's death. Then, Lawrence Brody. I'm sure he's probably already been apprised regarding the Miami situation, but if he needs any clarification…*

"Welcome onboard Delta Airlines, flight 2242 to Dulles International Airport. Flying time to Dulles is two hours, thirty-eight minutes. In final preparation for departure, please ensure that your seatbelts are securely fastened, your seatbacks and tray tables…"

Haul ass, Delta! McGregor was thinking as he closed his eyes and drifted off to sleep.

CHAPTER EIGHTEEN

While McGregor was away, fall had quickly changed to winter on his mountain, and some work needed to be done before the first hard freeze—one last mowing, for one thing, and firewood to be cut, split and stacked. Two weeks had passed before McGregor and Zeus realized that it was past time for them to make a trip to Hoppy's for lunch.

Even at eleven o'clock in the morning, McGregor noted as he looked out the window, *there's still a thick frost on the ground, and snowflakes have started to swirl in the air.*

"Zeus, I don't know about you, but I'm thinking that an open-faced, roast beef sandwich with lots of gravy is calling out for me. I'm volunteering at the airport tonight, but we have time to go to Hoppy's. Are you up for it? We'll bring something back for you, Annie."

Annie, as usual, put on her "long-suffering" face, but the delighted wag of Zeus's tail sent a clear message to McGregor that, as always, he welcomed going anywhere with his master, and Hoppy's was always a bonus. Zeus seemed to relish the vistas and the rolling hills of the Blue Ridge Mountains while continuously maintaining an attentive eye for what he considered to be fair game anytime, anywhere. White-tailed deer, either standing in a cautious freeze, or sprinting through the forest with their tails raised in alarm, simply begged to be chased.

As McGregor and Zeus pulled into the parking lot at Hoppy's Place, almost simultaneously with Zeus's tail excitedly announcing their final arrival, McGregor's cell phone alerted him to a text message. It was from Joan Taminelli.

"Hold on for a minute, Zeus," McGregor commanded.

> **Hi Cam!**
> **Sorry I haven't gotten back in touch—been busy**
> **at the office. If you've retired again and put your gold**
> **badge back in the drawer, I'd like to invite you up this**
> **coming weekend. Philly's beautiful at this time of the**
> **year. Let me know and I'll send you directions to my**
> **house in West Chester.   Joan**

"One more minute, Zeus; let me respond to this message," McGregor said.

> **Sounds good to me, Joan. My badge is back in mothballs.**
> **Send me time and place info...sounds like fun! Cam**

Mary Beth, Hoppy's wife, head waitress, and the behind-the-scenes secret of Hoppy's happiness and success over a very long stretch of time, was waiting to greet them as they made their way up to the porch.

"Too damn cold for you to be out here without a sweater, Mary Beth," McGregor hollered.

"Saw your truck out front," she hollered back. "And it's just way too cold for Zeus to be leashed to the porch swing. Bring that big boy in!" she demanded. "Hoppy and I've been waitin' for you to show your handsome face around here so he can show you...well you know," she whispered with a giggle, "our new plans!"

"Not until you feed us," McGregor said, giving her a hug. "Zeus and I are hoping you've got the fixings for a couple of open-faced, roast beef sandwiches, white bread please, with lots of gravy, and a side of mashed potatoes. Oh...and a small to-go container of beef and gravy to take home to Annie, too."

"Comin' right up," Mary Beth smiled as she took Zeus' leash and started to slip it under the leg of a table.

"No! you don't want to do that, Mary Beth," McGregor cautioned with a laugh. "If some big fat drunk comes in that front door and attempts to kiss you, and I come to your rescue— trust me, Zeus will flip that table right through your front windows as he comes to my aid. It happened just like that a few years back during a bar brawl in Maryland. Cost the service a fortune to have that window fixed," he said as he gently took the leash from Mary Beth's hand and slipped it under one leg of his chair.

"I ask you, Mr. Lawman! If some big fat drunk comes in that front door and attempts to kiss me, what makes you think I'm not going to...well, think about that while I shout up your order to Hoppy, who, I swear, is gettin' deafer every day. And when I tell him it's for you, well...be prepared for the happy-Hoppy blueprint show," she advised in a sing-song voice. "He's been busy spendin' that money," she giggled, whispering a bit louder.

This place has back-woods, small town atmosphere oozing from every cracked-vinyl seat, McGregor reminded himself as he looked settled himself in his chair. *And, the grub is exactly what you'd expect from a place located along a truck route at the crest of a mountain—food served hot, fast and in trucker-friendly portions. I hope Hoppy and Mary Beth don't get carried away and try to turn this place into a five-star palace of glitz and overstated glam!*

"Uh-oh, Zeus, here comes Hoppy out of the kitchen with a roll of papers tucked under his arm. Oh, Lord, and here comes Mary Beth, right behind him with our lunch. Brace yourself for trouble, big fella!"

"McGregor—Marshal, I mean—can I show you these plans while you eat?" Hoppy anxiously asked.

"No—you can't!" Mary Beth interceded, and nudged Hoppy aside.

"He can look and eat at the same time, don't ya think? Can't ya, McGregor?" Hoppy asked in a plaintive tone of voice.

"Why don't you *both* sit down for a minute and tell me—show me—what you've got!" McGregor suggested. "I'm in no hurry—I like to eat slowly, and actually, I'd enjoy visiting with both of you. Mary Beth, are you going to lay those plates down, or do Zeus and I have to tackle you?" She did, and McGregor enjoyed a few deep whiffs of the enticing aroma of beef and gravy before he dug in.

"Oh my, this is so good, Hoppy. You sure haven't lost your touch since you became wealthy—thank heavens! And, Mary Beth, you placed that plate in front of me just like a Playboy Bunny would. You're getting more beautiful by the day." Mary Beth giggled coyly and did a flirty pirouette before she and Hoppy sat down at the table.

"Okay, Hoppy, show me what you've got," McGregor said between bites. "It looks to me like you've been busy."

"Yep," Hoppy said with a grin. "I hired me one of those architect guys, and a contractor from Winchester City. I told them what we wanted, and, well, here it is! Whaddya think?"

"Well, looks to me like you're gonna put on a new front and a bigger front porch. I like that," McGregor said. "What's this, another dining room off the back of the room we're sitting in now?"

"Yep," Mary Beth chimed in. "Seats sixty people, and we're gonna have a buffet thingamajig built right in."

"Wow! You're gonna expand your parking lot too! That's great, and here it looks like you're gonna get a new and larger kitchen with all new equipment and ventilation. Am I right?" McGregor squinted at the plans.

"Nothin' but the best," Hoppy bragged.

"Now, I can't quite figure out what this room here is. Is it kinda off to the side of where we're sittin' right now? Looks like maybe you're going to put a door in over there," McGregor said, pointing to the east wall. "Are you gonna open a bar?"

"Beer only," Mary Beth said sharply while giving Hoppy a sour look. "Bad enough now how these loggers and gravel haulers drive their loads over this mountain as it is!"

"It's going to be a real man-cave, with big screen TVs and all that," Hoppy announced. "We're callin' it 'McGregor's Hide-a-Way.' We want a big picture of you to hang behind the bar!"

"I like the whole thing," McGregor said enthusiastically. "Except for one small thing, this is good work. When do you start construction?"

"Next week," Mary Beth said. "We want to have a grand opening in early spring. What's the small thing?"

"No picture of me behind the bar," McGregor insisted. "If you like I'll have a large picture of a Marshal's badge made for you."

"Hell, no," said Hoppy, "your picture would only scare away a few customers, but a badge around these parts—hell, you know I'd be outta business in a week!"

McGregor spent almost two hours eating and talking to Mary Beth and Hoppy about their renovation project, which included some major work on their house and land. He felt good about what he'd done to bring some of their hidden dreams to fruition. They agreed on a West Virginia Logo to be installed behind the bar.

"I'm honored to have a room in my name," he exclaimed as he pulled Zeus' leash from under the chair leg. "Time to go, Zeus, I've got a hot date with the airport at six o'clock," McGregor said as he picked up Annie's meal and walked to the cash register.

"Mary Beth, I understand that the caretaker I hired before my last trip racked up a tab while I was gone. It's okay, by the way; I gave him permission. I'm letting him live in the room over my garage, but I haven't had time to hire a contractor to put in a kitchen for him. And he's been too busy taking care of my dogs and horses, and fixing fences for me while I've been gone, to start the job himself. I'm going to hire him full time, so I'm sure he'll stop by once in a while, even after I get a kitchen up and running for him. So, I'll pay off his tab to date. Add it to my check, will you, please?"

"It on the house, Mr. McGregor—you're family here!"

"I appreciate that, Mary Beth. I really do, but, as a United States Marshal, I can't accept incentives or what you might call, freebies!"

"But you're retired!" Mary Beth said in a sad tone.

"That may be true," McGregor said, "and you and Hoppy *are* like family to me, and I appreciate your friendship more than you know, but I'm always going to maintain my code of professional ethics. That's just me. So, do you want me to come around the corner of this counter, and take a rolling pin to you, or what? Plus, Zeus is telling me he has to take a dump," McGregor laughed as he pulled two crisp one-hundred-dollar bills from his wallet and laid them on the cash register.

"Not enough? Start a new tab. Too much? Credit it to my tab. Gotta go now. Bye, Hoppy!" he yelled toward the kitchen as he and Zeus made a beeline for the front door and a grassy area at the far end of the parking lot.

"Good job, Zeus!"

163

CHAPTER NINETEEN

McGregor was still happily thinking about his afternoon with Mary Beth and Hoppy when he pulled his car into a parking place at Dulles that evening. As he put on his Travelers Aid badge and maroon sport coat and walked up the ramp from the short-term parking lot into the main terminal of an obviously busy airport, McGregor braced himself for the rush of problems and questions he was sure to encounter the moment he came into view of needy passengers.

Walk into any airport, it seems to me, he thought, *and you walk into an instant community of chaos, moving alongside an instant community of seasoned and savvy travelers—at times, pathetic, sad, and sometimes panic-stricken; at other times, routine, normal and ho-hum boring.*

He knew he'd be surrounded by people who have lost luggage, or can't find a phone that works; people who'd been left stranded by whoever forgot to pick them up; desperate tourists who neglected to make advance reservations and now couldn't find a place to stay—and those would be only a few of the multitude of other hard-to-fathom predicaments likely to crop up.

"Good evening, Molly and Dave," McGregor said. "Looks like you've had a busy shift. Perhaps you got everybody's problems solved and I can relax tonight?"

"Don't count on it, Cam; all the hotels in the Dulles area are booked up, buses are running late, and the taxis and shuttle buses are fighting to keep up with the business," Molly said stoically.

"What's goin' on?" McGregor asked.

"Nothing special that we can figure out," Dave answered. "Probably just a whole lot more of the same; it's Washington, you know!"

"How profound, Dave," McGregor laughed. "My God! Listen to that dude over there! Why is it that every time I'm at the airport there is always some annoying person on a Bluetooth remote telephone connection talking loudly, like there's no one else around? That guy's behavior is just plain arrogant and rude! The people around him shouldn't have to put up with his obnoxious behavior. Sometimes I believe that people like him take pleasure in knowing they're irritating; a 'me first, and only me' mindset. Don't you think?"

"Oh, I'm sorry, Cam," Molly acted surprised. "Were you talking to me? I couldn't hear a word you said because of that insufferable guy over there yelling at that device in his ear. Could you repeat whatever...?"

"Come again, Cam? I guess I wasn't listening!" Dave said.

"Never mind, guys; I'm just blowin' off steam," McGregor sighed.

"Okay, it's all yours, Cam. Come on, Molly, time to go. Let's let Cam solve problems for a while!" Dave said, handing Molly her coat. "Have a great shift, Cam!"

"Where have you been the past couple of weeks, anyway?" Molly asked as she and Dave exited the Travelers Aid booth.

"Thanks for asking, Molly. A good friend of mine passed away, and I had to go to Florida to help lay him to rest."

"I'm so sorry, Cam," she said sympathetically.

"Yeah, me too!" McGregor said. "I appreciate your sympathy."

"Excuse me, sir, the bus to L'Enfant Plaza?"

Off we go! McGregor thought. "No problem, that would be the 5A bus," he answered. "Take any door ramp down; go outside, cross the street, carefully mind you, until you reach the curb with the red awning. Look for a sign that designates 2E. The next bus leaves in...let me look...got it! —twenty-three minutes. Have a great trip!"

"Excuse me, sir, the restrooms?"

"Certainly" McGregor said. "Place your right foot toe directly behind your left foot heel and spin around one-hundred eighty degrees!"

"Uh...sorry sir, what does that mean?"

"The restrooms are right behind you," McGregor said flatly.

"Oh, I see them. Why didn't you say that in the first place?"

"You're right, I probably should have," McGregor admitted innocently. *So much for my attempt at military humor,* he thought as the man walked away.

"Hello, Loraine. You're early," McGregor said, as he reached over and opened the door to the Travelers Aid booth for his shift partner.

"Have Molly and Dave already left?" Loraine asked.

"Yeah," McGregor said. "I guess I was into one of my pontifical moods when I arrived and, well, they just bailed out!"

"So, what else *isn't* new?" she teased. "Regardless, I've missed you the past few weeks partner. Everything okay?"

"Great, actually," McGregor said. "You remember me talking to you about Hoppy's Place? Well, my dog Zeus and I had a wonderful lunch there this afternoon, and a great visit with the owners, Mary Beth and Hoppy Purcell. They recently came into some unexpected money, and they were anxious to show me their plans for an expansion of their restaurant. They're a great couple and just plain fun to listen to."

"You talk about going places with Zeus, but you also have a dog named Annie, I believe. How come you never seem to take Annie anywhere?" Loraine asked.

"Annie doesn't do cars well at all," McGregor explained. "She barfs before I even get out of my driveway. From there on, to anywhere, anytime, its gulp, gulp, barf all the way. Besides, I've convinced her, over time, that she's my

165

number one watchdog and needs to guard the house.... Uh, you've got a customer!"

"Hi, young lady, how can I help you?" Loraine asked.

"There are high-occupancy—HOV— lanes on the toll road leading to the airport. Right? The ones that require two or more people?"

"Yes," Loraine agreed. "You're absolutely right."

"Well," the young lady continued, "I'm pregnant. Do I count as one person or two?"

Loraine was quick in her response. "Hey, congratulations on your pregnancy," she smiled, "but in the HOV world, evidently you're still just one person. On the other hand, babies of any age count as a person. Just think, in a few months, you and your baby can use the Dulles HOV lanes anytime you want!"

"But, as a woman," the young lady lashed out, "do you think that's right? I mean wha…"

"Right or wrong," Loraine said calmly, "that's simply the way it is. Have a great evening."

"Well done, Loraine," McGregor commented after the young lady had left. "I couldn't have handled it better!"

"Oh, come on," Loraine snarked. "*You* would have botched that situation big time. I can hear your response now. Something like, 'well, you *chose* to get pregnant, and now you're blaming it on the HOV lanes?' Humph! By the way, speaking along those lines, how's *your* love life? Last time we talked you were hot for some chick who works for some association in D.C. I think I met her that time she came here to the airport looking for you. How's that going, Casanova?"

"Nowhere. Remind me to tell you about that situation sometime when we have a minute or two. She was something else......Yes, sir, how can I help you?" McGregor turned and asked a gentleman who'd just approached the counter.

"I just arrived on Turkish Airlines and I left my IPad in the seat pocket. I tried to go back and get it, but TSA wouldn't let me. What can I do?"

"I'll call the front desk at Turkish and we'll see if they can help. Hold on for a minute," McGregor said calmly. He spoke briefly on the phone for a minute and turned back to say, "Okay, my friend, I have a representative on the phone; he wants to talk to you. He's going to ask you for your seat number on that flight, if you can remember it, and then he's going to call out to the plane. They'll search for it. Here's the phone."

McGregor resumed his conversation with his partner, asking, in a subdued voice,

"So, Loraine, have you ever heard of Bellarmine's Cabinet? In downtown D.C.?"

Loraine gasped and turned three shades of red, before she whispered to McGregor. "Is *that* where you took her?"

166

"No, Loraine, *she* took me there. Hey, I can tell by the blush on your face that you..."

"No, I haven't! And my face is flushed, not blushed, simply because it's hot in here!"

"Well, it was hot in Bellarmines as well," McGregor smirked, as the man who was talking to the Turkish Airlines representative reached over the counter and hung up the phone.

"Any luck, sir?" McGregor asked.

"They found the case, but it was empty," the man said as he turned away from the counter. "I had hoped I'd be lucky, but..."

"You should file a police report while you're still here at the airport," McGregor quickly suggested. "I can call them for you if you'd like."

"Yeah, yeah, just forget it," the man responded in disgust and soon disappeared in the crowded terminal.

"Bellarmine's Cabinet?" Loraine whispered, "Isn't that a swingers club?"

"Yes, it is, but nothing happened," McGregor whispered back. "The date was a flop. The girl was just plain weird—actually, Loraine, the whole evening was weird. The second time I went out with her turned out strangely too." He shuddered a bit remembering Stacy's kinky behavior in contrast to her ethereal beauty.

"But...well... I recently met a woman who lives in Philly," he went on, "and I've got a date with her this weekend. There's something special about her. We've had lunch and dinner together, but we were both too busy to initiate a relationship beyond that. I gotta tell you, I'm really interested in knowing her better. I'm really looking forward to this weekend. I..." A nervous voice broke into McGregor's boyishly eager narrative.

"Excuse me, please, I've lost my mother. Her name is Claire Moody. The arrival board shows that her flight from St. Louis arrived at five forty-five and it's now almost seven o'clock. I called my sister, and she said that she did put my mother on that flight."

"Did your sister go to the airport and escort her to her flight?" McGregor asked gently.

"Yes, security let her go with her right to the gate because of, I'm sure, my mother's age and her very apparent confusion."

"Write down your mother's name," McGregor said, passing the young lady a pad of paper. "I'll page her for you."

"I've searched every part of the main terminal," she said, writing as she talked.

"Do you have a picture of her by any chance?" McGregor asked as he keyed in the password for the intercom system.

"I do, on my phone..." she said as he started his intercom announcement.

167

"Attention please! This is Travelers Aid. Would Ms. Claire Moody meet her daughter at the Travelers Aid information booth by baggage
claim number ten. Again, would Ms. Claire Moody meet her daughter at the Travelers Aid information booth by baggage claim number ten."

"Okay, ma'am," McGregor said in a reassuring voice, "while we wait a few minutes to see if mom heard that announcement and shows up here, I'm going to check and find out in which terminal and at what gate your mother's flight arrived. I need her airline and flight number. Do you have that information?

"I do," she answered, "and her carrier was Southwest, flight number 237."

"Okay, her flight de-planed its passengers at Gate 41, in the D terminal. Let me see her picture," McGregor said. "Okay, send that picture to my phone, and I'll go out to Terminal D and see if I can locate her. Here's my text info. Write down your name and your cell phone number so we can be in touch. Call me if she shows up here. I'll call you if I can find her. Do we have a plan?"

"You're wonderful, Mr. McGregor," she said, looking at his name tag.

"Oh, please don't tell him that," Loraine piped up, rolling her eyes towards the ceiling, "I have to work with him."

As McGregor made his way through the main terminal toward the employees' checkpoint to go through security and catch the shuttle to Terminal D, he heard a familiar voice call out his name. To his complete shock, it was Angelika Schafer.

"Cam, I was hoping you'd be here tonight! I thought I heard your voice on the intercom, and I was headed your way to find out. I just flew in from Miami—I'm on my way back to Berlin. I met a man who…"

"Is going to treat you right, keep you honest, and bathe you in gold?" McGregor said facetiously, as he gave her a hug."

"He'd better," she laughed. "I want to thank you so much for your kindness and understanding, that, interestingly, began right here in this airport. I'm catching my flight at ten o'clock—do you have time…"

"I don't, Angelika. I'm always on a mission—you know that. And, listen, I want to thank *you* for helping me in the Gonzales situation. We're even, okay? I wish you nothing but the best—drink a *Berliner Kindl* on tap for me!" McGregor said, as he entered the security checkpoint and disappeared.

That was interesting, McGregor thought as he stepped off the shuttle into the D terminal concourse. *Talk about surprise! Seeing her here again was a bit of a shock. Schafer and I started our acquaintance here at Dulles by accident, and we're ending it the same way. But the paths we followed in between were certainly strange. Hope she has a smooth flight back to Germany. At least it's a non-stop flight. Come to think of it, she's been on a non-stop flight ever since she and I first met!*

Within minutes, McGregor was able to spot an older woman matching the picture her daughter had shared with him, sitting alone in the middle of a row of seats in the waiting area just outside the door to Gate D 41. It was Claire Moody. Apparently, she thought her daughter would meet her there. He tried to call the daughter, but his call went immediately to voice mail. He disconnected that call and made another to the Travelers Aid desk.

"Loraine, Cam here. Please tell the lady waiting for her mother that I have mother Moody and will deliver her personally in about fifteen minutes."

"Good work, Cam! I suppose now you'll want some kind of reward or monetary raise out of your search and rescue mission?" Loraine smirked.

"Hmm, yeah, better make it thirty minutes. Mother Moody isn't all that bad looking," McGregor laughed as he abruptly ended the call.

The rest of the week went fast. Joan Taminelli sent McGregor the directions to her home in West Chester, along with a very inviting note. He'd be there for brunch Saturday morning by 11:00, and she'd gotten tickets for a musical at the Society Hill Playhouse in downtown Philadelphia for Saturday night. She hoped he'd spend Saturday night and as much of Sunday as he possibly could before returning home. McGregor didn't hesitate to respond positively on all counts.

As he backed his favorite Corvette out of the garage early that Saturday morning, his hopes for a wonderful weekend and perhaps a romantic interlude now and then, were interrupted by a call. The caller's name and number flashed on the car's console. It was Lawrence Brody.

"Larry! It's Saturday morning, for God's sake, take a break—get a life!" McGregor said, using his car's built-in Bluetooth connection as he coasted down the mountain to the highway below.

"Just wanted to share with you," Brody said, "that we got indictments on everyone we exposed in the MD 699 syndicate. Thirty-four to be exact, and we have charges pending on twenty-seven government people ranging from TSA, Immigration and Customs, Border Patrol, Dulles Airport Police, two Coast Guard officials, and three of my own agents. I think we've just about wiped out MD 699 as an active crime organization in the U.S.!"

"I hope you're right," McGregor said as he pulled off the road to talk. "But, well, think about this for a moment. Perhaps, just perhaps, De Smet felt, early on—even *before* the time I first ran into Angelika Schafer and the so-called security folks from the German Embassy—that, because you guys were getting close to exposing them, and were about to identify some of his big guns in the U.S. part of his syndicate—namely Girafalco and his bunch—he needed to set up a situation where, in a short period of time, we would able to flush them all out in the open. Kinda like what really happened! I'm thinkin', Larry, that De Smet set this whole thing up. He wanted to totally erase his U.S. operation so he could start all over with a clean slate—sort of a 'death by cop' scenario. Does this make any sense to you?"

"That's exactly what I want to talk to you about," Brody volunteered. "I *do* think we just finished a 'death by cop' cat and mouse game with this De Smet character, and I think that, if he's able to elude the arrest warrant out on him, he's got plans to rebuild his whole U.S. MD 699 branch—it may be already underway!"

After listening to what Brody had to say about the reason he was calling, it became quickly evident that Brody had something else in mind for McGregor than brunch in West Chester.

"Larry, you're a hard workin' cop!" McGregor said as he shifted his 'Vette from park to drive and slowly pulled back onto the road. "Speaking for the good citizens of the United States, I thank you sincerely for your efforts on everyone's behalf. However, my friend, *today*, I'm gonna take a break from trying to be *everything* to *everyone*. Today, I'd just like to be *everything* to *someone*. I'm gonna take a moment and make the best of it, without knowing what's gonna happen next. I'll call you Monday," he promised.

Casting off the momentary twinge of guilt at possibly pissing Brody off, and resetting his mind toward what might lie ahead—*another stage in the saga of my life?* —McGregor laughed out loud as he pressed hard on the accelerator, hitting the main highway north towards Philadelphia. Lying flat on the passenger seat beside him was a copy of that morning's Washington Post. He'd highlighted the first few lines of a cover story:

Aggressive FBI Tactics Produce Chilling Effects on MD 699 Crime Syndicate Activities

Justice Department Investigative teams have conducted extensive analysis to uncover internal links to Mirror Dot profile probe yet, and federal prosecutors are pursuing suspects in numerous high levels...

CHAPTER TWENTY

Stern winter loves a dirge-like sound. The line from a Wordsworth poem came to mind as McGregor stared morosely out the window at the snow-filled woods edging his northern Virginia home.

Fall has come and gone too quickly, he believed, and the winter season, well under way, seemed to cast an unearthly pall over the landscape. As he listened to the howls of the wind racing through the frigid air outside, it seemed, at least for the moment, as if he were stuck in a snow-white prison isolating him from the rest of the world. Through the blowing snow, he could barely see his handyman, Mike Soules, slowly maneuvering his tractor, blade deep down, crisscrossing the driveway leading to his house.

McGregor felt unusually restless that morning as he carefully added another log to the grate in the large fieldstone fireplace that rose grandly up the wall in his family room. He watched the flames embrace the seasoned wood as thoughts of the last few months turned over and over in his mind. So much had happened—disrupting the routine he'd established for himself in the three…almost four, now…years since his wife Polly died after a devastating struggle with cancer and his subsequent retirement from the U.S. Marshal Service.

When I was a recognized leader, I always had an identity. I always had a tag. I had an easy way of identifying myself to both myself and to others, he thought to himself. *What happens now that I don't have a purpose, when I don't have a place I have to be? The e-mail and phone calls will subside or perhaps completely disappear. My calendar will become unnecessary and replaced by a daily pill box that will dutifully inform me about days of the week.*

"OMG! I'm not going to know where to go in the morning, because it doesn't matter–it doesn't matter where I go…I have no fuckin' tag!" He shouted in frustration toward the view of Mike Soules and his tractor's running lights framed in the frosty window.

You know, Mike, there's never been a time in my adolescent or adult life when I'd ever question my "go to work, service to others," ideology. I mean, death might stop me, but aside from that I'm going to get to my job and play my real or perceived, but expected, leadership/service role—come hell or high water! But…what happens now…now that I've professed a screeching halt to such personal activities? How will I know who I am? he seemed to be asking the window.

"Whoa, partner! Keep perception and reality in sync!" would have been something that Polly probably would have told me about now," McGregor quickly reminded himself. *She would doubtless say that someone forgot to tell you that there is no leadership cookbook containing a final chapter title titled,*

"Taking the trash to the curb on Wednesday Evening, he surmised. *"Come on, perhaps it's not exactly that bad,"* she would undoubtedly exclaim. *You know that like every other system, organism, enterprise or person on this earth, shit happens. Life gets more complicated—nothing quite stays the same."*

His experience with a seemingly lost passenger at Dulles International Airport that had quickly and unexpectedly turned into a major and far-reaching take-down of at least a branch of the international Mirror-Dot (MD 699) crime syndicate, forcing him to temporarily abandon retirement, was, to a certain degree, "stuck" in his mind.

Maybe, he cautiously speculated, *the pull to be one of the "good guys" again is what's causing my restlessness this morning! The images of chase-driving and slamming on my car's brakes just short of the edge of a cliff, awesome rooftop chases in L.A., busting in the doors of sweet, multi-million dollar Manhattan apartments rented by elusive 20-something drug dealers, tracking down fugitives on private islands, and all those many road trips to somewhere and nowhere still seem fresh in my mind.*

These were the moments, memories and images that had showcased his life as a U.S. Marshal at the most vital and extraordinary points in his career, and McGregor knew that it was these flashback moments that kept enticing him to "re-up." However, it was common-sense that kept telling him that he'd done enough, and that it was time to just relax and enjoy his elder years in safety and comfort.

Dan Conroy, the FBI agent with whom McGregor had worked on the Miami murder of Roberto Gonzales, had surprised him when he took the job of Chief of Police in Key West—a position that had quickly opened after McGregor exposed the previous chief for an act of misconduct in office. Both Hans Mueller, now Assistant Chief of Police in Miami, and Conroy had asked McGregor to return to Key West for a few weeks to help Conroy reorganize the department and assist him in reducing a significant backlog of tricky cases that former Chief of Police Purvis Chapter had allegedly sat on—some of which, they suspected, had, and might still have, ties with the MD 699 syndicate. McGregor had told them that he'd think about it, but only after the completion of a diagnosis of the medical condition of his eldest horse, Whisper, who had been his wife Polly's personal favorite.

Over the past few months, Whisper had been showing signs of fast becoming a senior citizen with symptoms that were disturbing. Her gait had become choppier, and her overall energy level and appetite had decreased dramatically. McGregor's veterinarian friend, Steve Willingham, had looked at her during the past week and, at his insistence, McGregor had quickly delivered Whisper to Willingham's clinic for a series of diagnostic procedures, including a full-body ultrasound, an endoscopy of the respiratory system, stomach and bladder, and high resolution radiography if Steve deemed it necessary. Pushing his concern for Whisper to the back of his mind, he looked out the window again and saw that Soules had finished plowing the driveway and was now hand-shoveling the walkway leading to McGregor's front porch.

Bracing himself against the chill, McGregor opened the front door and leaned out. "Coffee break, Mike!"

"Heard anything about Whisper yet?" Soules asked as he stomped the snow from his boots. "She was not looking good when you loaded her up the other day."

"The vet's supposed to call me when they find out anything. Maybe later today...actually, perhaps right now," McGregor said, pulling his vibrating cell phone from his pocket and checking the caller ID. It was Willingham. McGregor braced himself for the worst.

"Sorry to have to tell you this Cam, but Whisper passed away last night. She went down in her stall— basically her heart gave out," Willingham said sympathetically. "She had advanced stomach cancer and she chose to go out on her own terms—she spared you the pain of having to put her down, which, by the way, was something you and I were going to have to visit about sometime today anyway. But now, well...she's running free in the wind and lying down in a grassy..."

"Please bring her to me, Steve," McGregor abruptly interrupted. "I wanna lay her to rest here," he said, terminating the call. This news was exactly what he'd been hoping *not* to hear.

"Get yourself some coffee, Mike! I need to go to the barn and talk to Shadow. Then meet me in the south pasture, just this side of the *roche moutonnée* formation. Please bring the tractor after you hook up the back hoe...leave the blade on the front, check the oil and hydraulic fluid—it's colder than a witches left tit in the pasture—don't forget to top off the gas tank," McGregor said as he pulled his extreme weather gear from the mud room closet.

Mike remained silent, but McGregor knew he was hearing every word he said and that he had deduced the news McGregor had just received from the vet. He knew what they were about to do. As McGregor turned to give him a silent signal of acknowledgement of their mutual grief, he couldn't help but notice the tears streaming down Mike's cheeks.

"You've not lost her, Cam," Mike said, swallowing hard, "just outlived her."

As McGregor slid the barn door open and approached Shadow's stall, he sensed that somehow Shadow already knew that Whisper would not be racing him through the woods that day or any day thereafter. McGregor stroked him softly between the eyes to calm him and let him know that he was in safe hands. Shadow slowly lowered his head so that McGregor could easily bridle him. As he finished saddling him up, he quietly reminded Shadow that they would have been much poorer if not for Whisper's shining presence in their lives. Shadow knew.

"Take me to the south pasture, my friend—Mike is waiting for us," he said to Shadow as they left the solitude of the barn. "We have important work to do!"

McGregor sat astride Shadow, huddled against the icy winter wind, as Soules gently leveled the ground over Whisper's final resting place.

"My good dear friend Whisper, I'll smile every time I see your bright eyes and perky ears in my mind," he said softly as Shadow quietly scuffed the freshly turned soil. "And I'll feel sad, not for what I've had, but for the people that go through life never having such an experience. You were my talker, Whisper—Shadow never has much to say," he said patting Shadows neck. "But you always had a whinny, whuffle, neigh or soft whicker for each situation. Today, Whisper, your voice fell soundless—except, for always, endlessly in my mind. Shadow knows."

CHAPTER TWENTY-ONE

Winter's biting chill was still full-on as McGregor inched his way down the mountain in his truck—his four-wheel drive fully engaged to help him plow through the drifts and hold him in place as he maneuvered the many S-turns that would eventually take him to the piedmont plateau at the base of Bull Run mountain. Despite weather conditions, Dulles airport was open 24-7, and TA volunteers made a special effort to be on hand, especially for those unfortunately stranded by canceled flights.

Everything at the airport seems to be measured this afternoon, McGregor noted as he walked past the slow-moving lines of people waiting at the security gates—all apparently over-anxious to get to their planes. Deeper into the airport, others fought the human traffic bunched impatiently around the baggage claims—all, it seemed, to be equally anxious to get the hell out of there.

Over the years, I've learned that the predominant cost of any type of waiting is often an emotional one for air passengers: stress, boredom, and for some, McGregor laughed to himself, *even a self-declared sensation that their life is slipping away.* He knew that: *the last thing people want to do with their dwindling leisure time is squander it in stasis, and their frustrations often play out in complaints to TA volunteers like me! I know from experience that the minute I put on my conspicuous Travelers Aid jacket and identification badge, I will immediately become a prime target for "air rage."*

"Approach airport difficulties with a sense of celebration," he'd advise frustrated travelers. "Say to yourself, 'I can get through this; I will get through this—it's part of the process; it is what it is'"—words that he knew, more often than not, would fall on deaf ears.

This could be one of those days, he supposed as he looked at flight cancellations and delays posted on the arrival and departure board as he approached his duty desk and greeted his long-time Travelers Aid partner, Loraine Pelliter.

"Let me guess, partner," McGregor smiled. "Cancelled flights because of the snow? Missed connections? Hotels booked up. Luggage misdirected to other destinations?"

"All of the above, and then some—just another day at the airport," Loraine sighed. "Mike Soules called me this morning about Whisper. I'm so sorry. I know…"

"Yes sir, can I help you?" McGregor was interrupted from his conversation with Loraine to direct a person to the international arrivals area to meet his son who was flying in from Paris. "Your son will be on the ground in about twenty minutes," McGregor said after checking arrival updates on his computer. "It'll take him about an hour and a half or so to get to, and though, customs and immigration, so you've got time for coffee as you walk to the other end of the terminal where you'll find the waiting area for people meeting and picking up international travelers. Anything else I can help you with?"

"Nope, that's all I needed to know. Thanks," the man said as he turned and headed toward the international arrivals area.

As he watched the man walk away, McGregor turned his attention back to his partner. "So, Loraine how ya been?" McGregor smiled.

"Well," she started, "glad you asked. "My friend Tommy and his brother are very successful businessmen in Baltimore. They have over two hundred employees working for them in a three hundred thousand square foot warehouse near the Baltimore Harbor. They're in the freight forwarding business, Burroughs Brother's Shipping and Containment, Inc., and both were close friends of my late husband."

"Excuse me, Loraine...Yes, ma'am, how can I help you?" McGregor asked a woman who approached him.

"Thank you, how do I get to my plane— Delta 4344 to Newark?"

"Do you have your boarding pass?"

"Not yet," she said.

"You need a boarding pass. Go upstairs—one floor up—the escalator or elevators, which ever you wish, are right there," McGregor said, pointing to his left. "The Delta ticket counter will be on your left when you get off. Have a great trip."

"Anyway," Loraine continued, "their trucks pick up goods arriving at the Port of Baltimore and then take them to their warehouse for storage until they receive instructions from their customers to size and package the goods and then ship the goods to their customers' retail stores across the U.S.A. and..."

"Excuse me, again, Loraine...Yes, ma'am, how can I help you?"

"I've been waiting for over twenty minutes for my luggage," a well-dressed women, a businesswoman, he assumed, declared angrily. "What's wrong with you people?"

"All due respect, ma'am," McGregor replied, "my partner and I do not work for any airline nor do we work for the airport. We're volunteers for Travelers Aid, and I can assure you—nothing's wrong with us—we're fine. That said, let's start again. How can either of us help you?"

"Okay, how the hell do I get my luggage from U.S. Air?"

"What baggage carousel have you been waiting at?" McGregor asked softly, glancing at his computer.

"Number five!" she said, softening her voice as well.

"Your luggage is on baggage claim 12."

"How was I supposed to know that?" she blurted, her voice rising again.

"It's posted on all of the arrival boards. If your luggage is not there, please come back and I'll help you track it down."

176

"Hmmph! Fine way to run an airport," the woman muttered under her breath as she stalked off toward baggage claim 12.

Loraine turned and grinned at McGregor. "Good job, Cam. Now, as I was about to say, my friends have done quite well financially over the years. Their company is also licensed by U.S. Customs to inspect incoming containers arriving at the Port of Baltimore, which is another lucrative business. They're..."

"Hi, Loraine...hi, Cam. How are things going?" a pleasant voice said as an efficient-looking older woman approached the counter. Mary McCory, from the main office of Travelers Aid in D.C., often stopped by to visit the desks whenever she happened to be at Dulles.

"Look around you, Mary! This place is a zoo today! First the west escalator broke down; then somebody's dog threw up down by the east ATM machine. More than the average number of people have had the clasps fail on suitcases, allowing for the disorderly display of a variety of objects, not to mention unmentionables. The human temperament quotient is off the chart, whatever that means, but, hey! Business as usual," Loraine said with a shrug. "Half of what we do is hand-holding, and...we're damn good at it!"

"I'm going to be waiting here for a few minutes to meet a passenger whom Travelers Aid is flying here from Santa Fe, New Mexico," McCory explained. "I'm told by our volunteer staff at Sunport International Airport in Albuquerque that the woman is willing to take a risk, to change her life for the better. According to our Sunport volunteers, this lady has been subjected to long-term physical and emotional abuse from her husband. Evidently, she's tried to flee before, but because her husband had total control over their money and friends, she was never successful. She would go to a safe house, but he would always find her and force her back home. She's been in this terrible situation for years, but this time, I'm told, she's determined to get as far away from her husband as possible and not leave a trail for him to follow."

"And, at this point, you're involved how?" Loraine asked.

"Well," McCory continued, "to make a long story short—early this morning, with previous guidance from Travelers Aid, she packed up her three children as soon as her husband left for work. When she arrived at the Travelers Aid desk at SunPort this morning, our social worker was there to meet her. He'd already arranged for plane tickets for them, using numbers instead of names—you know, to protect their identity—and he placed her and her children on a Southwest flight here to Dulles, where we've arranged for them to be taken to a safe house to begin their new life. Isn't that cool?" McCory said with a big grin.

"*Very* cool, Mary. Let us know if you need support," McGregor smiled as he turned toward a young man standing in front of the desk.

"You look a bit distressed, my man. How can I help?" he asked.

"Would you believe that no one in this airport will accept, much less break, a $100 bill! I've tried every store and, for God's sake, even the branch bank. And, no, I don't carry any credit or debit cards; therefore, I don't have an

177

ATM card—I believe in a cash only society! All I've got is this $100 bill and three $1 bills," the young man steamed.

"Okay," McGregor leaned toward the young man. "What am I'm missing here?" he asked. "What is it that you really need help with? I mean, I got the big denomination bill problem but…?"

"Other than a $100 bill," the young man interrupted, "I only have $3 in cash—I need $7 to get out of the airport's parking garage!"

"Got it now," McGregor exclaimed. "That's a problem I can solve for you right now," he said as he reached into his wallet and presented the young man with four $1 bills.

"Here's my name and address—send me $4 as soon as you can. In the meantime, you might want to rethink your aversion to ATM cards, especially when you travel."

"Wow, thank you, man, I can't believe it," the young man said. "Somebody's actually being nice to me."

"Right! Now go forth, young man; slay some dragons, free Willy, and protect the planet—but not before you rescue your car from the notorious airport parking garage, and… repay your loan," McGregor said in a pontifical voice. "Oh, and you should probably avoid toll roads after you leave the airport!"

"Submit a voucher, Cam," McCory advised. "We'll reimburse you your $4."

"Not necessary, Mary, but thank you, anyway. He'll repay me within a week's time, I'm willing to bet."

"Cam's an easy touch, Mary," Loraine laughed. "His win-loss record is standing at about fifty-fifty—far better, however, than his casino rating."

"At least casinos have bill-breaking machines," McGregor huffed.

McCory giggled. "That's all we need in this airport…more machines to confuse the public and break down at irregular intervals!... Oh! I'll bet that's the mother and children I've been expecting," she exclaimed, eyeing a tired looking young woman with three over-active children heading toward her.

"See you guys later, and thanks for your service."

"Thank *you*, Mary," they both chimed in unison as Mary scurried away.

"No doubt," Loraine noted, "she doesn't go out of her way as often as she does for some kind of an intrinsic reward. She gives selflessly. That said Cam, can we get back to personal issues?" Loraine insisted. "So, anyway, my friend and his brother were dating two women who were employees of the company. I know, before you say it—bad policy. Eventually both brothers became disenchanted with their girlfriends and broke up with them. Then both brothers went on to marry two other women. One wife is a friend of mine, and we had lunch together last week. That's where I heard about their predicament."

"Ah, hell hath no fury like a woman scorned," McGregor smirked. "And since there were two unhappy ladies—that translates into a kind of double…"

"*Please,* Cam! Get serious and pay closer attention. Here's where it gets a little complicated," Loraine continued, a serious look on her face. "One of the ex-girlfriends decided to marry an informant who was working for a Special Agent of the U.S. Immigration Service because she wanted to become a legal resident of the U.S.A.—she was from the Philippines. Her husband, the informant, and the immigration agent were also Filipino, and both were U.S. citizens. Are you following this scenario so far?"

"I'm trying. Hold on for a moment…Yes, ma'am, how can I help you?"

"Where can I plug my cell phone in? I need to charge the battery."

"Right over there," McGregor said, pointing to a bank of wall sockets. "You can use my desk phone if you wish."

"No, but thank you. It'll only take a moment for me to plug it in and make my call."

"Okay, Loraine, back to your story. One of the Burroughs brothers was dating a Filipino woman who was illegally in the United States. He dumped her, and she married the informant of a U.S. Immigration agent. Am I on track?"

"Yes, Cam, but then the U.S. Immigration agent fell for his informant's wife and decided to have an affair with her. The agent then sent his informant out of town continually so he could shack up with the informant's wife."

McGregor's eyebrows shot up toward his hairline. "Are you kidding me? This sounds like it's straight out of David and Bathsheba! You know…the biblical account of.…

"Rea-a-lly," Loraine continued. "Now, for any number of reasons, they— the ex-girlfriends—still burned from being dumped by the two brothers, decided they wanted to inflict some serious pain on their ex-boyfriends, my friend and his brother. So, the U.S. Immigration agent tells the two ex-girlfriends that he'll teach the brothers a lesson they'll never forget. Now, Cam, remember the agent's no paragon of virtue, as he's sleeping with his informant's wife—one of the ex-girlfriends. And, you'll recall that there were over two hundred employees working at my friend's warehouse. So, then, the agent waltzed into my friend's office one day and told him…yes, sir, may I help you?"

Loraine was interrupted for a moment by a man seeking information on the best ways to travel from the airport into the heart of downtown D.C. She deftly handled his inquiry and turned back to her conversation with McGregor.

"Anyway," Loraine continued, jumping back into her tale, "as I was saying, the immigration agent waltzed into my friend's office one day and told him that he was in violation of U.S. Immigration law, because, the agent claimed, nearly all of his employees were illegally in the country and that the fine for hiring illegals would be in the thousands. Now here's where the story stops being humorous."

"Wait, wait…hold on. What did I miss? What humor?" McGregor asked.

179

"Oh, Cam, you're getting old and stodgy. Anyway, the immigration agent suggested to my friend that all of this could go away if a small, under-the-table payoff was forthcoming. And then, believe it or not, after that conversation, the immigration agent goes to the FBI and tells them that he was bribed by my friend, and that my friend and his brother are transporting drugs throughout the United States via their delivery trucks. He also told them that my friend is paying off U.S. Customs agents to bring more trucks into his facility for inspection so he can make more money, and that he's paying his employees off the record and not declaring payroll tax."

"Is this for real, Loraine... are you bull-shitting me?" McGregor groaned.

"Then, to top it all off, my friend and his brother have discovered," Loraine continued, "that the ex-girlfriends have been breaking into their warehouse and stealing goods belonging to their customers."

"Loraine?"

"And then selling the goods at swap meets."

"Loraine?"

"Well, what do you think, Cam?"

"It's not so much what I think, Loraine, It's what I..." McGregor was interrupted by a man who was dressed, head to toe, in an outfit that, to some, including McGregor, that might lead one to think he was attempting to emulate one of Batman's arch enemies, the Mad Hatter!

Oh, my God! McGregor and Loraine rolled their eyes at each other.

"How can I help you," McGregor asked, holding back a snicker, "...love your hat!"

"I am well known for my green-colored hat which you may notice is slightly oversized, as it houses my mobile mind-manipulating devices. You know, of course, that the mind is the weakest part of a person."

"Ah, yes...I guess. So, again, *how* can I help you," McGregor asked a bit testily. "Or perhaps you could just manipulate my *weak mind* to know what you want, and then I could perhaps help you in some way?"

"Do you have the time?" the man asked.

"Yes, I have the time," McGregor answered while noticing that Loraine was on the phone with airport security. "What did you have in mind?"

"No! See, you have a weak mind. I want to know what time it is," the man asserted, and pointed sharply at McGregor's wristwatch.

"Oops, I guess your 'mobile mind-manipulating device' is not working. Sorry about that. It's exactly 7:48 p.m. Is there anything else I might be able to help you with?"

"Yes, what is your name so I can put you on my list?"

"Bruce Wayne, of course." McGregor quickly replied. "You may think I'm simply a volunteer here, but really, I'm a billionaire playboy, industrialist, and philanthropist," he said, killing time waiting for airport security to arrive. "Having witnessed the murder of my parents as a child, I swore revenge on criminals, an

180

oath tempered with the greater ideal of justice. Now, what's your name so I can formally introduce you to the Gotham City Police Department officers standing behind you?"

"Good job, Batgirl," McGregor said to Loraine as airport security led the man away to question him.

"You really shouldn't tease people like that, Cam" Loraine scolded. "Who knows what he was all about. Did you grow up on comic books?"

"*Au contraire*, Loraine, I wasn't teasing him, just keeping him well occupied and away from others in the terminal while you called security. Actually, you might say I was manipulating *his* mind. And, just so you know...comic books *are* my friends! I keep a stack in my bathroom to aid in my meditative moments." He grinned conspiratorially as Loraine sighed in exasperation.

"Now, about your friends, the brothers." McGregor pushed. "Clearly, *very* clearly, they *need* a good lawyer."

"Well," she frowned, "It seems like every time we've worked together lately, you're smack dab in the middle of some new investigation that, if I remember correctly, you swore when you retired from the Marshals Service, you'd avoid like the plague. But then...well...I just thought maybe you'd have a thought or two...or...perhaps you could..."

"Okay, listen, I'll think about it. Burroughs Brothers Shipping and Containment, Inc. Right? In the meantime—oops, excuse me. Loraine—back to you in a minute. It looks like we have a passenger in distress!"

McGregor quickly turned his attention toward an elderly gentleman approaching the desk.

"Yes, sir, you look concerned. I'll bet I can help you!"

"Your cell phone's ringing, Cam. I'll take care of this gentleman," Loraine said as she beckoned the man toward her end of the counter.

McGregor acknowledged Loraine's offer and answered his phone. It was the Marshals office in Philadelphia informing him that U.S. Marshal Joan Taminelli had been killed in the line of duty that afternoon. McGregor stood in shocked silence for a moment then thanked the caller for the information. While the call had automatically triggered a "fight or flight" response in his brain, the sheer weight of sadness drew him away from the counter and into a chair.

"It was bad news, Loraine, gotta go now!"

"Cam?"

"I'll be okay," he said as he pulled himself up from the chair, put on his coat, and walked toward an airport exit.

"I'll be okay."

Reaching his car, he got in and wearily leaned back against the headrest.

How many devastating losses can a person sustain in such a short time and still be...okay?

181

CHAPTER TWENTY-TWO

The temperature was falling fast, and a wind chill advisory was in effect as McGregor stood, stoic, near Joan Taminelli's gravesite at Philadelphia's Rocky Hill cemetery. The minister was talking, but McGregor was looking past Taminelli's coffin, his attention miles away.

Conch tastes like rubber bands to me, he'd told her during their accidental dinner meeting in Key West. Later, she'd revealed to him the scientific principles of *blobs and interblobs.* She'd given him her phone number before they parted that evening, and they'd become close in the months following that chance meeting. It was the silly exchange of banter that made that first meeting special.

"You okay, Cam?"

McGregor felt a hand on his shoulder. It was his friend, Lawrence Brody, Assistant Director of the FBI.

"This is FBI special agent Graham Blake from our Philadelphia office. He was at the courthouse when Marshal Taminelli was killed and the last person to talk to her. As soon as we're finished here, I want to get the two of you together to discuss why he thinks Taminelli *wasn't* personally targeted. Blake has some theories."

"Wasn't targeted! Hell, she's...never mind, I'm finished, gentlemen," McGregor said stiffly as he turned and headed toward the cemetery parking lot. The other two quickly followed him.

"It's colder than the last man's ass on a toboggan up here," Blake snorted as he tried to keep pace with McGregor.

McGregor shot him a stern look.

"She didn't suffer, Marshal," Blake offered," she ..."

"And you know that how?" McGregor barked. "Did you ask...forget it...sorry."

"She died instantly," Blake continued. "I was walking her to her car which was parked at the curb in front of the federal courthouse. As we got to her car, she remarked about how lucky she'd been to find a place right in front of the courthouse. 'An unusual event,' she'd commented as I continued walking toward my car which, as usual, was parked at least a block away. I recall my reply, 'great, Marshal Taminelli, you got really lucky today.' Suddenly I was knocked to the sidewalk by a fierce explosion and as I looked up—well— her car had been blown to smithereens— not much left 'cept twisted metal and lots of black smoke and fire. I didn't know her all that well, but..."

McGregor stopped abruptly. "Who did it, Agent Blake? Bottom line, who are you looking at?"

"I studied your work on the Mirror Dot 699 thing down in Florida," Blake began. "I'm seeing some of the same tell-tale M.O. in a syndicate currently working out of the Baltimore and Philadelphia areas—headed by a mobster who lives and works out of New Castle, Delaware. The case that was in adjudication in the federal courthouse in Philly, when Taminelli got hit, had to do with what I suspected was a middle management syndicate guy we had up on money-laundering and tax evasion charges. The bomb incident was a warning message to the court—probably ordered up from New Castle and had nothing to do with Taminelli—her car was just in the wrong place. I'm getting ready to…."

"Got a name and folder for the guy on trial that day?" McGregor interrupted.

"Yeah, I can get…"

"Got a name on the New Castle guy?"

"Oh, yeah, I…"

"And?" McGregor asked as he continued walking toward the parking lot.

"Lorcan Malachy," Blake said as he scrambled to keep up with McGregor's pace, "the scumbag currently on trial for alleged money-laundering and tax evasion charges, is a middle management syndicate guy who is probably not indispensable in the overall syndicate scheme. Nevertheless, the syndicate has to show its power and influence in his defense to keep others in the organization appeased and law enforcement advised that 'messing with the syndicate can mean dangerous misfortune for officials'—thus the bomb that was planted and detonated in front of the courthouse. I believe that one Redmond Satran from New Castle is calling the shots and…"

"I know you want probably want me on this, Larry." McGregor interrupted Blake again and looked straight at Brody. "I warned you in our last conversation, right after I finished my work on the Washington and Miami syndicate of MD 699, that I felt that the leader of the syndicate was playing games with us and had counted on us cleaning up his mess so he could start over with a clean slate. It sounds exactly like what's going down."

"I reactivated you the minute I heard about Taminelli's death," Brody said. "The case is yours if you want it."

"Which I don't, Larry! Period! It sounds to me like Blake has a handle on the situation. End of conversation!" McGregor turned, pulled the collar on his coat up as far as it could go and continued the trek toward his car. "Sorry about my impatience, gentlemen, blame it on the circumstances— including the weather. I'm outta here."

McGregor sat silently in his car for a moment looking back toward the blue canopy and the several blue velvet-covered folding chairs beside Taminelli's gravesite.

Between heaven, if there is such a place, and earth; between light and dark; between faith and sin, yet again, lies only my broken heart, he was thinking as he drove slowly away from the cemetery parking lot.

Story of my whole fuckin' life!

CHAPTER TWENTY-THREE

"Mirror Dot 699. Same M.O. In the Baltimore and Philadelphia areas—headed by a mobster who lives and works out of New Castle, Delaware," were the words that Agent Blake had used a few weeks earlier at Joan Taminelli's interment—words that were still fresh in McGregor's mind as he carefully watched an older model station wagon slowly inch its way up the serpentine drive to his house. He picked up his binoculars.

Three girls, one boy—look like college age kids. Maryland license plates, Maryland barcode Tax sticker on the left rear window. Rocker panel damage on the passenger side. 2004 Ford, worn tires having problems with traction in the light snow covering the driveway. Looks like they're lost—and now stuck. Mike has seen them too—is walking down the hill towards them. Perhaps I should make some hot chocolate? Hot chocolate? That's SO not like me! Where the hell did that come from?

"Zeus, head down the hill and help Mike if he needs you," McGregor said as he opened the front door and stepped outside for a moment.

What the hell, Mike's getting them out of the car and bringing them up here! Do I even have any hot chocolate mix?

"They're here to see you. Someone from the justice department sent them," Soules announced in a cell phone call to McGregor.

"Bring 'em inside, take 'em to the den, stoke the fire, and teach them how to drive in the snow and how to use the phone to make an appointment in advance to visit—I'll be there in a minute," McGregor muttered at his phone as he headed toward the kitchen.

"Who doesn't want hot chocolate on a cold winter day?" McGregor asked as he walked into the den balancing a tray with six mugs full of steaming hot chocolate.

"Two percent milk," he confessed. "Best I can do! No marshmallows, I'm sorry to say. Actually, I do have some, but they've turned to semi-white gummy things. So, who are you people anyway and why are you here other than the fact that your car is stuck in my driveway? Let me start. I'm Cameron McGregor and this is my foreman—I guess you've already met him—Mike Soules. These are my dogs, Zeus and Annie."

"Agent McGregor, I'm Cindy Henderson, and I'm a journalism student at American University. In fact, all four of us are Journalism majors."

Brown Uggs, black leggings, hooded sweatshirt, McGregor noted. *Great hair, beautiful complexion, wonderful smile…*

"And this is Bonny Covington, that's Susan Murray, and he's Trevor Wiley. Last week all four of us went to the headquarters of the U.S. Marshals and met with a gentleman named Corey Benjamin—Public Relations Officer. He said you knew him?"

"Yep, Benjamin and I worked together years ago when he was just a rookie. Good guy," McGregor volunteered.

"Well, bottom line, he couldn't, or perhaps wouldn't help us, but he suggested that I might contact you for some guidance on what we might do to get a case out of a 'cold file' status and people back in action. You see," Henderson continued, "my father, Eugene Henderson, was brutally murdered two years ago this week in a park just across the Potomac from D.C. Both D.C. and Virginia are classifying it as a cold case—and the FBI? Well—the same. You're a U.S. Marshal. You belong to what you guys advertise as 'a team that won't quit.' I'm here with my friends to ask you to..."

"Didn't Benjamin tell you I'm retired?"

"He suggested you might say that," Henderson retorted, "but he also said that you'd just finished a case and that you were reactivated."

"I'll go dig their car out," Soules quickly said, anticipating that the group would momentarily be making a quick exit. He thought to himself *this just ain't gonna happen* as he left the room.

"I was reactivated just for that specific case, nothing more, and nothing less. I'm retired and to tell you the truth, I'm..."

"Marshal McGregor," Wiley interrupted, evidently thinking that McGregor needed some "inspiration" for the request Henderson was about to present to him and launched into an oratorical rant that he thought might smooth the way for Henderson.

"You know," he leaned forward and intoned somberly, "when U.S. Marshal Matt Dillon, who kept the peace in rough and tumble Dodge City, crossed the street to the Long Branch Saloon where Miss Kitty was waiting for him—waiting just like she always was—Suddenly a shot rang out!"

"Gunsmoke? You gotta be kiddin," McGregor exclaimed. "Mr. Wiley, what the...?"

"Dillon could tell by the sound that the shot came from Chester," Wiley continued, "who was firing his 1873 Colt with ejector housing that allowed it to duplicate the single-action Peacemaker for fast firing. He owned the only one in Dodge City, so Marshal Dillon knew, without a doubt, that Chester was on the prowl."

"Oh... my... God," McGregor muttered.

"Chester could be heard in the distance bellowing 'stop, you sniveling, snot-nosed sidewinder before I shoot your ugly boots right off your nasty feet!'"

"Mr. Wiley," McGregor interrupted, "I don't know where that eruption of words came from. And I know I didn't lace your hot chocolate with weed, so what's this got to do..."

"Dillon heard other noises as well," Wiley continued, apparently unfazed by McGregor's reactions. "The inevitable dog was barking somewhere in a distant

187

alley, and the blacksmith was busy pumping his bellows to deliver air to his forge. But none of that was really important to him at that moment— Kitty was waiting. Dillon was hungry and *not about to quit* in his relentless quest for Kitty's fantabulous fixin's, much less her…"

"Mr. Wiley," McGregor interrupted again, "where the hell are you going with this vintage story-line histrionic nonsense?"

"But Marshal Dillon, knew," Henderson interrupted in turn as McGregor sat gaping in astonishment, "without any doubt at all, that Chester would corral whatever culprit he was chasin' even if he had to chase him from Dodge City all the way to San Fran-cisco. Chester was a Deputy Marshal—he was part of a *team that won't quit*! *Your* team, Marshal McGregor! Retired or not," she exclaimed as she pointed her finger toward him. "My father was executed—shot and dumped in a storm sewer. My family wants to know why and who did it. It's not a cold case to us! The only thing cold about this situation is the 'turn-off attitude' we keep getting from federal, state and local authorities."

"Okay, let's get serious here," McGregor insisted. "Put your finger back in its holster, Cindy Henderson! What is it you want from me? This isn't Dodge City I'm not Matt Dillon, and this is not drama school! This is here…and…now! Your father's death probably isn't a story about hot summers, rain on the asphalt, the woman with the lipstick or the guy in the fedora. That's the stuff TV mysteries and cheap novels thrive on, and this is neither! No cigarette ash and alienation. No souped up cars, tough guys, snub-nosed pistols, the ice melting in the bourbon. I don't have to tell any of you that this is real life and real death. Bottom line—I don't know anything about your father's case and…"

"I want to hire you to find out who killed my father and why!" Henderson thundered.

"Hold on a minute, Cindy," McGregor said quietly but firmly. "First, I'm not for hire at any price—sorry. Second, you're assuming I have the time for this—sorry again. Third, I'm unhappy that you made this trip for nothing, and finally, well, drive carefully when you leave—I'll walk you to the door."

McGregor growled as he watched the Ford and its young passengers carefully work its way down his drive toward the main road.

"What the fuck! Zeus! Damn it! You coulda helped me out instead of just sitting next to me and yawning. And Annie…!"

Over the next few days, McGregor's mind kept returning to the look on Cindy Henderson's face when she mentioned her father's murder. Her eyes had locked onto his as she pleaded for his help.

That look in her eyes. Her father. If she'd been my daughter and something had happened to me…what would my daughter…? Somewhat reluctantly, he picked up the phone and called Marshal Corey Benjamin's office. He asked for the complete file on Eugene Henderson.

188

"No, Corey, you got me into this, and you can damn well deliver the file to me in person and bring me up to date on anything else about this case!" he'd demanded. "Otherwise there's a post in Adak, Alaska just begging for your personal attention and consummate services. Remember, as Cindy Henderson and her friends recently reminded me, you're part of a *team that won't quit*! Yes, Corey, you got yourself into this thing—yep, all by yourself. Yes, this afternoon will be fine. I strongly recommend," McGregor chuckled, "that since you're a city boy, you might consider requisitioning a four wheel drive for your trip—and, while you're at it, bring me either your files and/or the FBI's current files regarding two additional investigations. Lorcan Malachy and Redmond Satran. Also, see if you can find anything from the U.S. Immigration and Customs Enforcement files concerning a situation involving Burroughs Brothers Shipping and Containment, Inc. in Baltimore. And, Corey—seriously—enjoy the drive out here."

"Cam," Benjamin warned before he hung up the phone. "If you're thinkin' about getting involved in the Henderson situation, I need to advise you, as a friend and colleague that Christine Henderson, Eugene's widow, is not someone you're gonna find easy to get a handle on and that's all I can say about her. I'll bring you whatever info I can concerning the Henderson investigation and anything I can find on the other stuff. See you later this afternoon or this evening."

Benjamin had just—purposely, McGregor figured—tossed him a clue in his warning about Christine Henderson. His statement "all I *can* say about her" as opposed to all I *know* about her usually meant that the party in question had something to do with some form of covert operation and that Benjamin had information that he could not legally or professionally reveal.

"Interesting," McGregor thought as he glanced out the window as snow began to fall again, drifting against the windows, rudely begging entrance and then falling with apparent futility to the ground."

CHAPTER TWENTY-FOUR

Foxstone Park? What the hell was Eugene Henderson, Cindy's father, doing in Foxstone Park when he was killed? McGregor asked himself as he examined the Henderson file that Corey Benjamin had begrudgingly delivered to him. Foxstone Park is one of the places where the notorious FBI employee Robert Hanssen was alleged to have been meeting foreign agents, under a bridge, and passing secret information to them. Until Hanssen's arrest, McGregor had never heard of Foxstone Park. But right after the arrest, McGregor's curiosity led him to drive to the park to try to figure out why this location was chosen. He still couldn't figure it out except for the possible proximity to Hanssen's home.

Nothing in Henderson's file explains why he was in that particular park. Who did Henderson work for? "Uh huh," he said out loud as he flipped over another page in the Henderson file. "The World Bank— a senior Hydropower Specialist in the Energy and Mining Division stationed in D.C." *This case is only two years old! Why are they classifying it as a cold case? Have they run out of leads...or is something else going on? Who moved this file from active investigation to cold case status? I need that information,* he was thinking as his phone rang. Oddly, he saw on his caller ID, it was Christine Henderson, Cindy's mother. McGregor quickly learned that Cindy had told her mother about her surprise visit to McGregor's house and the disappointment she was feeling with his apparent lack of interest in her father's murder.

"I'm so sorry about Cindy's uninvited visit to your house a few days ago. She told me about it this morning," Henderson said in an apologetic tone. "Cindy's still very upset about her father's death and…"

"I understand, Mrs. Henderson," McGregor interrupted. "Cindy was very industrious in her quest to find me and, I might add, contrary to what she's thinking, to get me interested in her father's case. I was just looking through his file when you called. No promises, but Cindy and her friends kinda piqued my interest. Do you know who decided, other than the FBI agent who was the lead investigator, that your husband's case should be delegated to cold case status?"

"Not really," she said. "The investigator simply told me that if anything came up, he'd call me. I asked him what was happening at that point, and he repeated that he'd call me if anything new was discovered and hung up."

"Mrs. Henderson, who do you think killed your husband?" McGregor bluntly asked. "I'm sure you were asked that question during the initial investigation, but there's nothing in your husband's file to verify …."

"It should be in there somewhere," she quickly responded. "I told them that he was worried about something on the job—something about being…he used the term… 'outed.' I had no clue at the time what he meant, and I still don't today. I remember getting kind of a strange look from the investigator when I told him that."

"Your husband worked for the World Bank? Is that correct?" McGregor asked.

"Yes, for many years," she said. "He was a ...."

"Tell you what I'd like to do," McGregor interjected. "Again, without any promises, and before I consider jumping into this investigation with both feet, I'd like to meet with you personally. Perhaps you can fill in some apparent gaps in this investigation for me. You live in Vienna, Virginia—how about meeting me for lunch tomorrow at Amphora Deli on Maple Ave?"

"What time?" Henderson sounded eager.

"Let's miss the lunch crowd and make it 1:00," McGregor said.

"How will I recognize you?" she asked.

"I'll find you. That's my old job," McGregor laughed. "We'll see if my instincts are still sharp."

Within seconds after he'd talked to Henderson and before he'd had an opportunity to refill his coffee cup, McGregor's phone rang again. It was Lawrence Brody, Assistant Director of the FBI.

"I'm bettin', Larry, that someone plopped a note on your desk this morning that one C. McGregor had on his desk the files regarding the murder of Eugene Henderson, investigation notes on Lorcan Malachy and Redmond Satran, and an inquiry into the activities of Burroughs Brother's Shipping and Containment, Inc., Baltimore," McGregor reckoned. "Now, you're calling me why?"

"Glad to see you back on board," Brody laughed. "I don't know anything about the Burroughs Brothers situation, but I'm happy to see your request for the Malachy and Satran files. Be careful! That's all I need to say about that situation. But I do want to share some info with you that you *won't* find in the Henderson file and perhaps save you the trouble of a dead-end investigation that could be marked with potential danger."

"Danger for who?" McGregor asked.

"You," Brody retorted. "The Henderson case went cold when we were ordered by the CIA and Justice Department to 'back off.' We had some evidence from Henderson's home computer and some crime scene evidence that led us to believe that Henderson was possibly a double agent, working for both the CIA, under the cover of his position at the World Bank, and some foreign agency at the same time. However, the evidence was very weak. We also found evidence at the crime scene, a storm sewer in the park to be exact, that another person had been killed or severely injured at the same time and place that Henderson was killed. No other body was found, and whoever removed it did a haphazard job of physically sterilizing the scene *before* the police, and eventually we, entered the picture. We found a gun beside Henderson's body with a full magazine. He had no powder residue on his right or left hand between his thumb and index finger or his wrist. DNA from blood samples we took at the scene showed *two* distinct types. Now, none of this information appears in any file you'll be able to get ahold of, nor, I'm positive, will ever appear anywhere. The CIA confiscated our files with a court order; however, we still have the DNA results. So, if you're looking to get involved in this particular case, you'll get nowhere. However, for what it's worth, here's what we were thinking at the time we were ordered off the case.

"As I said," Brody continued, "we think Henderson might have been a double agent. During a meeting with his contact at Foxstone Park in Fairfax County, they were interrupted by somebody—possibly CIA agents. During an exchange of gunfire, Henderson was shot and killed by either his foreign contact, the CIA, or someone else. The CIA, or that someone else, took the contact, either dead or wounded, from the scene. So, who killed Henderson? We'll never know. Why he was killed? I guess it was just the cost of being involved in that kind of business, but again, we'll never know. So now, what's your interest in this case?" Brody asked in an official tone of voice.

"Not a whole lot of interest," McGregor responded. "I was asked by Henderson's daughter if I would look into the situation. I'm guessing no one has talked to her in any detail to date, other than to inform her that the case has been put on the back burner. She's distressed and is simply seeking advice. Bottom line...I'm just fishin'. *An old fashioned sorta place—been here for years,* McGregor was thinking as he opened the door and walked into the Amphora Deli, *—lookin' kinda tired but still, a 24-7 option for food when you aren't in an IHOP or Denny's mood.*

He quickly checked the restaurant's patrons against what Mrs. Henderson's daughter looked like. A lone woman sitting at the bar sipping on what looked to be tonic water with a lime twist caught his eye. He was right. *Christine Henderson is a tall woman, probably played high school and college basketball,* he noted as he found a table for them and settled in for lunch. *Mid to late 50's, dressed in business casual, a shirt with a button-down collar under a plain sweater, khakis, and loafers. Agent Benjamin's statement "all I can say about her"* flashed across his mind.

"Let's get right down to business, Mrs. Henderson" McGregor suggested after they'd ordered lunch and shared a few social pleasantries.

"Please call me Chris, Cameron. Where should we start?"

"Again, Chris, who do you think killed your husband? That's my usual starting question," McGregor opened.

"He was well liked and..."

McGregor interrupted her. "You're aware that he was, along with his work at the World Bank, working undercover for the CIA."

"Not true, Cameron. Eugene had some quirks," Henderson began, "but he was the typical nine to five guy who works in an eight by eight, fabric-decorated cubicle, shuffling papers all day. I had suspicions once that he was doing some moonlighting that wasn't necessarily connected to his World Bank position. I confronted him. But he said that he couldn't talk about anything concerning his job with the WB. I thought maybe he had some outside contracts that he was dealing with—some outside consulting or perhaps spin-offs from WB clients. He wouldn't talk about his job at all. The CIA? No, it's simpler than that. He was having an affair with another gay man and they often used the park as their meeting point."

Henderson's eyes had been calm and emotionless up to this point, McGregor noted, but now she was perusing her surroundings very carefully. Whenever her eyes met his they held within them a strangely knowing look. It was as though she could see right into his mind and know exactly what he was thinking. Maybe she could, but McGregor was good at avoiding someone else's speculative thinking. He was also good at rattling a reluctant potential witness's reluctance to share information. At least he thought he was.

"So is this what you're telling me," McGregor queried "that your husband was having an affair and had been meeting a *man* in Foxstone Park off and on before his murder, and was, in fact, the very night he was murdered, in the park to meet this man again? Who was the man he was meeting? Why is the CIA involved in this case?"

"His name is Patr Sokolov," Henderson responded flatly. "As I said, it's pure nonsense that my husband was a spy. He and Sokolov met at a conference in Germany a few years ago and have been lovers ever since. If he, Sokolov, was a spy, so what? That was neither Eugene nor Sokolov's reason for meeting. They had something more prurient in mind, I can assure you. I chose to ignore the whole situation and pretend I knew nothing about it. I didn't want the humiliation that would come naturally if others—our daughter—our friends—found out that my husband—Cindy's father—was gay. I certainly didn't then and still don't want anyone to know!"

McGregor leaned across the table and deliberately whispered for effect. "Talk to me, Chris. I don't really have time to play games. Your daughter wants closure and…well, again—who do you think killed your husband?"

The expression in Henderson's eyes quickly changed to a clearly focused glare. "I *know* who killed my husband and I can assure you that you or anyone else's speculation is…well…just that. In other words, it is a cold case and it will stay that way," she challenged. "My daughter is just going to have to live with the fact that the truth about her father's death will never come out—at least from me."

"So, what you're saying is…" McGregor began.

"What I'm saying is simply that my husband was *not* a spy—he didn't have any information that a foreign government wanted. All his work was out in the open. He was simply a gay man who happened to be hooking up with another gay man. However, since Sokolov was evidently known by the CIA to be a spy, the whole thing has been effectively wrapped in a cloak of permanent CIA secrecy. It's a dead issue, if you'll excuse the pun."

193

"Or perhaps," McGregor added, "simply a challenge for law enforcement."

"Take it for whatever you want, Agent-emeritus Cameron McGregor! Thanks for lunch and the stimulating conversation," she said as she stood up. Henderson sounded agitated. "Getting back to espionage for a moment," she continued, "the connection you're looking for between Malachy and Satran, and, as you're going to soon find out, their connection with the Burroughs Brothers and, as a matter of fact, the federal courthouse car bomb incident that killed your girlfriend, is, well, think *conspirers*—think *deep-dark-web*—but be careful. I really mean that! By the way," her voice lightened, "I like the Sig P226 you're carting in your shoulder holster— good choice—just like the one I have in my handbag. Call me when you want to talk about something other than who killed my husband."

McGregor was caught entirely off guard and Henderson was up, out the door and long gone before he could attract the waiter's eye and pay the check. *"What the hell was that all about? How did she know I...who does she know? WTF?*

It didn't take long for McGregor to realize he'd been set up—big time! The CIA, he concluded, was playing a "back-off" game and Christine Henderson, at the expense of her daughter Cindy, was somehow tapped to deliver the message.

Perhaps she was right, he reasoned. *The murder of Eugene Henderson might have been a planned CIA hit, and she may have even been the primary instigator. In any case, the people or person involved with the hit and the rationale for the hit may never be exposed. Christine Henderson is a CIA operative.*

He wondered more about how she knew about the other situations he'd asked Benjamin about—the Malachy and Satran state of affairs, not to mention the bombing or the Burroughs brothers. What kind of game is she playing? Her statement that she knew who killed her husband would haunt McGregor over the next few days. He wondered if it was a CIA hit job or something as simple as Henderson using the meeting between her husband and Sokolov as an opportunity to get rid of both of them to protect her social standing—as well as her self-perceived sexual prowess. One thing he knew for certain, he didn't *have* to get involved in *any* of this. On the other hand, what's with the conspiracy thing she insinuated?

194

CHAPTER TWENTY-FIVE

Wintry Weather had come and gone, McGregor noted as he stopped to enjoy the fresh Spring air and catch his breath after a vigorous walk from his car toward the Dulles lobby. *It's clearly a busy day at Dulles,* he observed, watching the ebb and tide of pedestrian flow to and from the main terminal.

"We seem to have a migraine of children in the airport this morning," he laughingly announced to let Lorraine know he'd arrived at the Traveler's Aid counter and was ready to go. She turned to respond but McGregor was already attending, with eyebrows cocked, to his first request for assistance.

"Sir! How 'bout, a splendorous Big Mac, a monster Coke, crisp fries with a ton of ketchup, a side of onion rings, and a bale of napkins," said the seemingly self-entertaining, sing-songing young man approaching the counter that evening. "To go, if you please," he continued.

"Got it," McGregor quickly smiled. "Let me repeat your *directive* to make sure I heard you correctly. You asked for a stick of gum, a side of beets, a teacup of fresh bee's nectar and a swift kick in the butt—straight up please. Am I right?"

"Hold the beets," the young man laughed. "And... while you're holding them, can you direct me to the Hertz Car Rental Station?"

"Can you eat and drive? McGregor queried.

"Sir! Can you lift your leg high enough to kick me in the butt?"

"All right," McGregor laughed. "Let's call a truce in this farcical *tete-a-tete*! The Hertz counter is down that ramp," he said, stifling a prolonged snicker while pointing the way. "Go outside to the bus marked Rental Cars, hop on and you're on your way. Have a good trip wherever."

"Thank you, sir, and...your beets are, mysteriously, but regrettably, dripping!"

"Hey, kid! You're like a Slinky," McGregor retorted! "You know, not really good for much, but you're really gonna bring a smile to my face when I push you down the stairs!" They both laughed.

"You know, don't you, that they're going to have to lock you away very soon, Cameron McGregor," Loraine declared as she gingerly restocked the plastic information brochure holders displayed randomly around the counter area. "You *do* know, of course that that kid was *way* too young to know what a *Slinky* is! That was a fake laugh, I bet!"

"Eavesdropping as usual, Loraine?" McGregor snickered as he picked up a stack of brochures to help. "If it's my people skills that worry you, they're just fine, my dear; it's my tolerance for idiots that needs work! You know," he concluded, "the next time a stranger talks to me, I'm not kiddin', Loraine! I'm gonna look at them shocked and whisper the question: *You can see me?* Then, of course, you'll get all the questions and I'll just do the paper and pamphlet-stocking work. Ok?" he smiled.

His shift that day displayed all the usual elements of traveler nervousness mixed with the occasional self-perceived misery and self-pity. Regardless of myriad one-after-another distractions, he couldn't shake the feelings of confusion and dismay he'd felt after the Christine Henderson meeting.

Brody is the only one who could have informed Henderson about my interest in the Malachy and Satran situation. What's their connection and who ordered Henderson to attempt to get me to back off? Did Henderson put a fatal slug in her husband? What the hell is 'Deep Dark Web'? Is Brody the protagonist in this scenario or simply a villain in camouflage?

McGregor didn't like being set up—especially by someone he was beginning to consider to one of the good guys! Regardless, he'd soon find out what Henderson meant about Deep Dark Web—actually, the next morning!

As he usually did, McGregor read the Washington Post carefully that morning. The Justice Department, the FBI and the U.S. Immigration and Customs Enforcement offices had just announced that they had shut down what they identified as a major agglomeration of dark web drug marketplaces and arrested the alleged owners in what federal prosecutors say was a first-of-its-kind operation. McGregor was instantly alert. His supposed friend, Special Agent Lawrence Brody, whom the Post identified as Assistant Director, headquarters, F.B.I., announced that "the so-called darknet or dark web was a part of the internet that could be accessed only by specialized software or hardware and contained clandestine sites not found through ordinary search engines." "Deep Dark Web," McGregor learned it was called, was a website, he read, "that provided a directory with direct contact to a framework of darknet marketplaces selling illegal narcotics. The website also provided access to marketplaces for firearms, including assault rifles, and for malicious software and hacking tools."

McGregor was suddenly having his "aha moment" of the day. Brody was also quoted as saying that "F.B.I. special agent Graham Blake of the Philadelphia office had been the lead in the investigation," which McGregor found interesting.

According to the Post, the alleged owners, "Lorcan Malachy, 49, and Redmond Satran, 37, both from Israel, were arrested Monday in Baltimore along with Klinedare Burroughs of the Burroughs Brothers Shipping and Containment, Inc., located in Baltimore. The three defendants allegedly received kickback payments through bitcoin when someone purchased an item on the darknet sites found through the directory, earning more than $15 million in fees since October 2013, according to sources familiar with the arrests.

"The closing of a directory like Deep Dark Web is significant," Brody said, "because it should stifle hundreds of millions of dollars in illegal purchases."

McGregor wondered if this Burroughs was the guy Loraine was referring to who was dating a Filipino woman who was illegally in the United States, who

196

then dumped her, and she went on to marry some informant of a U.S. Immigration agent? He'd ask Lorraine, but not before he contacted FBI special agent Graham Blake from the F.B.I.s Philadelphia office to congratulate him on the Deep Dark Web bust and ask him about any information he might have learned in the Baltimore situation regarding the car bombing incident that killed Joan. He hadn't forgotten that Blake was at the courthouse when Marshal Joan Taminelli was killed and the last person to talk to her. Brody had said that he thought Taminelli *wasn't* personally targeted but had some theories. McGregor now needed to follow up.

"Special Agent Blake! This is Cameron McGregor who you might remember from Agent Taminelli's burial ceremony. Do you have a moment—I have a few questions regarding your recent Deep DarkWeb bust and whether or not you uncovered any connections to...."

"Bingo, McGregor! You were on my list to contact today. We not only have a prosecutable connection between Deep Dark and Taminelli's death, but we also have in our possession the definite cell phone that was programmed and used to set off the car bomb off that killed her. We identified the device as a vehicle-borne improvised explosive device, aka, VBIED. Lorcan Malachy, the ostensible 'boss' of this cartel—evidently not the sharpest crayon in the box—left it on the same workbench where he allegedly built the bomb that was placed in the car that was meant to explode and kill Taminelli and anyone else who just happened to be walking by! He even left us the *easy-to-follow* internet tutorial he used to modify the cellphone into a trigger. And, as you know, all it takes is a phone, five bucks worth of parts, and a few minutes of tinkering—plus, for first timers like Malachy who is, by all observations, a few peas short of a casserole, any one of scores of DIY stuff on the Web. Then, apparently from a safe distance that day, he dialed the number of the phone attached to the detonator. Boom! The murder of Marshal Joan Taminelli is listed separately on the indictment as a homicide committed exclusively by him in the writ of allegations we've filed in Federal Court—Malachy is your man!"

In his usual calm, soft voice, McGregor concluded the conversation abruptly with a congratulatory note, "Good work, Graham. Thanks," as he turned away from the phone, his mind taking in the view from his window. He badly needed some down time.

CHAPTER TWENTY-SIX

Zeus and Annie lay quietly at his feet as McGregor scribbled some notes in a well-worn notebook he reserved for what he called "his imprudent musings." It had been two weeks now since he talked to FBI special agent Graham Blake and learned of Marshal Joan Taminelli's found killer. Today he was thinking about Whisper.

The thundering of hooves split the silence as a lone mare galloped through the bleak landscape, he penned. *The wind tossed her mane into the air like flames; after all she was a flame colored chestnut. Whisper was her name. Her muscles rippled beneath her freshly groomed pelt and in her powerful legs. They propelled her forward and kept her going as she powered over the land.*

He laid his pencil aside for a moment. He missed Whisper—he missed Joan.

I stare gravely towards the advancing mare, he continued... *her gleaming coat matching the impenetrable horizon. Her ears pricked, as she moved swiftly, powerful limbs tearing into the barren earth. My knuckles are white, as I clench them against the bone-jarring wind while I watch....*

The murder of Marshal Joan Taminelli and the apprehension of Lorcan Malachy could not be easily forgotten by McGregor, even though he forced himself to move on. He would, at least, attend the Malachy trial in Baltimore in memory of his relationship with Joan.

"Come on, Annie, up and at 'em, Zeus, let's take Shadow for a romp in the woods," McGregor grunted as closed his notebook, quickly stood up from his desk, and stretched. "Gotta get some wind back in my sails. Annie! For God's sake, you cute, loveable, soft furry hair ball, stop lookin' so put-upon—you need the exercise—you play the victim so well, I'm surprised you don't carry your own body chalk! And Zeus, you fast, fiery, confident, hard-working companion-in-pursuit, you're already at the door, I see! Figures."

Shadow, not unlike the horse Mark Twain described in "A Connecticut Yankee," was not much above medium size, but he was alert, slender-limbed, muscled with watch springs, and just a jet-black fire-eater. He was a beauty. Glossy as silk, and naked as the day he was born, except for a bridle and a western design saddle—Zeus is his best running pal!

McGregor could feel the heat of that day's sun beating down on his back as the leather reins rubbed gently between his fingers. It felt warm. It felt good.

198

Whisper was my pride and joy, he thought to himself. *She had soft eyes that you could stare into forever, seemingly all-knowing, reflecting promise. A heart made of love, a slender profile, and a gorgeous chestnut coat.*

He was still in mourning.

Shadow, on the other hand, he noted, *has always been right there for me in the darkest days, when it felt like my life was a hurricane in an endless sea. I will never forget the days I spend with her either. Shadow shines in my life today! Whisper shines as...well, a shadow.*

McGregor was preparing himself emotionally for the next bite on his plate. And even though he didn't need to approach the plate at all on this one, his personal and emotional, as well as his U.S. Marshal-trained curiosities, kept returning to the look on Cindy Henderson's face when she mentioned her father, Eugene Henderson's murder. Her eyes had locked onto his as she pleaded for his help.

That look in her eyes, he remembered, *her father had been murdered. If she'd been my daughter and something had happened to me...what would my daughter...?*

Somewhat reluctantly, he'd picked up the phone soon after that meeting with Cindy and called the office of Marshal Corey Benjamin, the U.S. Marshal who had given Cindy his phone number. He'd asked for, and received, the complete file on Eugene Henderson and Cindy's mother, Christine Henderson. He was about to contact Christine for a second round of what he called a "date-designed grilling." She'd skillfully left him hanging, proverbially "gasping for air," after their first encounter. Perhaps not this time, he hoped.

CHAPTER TWENTY-SEVEN

McGregor knew full well that women, not unlike Christine Henderson, make "damn good spies."

Women spy well, he knew, *because women spies have proven, over time, statistics and action accounts support, to be good at multi-tasking as well as being superb at tapping into different emotional resources. Perhaps,* he reckoned, *the most important attribute possessed by female spies is, in fact and practice, prejudice—the implication that spying is a "man's job" is possibly the biggest reason women like Christine make good agents.*

However, contact with her would have to wait. Her daughter Cindy had phoned and wanted to meet once more with him; she had "new information" she wanted to share. He'd agreed to meet her in a pubic setting, and suggested Hoppy's Place. He also advised that she bring a friend; he was uncomfortable meeting with her alone. Zeus, as always, would be accompanying McGregor to, at least, Hoppy's front porch.

"My father, Eugene—he went by Gene—was a gay man," Cindy began as her friend Trevor Wiley, the young man who so vehemently argued Cindy's efforts to get McGregor involved in the first place, sat quietly listening.

"I found some notes he wrote to his friend, a Russian man named Patr Sokolov," she went on. "It seems they had a long-term relationship that started almost two years before my father was murdered. Bottom line, I think Patr what's-his-name, simply murdered my father as a result. It...it was a lover's quarrel. Whether my mother knew anything about this...I don't know, doesn't matter I'm satisfied, case closed—what's for lunch?"

"Hoppy makes a mean Virginny Mountain-Momma Bear-Meat hot dog with all the droppin's, uh.. toppin's," McGregor laughed as he leaned across the table. "Cindy, you sure you're content with your assumptions about your dad and his death?" he leaned across the table and asked. "I mean..."

"Yes, enough said." She cut him off sharply. "What you gonna have, Trevor?

It was clear to McGregor that Cindy had dealt with the whole situation, as she understood it, and had internalized her findings. There was no reason for him to mess with her mind by introducing other implications or innuendo. However, by asking him to effectively "bow out," she'd inadvertently raised some suspicions in his mind about her rationale and had provided McGregor with a reason to contact Cindy's mother. *Had her mom told her to back off?* he wondered. He would use that contact to attempt to arrange a follow-up meeting to let her know that he and Cindy had met, as well as bring her up-to-date regarding his interest in the Burroughs Brothers situation. *As if she didn't already know,* he thought as he untied Zeus from Robbie's porch rail.

"Let's go Zeus, there's a tree yonder beckoning for your attention before we head home!"

CHAPTER TWENTY-EIGHT

"You lost your wife a few years ago. How, if I may ask, did you handle that loss? I'm still having difficulty dealing with the death of my husband," Christine Henderson rested her glass of wine and leaned across the table towards McGregor. "I get tired of people asking how I'm doing—how I'm handling it all, you know?"

"Chris—can I call you Chris? McGregor asked. "Short answer here. You know, I get frustrated when the only idea people seem to have of widows or widowers is that we lose everything—the partner, the job, whatever. I'm very aware that there's a tendency for people in grief to isolate themselves. I hope that's not you; I work hard against that. The other short answer," he smiled, "is that we're not alone—a lot of other people go through this with grace and poise. I want to be one of those people and not make a federal case out of it, if you'll excuse the obvious pun. I should be allowed to hurt in my own way and so should you—without people interfering. Make sense?"

"Almost," she laughed. "I'm glad you called and invited me for dinner. I promise I won't mention you're still packing heat tonight. I'm glad you met with Cindy and her friend and helped her put her father's death in a more comfortable place for her. Now, just to start the evening off with bit of a common, albeit judicial, interest, let's talk about your relationship with Angelika Schafer and Maggie Douglas," she smiled cunningly, "that's much more interesting!"

McGregor went very still. "Is there anything about me you *don't* know?" McGregor growled suspiciously.

"I'm still working on that—ask me later," she grinned. "However, here's your big surprise for the evening—don't, my friend, even think of asking me how I know all of this—dinner and wine alone will not get that information from me—I'm a trained and certified necromancer."

"Necromancer?" McGregor questioned.

"Bitchy-Witch," Henderson smiled. "You got royally fucked by both women, Agent McGregor, and, while they both seem to be out of the picture right now, your real nemesis is still out there. For dessert, I'll be glad to share with you what information I know about that matter—you're not going to be pleased and I don't want to upset your tummy before our main course is served. I'm starved!"

Over the Brazilian restaurant's signature dessert, *mini guava cheesecake*, which they both ordered, Henderson unveiled a scenario almost too unbelievable for McGregor to believe, even when considering the source.

"Your so-called friend and confidante, Maggie Douglas, whom you think poisoned herself,"Henderson said, "had a long-running affair with, surprise, Lawrence Brody, whom you identify, and rightly so, as the assistant director of the FBI at their D.C. headquarters. The CIA had a watch going on them for almost a year before the Mirror Dot organization faked her death and found her a new name, a home, and a job in Vermont. I was then, and still am the agent in charge in that bit of action. It wasn't the affair we were interested in, but rather their direct ties to the very top of the Mirror Dot organization, which you guessed quite a while ago wasn't as confounded or disrupted as much as you and others in the FBI were led to believe after the Florida muddle. You did good work on that mess, by the way. but, in the end, you were an unwitting fall guy for Mirror-Dot. We knew, and now you know, Brody is one of the top covert executives in Mirror-Dot!"

Although he was already suspicious of Brody, McGregor was still shaken by the
information Henderson was sharing.

"Brody was introduced to me by my old friend and colleague, FBI Agent Allen Beck, who, at the time, was special agent in charge of the Southwest territory for the FBI," McGregor bitterly said. "Beck and I had worked together on several high-profile cases in the past. Hell, Beck gave the eulogy at my wife's funeral, for Christ sake! Beck told me that Brody, like me, hated cops and agents who had, in the vernacular, 'gone over to the dark side'." McGregor rumbled, "and Maggie," he cut himself off in mid-sentence… "who else has Brody led astray over the past few years?" he angerly asked.

"Beck," she answered coldly. "Clearly you forgot your scriptures," she smiled as she attempted to lighten up the conversation. *Beware that you are not led astray; for many will come in my name and say, 'I am he!' and, 'The time is near!' Do not go after them!*
"Waiter, could we each have a bourbon on the rocks, two times please," she turned and asked a passing server."

"That's a start, Chris," McGregor growled. "The drinks mind you, not the scriptures. That was from Luke 21:8, I believe," he smiled in a "smart-ass" way.

"Cam, Maggie was given a beta-blocker combination by her handler to use at a moment like that," Henderson continued. "It stopped her heart momentarily so you and the paramedics, in your rush to get her to the hospital, thought she'd lost her pulse and was dead. She faked her death by taking a lozenge that slowed down her heart rate. She was guessing that you and the emergency personnel would probably only check for her pulse for just for a second or two."

Perceiving that McGregor was about to explode at any moment, Henderson gently reminded him that they were in a public place and that she was simply a messenger!

"A messenger from Hell," he remarked. "I'm okay…just need a minute."

"I knew you were coming," McGregor remembered Maggie's voice in his mind. *"got a call last night—from Porter —saw cars surround the place just a*

little while ago. I'm sorry, Cam, I called the hit on Roberto. I'm so sorry," were
her final words to me, as she slumped to the floor.

"Chris, I was still giving her CPR when the rescue squad arrived! By all intuition, I knew she was dead already, but I was not ready to give up. Now, you're telling me it was all a hoax?"

"Listen Cam! You mention 'intuition.' And I know that a lot of your success in your career in law enforcement has been based on your ability to be intuitive. What happened in the whole Mirror-Dot end game, and especially with the situations surrounding the personnel you know as Maggie Henderson and Lawrence Brody, was based on your intuition. Now, the question, simply asked in this case—was your intuition real or did it fail you? The truth of the matter is that your intuition will almost never fail you. But I need to add that, under certain circumstances and without understanding, in this case, the Mirror Dot situation, coupled with your personal emotions and belief systems, your intuition did fail you badly and ultimately led you astray. And even though chance has brought us together at this juncture in our professional lives, I've had Brody in my sights for almost three years now and have watched your work on the Mirror-Dot case meticulously for the past year or so. Bottom-line? I, as the Agency's lead investigator regarding Brody's activities, want you to join up with us, the CIA, as a special agent. You're cleared for highly covert service all the way to the top. We want to put Brody behind bars, and *as* his so-called friend and confidant, even though he probably really sees you as a dupe," she chuckled, "you could play a major part in bringing him down, big time! And," she added, "I think we'd make a good team! Mind you, I'm not telling you this will be an easy task, but I am telling you it's going to be worth it. Nothing more, nothing less. So, Cameron McGregor, U.S. Marshal *extraordinaire,* even though, at this moment, your mind is probably spinning, what does your infamous intuition say about all of this?" she laughed. "We need you—I need you! We both need another bourbon! This is the kind of crazy-ass case no one ever warned you about—because, simply stated, no one knew this level of craziness existed in real life!"

CHAPTER TWENTY-NINE

Even though McGregor had been successful in shutting down some of Mirror-Dot's clandestine and dicey U.S. connections, he still felt the effect of the excruciating murder of his good friend and professional colleague. U.S. Marshal Roberto Gonzales who was brutally decapitated and dumped in the Miami River by Mirror-Dot heavies. McGregor had a stalwart emotional investment in Gonzales—the same was true for his investment in the U.S. Marshal's service. But he was still bitter over the betrayal by a few of his fellow law enforcement partners, especially those associated with the F.B.I., that were participating in the Mirror-Dot exploit. In addition, and perhaps the most difficult for him to accept personally was his deep distress caused by his *own* failure to identify the fact that he was being mismanaged and misled by so many of the cohort actors that had surrounded him over the past year. McGregor knew how to get past this. He would have to deal with his emotions, as always, in his own way, by uncomplicating the story line, rediscovering factual truths and refreshing himself through an self-examination of who he was before Mirror-Dot, who he is now, and where he wants to be tomorrow.

"Come on, Shadow," he gently commanded as he lifted his boot to a stirrup and swung his body into Shadow's age-polished saddle. "We need to soak up some sunlight and fresh air. You know, the sun rises, then the sun sets. It's as simple as that. But, sometimes, the people around us seem to complicate that process. Here's our challenge today," he exclaimed. "Let's you and I *uncomplicate* things straight away!"

The flecks of golden sunshine mingled with the wispy clouds in a sky that offered no signs of rain as he and Shadow cut northeast across the field from his house, frightening up a cottontail or two in their wake. It was the perfect weather for clearing one's mind, McGregor hoped.

"Failure is not a sign of personal incompetence; it's just one experiment that's gone wrong," McGregor assured himself as he fixed his boots firmly in the stirrups and leaned forward into Shadow's jet-black mane. "If you don't have room to fail, you don't have room to grow, Shadow" McGregor said and gently kneed Shadow's girth. He immediately felt the wind on his face quicken with the horse's steady acceleration from a walk to a working canter.

"I need to accept that I don't always make the right decisions, and that I screw up spectacularly sometimes. And, Shadow, just so you know, I'm presently experiencing life at a rate of several WTF's per hour," he laughed and lowered his voice as he reined Shadow back to a steady walk.

"With that thought in mind, let's take the long way through the west outer basin on our way home—past Whisper's grave—no hurry! I need to make a call, but it can wait. Christine Henderson has already waited for a week to hear whether I'm going to be involved in the Brody investigation. And, to be honest, Shadow, it will be good to hear her voice again—but, well…hell, you already figured that, didn't you! Shadow knows," McGregor expressed slyly with a smile that was just barely hiding his typically stifled, but always quietly lingering, thoughts of eventual payback.

"You know, Shadow, to win, you must lose, and then get royally pissed off," he sighed. "I've been betrayed by people who carried the badge of official authority. People who swore, on their honor, to never betray their badge, their integrity, their character or the public trust and who swore an oath to enforce the law and have the courage to hold themselves and others accountable for their actions."

They stopped at Whisper's grave and communed with her gentle spirit for a moment. McGregor stepped down from the saddle and pulled a few weeds from the gravesite. As he remounted he adjusted his hat and quietly, but forcefully declared, "Their barefaced betrayal of the law has really pissed me off! Take me home, Shadow, I'm ready to win again—big time!"

CHAPTER THIRTY

Nothing new seems to be going on here, McGregor observed as he opened the half-door to the Travelers Aid desk at Dulles that morning. *The same messy desk, the same yellowed announcements posted on the bulletin board, the clock that never seems to move fast enough, the hubbub of voices surrounding and passing by the desk— it smells like a bologna sandwich in here,* he noted silently. In plain sight and placed squarely in the middle of the desk was a well-worn book with a "sticky note" on the cover addressed to him.

> *Cameron, waiting for your call,*
> *Enjoy the book, especially <u>page 147</u>.*
> *<u>For inspiration, of course</u>! Chris*

The book, "A Coffin for Dimitrios" by Eric Ambler, by title alone seemed rather ominous to McGregor. And, as promised, in blaze-orange on page 147, Henderson had purposely highlighted the line:

> *"It is not who fired the shot but who paid for the bullet."*

Before he had even a moment to muse the situation, as well as the message, he was interrupted by his first question of the shift.

"Sir, I don't mean to disturb your reading but, well, where do I find my luggage?

"What was your flight number, my friend?" McGregor inquired with a Traveler's Aid smile.

"United 2057, Sir."

"Baggage claim 6" McGregor responded. "Have a great day, and welcome to Northern Virginia and Washington, D.C."

It's neither who fired the shot nor who paid for the bullet, it's who screwed McGregor, McGregor growled to himself as he dialed Christine Henderson's number on his cell phone. The call went immediately to voice mail. McGregor quickly left a terse message.

"Hi, Chris, I'm busy right now at Dulles, but I'll be enjoying an *economy* dinner at Hoppy's restaurant tonight at 7:00. If you can find the place in the mountains west of you (I suggest you use your GPS) and want to discuss Ambler's book in person, I'll spring for your hot dog and, if you're lucky, perhaps a beer."

"My new best friend!" a person addressed McGregor at the desk. "I've just arrived here and I'm looking for a hotel close to Tysons Corner in Virginia. Can you help me?"

"I can," McGregor quickly responded as he picked up the desk phone and dialed a number. "Please hold for a customer," he replied to an answering operator and handed the phone to the traveler. "She can help you," he said as he turned towards a young lady who seemed to be upset and crying.

He smiled and handed her a tissue "I think you need a buddy" he said in a fatherly voice. "What's the guy's name and I'll stomp him for you," he joked.

"I'm running away from home and I had only enough money for a plane ticket. My aunt lives somewhere close here and I need to call her."

"My phone is tied up at the moment young lady," he responded in a serious voice. "What's your aunt's name and number and I'll call her for you on my cell phone. Is she expecting you?"

"No" she replied, "but she'll help me."

"Write down her info for me," McGregor said handing her a note pad. "How old are you?" he gently inquired.

"Thirteen," she responded as she combed through her backpack for what he assumed was her aunt's contact information."

"God, I hate these kinds of ever more common situations," he grumbled in his head.

"Thank you, my friend," the hotel-seeking man said as he hung up the desk phone. I have a room and a limo is on its way to pick me up at ..." he glanced at his notes, "door 5, I'm told. In about twenty minutes."

"Starbucks. sixty yards that way" he pointed. "Then, down the stairs next to the counter, go outside— that's where your limo will be waiting. Glad I could help, have a great evening and even a better tomorrow," he smiled while quickly glancing at the young lady, still wrestling with her backpack.

He quietly contacted airport police on his cell phone to alert them of a possible juvenile runaway situation that needed their immediate attention and investigation. They responded swiftly, and gently escorted her away for questioning. Later during his shift, McGregor was informed that the young lady was released to her aunt by juvenile authorities.

McGregor left the airport that day, knowing that he'd helped a few individuals with their travels through the airport, realizing he'd pissed off one or two idiots, and that he'd intentionally disregarded the usual number of expected invectives directed at Travelers Aid volunteers by a few irate passengers. He silently flattered himself for resisting the urge to tell a couple of irrationally impatient people that he didn't *give a rat's ass* where their luggage was, and he refrained from telling an incensed women who decided to curse loudly at everyone in sight because she missed her airplane by thirty minutes that her plane departed without her because *nobody likes you*! The mere fact that he was able to help anyone that day was, he knew from years' experience, the sole gratification any of the volunteers needed to make their TA shifts meaningful.

That evening, McGregor ordered his usual at Hoppy's, with a side order, of course, for both Annie and Zeus who didn't mind being temporarily short-tethered to a front porch post. Annie had adjusted to car riding over the past year and was now able to see Hoppy's Place firsthand. She was happy to occasionally turn over her house guarding gig to her pal Mike Soules, the caretaker.

Zeus seems to like to practice the art of methodological smell-tagging customers who visit this particular roadside sanctuary, McGregor knew from past practice. *Annie will learn the art quickly,* he surmised.

It was almost 8:00, and he was on his third beer, when Christine Henderson, dressed, for some unknown reason, in semi-sexy camouflage gear, waltzed through the door, spotted him immedicably and quickly moved toward his table. She was not alone.

"This place is so," she hesitated, "so, uh, —I'm looking for just the right word here," she said looking around the place.

"Quaint?" McGregor said with a straight face.

"And the dogs on the porch, do they live here?" she asked as she positioned herself in a way that would allow her to introduce her friend.

"No," McGregor slowly rose from his chair. "I belong to Zeus and Annie," he said stepping forward to give Henderson a kiss on the cheek while offering his hand to her friend.

"This is Anastasia Sokolov. She works with me at the store." Henderson carefully offered. "Her husband was Patr Sokolov," she whispered. "If you recall, he was my late husband's friend who was murdered in the park at the same time as my husband. We found out later that his body was claimed by Russian officials and spirited away before American officials found my husband—we can talk more about that later," she abruptly interrupted herself and smiled. "Anyway, Ana buried him, Patr, in their hometown of Kostroma. Her brother is a banker there, and her sister is a teaching nun at the Epiphany Convent, also in Kostroma."

Henderson concluded what seemed to McGregor to be a highly nervous, almost hesitant introduction.

She's chattering like a sparrow attempting to threaten off a cat! He wondered why.

Through it all, McGregor managed to discern the fact that Henderson was introducing Anastasia Sokolov as a new CIA operative recruit, and that her husband had also been an operative, but with the KGB. He was conceivably killed because of his association with Christine's husband.

To say the least, a not surprising situation in the spy versus spy world, but the unusual introduction to murder victim Patr's wife he'd just gotten from Christine, the wife of the other victim, Eugene—well—just a bit strange, McGregor considered as he pulled out chairs for his late arriving guests.

Is this what she was trying to tell me by quoting Ambler's "It's not who fired the shot but who paid for the bullet? What's she not sharing with me?"

"It's a pleasure to meet you, Anastasia," McGregor said. "I'm really anxious to hear more about business at the store," he grinned at both. "Please order while I take a moment to walk my canine family a bit. They have a preferred grove of trees that I'm very confident is hastily beckoning them! I'll be right back."

After a bit of small talk, McGregor was able to establish, at least in his own mind, why Anastasia was invited to this meeting with him. *She's been professionally involved with Christine Henderson for quite some time, following and collecting information and potential evidence concerning the entire Mirror-Dot organization and, perhaps, most important, Lawrence Brody's covert leadership contribution. She's developed an on-going personal relationship—best friends and constant communicators—with Maggie Douglas, (Brody's alleged mistress, newly resurrected from a fictional death) who's currently ensconced in a witness protection program, stashed somewhere in rural Vermont.*

"So, tell me this, as best you can in the present environment," McGregor asked bluntly as he looked around the room. "Your husbands were mutual friends—let's leave it at that. However, I have some questions. First, the obvious, who killed them, and why? Second, Chris, why are you so outwardly uptight and nervous? Unlike your usual calm self, you've been chattering like an auctioneer since you got here. If it's because I haven't yet given you a *'buy in'* to your *'project'*—look, I'm in! So, if that's the problem, you can calm down. Now, with that," McGregor continued, "Chris and Ana, both of you are invited to bail out of here, follow me and my canine sweethearts down the mountain to my place, and we'll continue our conversation, in a less public, more relaxing arena. You know," he mused, "the older I get, the more I become an apple pie, sparkling hard-cider kind of guy. For your info, my housekeeper baked a fresh apple pie this afternoon before she left, I've got ice cream in the freezer, and some truly spirited cider on tap—how 'bout it," he grinned. They gamely accepted his offer.

That was damn good cider! McGregor muttered to himself as he looked at the alarm clock alongside his bed the next morning. *These ladies are going to be very late to work,* he noted as he walked down the hall to the guest bedroom where he'd suggested they stay overnight. They were in no condition to drive, and, with his resolve that there would be no *ménage à trois* last night, their disappointment, combined with the effects of the cider, soon dictated their need for sleep.

"Haul ass, ladies," he hollered as he knocked on their door. "You're going to be late for work!"

"Oh my!" he heard them say.

"Cam, how many deals did we consummate last night?" Christine asked in a sly voice from behind the door.

McGregor smiled. He'd let her curiosity continue *ad infinitum.*

CHAPTER THIRTY-ONE

Shadow, Zeus and McGregor paused for a moment before advancing through the middle of the green sea of grass. McGregor was in no hurry that morning as he motioned Shadow forward. He smiled as Shadow paraded through the weeds, head held high and proud—his silky black mane flowing down his neck and pouring off his shoulders in a churning, inky waterfall—his tail flowing carelessly behind like the flag of a bold country, waving in a proud victorious fashion.

He loves strutting his stuff in this particular pasture. Actually, in any pasture, McGregor noted.

Suddenly, without warning, Shadow briskly gathered his legs under himself and hurtled into the air, swinging his massive head like a weapon—sharp and dangerous. The problem, McGregor quickly discovered, was a tightly coiled black snake. It wasn't a large snake by any means, but evidently chilling enough to cause Shadow to perform an oblique acrobatic maneuver to evade contact. As McGregor reached down to place a comforting hand on Shadow's flank, and as Zeus raced to the rescue to quickly drive the snake out of sight, he noticed scuff marks in the grassy pasture.

Tire tracks from a dual tire vehicle?

After calming his horse and checking the adjustment on his saddle, McGregor alertedZeus to follow the track while he and Shadow attentively trailed.

"Good morning, gentlemen," McGregor shouted to advise the men standing alongside a dual-wheel truck, outfitted with a pole-setting apparatus and parked at the edge of a weedy knoll, that they had company.

"You're on private property. What's the deal?" he asked as he dismounted, dropped the reins to the ground and approached the two workers. On silent command, Zeus crouched in the grass and scrutinized the action carefully.

"Don't have any details, mister, other than...well...according to the coordinates the boss gave us late yesterday, this is where we're supposed to plant a pole this morning. Other than that, your guess is good as ours. Here's the company's name and phone number, if you want to call them. We'll be glad to wait."

McGregor glanced at the coordinates and made note of the contact information.

"Just planting a pole...no lines or attachments?" he asked.

"No sir!"

"Can I check your truck?" McGregor asked.

"Go for it," they said.

"Have a great day, gentlemen," he said as he finished his walk-around of the rig. "Work carefully—please leave things neat when you leave," he said, as he picked up Shadow's reins, swung into the saddle, and urged his horse forward.

No need to question them further, he figured as he moved Shadow to a canter. *I'm betting that pole is going to have some transmittal paraphernalia attached to it very soon. I'll wait a couple of days to find out what the game plan is.*

Later that day, McGregor and Shadow revisited a grove positioned close to the spot where the new pole was now well-planted. After selecting an appropriate tree, he securely attached a hunter's stalking camera to it and carefully aimed it squarely at the newly placed pole.

I can now watch from the comfort of my recliner, he grinned. *Much better than the old days of lying in the cold damp grass with binoculars getting eaten by chiggers and chattered at by hostile squirrels…much better!*

"Take me home, Shadow," he said as he deliberately snapped his boots into their respective stirrups. With a muffled snort, Shadow went immediately from trot to canter to all-out gallop, soaring into the late afternoon breeze. The ground was rigid from lack of rain and Shadow's steps sounded sharp—*like gunshots*, McGregor noted, popping brazenly on the ground as he shot himself forward.

When he runs, McGregor marveled, *he leaves nothing behind him and runs towards everything.* He could feel Shadow's entire body tremble with joy when they reached the stable. Shadow loved the run; McGregor loved the journey.

By ten o'clock the next morning McGregor's carefully placed game-spotting camera had chronicled the complete installation of a wireless transmitter/receiver apparatus with appropriate antennas on the targeted pole in the far-north pasture. Less than an hour later, his hi-tech home security monitoring system was alerting him to intrusion efforts directed toward his cell and land phones and computer equipment. By noon, McGregor was back in the saddle with Zeus in the lead. Shadow was carrying a saddlebag carefully packed with what McGregor laughingly referred to as his "zip-bang-sky-high, portable elevation apparatus." In case the pole was being protected, McGregor, cautious as always, had his P226 Sig holstered at his side. He arrived at the pole at exactly 1:12 p.m. After a quick review and mental analysis of the terrain surround the pole, he cautiously buried two sticks of straight dynamite about eighteen inches below the base of the pole. Each stick consisted of nitroglycerine, sodium nitrate, and a bit of wood pulp wrapped in cylindrical packages of newspaper. After calculating that a ten-foot long internal-burning fuse would give him enough time to remove himself and his entourage to a safe distance from the effects of the subsequent blast, he attached the long fuse to the dynamite's short fuse, which he'd purposely left uncovered just above the surface of the pole's dirt base. Stringing the long fuse out its full 10 feet, he lit the fuse with a legendary "flick of the Bick" and cracked a knowing grin. McGregor considered that they had four minutes to reach a grassy knoll about 200 yards from ground zero—an easy jaunt that gave them just enough time to turn and see exactly how high McGregor's calculations would send the pole and its contents. The blast itself was a large, but muffled thump. The crash of the pole and its contents was much more dynamic, and extremely satisfying, sending parts and pieces of apparatus everywhere within a seventy-five-foot radius.

Kinda gives a whole new meaning to pole dancing, McGregor smiled.

"Mission accomplished, partners—drinks on the house when we get home," he announced as the last smoke from the blast drifted above.

Message sent, he reckoned as he signaled Shadow and Zeus that it was time to go.

CHAPTER THIRTY-TWO

Prior to the pole planting incident, the preliminary plan that had been discussed between McGregor, Henderson and Sokolov had been based around an attempt to get Maggie Douglas to become a federal witness against Lawrence Brody. Henderson had started developing the papers necessary to be able to provide Douglas with an opportunity to utilize a federal arrangement built around the "Use and Derivative Use Immunity" policy, to protect her from criminal action. It would prevent the prosecution from using the witness's statements or any evidence derived from those statements against her in a criminal prosecution, and protect her from federal prosecution for anything pertaining to Brody's actions or inactions regarding his role with the F.B.I. and/or his relationships with the Mirror Dot syndicate. In the meantime, Sokolov was developing a plan to "soften-up" Douglas with efforts to persuade her to become a federal witness. They had decided not to involve McGregor in any preliminary planning because of a statement he'd made regarding putting a gun to her head and threatening to blow her brains out if she didn't cooperate.

"What? You think my method is too damn harsh?" he'd asked them in the heat of discussion.

He settled for the Henderson and Sokolov approach in exchange for their agreement not to offer Douglas "transactional immunity"— the *broadest* type of immunity because it offers complete protection from future prosecution for *any* and/or events mentioned during testimony.

"I'm not going to support total or blanket immunity for Douglas in any way," he'd declared. "No exceptions!"

Here's what I'm thinkin' right now, based on what's just taken place, McGregor thought to himself while appreciating the view from his breakfast room windows. *Yesterday somebody ordered a device strategically placed on my property to monitor my communications. By destroying their equipment so quickly I sent an immediate message to either Mirror-Dot, Brody, or both, that I knew they were up to something. Did my meeting with Chris and Ana have anything to do with the monitoring equipment suddenly appearing? It would seem so. Were they followed the other evening? Was there already some kind of shadowing of my house going on? Do we have a leak? Chris? Ana? Do I have some other adversaries out there that want to do me harm? Am I being set up again?*

As he often did when mysteries started to mess with his head, he decided to take a couple of boxes of shells and walk down a path behind his barn, past Whisper's grave site and down a steep hill to a sand pit where, over time, he'd build a firing range for both pistols and rifles unmatched by any governmental site he'd ever used to satisfy the U.S. Marshal's requirement of time and accuracy.

I've buried a lot of lead in here, and I've killed a whole of bad dreams in here as well, he mused to himself as he filled a couple of extra clips for his Sig. and stuck them in his back pockets. He unrolled a target from his backpack and walked to a frame embedded in the sand.

"I'll start from twenty-five yards today, twenty bullseyes, four close-enough for government work, two outsiders. Twenty-six shots, thirteen a clip" he announced to the target as he backed away and starting firing. An hour later he'd obliterated five targets and dug a hole in the backstop big enough to bury all the bad things he wanted destroyed and a few more just for amusement. He was far from getting his predetermined goal of twenty bullseyes per every twenty-six shots, but with fourteen, he still had his touch, he felt.

One more target before quitting time. My wrist is getting tired and I've got to get some lunch, shower, and be at the airport for a shift today from 4:00 to 7:00, he said to himself as he walked back from pinning up his final target.

Inserting a fresh clip in his gun, he turned to address the target. As he was aiming, but just before he could squeeze out his first shot, six shots whizzed past him nailing the target dead center. McGregor automatically dropped to the ground, spun around and looked for the shooter. He could smell the gunpowder. He could see gun smoke, but the shooter was nowhere in sight.

"Cam, it me—it's only me!" a voice quickly shouted from behind an old growth tree situated about twenty-five yards behind him. "It's me, Ana Sokolov, can I show myself?"

"Holster your gun, lady. Step out from the tree and show me both hands," McGregor ordered.

"My holster is in my bag, Cam. I'll put it away and toss out my bag first. Okay?"

"Just show me both hands when you step out," McGregor snapped.

"Did I hit the bullseye?" she asked, still concealing herself behind the tree.

McGregor remained silent.

"I'll bet I did," she giggled. "I'll bet you're jealous!"

McGregor was not about to take his eyes off the tree she was behind.

"Here's my purse. Here's my hands, here's the rest of me." Ana said in a serious tone as she stopped and slowly recovered her purse as she warily walked toward McGregor.

McGregor holstered his gun. "What the hell, Ana?"

"I'm good aren't I, Cam?"

"Damn good, Ana, but you scared the shit out...."

"We need to talk, Cam. Now!" she abruptly declared. "Let's walk back to the house."

She means business, McGregor recognized.

215

"You're in great danger," she continued. "Mirror-Dot must dispose of you now! Brody *wants* you to come after him personally, so he has an excuse to kill you as a rogue cop who's looking for revenge on him for whatever's in your warped mind. You've been set up and groomed by Christine, who's also on the Mirror-Dot payroll and being directed by Brody."

McGregor stopped, turned to her and asked in sheer exasperation, "and you know this how?"

"My company knows this but can't prove it. Chris killed her husband as well as mine. My company knows this—period."

"That, I suspected," admitted McGregor. *Why should I be surprised about another setup!* he thought to himself.

"Maggie Douglas *is* dead," she continued, "but, as you can see now, is still being used to manipulate you. In the next few days, Chris is going to suggest that you go to Vermont to negotiate with a completely hypothetical Douglas. My guess is that she and Brody will be waiting for you there. At this point, Chris, who you thought worked with the same organization that I do, but who was really a contract person assigned to us by the F.B.I., appears to have gone mysteriously missing.

"Now, stop walking, take a deep breath and look at me." Sokolov demanded. "I could have easily killed you a few minutes ago. I just wanted your immediate attention and I wanted you in an angry, fighting, state of mind. My company, and you know only too well who I work for, is fully aware of what's going on around us and fully aware of my reason to be here today. We're not alone, but you and I are going to bring this situation to a head with us being the winners. You have to trust me!"

"You're one in a line of many in the past year who have said those same words to me, Ana. I'll trust you only after I verify," McGregor spoke firmly. "Sorry, but words alone are no longer enough in this game. Please stop here, remove your gun from your purse and hand it to me. Butt end first, please!"

Sokolov was immediately compliant. She knew that McGregor would take her gun, pull the clip, check to see if there was still a round in the chamber, and check to see if any bullets remained in the clip.

She fired six rounds, McGregor readily recalled, *said she could have killed me. Did she run out of ammo after six shots? Nope,* he discovered. *One in the chamber, and six left in the clip. A thirteen-round clip—she had ammunition left!* He ejected and cleared the chamber, placed the previously chambered bullet back in the clip, and handed the gun back to Sokolov, barrel down and barrel first. He watched her carefully as she placed it back in her purse.

"Thanks for the unusual heads up introduction, Ana," he laughed. "And especially thanks for the update info. You've, in fact, set my mind at ease. I'll be in touch with you in the next few days. We'll go from there," he said as he escorted her to her car.

216

She watched him carefully as he wrote down the VIN number behind her windshield. She knew he was going to determine the registered owner of the car. It would be the federal government, she knew. The verification process had begun.

Within a few days, using the resources and the know-how gained from his years as an agent with the U.S. Marshals Service, McGregor was able to uncover several provocative facts.

Ana Sokolov was who she said she was, but her connection with Christine Henderson was still unclear and questionable. Christine Henderson had disappeared and not, according to his sources, unexpectedly—the CIA had no record of her ever being employed by them. She no longer lived at her previous address and she had no phone service listed or unlisted—the F.B.I. had personally wiped her file clean, according to his F.B.I informant. Christine Henderson did, in fact and under her own discretion, kill her own husband as well as Patr Sokolov, Ana's husband. Maggie Douglas was stone-cold dead, and he had the coroner's report and death documentation to verify it. The receiving and transmitting station invading McGregor's telecommunications and property was sanctioned by the F.B.I., and approved, namely, by Brody. Brody had probably disposed of Christine Henderson—most likely permanently.

He determined that he needed to confront Brody directly, and that he also needed to question Sokolov about her alleged relationship with Henderson. He called Ana Sokolov. "We need to talk," he suggested. "How 'bout dinner at Hoppy's Place Friday evening?"

They settled on 7:00 p.m. after conceding that, most likely, they would be under surveillance and necessary safeguards should be taken. They agreed that they would both be practicing an "on-duty," but undercover, method of operation. Before hanging up, he asked if she'd heard anything about, or from, Christine Henderson. She briskly replied, "we'll talk!"

Sokolov's assertion that *Brody wants you to come after him personally,* brought Samuel Johnson's words regarding the legality of "dueling to death" to mind.

A man may shoot the man, he'd written, *who invades his character, as he may shoot him who attempts to break into his house.*

McGregor had fully established, in his own mind at least, that his reputation as well as his character had been tested and damaged by Brody and Mirror-Dot. He knew full well that, with the attempt to monitor his communications, Brody was in the launching stages of setting him up for something.

It was crucial for him to *quickly* determine—what, when, and how! He couldn't afford to guess. In the back of his mind, he was hoping that Brody had captured his earlier call to Ana Sokolov.

After lunch on Friday, he whistled up Annie and Zeus and ambled toward the barn where Shadow was eagerly awaiting. *Maybe they'll come after me tonight*, he considered. He could almost sense the bad guys thinking, *it's about time*!

He shared his thoughts and fears with his loyal friends along the trail, as he always did. He knew Whisper was probably listening as well. Zeus would be riding shotgun that evening as usual. Annie would be tending the house, and Shadow would be "in touch"—Shadow always seems to know what was up! *Horse intuition and sensitivity*, McGregor figured.

Their romp through the fields had to be a bit short that afternoon to give McGregor enough time to shave, shower, and be at his Travelers Aid desk at the Airport for a three hour shift that late afternoon, prior to meeting Sokolov at Hoppy's for dinner. He also needed to allow enough time for him to arrive in the vicinity of the restaurant early so he could "scout" the area prior to his conceivably pre-publicized arrival time. *Risk-management is my middle name*, McGregor thought grimly.

He'd trade his Corvette for his pickup that evening. *Metal is better than fiberglass when bullets are concerned*, he knew from experience. Just in case, his shotgun, as well as a 30-06 and extra shells for both, were on board in a locked compartment concealed beneath the rear seat.

"Can't be too safe where bears abound," he sang off-pitch as he kicked the front tire of the truck, tapped his ankle area to make sure his Sig. was securely in place, and keyed his Corvette. He looked forward to his late afternoon stretch at the airport.

His long-time Travelers Aid partner, Loraine Pelliter was already at the desk and greeted him with her usual, unsurprisingly sarcastic but always endearing welcome message. He took her aside for a moment and told her the closing story about her inquiry into the so-called "Burroughs brothers" and their Baltimore business enterprise. She could now share the story with her girlfriend.

"Okay," McGregor said in a voice that signaled Loraine that he was ready for action. "What's up?"

"All's quiet on the Western front, somewhat evil smelling on the Eastern." she started. "I think the exhaust fan is broken in the Sudanese fooderie. The South is thinking about rising again, and the North is…well…just acting north of it all," she announced with an embellishment of arm and hand gestures. Oh…and the guy that was here a while ago, maybe…some time last year…that was looking for Jesus? He's back, and still looking. If he comes here again, be nice. Okay? I remember what you did to him last time! Gave him a hooker's phone number!" she scoffed.

"Ahh, Loraine. I regard you with an indifference bordering on aversion." McGregor reparteed with a grin.

Suddenly their *tete-a-tete* was loudly interrupted by a woman physically attacking a man about twenty feet from the Travelers Aid desk. She was forcefully

218

reciting every word in the "bad girls dictionary" while battering the man with her purse. While Pelliter grabbed the strap on the handbag the women was using to belt the man, McGregor quickly stepped between them. He ended up having to quickly wrap his arms around the women to ward off her continuing advances.

This chick wants to destroy this dude, McGregor thought as he struggled to contain the women's anger. By the time airport security was alerted and showed up on the scene, the assaulted man had fled the area.

"It was just a husband-wife spat," the winded women announced with scorn as she pulled away from McGregor. "No, I don't want to press any charges. But you can bet your sweet ass he's on my shit-list," she snarled, as she headed in the direction of the closest exit.

"Good work, Lorraine," McGregor smiled as he re-tucked his shirt and straightened his collar.

"Was that the best hug you've had today?" she laughed. "She was actually trying to wrap her legs around you and take you to the floor. She would have…"

"Excuse me, folks, can you help me," a rather timid looking young woman, with a nearly inaudible voice, asked as she cautiously moved toward the TA desk.

"I'll bet we can!" Pelliter smiled at the young lady, motioning her closer to the desk.

"It's like this," she said nervously. "The guy who was attacked by that women a moment ago paid for my plane ticket here. We met online and I agreed to spend the weekend with him somewhere close by the airport. Did I hear her say something about a husband-wife thing? He told me he was single. I seem to be stuck here. I think I need to go back home."

Pelliter turned and looked at McGregor who, she knew, was probably in a "the plot thickens" state of thinking.

"He was going to get me my return ticket for day after tomorrow, back to Duluth," she continued. "He was going to pay for the ticket. I don't have any money, and my credit card was maxed out last week buying lingerie for this trip."

Pelliter continued to look at McGregor. She was hoping he wouldn't break into laughter and embarrass the women even more. Although, she later admitted that "actually, the woman didn't look embarrassed at all!"

"Sorry, Loraine, McGregor smiled, "I need to go and find the guy looking for Jesus and show him the way…I…"

"No, you don't, Cam! I need you right here.," she demanded.

"Okay," he grinned, "I suggest we call the TA social worker, as well as the county welfare office, and see if we can get one or both to help this young lady out. You call the TA office and I'll contact the county."

Within the hour, with the assistance of a TA social worker, the young traveler from Duluth, Minnesota had a ticket for a flight later that evening that would take her to Chicago, then on to Duluth. She would be home by 10:30 the next morning.

"I hope she learned a lesson from this!" Pelliter heaved a sigh of relief.

"Trust, but verify," McGregor quietly replied.

McGregor left the airport at the end of his shift that afternoon experiencing what he called "a normal deer in the headlights immersion experience," readily admitting that there's nothing that delivers more of a feeling of empowerment than being of service to someone in need. However, he really didn't mind *not* crossing paths with the fellow seeking Jesus and a bit of loose change.

"If, sir, you have some," would have been his plea.

CHAPTER THIRTY-THREE

Later that afternoon, after a shower and shave, he rolled into the seat of his pick-up, signaled Zeus into the passenger seat, and watched his GPS deliberately outline the path to his pre-planned dinner with Ana Sokolov. He was leaving his place early so he could eye-ball the road-side zones along the only route possible to Hoppy's Place. He recalled his earlier conversation with Ana that he hoped Brody might have intercepted. A conversation which might have prompted him to determine the need to bring McGregor's intrusions on his Mirror-Dot activities to a screeching halt. McGregor knew Brody had the know-how and the badge to be able to pull off the final demise of the interrupted retirement/restarted career of Marshal Cameron McGregor. He had to outthink and outsmart Brody, and Sokolov was still *not completely verified—still a work in progress,* in his mind. He'd worry about her later. "One problem at a time," he muttered to himself.

Hoppy's Place was precisely 12.7 miles from McGregor's barn. Just past the 6.3 mile marker was a cliffside pull-off with a water source that logging trucks regularly used to top off their radiators before cresting the mountain at Hoppy's and freewheeling down the steady decline to highway 81 and the sawmills that dotted the road all the way south to North Carolina and beyond. As he passed the 6.3 pull-off, he noticed a white Toyota Prius parked close to the edge of the cliff partially veiled by a grove of azaleas. He knew the FBI was using this vehicle as their executive-level company car. *Could that be Brody hiding back there*? he wondered.

At a smaller pull-off at the 7.0 mile marker, McGregor wheeled his truck to a stop and removed his Sig from his ankle holster. He placed it on the console beside him and activated Brody's cell number on his Bluetooth-powered dashboard phone. The ring reverberated on the truck's speaker system as McGregor turned the truck around and headed back towards the 6.3 pull-off. McGregor drove slowly into the pull-off, effectively blocking the only escape route of the Prius. McGregor picked up his binoculars, even though the vehicles were less than seventy-five yards apart. He could see Brody fumbling for something in the car.

"Checkmate, old man!" he shouted, as he saw Brody find and answer his phone.

"Hell, I remember when we were both the *good guys* in scenario's like this," McGregor announced as he slowly rolled his truck closer to Brody. "If you're considering shooting your way out of here, remember you're the bad guy now, saddled in a Prius, for God's sake, at the edge of a cliff and I'm staring you down from behind a Ranch Hand Legend Series truck with a grille guard and front bumper built with schedule 40 pipe and diamond-plate steel for maximum protection from impact with a thousand-pound Moose at a hundred miles per hour. That big ol' front end is pushed headfirst by a 450 horsepower, 4-wheel drive truck, asshole," he laughed and waited for a response.

Brody was silent except for heavy breathing and the distinctive sound of a clip being inserted into a government-issued Glock 19-millimeter pistol.

"One shot from you and you're going over that cliff behind you," McGregor warned.

Silence.

"It a long way down," McGregor challenged and adjusted his binoculars.

Zeus was sensing danger and remained at ready alert as McGregor waited for Brody to make his next move. He was honestly hoping that Brody would give up, want to talk, and admit guilt to law-enforcement authorities regarding his role in the Mirror-Dot domain. He could see that Brody had obviously put McGregor's call on his car's Bluetooth speaker and was talking to someone on a different cell phone.

A second cellphone? Perhaps calling for backup? McGregor wondered who Brody was calling?

Adjusting his binoculars further he could see that Brody was obviously distressed and it looked like he was crying. He would learn later that Brody had called his home and left a message for his wife—a message McGregor didn't want to hear about.

"Your move," would be McGregor's last words to Brody before a bullet whizzed through McGregor's open side window and embedded itself in the truck's back seat head rest. McGregor estimated the distance between Brody's car and his truck and contemplated closing the distance and moving his truck into a head-to-head position with the Prius as additional shots rang out.

"Wrong move, bad cop," McGregor shouted at the phone as he skillfully placed his truck in 4-wheel drive, pulled swiftly ahead, aligned his front grill with the hood of the Prius, and slowly pushed Brody and his car over the edge of the cliff until they disappeared in the deep ravine.

As the car fell, McGregor heard a single shot—*suicide* flashed through his mind.

Even with a small car gas tank, that fire is remarkable, McGregor marveled as he disconnected his call to Brody and dialed 911 to report an accident and fire at the pull-off just shy of the 6.4 mile-marker.

It was 6:47 according to his watch, as he headed up the road to Hoppy's Place. If he pushed it, he'd arrive at Hoppys with about a minute to spare.

The fire apparatus will be coming up the mountain behind me—the ambulance the same. State and local cops will be converging from all directions, he knew for sure when a sheriff's car sped down the mountain past him. He thought he heard an explosion—*there won't be a survivor,* he surmised.

222

If she's not here already, Ana may be caught in any backup near the pull-off site, he realized as he pulled into the parking lot at Hoppy's.

He re-holstered his Sig and leashed Zeus as they walked towards a grassy area where McGregor could get a good look at the grill guard on the front of his truck and Zeus could relieve himself.

No white paint scars, no visible damage— "Ranch Hand" truck fittings came through for me, he smiled. A quick walk-around of his truck didn't disclose any other damage. He'd have to get the backseat, driver's-side, head rest re-upholstered.

The metal main stay in the padding must have stopped the bullet, otherwise I'd be replacing a back window as well. Brody should have spent more time at the firing range, he reasoned as he leashed Zeus on the front porch, checked the level of the water in the 'always there' bowl, and walked through the door, To his surprise, Ana was already there and enjoying what looked to be her second beer. McGregor took a deep breath, acknowledged a couple of familiar faces, and headed for her table. He felt relaxed for the first time in weeks.

He let Sokolov take the lead in most of the conversation that evening. She was able to fill in enough of the missing links to satisfy McGregor's *need to know* way of thinking and definitively put Mirror-Dot to rest.

Later that night, under the cover of moonlight, he, Shadow, Annie, and Zeus would take a peacefully walk to Whispers grave and back.

"No reason," McGregor explained to his entourage, "just a little outing, just need the wind-down time."

"The wind— a torrent of darkness among the gusty trees," he reminisced a line from *The Highwayman* by Alfred Noyes.

"The moon— a ghostly galleon tossed upon cloudy seas" he continued, "the road— a ribbon of moonlight over the purple moor." Then, he tugged at his rein in the moonlight and galloped away to the west, the dogs racing along in his wake.

A few days later, on his way to his usual shift at the airport, he received a text message reinforcing his thinking that a post-mortem on Brody would probably list suicide as the *fundamental motive,* as well as the *definite cause,* of his death.

Dead issue—closed case, he reasoned as he parked his car and instantly merged with the airport throng. As usual, he promptly became a participant in what he called the "genuine domain of the truly lost and found."

May all the good folks I meet today actually be aliens or animals masquerading as people, he chuckled to himself as he stepped behind the Travelers Aid desk. *I'd rather not have to deal with any actual human beings today,* he thought as he surveyed the passing crowd and took a deep breath. *I've learned over time, that humans are clearly unique in having the ability to learn*

223

from the experience of others but are also <u>remarkable</u> for their apparent <u>reluctance</u> to do so.

"Excuse me sir, where's the nearest drinking fountain?" A young lady carrying a small dog in her arms asked graciously.

"Just inside the corridor to the ladies' rest room," he responded indicating the restroom sign just a few steps down the hallway. "Here's a paper cup for your pup," he said, smiling at the pair of them.

In the adjacent hallway, McGregor couldn't help but notice a reasonably well-dressed man nonchalantly strolling through the crowd and carrying a hand-scrawled placard boldly declaring that:

The End of the World is Here!

McGregor, being McGregor, couldn't resist facetiously addressing the man's efforts by loudly announcing that:

"It's already tomorrow in Australia, my friend!"

"How do you know that?" the man asked vigorously, while maintaining his forward pace.

McGregor, not wishing to insult the man's already problematic intellect, merely replied: "Sir! I respectfully decline to answer that question on the grounds that I simply don't know the answer."

The man shrugged and marched on, apparently pretty much unmoved by McGregor's witticisms.

Australia will have to wait, I guess, McGregor surmised.

Meeting people, helping them resolve airport travel as well as humanitarian issues while having fun, were, and still are, McGregor's reasons for becoming a Travelers Aid volunteer in the first place. McGregor was never going to allow himself to become a casualty of what he traditionally labeled as *boredom burnout*. Not now, he pledged, nor had he done so in his lengthy record of service with the United States Marshal's Service.

Hoping to be unnoticed, in a semi-secluded corner tucked between some lockers and a connected airport information sign, McGregor spotted a young couple, holding hands and swapping what looked to be happy thoughts—not a common sight in a busy airport, he observed. He was quickly and happily reminded that author Nicole Krauss may have conceivably witnessed the same scene, when she wrote:

"Once upon a time there was a boy who loved a girl, and her laughter was a question he wanted to spend his whole life answering." He took another deep breath and thought of Polly.

Life and continuous questions endure for Cameron McGregor! The remainder of his story? —well —*Shadow knows*!

"Yes, Ma'am! The trip by cab from here at Dulles to the center of Washington, D.C., at this time of the evening, is about 35 minutes—it's a pleasant drive. If you and your party wish to wander around and look at the National Mall, it's beautiful at night, and the weather will be ideal. The cab stand is at the top of that exit," he motioned. "Here's a map! If you're staying at a downtown hotel, I suggest you check in first, and put on comfortable shoes for your adventure. Most of all—enjoy!"

Maybe, he thought to himself. *I could turn my recent law enforcement endeavors into a virtual handbook on how <u>not</u> to get royally screwed!*

Duped: Double Lives, False Identities, and the Con Folks in my Life!

Best seller, no doubt! Movie rights—a TV series…
Conceivably…

"Oh! Hi folks! No, you're not lost," he laughed. "I am! But, not to worry," he promptly assured them. "It's all in a day's work for me! "Together, we will resolve this pressing issue triumphally and persevere collectively. That said, how can I help?"

About the Author

Dennis Russell Dunklee, Ph.D., (*Denny*) is an emeritus professor of Law and Leadership at George Mason University, and was, for many years, one of many volunteers at Dulles International Airport.

Although he has authored and co-authored many non-fiction articles and textbooks in his academic areas of expertise, *Non-Stop Flight (2013)* and *Shadow Knows, (2020),* presented here in a *combined* edition, are his first works of fiction.

Dunklee lives in Historic Falmouth, Virginia which is situated on the north bank of the Rappahannock River at the falls, north of and opposite the city of Fredericksburg, Virginia.

Sincere appreciation to my wife
Lorna Westfall Dunklee,
who loves to catch my big and little errors,
tighten up my prose, and make my writing better.
You are my ~~typo~~ type!

Made in the
USA
Columbia, SC